Caroline Graham was born in Warwickshire and educated at Nuneaton High School for Girls, and later the Open University. She was awarded an MA in Theatre Studies at Birmingham University, and has written several plays for both radio and theatre, as well as the hugely popular and critically acclaimed Detective Chief Inspector Barnaby novels, which were also adapted for television in the series *Midsomer Murders*.

**Detective Chief Inspector Barnaby novels
by Caroline Graham:**

1. The Killings at Badger's Drift
2. Death of a Hollow Man
3. Death in Disguise
4. Written in Blood
5. Faithful unto Death
6. A Place of Safety
7. A Ghost in the Machine

Other novels by Caroline Graham:

Murder at Madingley Grange
The Envy of the Stranger

FAITHFUL UNTO DEATH

CAROLINE GRAHAM

headline

First published in paperback in 1996 by
HEADLINE PUBLISHING GROUP

First published in this paperback edition in 2007 by
HEADLINE PUBLISHING GROUP

8

Quotation from 'Ridge House' by U. A. Fanthorpe by
kind permission of Peterloo Poets

Cataloguing in Publication Data is available from the British Library

ISBN 978 0 7553 4219 8

Typeset in Sabon by Avon DataSet Ltd,
Bidford-on-Avon, Warwickshire

Printed and bound in Great Britain by Clays Ltd, St Ives plc

Headline's policy is to use papers that are natural, renewable and
recyclable products and made from wood grown in sustainable forests.
The logging and manufacturing processes are expected to conform to
the environmental regulations of the country of origin.

HEADLINE PUBLISHING GROUP
An Hachette Livre UK Company
338 Euston Road
London NW1 3BH

www.headline.co.uk
www.hodderheadline.com

For my friends
Lili and Neville Armstrong

Dramatist to this house is Death. Austere,
Withdrawn, the scripts he writes.

U. A. Fanthorpe, 'Ridge House'

Chapter One

Simone Hollingsworth disappeared on Thursday, 6 June. You could have said she had a wonderful day for it. A warm breeze was circulating beneath a sky so clear and bright it was almost colourless. The hedges were thick with blossom and in the fields rabbits and hares were larking about from sheer *joie de vivre*, as is the way of very young creatures who have not yet twigged what the world has in store for them.

The first sign in St Chad's Lane that all was not quite as it should be was observed by Mrs Molfrey, tottering past the house next door on her way to post a letter. Sarah Lawson was struggling to open the Hollingsworths' gate inwards with her foot while holding in her arms a large cardboard box.

'Let me help you,' said Mrs Molfrey.

'I can manage if you could keep this open.'

'It looks jolly heavy,' said Mrs Molfrey, referring to the box. She eased back the wrought and gilded iron. 'What on earth's in it?'

'Some Kilner jars for my stall at the fete.'

They walked along the lane, Sarah courteously moving at a quarter of her usual pace, for Mrs Molfrey was very old. The clock on the flint and stone church tower struck three.

'Simone invited me for tea as well but she seems to have gone out. I found these on the patio steps.'

'How odd. That's not like her at all.'

'Can't say I'm sorry.' Sarah hefted the box up in her arms with a groan. 'Once you're in there it's goodbye to the next hour at least.'

'I expect the poor girl's lonely.'

'Whose fault's that?'

They paused outside Bay Tree Cottage where Sarah lived. Here there was no need for Mrs Molfrey to do the honours, for the gate was permanently hanging off its hinges. This slovenly departure from the approved norm was accepted with a resigned shrug by the village. Sarah was known to be artistic so naturally allowances had to be made.

'Simone can't have gone far without wheels. And she's bound to be back soon. It's bell-ringing practice at five.'

'Oh, that's the latest thing, is it?' Sarah laughed. 'I suppose there's nothing else left.'

'Did she stick at your course?'

'No.' Sarah put the box down and produced a key from her skirt pocket. 'Came for a few weeks then lost interest.'

Mrs Molfrey posted her letter and turned homewards, silently reflecting that, as far as Simone was concerned, there was indeed not much left for her to play with.

The Hollingsworths had moved into Nightingales just over a year ago. Unlike most newcomers who were invariably anxious to understand, appreciate and embrace every aspect of village life before the removal vans were out of sight, Alan Hollingsworth had never shown the slightest interest in either the place or the people. He could be glimpsed only when climbing into his black and silver Audi convertible, waving goodbye to his wife and crunching off down the drive. Or, long hours later – for he had his own business and worked extremely hard – driving smoothly back up again and kissing her hullo.

Simone always appeared in the doorway the moment the car door slammed as if she had been poised in some concealed lookout, determined that the man of the house should not go unwelcomed or unreceived for a single second. When kissed, she would stand on tiptoe with one leg flicked up behind her like an actress in a forties movie.

Unlike her husband, Mrs Hollingsworth, having time on her hands, had made an effort to become involved in local activities. It had to be acknowledged that these were pretty limited. There was the Women's Institute, the Embroidery Group, the Bowls Club, a Homemade Wine Circle and, for the truly desperate, the Parish Council. The vicar's wife chaired that.

Mrs Hollingsworth had gone along to the Institute on a couple of occasions and had sat through a talk on corn dollies and an illustrated lecture on the botanic discoveries of John Tradescant. She had applauded the winner of the most interesting apron competition and enjoyed a slice of Madeira cake. Asked several mildly probing questions about her past and present circumstances, she had replied with a sort of willing vagueness that managed to be both unsatisfactory and unobjectionable. At the third meeting (Intrigue Your Friends With A Tudor Posset) she was seen to sigh a little and was, regretfully, unable to stay for tea and a lemon curd butterfly.

Bowls came next. Colonel Wymmes-Forsyth, the club secretary, watched, goggle-eyed and half fainting with horror, as her four-inch heels, narrow as wine glass stems, stabbed and mangled their way across his exquisitely striped green. She was dissuaded without too much difficulty (everyone was *so* ancient) from joining.

The wine circle and parish meetings, which took place in the evenings, knew her not. Neither did the embroiderers' group although Cubby Dawlish put a delightfully illustrated little notice as to their times of meeting through Nightingales' letter box.

It was thought that either shyness or a sense of decorum led her to ignore the simplest and most pleasurable way of getting to know people, that is, a visit to the Goat and Whistle. Most new immigrants were in there at the drop of an optic. They asked for a pint of the landlord's best then, foot on the bar rail, would hesitantly broach a subject or drop an agreeable remark into an already established conversation, trying to make friends.

Invariably warmly welcomed, they would return home confirmed in the belief that it was only in the country that people really had time for you. Most remained happily unaware that it was merely the stultifying boredom of seeing the same old faces day in day out that promoted such keen interest. They did not even notice when they, in their turn, became stultifyingly bored.

Bell-ringing, as has already been mentioned, was Mrs Hollingsworth's latest humour. To date she had attended half a dozen sessions without apparently exhausting her interest. But she was not always prompt and so, when she hadn't arrived at half past five, no one was either surprised or concerned.

The vicar, the Reverend Bream, listened with half an ear for her approach whilst tidying a pile of church guides desktop published by his wife. Priced modestly at fifty pence, they were very popular with visitors, at least half of whom put something, if rarely the full amount, in the box.

Mrs Molfrey wandered in, apologising for her lateness and doing a quick head count.

'She's not come back then, Simone?' After she had explained the background to this remark, the vicar decided to wait no further and they all hove to.

The practice was for a funeral the following day. Usually requiring nothing more than a somnolent ongoing toll, the bereaved on this occasion had requested a rendering of Oranges and Lemons, a childhood favourite of the dear departed. It was not a peal with which the Fawcett Green campanologists were familiar. But the vicar, who knew it well, had written it out on cards. This was their third run through. Substituting now for their absent colleague, the Reverend Bream swung rhythmically. Arms stretched, he took deep regular breaths, while the heels of his elastic-sided black boots rose and fell and the coarse red, white and blue hemp slipped through his fingers.

Next to him little Mrs Molfrey shot up into the air, her ringlets flying and unlaced tennis shoes hanging off her feet before descending gravely to the worn flagstones. The team rang for half an hour then, as was usual, repaired to the vestry for refreshments.

Avis Jennings, the doctor's wife, put the kettle on an old electric boiling ring. The vicar broke the seal on a pack of arrowroot biscuits. No one liked these much but Mrs Bream insisted on supplying them, having read somewhere that arrowroot was not only nutritious but calming to the nerves.

Just before Christmas, Avis had introduced a box of homemade hazelnut clusters. Someone, no doubt over-stimulated by excess protein, had let this slip. A definite coldness emanated from the vicarage and, as a result, Avis Jennings was left off the church flower rota for three months.

Mugs of well-sugared tea were now handed out. Everyone sat, in varying degrees of comfort, among coils of chicken wire and green Oasis, choirboys' surplices, the Sunday School's paints and brushes, Bible storybooks and towering piles of dusty hymnals.

The vicar took a sip of tea, far too strong for his liking, and turned the conversation once more to Mrs Hollingsworth's absence.

'Have you seen her at all today, Elfrida?'

'No, I haven't,' said Mrs Molfrey in a squeezed-up voice for she was bending over threading some tape through the eyelet of her plimsolls.

'What about you, dear heart?'

Cubby Dawlish turned very pink and tugged at his brief white beard, more of a sparkly frill really, which ran neatly from one earlobe to the other. Then he cleared his throat shyly before also admitting ignorance of Mrs Hollingsworth's whereabouts. 'But I don't think she could have gone far. I'm sure I would have noticed if Charlie's taxi had turned up. I've been outside nearly all day.'

Cubby also lived next door to Alan and Simone Hollingsworth in a grace and favour residence placed discreetly among the fruit trees in Mrs Molfrey's orchard. In lieu of rent and in gratitude for her kindness, he spent a great deal of time working in the garden.

'I'm not sure,' began the vicar, urging his plate of pallid soporifics to little effect, 'if there's a lot of point in her coming tomorrow. She's not really familiar with the peal and we don't want anyone dropping a clanger.'

Mrs Molfrey gave a whoop of pleasure at this felicity, slapping her thin haunches and releasing puffs of dust from her rusty chenille skirt.

'Especially,' added the Reverend Bream sternly, 'at a funeral.'

It took a lot more than this to subdue Mrs Molfrey who chortled again and nudged Cubby so hard he almost overbalanced. Reaching out to save himself, he knocked over a watering can and blushed even more deeply than before.

'I'll call round after I've locked up,' said the Reverend Bream. 'If she hasn't returned, no doubt Alan will have some sort of explanation.'

'I wouldn't trouble,' said Avis Jennings. 'He's a workaholic. Never back before eight, Simone said. And that's early.'

'It's no trouble,' said the vicar. 'I have to call on old Mrs Carter and they're practically on the way.'

Nightingales was one of three houses set a little way back from St Chad's Lane, in an area not quite large or clearly defined enough for the post office to designate it a close. On the left of the Hollingsworths' was a 1930s pebble dash, complete with glass door panels in harsh, fruit-gum colours. Patchily stained bits of wood had been fixed to the walls in an alternating series of Y shapes and inverted chevrons. These were, in the opinion of Avis Jennings who came from the North, neither use nor ornament. A polished wooden shingle read 'The Larches' though not a single arboreal specimen supported the bold claim.

On the other side of Nightingales were Mrs Molfrey's twin cottages discreetly transformed into one. Only thirty years older than the hideous mock Tudor, Arcadia exuded a stable and serene charm. The gardens were exuberant, fruitful and very lovely.

The Hollingsworths' residence was totally out of place in

this small enclosure. 'A Desirable Executive Country Dwelling' according to the pre-sale literature, it had been built in 1989 by an enterprising money man with a nose for a snip. He had bought the row of three decrepit workman's hovels previously standing there, demolished them and erected the type of building usually only seen fraternising with a group of select fellows on camera-ridden, landscaped grounds behind fully charged high-wire fences.

The village had protested fiercely once the scale and pomposity of the entrepreneur's vision was revealed but to no effect. Bribery in the planning offices was suspected.

Alan's car was parked a few feet from the double garage. The gravel was all swirly and churned about as if he had driven up to the house in a great hurry, skidded and slammed on the brakes. The gates were wide open. Walking up to the front door, the vicar lifted the tail of a brass mermaid and rapped firmly several times.

No one came. The Reverend Bream hesitated, wondering what to do next. He waited, enjoying the scent from clusters of white nicotiana flowering in fat Italian pots. Then he rapped again.

Afterwards the vicar was to say that he sensed, even at that early stage, that there was something very wrong. But the truth was, within seconds he had got bored and would have simply given up had it not been for the car, so plainly visible a few feet away.

As the unexpected silence continued, curiosity overcame him. Not thinking for a moment how such behaviour might strike the casual passer-by – he had never known embarrassment in his life – the vicar crossed over to the sitting-room windows and, cupping his hands against the early evening sunlight, peered in.

A lush room. Peach walls and hangings, clotted cream

carpet, pretty puffed-up silk sofas and armchairs. Gilt and ormolu and crystal. Masses of flowers and several table lamps, none of which were switched on. No human life at all.

A creaking sound some short distance away caught his attention. The door of a shed was being closed in the garden of The Larches. Discreet footsteps tiptoed away. The Reverend Bream guessed it to be the master of the house. Like everyone else, he was familiar with the Brockleys' sly, concealing ways. Not for them the frank enjoyment of a bit of a gossip in the village shop or a good stare over the fence. Whilst being passionately interested in everyone else's business, they presented a united front of absolute indifference. Metaphorically they would cover their eyes and ears and mouths in self-righteous repulsion should even the merest morsel of titillation drift their way. Mrs Bream said they reminded her of the three wise monkeys. She could be very unChristian at times.

Naughtily, the vicar called out, 'Good evening, Mr Brockley!' Then, as the footsteps hastened away, he went back to the mermaid and knocked again.

Inside the house, to be precise in the kitchen doorway, the quarry stood, motionless, head resting on the painted white wooden frame. On the point of entering the hall when his visitor first knocked, Alan Hollingsworth had frozen on the spot, staring at the panel of thick, wavily patterned glass through which the vicar's distorted figure could be seen but not recognised.

Alan closed his eyes and moaned silently. The seconds passed, marked by the soft whirring of a grandmother clock in the dining room and the strained beating of his heart. He cursed himself for not putting the car away. Weeks – no, years passed. Whoever it was still stood there.

The ridiculousness of his position and the impossibility of maintaining it indefinitely filled him with humiliation and distress. He knew that, even if whoever it was out there gave up, someone else would sooner or later take their place. Villages were like that. People were always calling round collecting or stuffing leaflets through the letter box or asking you to sign petitions. Even though he had remained pointedly uninvolved in the day-to-day life of Fawcett Green, no one escaped entirely. Eventually neighbours, receiving neither sight nor sound of the inhabitants of Nightingales, would start to wonder if they were still *in situ*. If they were 'all right'. Someone might even call the police. A cold sweat broke over Alan's face and vile-tasting liquid surged into his throat.

The tapping started again.

Telling himself that the first time would be the worst and the quicker he got it over the better, he turned his head and called, 'Coming.'

The vicar fixed an expression of concern to his face. An expression he had no trouble whatsoever maintaining when the door was finally opened, for Hollingsworth looked quite dreadful. His face was pale, the skin sheened with moisture as if he had just completed a vigorous workout. His eyes stared wildly and he was frowning; struggling to remember where he had seen the man facing him before. His tangled hair stood on end as if he had been tugging at it. When he spoke his voice was loud and he seemed to have trouble breathing normally. This resulted in his sentences being oddly punctuated.

'Ah Vicar it's. You.'

Agreeing politely that it was indeed him, the Reverend Bream took Hollingsworth's involuntary step backwards as an invitation to enter and was on the hall carpet in a twinkling. He asked if all was well.

'We were a little worried when Simone didn't come to practice,' he elaborated. 'And I'm really calling to tell her not to bother about the funeral tomorrow.'

'Funeral?'

'Two o'clock.' The vicar became increasingly concerned. The man looked almost demented. 'Are you quite well, Mr Hollingsworth? You look as if you've had rather a shock.'

'No, no. Everything's.' The rest of the sentence seemed either to escape or defeat him. He glanced aside, rather longingly, it seemed to the vicar, at the now wide open front door. But the Reverend Bream, faced with an obviously deeply distressed parishioner, was nothing if not aware of his duty.

'May I?' he inquired and, without waiting for a reply, sailed into the Viennese pastry of a living room. He lowered his ample rear on to a heap of heart-shaped satin cushions, slid off and replaced himself more securely. He then turned a determinedly benign smile on Hollingsworth who had reluctantly followed him in.

'Now, Alan,' said the vicar, 'if I may call you that?' His kindly glance was momentarily distracted by the sight of a splendid silver tray holding two cut-glass decanters and several bottles including a Jack Daniel's, nearly full, and a Bushmills, half empty. There was no way, on his stipend, the vicar could afford either of these splendid beverages. He heaved himself upright again saying, 'You look as if you could do with a drink. Perhaps I could—'

'Simone's. Don't worry I'll pass. The message.'

'She isn't here then?'

'No. Her mother.' Hollingsworth shook his head and made a despairing gesture with his palms upturned.

'I'm so sorry.' The vicar gave up all hope of the Jack

Daniel's. Even lusting after it now struck him as slightly improper. 'I do hope it's nothing serious.'

'A stroke.' Alan said this without thinking but immediately recognised it as an invention of genius. Unlike other illnesses, where one either got better or worse, strokes could incapacitate indefinitely, engendering a more or less permanent need for attention. So if the worse came to the worst. The very, very worst . . .

'Oh dear.' The vicar reprised his condolences and made a move to leave. For the first time since he had answered the door, Hollingsworth's face relaxed slightly. Relief would be too strong a word. Just a small decrease in wariness and tension.

'Does she live far away?' asked the Reverend Bream.

'Wales,' said Alan. 'The Midlands.'

'That's not so bad,' said the vicar. 'Perhaps you'll be able—'

'I don't. Think so business.'

'Of course.' The Reverend Bream nodded understandingly while trying to recall what Hollingsworth's business actually was. Something to do with computers. The vicar's brain turned to custard at the very thought. One of his flock had recently presented St Chad's with a second-hand machine on to which had been transferred every scrap of data relating to parish matters. Now the vicar could not even find his verger's phone number. He had thought the dark night of the soul a mere metaphysical concept until pitched into its shadows by the demon Amstrad.

Now, with one foot on the front step, the thought struck him that Evadne, once advised of this present set-up, would chide him for not extending a supper invitation. He mumbled something along the lines of 'cold collation' and 'stretching to three'.

Much to his relief, for he had spotted the game pie in the larder at tea time and thought it a very small one, Hollingsworth immediately declined.

'Freezer. Full,' he said and closed the door before his visitor was properly outside.

Walking away, the Reverend Bream turned and looked behind him. Alan Hollingsworth was resting against the wavy glass panel. As the vicar watched, the dark shape, its outline shimmering as if beneath deep water, gradually started to slip and slide downwards until, within a matter of seconds, the man was slumped on the floor.

'The vicar's just called at Nightingales.'

Iris Brockley, her nostrils satisfactorily filled with the rich smell of Windowlene, bent a frilled net curtain rigid with starch to the side and took a discreet step backwards. When it came to surveillance, Iris could have given tips to the FBI.

'Does he have a collecting tin?'

'No.'

'That's all right then.'

Iris lifted her husband's cup and wiped the saucer where the spoon had made a mark, wiped the spoon, wiped the plastic tray hooked over the arm of his chair and replaced the flowered, gold-rimmed crockery. Then she perched on the edge of the pale green Dralon stool attached to the knee-high telephone table. The darker green piping pressed into the back of her plump thighs.

'I wonder what he wanted.'

'I'm sure I couldn't begin to comprehend.'

'I hope there's nothing wrong, Reg.'

'Won't be our business if there is.' Mr Brockley closed the *Daily Express*, smoothed it front and back with the palm of his hand, folded it into a precise half and placed it in a bamboo rack by his feet.

'Have you finished with that?' Springing up when her husband nodded, Iris snatched the newspaper out again and disappeared to the kitchen.

Reg closed his eyes, waiting for the thwack of the pedal bin's lid as it hit the wall and the clang as it fell back. When this had been followed by a cry of, 'Get back into your basket *please*, madam!' he drained his tea, unclipped a pen from his breast pocket and opened the *Radio Times*. All of his movements were cramped. Completed almost before they began.

When Iris returned he was drawing three neat rings round their evening's viewing: *Question Time, May To December* and *The Travel Show*. Not that the Brockleys ever went anywhere. Leafy Bucks was good enough for them, thank you very much. But they enjoyed programmes about foreign climes, especially when the unfortunate tourists were stranded, struck down by some exotic virus, mugged or, best of all, asphyxiated in poorly ventilated hotel rooms.

Having replaced the magazine, Reg now stepped out through the French windows as he did every evening about this time in clement weather. He would perambulate around the garden, returning on the dot for the six o'clock news and the arrival, also on the dot (bar her late night) of their daughter Brenda.

It was a lovely evening. The soft, sweet air pressed against Reg's plump cheeks and stiff little moustache. All he needed was a cherrywood pipe and copper-coloured spaniel and he could have stepped straight into a Metroland poster.

Next door's clematis was climbing exuberantly over the trellis and trailing down the Brockleys' side. Reg and Iris had had many weighty discussions about this beautiful plant but refrained from any direct comment. This would mean 'getting involved', which was out of the question. A comment about the weather, a tut or two regarding the increase in village vandalism, a brief, insincere compliment with respect to each other's floral landscapes, this was the limit of the Hollingsworth/Brockley discourse.

A handle turned a few feet away and someone stepped on to the patio. From the weight of the footsteps, Reg guessed it must be Alan. Although present first, Reg immediately cast himself in the role of invisible eavesdropper. He stood very still, breathing silently through his mouth and hoping he wouldn't need to swallow.

Hollingsworth started to call Nelson, the cat, in a voice that struck Reg as rather strange and croaky. As if he had a cold.

Reg tiptoed back into the house to pass this snippet of information on to Iris. She was as intrigued as he, for it was well known that Alan had paid the creature no mind since the day it arrived. It was Simone who had taken pity on the tabby kitten, found abandoned nearly a year ago. She who fed and brushed it, who cooed and whistled softly to persuade it home at the end of the day. The Brockleys were still discussing this unusual state of affairs when Brenda arrived.

As the dark brown Mini Metro slid past the kitchen window to park beneath the car port roof of corrugated plastic, Iris donned her frilly apron, got an M & S Welsh rarebit out of the freezer and switched on the microwave.

Iris and pre-prepared meals had been made for each other. Acutely aware of her duty as a wife and mother to put hot, appetising food on the table at regular intervals, she had struggled throughout her married life to do so. She washed superior cuts of meat (never offal) and gutted fish until the water ran clear. She forced herself to make pastry even though the fat got under her nails and no amount of scrubbing ever convinced her they did not always remain ever so slightly greasy.

Now, as she slid the little aluminium tray from its temptingly illustrated sleeve, she thought how very reassuring frozen comestibles were. Constrained beneath a glittery crust of sterile crystals, they did not leak or smell or ask to be in any way humanly dealt with but were quickly transformed, as if by magic, into comforting, tasty nourishment. Iris sliced a tomato for freshness and put the kettle on.

Brenda entered the house and ran swiftly upstairs. Her routine never varied. She would hang her coat in the wardrobe, tidy her hair then wash her hands. Shona, a white poodle tucked away in a wicker basket between the washing machine and the fridge, started to whine with happiness the moment this recognisable procedure began. As the toilet flushed, Iris warmed the pot and by the time her daughter came into the kitchen everything was ready.

Brenda ate very daintily. Small portions chewed with her lips closed as she had been taught from early childhood. Mr Brockley regarded his offspring's neat maroon skirt and jacket and white blouse with pride and thought how smart she looked. Her short brown hair was brushed neatly away from her face and a red and gold pin in her left lapel displayed her full name. Reg, who had never flown, thought she looked like an air hostess.

He and his wife often discussed their daughter's future with respectful seriousness. A business career was all well and good but they were full of hopes that she would, fairly soon, marry a nice, respectable man. Living nearby she could then, at judiciously spaced intervals, present them with two nice, well-behaved grandchildren. They called it settling down though a disinterested observer might have got the impression that Brenda was already so firmly settled it would take a ton of dynamite to move her.

She was sitting now, little finger eloquently crooked, sipping tea and answering the customary questions about her day in copious detail. Brenda knew how much her mother – and father, too, now that he had retired – anticipated this daily exposure to the hurly burly of high finance.

'Then to top it all Hazel Grantley, from Accounts, chimed in. As she always does, given half a chance. "Don't tell me," she said, "that interest was miscalculated. Machines don't make mistakes."' Brenda licked the tip of her finger and dotted up a final crumb of toast. 'No one gets on with her.'

'You said.'

'Including her husband.' Brenda spoke with some satisfaction. Like many unhappy single people she relished tales of marital discord. 'Then Janine, who was really upset by this time, came back with "Why not? They're only human." Of course everyone laughed, upon which what should she do but burst into tears? And all this with a customer at the counter. I don't know what Mr Marchbanks would have said.'

'Wasn't he there then?' inquired Iris.

'Dentist. Then no sooner had all this blown over when Jacqui Willing's pen walked.'

'As per usual,' said Iris knowledgeably.

'Trish Travers from Personnel said she'd seen it in the toilet. Jacqui said *she* wasn't so old she had to keep running in there every five minutes. Unlike some.' Brenda, having wrung every possible drop of drama from her day at the Coalport and National Building Society, now dabbed at the corners of her small mouth with an embroidered napkin.

Reg and Iris exchanged glances of arch complicity. Without conferring on the matter, neither had mentioned the unusual state of affairs next door, both believing the most toothsome morsel should be left till last. Now, as Brenda checked the time on her diamanté cocktail watch against the gingham plate on the kitchen wall, Reg cleared his throat and Iris underlined the importance of the moment by taking her pinny off. Brenda looked surprised when they both sat down at the table.

'Something's happened next door, dear.'

'Next door?' Brenda was stacking her cup and saucer and plate together ready to take to the sink. There was a sudden clatter as they all rattled on the Formica.

Iris said, 'Careful.'

'What sort of thing?' Brenda's voice was dry. She gave a scrapy little cough before continuing, 'Everything looked as usual when I drove by.'

'Mrs Hollingsworth's not there.'

'Simone?' Brenda started looking round the room. Darting glances accompanied by quick jerky movements of the head, like a bird looking for food. 'Who told you that?'

To the Brockleys' surprise their daughter got up, crossed over to the sink and turned on the hot tap. Brenda never washed up or even helped to clear away. It was not expected. There was the unspoken assumption that her contribution to the household's expenses, or 'keep' as Iris put it, not only covered her food but relieved her of all domestic duties. Apart from cleaning her room which no one could get into as it was permanently locked.

'I'll do those, dear.'

'It's all right.'

'At least put some gloves on.'

'So . . .' Brenda plunged her hands into a pyramid of iridescent bubbles and started clashing cutlery about before rephrasing her question. 'Where did you hear that?'

'No one actually told us,' said Iris. Catching her husband's eye, she was unable to conceal her anxiety. Brenda had gone very pale except for a bright flush across her cheekbones and was now sloshing about in the sink so vigorously that the sudsy water was splashing over the edge. 'It was just something Daddy . . . um . . .'

'Deduced.'

'Yes, deduced.'

'You see, Brenda . . .' Reg frowned at the rigidly upright back and furiously working elbows. 'Couldn't you stop that for a second?'

'I'm listening.'

'There was a bell-ringing practice late this afternoon – and very unusual chimes they were too – but Simone couldn't have turned up because I happened to be in the front garden when they finished and she didn't come home.'

'Then the vicar—'

'All right, Iris.'

'Sorry, dear.'

'The Reverend Bream called at the house shortly after this and I think it reasonable to infer that he was inquiring about her absence. Not only was it a very long time indeed before the door was opened but he was no sooner in the place than out again. And then—'

'This is the best bit.'

'Alan came out into the back garden *calling the cat*.'

'Well, he'd have to, wouldn't he? If she wasn't there to do it.' Brenda pulled the plug and dried her hands very vigorously on the tea towel. 'I think you're making a mountain out of a molehill.'

Reg and Iris stared at each other in disappointment and dismay. There had been many an occasion when a mountain if not indeed a whole cloud-capped range had been made of detail not nearly so rich in dramatic potential. And Brenda had been the first to relish such discussions. But now she simply flung the cloth down, clicked her tongue in the direction of the dog and left the room. Shona, full of joy but with more sense than to express it by barking, leapt from her basket and trotted after. There was a breathing space when the Brockleys could hear the bell on the dog collar tinkling as her lead was attached. Then the front door slammed and they were gone.

Reg and Iris rushed to the picture window in the lounge and watched as the pair made their way down the drive. The poodle dancing and prancing, ecstatically exercising her vocal cords; Brenda walking carefully with neat, even steps. They hesitated briefly outside Nightingales before walking on into St Chad's Lane.

Reg and Iris returned to the kitchen. Iris picked up the tea towel – a nice view of Powys Castle – prised open a turquoise plastic peg and hung the towel up next to her rubber gloves.

Her husband said, 'What's got into her tonight?'

'Nerves, Reg. I blame these high-powered meetings. Remember how you used to come home?'

Heather Gibbs gave Arcadia a good seeing-to every Friday. Two hours, twelve pounds. Generous in comparison with the usual but, as Heather's mum pointed out, if you're batty as an egg whisk you're going to have to cough up just that little bit extra.

Mrs Molfrey sat in her faded petit-point wing chair, feet up on a beaded footstool, and watched Heather with deep satisfaction. When the girl had first turned up some months ago now, clomping into the sitting room on shoes like great blocks of wood and bawling her head off, Mrs Molfrey had trembled on behalf of her delicate glasses and fragile ornaments. But Heather, though lumberingly uneconomical in her movements, handled every one of these treasured artefacts with the most gentle and precise movements.

At the moment she was carefully going over an ornately carved, many-mirrored overmantel with a feather duster. Mrs Molfrey's satisfaction deepened when she glimpsed, through a gap in the sitting-room door, her gleaming kitchen. Aware from a certain amount of static from the shiny pink box on her concave chest and the liveliness of Heather's lips that she was being spoken to, Mrs Molfrey switched on her deaf aid. She waited till the girl was looking elsewhere for she felt it was rather rude to have switched it off in the first place.

'So I said, what time do you call this and he only said "nookie time" didn't he? In front of me mam and the kids and everything.'

'Who was this, Heather?'

'Kevin's dad. He's never off the nest. Know what I mean?'

'Which dad is that?' asked Mrs Molfrey, for she had still not disentangled Heather's assorted progeny let alone grasped the ramifications of an extended family that seemed to cover half Bucks county.

'Barry. The one with the Harley Davidson.'

'Ah. The musician.'

Heather didn't bother to put her right. It wasn't worth it. She'd have forgotten by next time. And really Heather only chatted to be polite. Given a choice she'd as soon bring her Walkman and a tape of Barry Manilow. But the old lady must crave a bit of conversation what with only the old geezer in the caravan for company. He cooked for her every day too. Sweet really.

Now, giving a final polish to an emerald glass lustre, Heather asked Mrs Molfrey if she was ready for her cuppa. This was Heather's last chore. She would leave the tea and a piece of cake on the little piecrust table by Mrs Molfrey's chair.

Mrs Molfrey always asked Heather if she would like to join her but Heather had only done this once. The tea was disgusting. A funny colour and a worse smell. And there wasn't any other sort. Just looking at it, thought Heather, was enough to make you heave. Like dried up black worms all mixed up with yellow flowers.

Now, as she put the kettle on in the kitchen, Heather heard the thocketer, thocketer of a 500cc engine and saw, through the kitchen window, a Honda scooter bouncing gently over the grassy approach to the back of the house.

'It's Becky,' she called through to the other room.

'She'll be bringing my hair,' called back Mrs Molfrey. 'Chuck another spoon in the pot. And dig out the cake tin. There's a WI lemon drizzle.'

Becky Latimer, a sweet-faced young woman with a lightly freckled skin, smooth and brown as a hen's egg, lifted the latch and walked into the kitchen. She carried a wig block under one arm and a customised plastic carrier on which a crossed brush and comb surmounted the words 'Becky's Mobile Maison'.

'All done for you, Mrs Molfrey.' She smiled at the old lady. 'How's the world treating you today?'

'You'll stay for tea, Becky?' Mrs Molfrey laid an

arrangement of knobby bones covered loosely by gingery spotted skin urgently on the girl's arm.

'Course I will,' said Becky who was already running twenty minutes late. 'Just a quick one.'

As Heather brought out Mrs Molfrey's tray, Becky brought up Simone Hollingsworth's name, asking Mrs Molfrey if she had seen anything of the woman. 'Only I was giving her a cut and blow dry yesterday half three and when I turned up she'd gone out. She didn't cancel or ring or anything. It's not like her at all.'

'I heard she was looking after a sick relative,' said Mrs Molfrey, 'and had to dash off. No doubt it put the appointment right out of her mind.'

'Yes, it would,' said Becky with some relief. She was trying to build up her business and had feared that Mrs Hollingsworth had become dissatisfied with her work. Simone was a demanding client and her soft, white-gold hair was far from easy to handle. Unlike most of Becky's customers she wanted something different every week, if only in some small detail. When Becky arrived there would often be a *Vogue* or *Tatler* lying open on the sitting-room table and her young heart would sink as she was shown some elaborately styled or brilliantly cut coiffure and asked to copy it. Still, so far, fingers crossed, she seemed to have done OK.

While these thoughts had been passing through Becky's mind, Heather had taken the cling film off the cake, cut it in slices and poured a second cup of tea. Now, having put her outdoor coat on, she stopped in the middle of saying goodbye and said instead, 'Hey, Becks. You talking about Mrs H from Nightingales?'

'That's right.'

'She was on the market bus.'

'On the bus?'

'That's right, Mrs Molfrey.'

'But she never goes anywhere.'

'Well, she went to Causton.'

'Was that the two thirty?' asked Becky.

'No, half twelve. Got off outside Gateways. And I'll tell you another funny thing. She hadn't got no case nor nothing. Just a handbag.'

'You'd think,' said Becky, 'if she was visiting this sick relative she'd have got off at the stop near the railway station.'

'It's a right mystery,' said Heather. She swung round and her full skirt floated about her, describing a wide circle.

There really should be a shipping warning when people like Heather entered one's natural orbit, thought Mrs Molfrey. She closed her eyes and prayed.

'Ah well,' said Heather, now safely on the threshold. 'Ta-ra again.'

'Could you knock on Cubby's caravan as you go by, please?' asked Mrs Molfrey. 'Tell him the lemon drizzle's up.'

Becky sipped a little of the tea which she disliked quite as much as Heather.

'Isn't that extraordinary, Becky?' said Mrs Molfrey, inhaling the jasmine fragrance with a sigh of pleasure. 'Going off to care for someone who's ill with no more than a handbag. You'd think at least they'd take a little Benger's. Or some beef jelly.'

'P'raps Mr Hollingsworth's going to drive over later.'

'Perhaps. What I can't understand,' continued Mrs Molfrey, 'is why she took the bus. It takes nearly an hour to cover the distance Charlie's taxi does in fifteen minutes.'

'Well, can't be to save money, Mrs Molfrey.' Becky

glanced at her watch. 'Sorry, I have to go now. I'm running a bit late.'

'Dear child,' cried Mrs Molfrey. 'Why didn't you say?'

For the next couple of days Fawcett Green attempted to observe the owner of Nightingales in what it regarded as a discreet manner. This involved slowing up, often to a marked degree, when passing the house and looking in the windows. Listening keenly for the laser whir and soft metal clunk of the garage door being opened or closed. Or strolling down Mrs Molfrey's back garden and casually glancing over the fence. But in every instance Fawcett Green was unlucky. The object of their interest did not show himself.

It was plain, however, that Simone had not returned, which left a male person living on his own. Naturally it was thought, for there is nothing more conservative than an English village, that such a man must be in need of assistance. Immediately this need was diagnosed, a support group rallied to satisfy it.

The group did its best. An apple pie, some fresh eggs and a jar of green tomato chutney were placed on the doorstep of Nightingales and stayed there until they were aggrievedly taken back. A message slipped through the letter box offering to collect and return any necessary washing was also ignored. As was a note asking if any shopping was required and an offer to cut the hedge. Umbrage was well and truly taken when it was discovered that a boxful of convenience foods had been ordered by telephone and delivered by Ostlers, the village store.

After this the frustrated Samaritans, acknowledging that you just couldn't help some people, gave up any direct approach. A sharp eye was still kept, though, and the village noted, not without some satisfaction, that only twenty-four hours after Mrs Hollingsworth's departure, things started to take a definite turn for the worse.

On Friday the curtains remained closed till lunchtime. On Saturday and Sunday they were not opened all day. Determined to regard such moral laxity as a cry for help, the team renewed its efforts by tapping on the front door and, when this was ignored, repeating the procedure at the rear, in both cases with negative results.

When the milkman called for payment, there were three full pints on the step. He rapped the knocker several times and shouted, 'Milk-oh!' through the letter box. Eventually the door opened a fraction, a ten pound note was pressed into his hand and the words 'Don't leave any more' were breathed through the opening on whisky-soured breath.

Naturally this was all round the place in no time. Later, further verification of Alan Hollingsworth's debauched state was provided when a stream of bottles descended from his wheelie bin into the masticating maw of Causton Borough Council's refuse lorry. Avis Jennings said it sounded as if someone was disposing of a greenhouse. The vicar, put in the picture by his spouse, thought of all that Jack Daniel's consumed in lonely isolation and wondered if he should once more attempt to offer solace.

In the Goat and Whistle the regulars discussed Simone's absence among themselves. No one believed the 'illness in the family' story. The landlord, no doubt chagrined that not a single swallow of Hollingsworth's river of forgetfulness had been purchased at his establishment, was especially scathing.

'A load of old cock,' he said, pulling a Beamish for a puce-complexioned man in a Tattershall check waistcoat.

'She's buggered off to get a bit of life for herself. And I for one don't blame her.'

There was a rumble of assent. Neglect a pretty wife, was the general theory, and you're asking for trouble. Not everyone agreed. An advocaat and lemonade snowball thought that, far from being neglected, Mrs H was kept on such a short leash that boredom and frustration had driven her to snap it. This was also not universally acceptable.

'You work your fingers to the bone for 'em,' said the Beamish, 'buy them everything they want and where does it get you? Bloody nowhere.'

A female with arms like Popeye and a leering, pock-marked face threw darts with savage accuracy. She pointed out how totally pathetic it was that men let themselves go the minute they didn't have some poor drudge of a woman running round after them.

'I can think of one party who won't be heartbroken,' said the snowball very quietly. She winked and tapped her nose which was tiny, soft and porous like a mildewed strawberry. 'After what Hollingsworth done to him. Dancing on the ceiling, he'll be.'

'Cruel, that was.'

'I wouldn't be surprised if he'd run off with her hisself.'

'Nah. He's got other fish to fry.'

Everyone turned and looked down the room to where a solitary drinker sat nursing a half of bitter. He didn't look as if he was about to start dancing on the ceiling. More as if he was expecting it to fall on him any minute. He'd hardly spoken since he came into the bar and now, draining his glass, Gray Patterson got up and left without a word.

It had actually been in the Goat and Whistle that Gray had met his 'other fish'. At the time he had not appreciated just how unlikely such a contingency was. She had visited the pub no more than twice in the five years since she had moved to the village. On this, the second occasion, Sarah Lawson had dropped in for a box of matches, the village store having run out.

He knew who she was of course – in such a small place everyone knew everyone else by sight – and a little about her. She taught part-time in adult education, had hardly any money, her house was falling down. She made models out of clay and also worked with stained glass. It was rare to walk past Bay Tree Cottage without hearing music, powerful operatic bawling that Fawcett Green accepted with a resigned shrug, for artists were known to need a creative ambience.

Gray was intrigued by Sarah's looks and the way she dressed. By her gravity and by the fact that she appeared genuinely not to give a damn as to what anyone thought either of her or her way of life. And so, following her out of the Goat and Whistle and catching up in St Chad's Lane, he introduced himself.

'Oh, I know who you are,' responded Sarah. 'From the front page of the *Causton Echo*.'

'You make me sound notorious.'

'Doesn't take much in a place this size.'

'You mustn't believe everything you read in the papers.'

'Sounds like a useful, if slightly patronising, tip.'

'Sorry.'

A bad start. They walked on in silence while Gray sought to repair the damage. He had more sense than to attempt a personal compliment which he felt would be judged both clumsy and impertinent. But he could, in all honesty, praise her garden.

'Every time I come down this way I admire it.'

'I can't imagine why.' She had a calm, clear voice. 'It's an absolute shambles.'

'The balance, I think. You seem to have something of everything but not too much of anything.'

'Can't take credit for that. My father created and cared for it. Almost to the last day of his life.'

'Ah, yes.' He remembered hearing that the house had belonged to her parents. 'Did they bequeath any advice on horticultural matters? I could do with a few tips.'

'Start with clean healthy soil. Feed it properly. Plant only top quality stuff. And if ugly or poisonous things turn up, yank them out and burn them.'

'Not a bad recipe for life when you come to think of it.'

Sarah gave him a sharp, interested look. How bright her eyes were! Unflecked, shining, brilliant blue. Gray was still surreptitiously studying her severe, elegant profile when they arrived at Bay Tree Cottage.

Sarah dragged the unhinged gate to one side.

'Could I come in for a minute?'

'What for?'

'Oh.' Though he had spoken on impulse and half anticipated a refusal, Gray found himself already standing on the path. 'Just a talk.'

'No.'

'I'd like to get to know you.'

'Why?'

'Because . . .' Gray felt rather at a loss. Most women would not ask that question. They would know why. And yet he could see she was being neither *faux naif* nor coy.

'Don't you ever fill conversations out, Sarah?' He stepped back on to the verge. Lifted the gate into its previous position. 'Qualify, elaborate, make excuses, crack jokes? Hand out recipes?'

'Not really. What's the point?'

'I hate unanswerable questions.'

'And I feel they're the only sort worth asking.' She smiled then but to herself, shutting him out. 'So you see we shall never get on.'

'I could change. I'm a flexible man.'

'Goodbye, Gray.'

He loved the way she spoke his name. A slight slurring of the R. Not an impediment, and certainly not a lisp; more a rough gliding over. It was irresistible.

He called out,'Would you like me to mend this?'

'Certainly not. Took years to get it to that state. Anyway,' she turned on the step and stared amusedly back at him, 'if I want it mending I can mend it myself.'

All that had taken place nearly three months ago. He had not given up. He had run into her 'by accident on purpose' a few times and fallen into yet more amiable conversation. Once, out walking his dog, he had let the leash slip and had to rescue the animal from Sarah's vegetable patch. Unfortunately he chose a Wednesday for this ingenuous ploy, which turned out to be her working day. He had appeared a couple of times with some flowers or fruit from his own garden. The offerings had been graciously accepted, with thanks, and the door shut firmly in his face.

He asked one or two people discreet questions about her then, afraid she might get to hear about this, stopped. In any case he discovered very little. Her parents had only bought the house when they retired. It wasn't as if she had grown up in the village. In fact, people seemed to know hardly any more about her than he did himself.

If she had appeared actively to resent his attentions then naturally he would have ceased to make them. But in a dry, detached manner she seemed prepared to put up with it all.

Gray's guess was that she regarded him as some sort of mild divertissement.

But then, six weeks ago, everything had changed. He had brought along a small tray of seedlings, hellebores which she appeared not to have. She took the tray, smiled and asked him in. He stayed about half an hour. Her manner, Gray had to admit, was rather perfunctory. Still, he was over the threshold. That was the main thing.

On that occasion and on most of the ones that followed they spoke mainly of mundane matters. Gray, who had a mercurial temperament at the best of times, quickly became downcast. He told himself these were early days but couldn't help feeling that he was merely marking time. He tried to get her to talk about herself or her work but without success. Once, greatly daring, he asked if she had been married. A flinty reticence descended. Eventually she admitted to having lived with someone once for a year or two but preferred being on her own.

She would never go anywhere with him. In spite of his dire financial state, Gray had asked her out for dinner. And, when this offer was refused, to a movie or the theatre with much the same result. Once or twice they had been for a drink at the Goat and Whistle but mainly they just sat talking in the garden.

This present Saturday morning they were discussing – who wasn't? – the Hollingsworths. Gray was sitting on a rather battered sofa sipping a small cup of bitter Javanese coffee. Sarah was looking at her watch.

'My theory,' said Gray, 'for what it's worth, is that she has hied her to a nunnery.'

'Simone?'

'Having finally realised how meretricious are the sybaritic luxuries of this sinful world.'

'That'll be the day.'

'Have you been in their sitting room?'

'Yes.'

'The perfect setting for a *poule du luxe*, wouldn't you say?'

'What makes you think I'd know?' Sarah shook her watch and held it to her ear.

'I can just see Mrs H, gold-sandalled feet on a fluffy pink foot-stool, Malibu plus ice and a little parasol on her onyx side table eating chocolate truffles, varnishing her toenails and reading Jackie Collins.'

'She wasn't that dextrous on my course.'

'A sugared almond on legs.'

'What were you doing at Nightingales anyway?' Sarah came over, collected his cup and saucer, stacked it on top of her own and took them to the kitchen. 'Delivering the ass's milk?'

'We were friends, him and me. Well, sort of.'

'I knew you were business partners.' Standing in the doorway she gave him a strange look. Interested, curious but without a trace of sympathy. 'It was on the—'

'Front page of the *Causton Echo*.'

'That's right.'

'I trusted him.' Gray shrugged. 'The more fool me. When money comes through the door, friendship, it seems, buggers off through the window.'

'Did you really beat him up?'

'Yes.'

'And you lost everything?'

'Not quite. I haven't lost my negative equity – around fifty at the last reckoning. Or my debts. Or my dog – she's still hanging round. So let's look on the bright side.'

'You're taking it better than I would.'

'I'm suing the bastard for all he's got. That's how I'm taking it.'

Sarah put on some music, '*Di*', *cor mio*' from *Alcina*, and started to peel a damp muslin cloth away from a mass of clay on a marble slab. A narrow elongated male head with a long nose and a thin-lipped, down-turned mouth emerged. It was eyeless and appeared mutilated to Gray even though he knew the piece was in the process not of being destroyed but created.

Gray picked up his jacket and prepared to leave as he always did when he sensed his time was up. He was determined not to push his luck. As it was, he had a very strong feeling that the minute he was off the premises she forgot his very existence.

He turned at the door. Bending closely over the table, Sarah pressed her thumb hard into the clay, moved it slightly, took her hands away.

Suddenly, although it was merely an empty socket, intelligence sprang into being, informing the face. Giving it life. And Gray wondered how, with one simple movement, such a thing could be.

As this conversation took place, something else was happening which, though not directly connected with the Hollingsworth mystery, nevertheless prompted a response that drew the attention of a slightly wider world to Simone's disappearance.

Ostlers, the village store (Prop: Nigel Boast) was situated in the main street of Fawcett Green. This ran, like the bar on a capital T, across the top end of St Chad's Lane. A note on the door informed children that their presence was welcome one at a time.

This stern directive had cut down petty pilfering

33

considerably but there was still a certain amount of leakage. Mr Boast, who watched his young customers as would a hawk a fledging dove, could not understand this. It never occurred to him or Doreen, his 'good lady wife', that the culprits might be grown up.

The shop was very Tudory. The price tickets were written in Olde English, as was the notice behind the till: Pray Do Not Ask For Credit As Ye Refusal Oft Offends. Originally all the s's had been f's which was, as Mr Boast tirelessly explained, authentically correct. But no one was impressed by this conceit. Customers kept winking and asking for 'a pound of foffages' and 'fome tomato foup' so, after a while, Nigel and Doreen reluctantly reverted to more contemporary Elizabethan.

Cubby Dawlish, who was encouraged by Mrs Molfrey to sell surplus produce from her garden to eke out his pension, came in around half past ten with several pounds of broad beans. Handing over the laden wooden tray, Cubby forbore to haggle over the going rate, even though he was aware the eventual mark-up would probably be three times as much.

While the beans were being weighed, Cubby looked about him at the whitewashed walls and wooden beams. The latter, though artificial, were nothing like as false as the beam in Mr Boast's eye as he offered ten pence a pound, there being a glut at the moment. There was always a glut. Or an unexpected surplus. Cubby sometimes thought if he came in during the depths of winter with freshly picked raspberries some miraculously cheap source of such a delicacy would only that second have franchised itself to Ostlers.

While putting the coins in his pocket and commenting pleasantly on the sweet and balmy weather, he was asked, in his capacity as a very near neighbour, if he knew how Mrs Hollingsworth's mother was prospering after her stroke.

Cubby begged the shopkeeper's pardon and, when the question had been repeated, asked if it was in fact the case that Mrs Hollingsworth's 'sick relative' was, in fact, her mother.

'Verily,' replied Mr Boast who often slipped into high Tudor, especially after a session with the Civil War Society. 'Alan told the vicar in person.'

After declining to spend his earnings on some reduced Jamaica ginger cake, Cubby made his way back to Arcadia where his first task was to make a cup of banana-flavoured mineral-enriched Vita Life for Elfrida's elevenses. Whilst getting out the remains of the lemon drizzle, he passed on this snippet of information. She stared at him for a long moment in complete surprise.

'This is most disturbing, Cubby.'

'Why is that, my love?'

'Simone doesn't have a mother.'

'Doesn't . . .' He stood, a scoop of the vitamin supplement tilted near the opalescent beaker.

'You're spilling some.'

'Sorry.' He sprinkled in the rest of the powder. 'How do you know?'

'It's all over the draining board.'

'I mean,' Cubby blew the spillage into the sink, 'about Mrs Hollingsworth senior.'

'Simone told me herself. I was in the greenhouse a few weeks ago dividing some narcissi and she came wandering by. You know what she was like, poor girl. Always looking for something to do.' Mrs Molfrey spoke in the uncomprehending tones of someone who had so far been vouchsafed eighty-three years and had not found them nearly long enough to pack in all that she wanted to do.

'More to make conversation, I suspect, than out of real interest, she asked what I was about. When I explained, she said narcissi had always been her mother's favourite. And that she – Simone, that is – had ordered a wreath, a harp I think it was, made entirely of Pheasant's Eye, on the occasion of her mother's funeral.'

'How extraordinary.'

'Oh, I don't know. I should have thought a harp entirely suitable under the circumstances.'

'I meant—'

But Elfrida was retreating to her favourite armchair. Cubby followed, carrying her drink and his own, a midmorning pick-me-up of elderflower cordial, freshly squeezed lemon and English clover honey.

'So,' said Elfrida as she rested her thin, trembly shanks against the embroidered unicorns and dragons and roses with golden thorns, 'Alan Hollingsworth has been deliberately lying. Hmm.'

Cubby put the beaker carefully into Elfrida's hand, gently pressing her fingers round the glass, then sat down himself in a large, Chinese basket chair. He knew what was coming and the pointlessness of attempting any diversion.

'This would explain why she went the long way round on the bus and took no luggage. After all, even for the briefest of visits, one hurls some cologne and a few unmentionables into a Gladstone. There was no journey, as such, at all. She was simply going into Causton, either to shop or meet someone. *So where is she now?*' Elfrida paused for breath and a swig of her drink. 'It's all very slippery-snakery.'

'But not necessarily sinister, dear.' Cubby hesitated,

unsure how to continue. The truth of the matter was that this sort of situation was not unfamiliar. Ever since he had persuaded Elfrida to buy a television set almost five years ago she had been passionately addicted to all programmes, whether fictional or no, which had even the most slender connection with crime. Her dearest wish was to assist the police with their inquiries and if she had so far failed to do so it was certainly not for want of trying. Cubby had had great difficulty, after Elfrida's last foray, in saving her from an assault charge.

It had all come about after she had seen an Identikit portrait on *Crimewatch* and became convinced that the miscreant, who had held up a building society with a sawn-off shotgun, was none other than Fawcett Green's relief Christmas postman. She had been dissuaded with great difficulty from contacting the authorities and had agreed only on the condition that Cubby be present at the cottage from that day onwards at delivery time.

Once, he had been a few minutes late. Elfrida, quaking with panic, had armed herself with a broom handle. When the postman attempted to insert tidings of comfort and joy into the letter box, she had thrust the handle violently back. Emerging from his caravan, Cubby had discovered the poor man staggering blindly round the garden, bent double in agony.

'The quinces are ripening up well,' Cubby said now, very firmly. 'Would you like me to make some lemon and japonica jelly?'

The attempt was futile as he knew it must be. Being firm with Elfrida was like speaking to someone in a completely alien language. She could hear that your voice had got rather louder than usual (providing her box was switched on) and that you were standing four square in a very sturdy sort of way. She just didn't understand your problem.

'All this talk of jelly is by the by,' said Elfrida. 'The point at issue surely is what we are going to do about Simone.'

'I don't see why we have to get involved at all.'

'Bosh! Show some gumption, Dawlish.'

'What do you think we ought to do then?' asked Cubby, anticipating and dreading the reply.

'It's plain as a pikestaff.'

'I was afraid it would be,' he sighed and put his cup down. 'Righto. I'll bike over to Ferne Bassett and—'

'Forget Ferne Bassett!' cried Elfrida. 'Ferne Bassett is small potatoes. We're almost certainly describing a serious crime here. Mark my words, that man has done away with his wife. And with calumny of such magnitude there's little point in pussyfooting around with the infantry. It's not the local boys in blue we're after. It's the top brass.'

'But Elfie—'

'On the blower hotsy totsy, Dawlish, and order a Hackney carriage.'

At the sound of the taxi drawing up, Brenda Brockley's heart pounded. Ignoring her parents' disapproving glances she rushed to see what was happening and immediately afterwards rushed straight upstairs, thus avoiding any discussion or lecture on her odd behaviour.

She locked her door and went over to her pretty little writing desk which was placed in the large bay window. The chair on which she sat was pretty too. It had a tall, narrow back: two upright slats and a crossbar made of varnished papier-mâché inlaid with mother-of-pearl. An amber silk cushion patterned with silver fleur-de-lis was tied to the seat with narrow velvet ribbons. Facing her, on the sill, was a vase of deep red carnations.

These two pieces of furniture were deliberately different from anything else in the room. It was not that Brenda thought the other things boring or tasteless – though they were – but that she recognised their absolute unsuitability to play even the most humble part in a scene in which her grand illusion would be allowed to hold full sway.

She took a tiny gold key from a box covered with shells, unlocked the desk and rolled back the lid. From the interior she removed a large, shagreen-covered book labelled with the word *Diary* and filled with unlined pages of creamy yellow paper. Just inside the front cover was Sellotaped a photograph of Alan Hollingsworth which she had obtained in the spring of the previous year.

One Sunday afternoon when Reg and Iris were out buying a large supply of Paraquat from their nearest garden centre, Brenda, fortified by a schooner of sweet sherry, had approached the Hollingsworths over the larch lap divide. Explaining that she had just one shot left and Shona seemed to have quite lost interest, Brenda asked if she could take their picture. Somewhat surprised, they agreed.

Brenda adjusted the viewfinder with great care and got exactly the snap she wanted. A clear head and shoulders of Alan and no sign of Simone.

Brenda would have liked to have framed the photo. It deserved a beautiful silver one like those she had seen in antique shops; all flowing acanthus leaves and arabesques of lilies. But she was afraid that one day she would forget to lock it away in her desk. And that such a time might coincide with one or the other of her parents popping their heads in while she was having a meal or in the bath, to sneak a quick look round.

She wrote in her diary only at the weekends when there were enough hours to do it justice. Sometimes, and this was more exciting by far, she actually spoke to Alan. The smaller window in her room overlooked the forecourt of Nightingales and, when he was due to arrive home, she would open it with trembling fingers, lean out and call, 'Good evening.'

Brenda had pondered to an agonising degree as to how frequent these greetings should be and had finally decided on a ratio of one to ten. More frequently and she feared he would guess that her appearance was not accidental. Less and the fear was that she would be unable to bear the waiting.

The occasions of her calling out were carefully marked by an asterisk in her shagreen book with a special pen, the sort used at Christmas for labelling parcels. Filled with powerfully smelling runny liquid, it dried shining silver like a snail's track.

Once a month she and Alan actually conversed. These stomach-churning encounters were marked with a golden pen of the same type with the asterisk surmounted by a red felt-tipped drawing of a heart.

The conversations could only be brought about by a certain amount of artificial loitering which involved hanging around the front garden sniffing the roses and pretending to weed or playing outside in the lane with her dog. As Alan closed the garage door, Brenda, nauseous, her skin prickling with nerves, would toss a casual 'Hullo' in his direction.

He replied of course but the ensuing conversations were necessarily brief. How many responses were there after all to a suggestion that today had been uncertain/awful/ wonderful/changeable? Or that the news didn't seem to get any better. She would follow through with, 'And how are things at Nightingales?'

Alan would then assure her that things were fine. Although he only rarely asked how matters at The Larches were faring, Brenda was never unprepared.

Recognising that her replies must not only be short and light-hearted but, hopefully, amusing, she would practise them right up to the last minute, a throwaway almost negligent style being her aim.

There was no one to whom she could sing her love. At work, where her shyness was mistaken for slyness, she had no friends. And the thought of telling her parents was utterly appalling. Even thinking of it chilled her bones. They had always seemed to Brenda antiseptically unaware that such a thing as romance existed. She had never heard a sound smacking even remotely of eroticism from their bedroom. The only rhythmical vibration occurred when the alarm clock went off. Sometimes, regarding the straining hospital corners on the chaste, single beds, Brenda wondered if she was a changeling found under a gooseberry bush.

Like everyone else in the village, but to an intensely more passionate degree, Brenda's thoughts were engaged in the matter and manner of Simone's disappearance. Plainly she had been forcibly abducted. Or lured away, perhaps by a false message purporting to come from her husband. Obviously no woman lucky enough to be married to Alan Hollingsworth would leave home voluntarily.

It might be thought that Alan's newly unyoked state would fill Brenda with wild hope and delight but such was not the case. It was the stable impenetrability of the Hollingsworths' lives that held Brenda's dreams together. Now that background had been torn apart the whole tapestry seemed about to unravel. She dreaded what the future might hold. Overwhelmingly paramount was the fear that, if Simone did not return, Alan might decide that Nightingales held so many unhappy memories he could no longer bear to go on living there.

For the first time she found herself regretting her parents' reclusive existence, her mother's finicky revulsion against any sort of close relationship. If only she had been the sort to run around with a dish of something sustaining. And what then would be more natural than that her daughter should call to collect the empties.

Brenda had even, shaking in her shoes at the thought of such audacity, imagined going round alone. Alan hadn't been out for two days now and must surely be in dire need of assistance. In her imagination she placed a wicker basket on his table and lifted a snowy cloth to reveal French bread and rosy apples, a honey pot shaped like a beehive, crisp frilly lettuce and a wedge of cheese wrapped in waxed paper. Finally, a long-necked dark green bottle of wine.

Alan would be sitting, sad and solitary, staring at the wall. She would need to speak two or three times before he became aware of her presence. It might even prove necessary to touch his arm.

Brenda sighed and returned to a worrying present. She unscrewed the cap from her fountain pen, mottled tortoiseshell with a gold nib. It had been bought especially and at great cost for inscribing her private thoughts and was never used for anything else.

She pondered her first line carefully, for the text was sacrosanct. Nothing was ever altered or crossed out. She would have regarded such mutilations as ill-omened.

A movement in next door's garden caught her eye. Alan! First sighting since he had been so cruelly abandoned. He had his back to the house and was carrying a spade. As

Brenda gazed hungrily down, he pushed it into a large, wet patch of earth near the patio.

Brenda had sat, just so, looking down and longing, on hundreds of occasions. She believed herself to have exceptional sensitivity as far as Alan was concerned and was sure that, should he happen to look up, she could lower her eyes and turn away in time. Certainly she always had till now.

But then something happened which gave the lie to such confidence. He thrust the spade down hard by a clump of day lilies, withdrew it then turned away, apparently in some disgust. As he did so he raised his head and stared straight at Brenda's window. Caught out, all she could do was stare straight back.

Their eyes met as they had done so often in her dreams. But in real life it was all very different. His glance was dark and unfriendly, almost a glare, and struck her like an arrow. He made a forceful movement with his free hand and, for one terrible moment, Brenda thought he was threatening her with his fist. Then he flung the spade down with a great clatter on the patio slabs and strode back into the house.

Brenda was devastated. What must he think? What must any person think going about their business, with every reason to presume themselves unobserved, only to discover they were being spied on? No wonder he was angry. Brenda felt shattered, as if they had had a lover's quarrel.

She closed her book, replaced the cap on her chunky pen and blew her nose loudly. It would do no good to cry. Nor was there any point in abandoning herself to morbid self-scrutiny. Quarrels were made to be mended. And it would be up to her to find a way to do it.

'I had to get all worked up to come.' Mrs Molfrey tossed

back her shoulder-length blonde ringlets with such vigour that her hat nearly fell off. 'I hope I have not been misinformed as to your rank and station.'

Detective Chief Inspector Barnaby tried to hold in place the mask of courteous inquiry invariably assumed when presented with an unsolicited visit from a member of the public but it was hard, very hard indeed, not to stare.

An excessively raddled old lady sat facing him. She appeared lost inside a voluminous girlish dress with puffed sleeves. It was made from what appeared to be furnishing fabric: glazed chintz, patterned with blowsy cabbage roses. She also wore white lace gloves and rather muddy, elastic-sided shoes with holes punched into the ivory leather. Her face was so thickly layered with pink and white cosmetics that when severely frowning or expressing emotion with any degree of vivacity motes of it became detached and drifted in the air like perfumed dandruff. Her eyelids were the harsh and dazzling blue once called Electric. If Mary Pickford were still alive, thought Barnaby, this must be pretty much what she would look like.

'They tried to palm me off in your front office with a constable. In his shirt sleeves.' Mrs Molfrey lowered eyelashes so black and stiffly curled they could have been coated with pitch. 'But I insisted on speaking to someone of the highest authority.'

Sergeant Troy had passed through reception during Mrs Molfrey's argumentative discourse. Sussing the situation, he had popped her in the lift, whisked her up to the third floor and left her on Barnaby's Welcome mat. Whether his bag carrier had been motivated by sportish malice or the suspicion that an entertaining diversion was required, the Chief Inspector had yet to discover.

'So what seems to be the problem, Mrs Molfrey?' asked

Barnaby aware, as soon as the words were out, that he had assumed an avuncular, almost condescending manner. Attempting equilibrium he added, more formally, 'How can I help you?'

'It is I who can help *you*,' replied Mrs Molfrey, tugging off her left glove. 'My neighbour has disappeared. I thought you would want to know.'

'His name?'

'Her name. He's still on the spot. And thereby, if you ask me, hangs a very long tale.'

Barnaby, who had anticipated that what Mrs Molfrey had to say would be as dotty and uncoordinated as her appearance was pleased to be proved wrong. Even if elaborately presented and quirkily phrased, her meaning seemed crystal clear.

'It's Simone Hollingsworth,' began Mrs Molfrey. She paused for a few moments, frowning severely at an antitheft poster and dislodging a few more flakes of pastel pargeting. 'Aren't you going to write it down?'

'Not at the moment, Mrs Molfrey. Please continue.'

'She vanished last Thursday. Into thin air, as the saying is, though I've never understood why. Surely if a person is to be concealed the air would have to be extremely thick. Rather like the old pea-soupers.'

'If you could—'

'Don't chip in, there's a good fellow. When I've finished I'll give some sort of signal. Wave my handkerchief. Or shout.'

Barnaby closed his eyes.

'I became suspicious the very first evening. I remember it precisely and I'll tell you why. The sunset, from which I usually derive considerable refreshment, was a great disappointment. A dreadful common colour, like tinned salmon. Cubby was feeding my onions – renowned, I might add, for their splendour – and I was rootling around with my little hoe anticipating a word or two with Simone. She would usually come out around that time to call her cat and we would exchange pleasantries, the latest bit of village gossip from her side of the fence whereas I would discuss the progress of my plants, curse all winged and crawling predators and inveigh against the weather, the way keen gardeners do.'

Barnaby nodded. He, too, was a keen gardener and had been known to inveigh against the weather in his time in a manner so robust it caused his wife to slam the French windows with such vigour the panes rattled.

'But who should emerge instead but Alan – that is Mr Hollingsworth – calling "Nelson, Nelson" as if he had ever cared tuppence for the poor creature and rattling a box of crunchy stuff.' Mrs Molfrey leaned forwards. 'And that's not all.'

These last few words had a throbbing undertow bordering on the melodramatic. Barnaby recognised the note; he had heard it many times. It nearly always indicated a possibly genuine concern for the welfare of a fellow human plus an inability to believe that that welfare was not at risk, usually for the most lurid and sinister of reasons.

'I had already discovered three more disturbing pieces to this mysterious jigsaw. On the afternoon of the day Mrs Hollingsworth vanished, Sarah Lawson, our artist in residence so to speak, had been invited to tea. Half an hour later Maison Becky also turned up on her flying bicycle plus all the coiffure folderols for a pre-arranged hair appointment. But Simone had taken the twelve-thirty omnibus to Causton without letting either of them know!'

Mrs Molfrey, who had ticked off these peaks of high drama on gnarled fingers tipped with brilliant vermilion nails, now concluded, 'Nothing could be more out of character.'

The process wherein a slightly unusual or vaguely inexplicable occurrence was fancifully expanded into an event of *Grand Guignol*-like style and content was also very familiar. Barnaby controlled his impatience.

'But if you find all that baffling,' Mrs Molfrey paused and looked at the Chief Inspector in such keen and collusive anticipation that he did not have the heart to disappoint her. An expression of mild curiosity briefly possessed his craggy features. 'Wait till you hear *le mot juste*.' She leaned forward, severely mangling, in her excitement, a large raffia bag on her knees. 'Questioned by the vicar, who was naturally concerned at finding himself one campanologist short for the funeral, Alan Hollingsworth said his wife had gone to visit her mother. Hah!'

Uncertain whether this was a forceful expression of disbelief or the shout that signalled he was now free to chip in, Barnaby cleared his throat and, when no reprimand was forthcoming, said, 'Was this something out of the ordinary then, Mrs Molfrey?'

'You could say that. She's been dead for seven years.'

'Then it was plainly an excuse made up on the spur of the moment,' said the Chief Inspector. 'People don't always tell the truth about their personal affairs. Why should they?'

'I do,' said Mrs Molfrey with the simplicity of a child.

There was no answer to this and Barnaby wisely did not attempt one.

'Don't you think,' continued Mrs Molfrey, 'it all sounds rather,' she searched her mind for an adjective which would adequately sum up the dark and terrible complexities of the matter in hand, 'Sicilian?'

Barnaby thought it sounded about as Sicilian as a stick of Blackpool rock. 'Would you expect to hear from Mrs Hollingsworth if she's away for any length of time?'

'Probably not. She was an acquaintance rather than a friend. But that does not mean one is not concerned.'

'Indeed. And have you discussed this with anyone else?'

'Only Cubby – my *innamorato*.' The Chief Inspector kept his face straight by a supreme effort of will. 'He feels it's really none of our business but then he's getting on a bit for any sort of arsy-varsy. Fruit-bottling, making faggots and appliqué embroidery – that's all he's good for. Typical male. That's a nasty cough you've got there, Inspector.'

'No, no.' Barnaby wiped his eyes. 'I'm fine.'

He got up then and Mrs Molfrey got up too, pushing on the tubular steel arms of her chair for leverage and looking crisply about her.

'Thank you for coming, Mrs—'

'Don't I get a form to fill in?'

'Just leave the Hollingsworths' address with the desk sergeant.'

'They do on *The Bill*.'

'I can assure you, Mrs Molfrey, the matter will be looked into.' He'd get a call put through to the village beat officer. Get him to ask around discreetly. She sounded reasonably *compos mentis* but might well have got completely the wrong end of the stick. The last thing the station needed was complaints of wrongful accusation.

Barnaby came round from behind his desk to open the door. As he did so, Mrs Molfrey held out her hand. The Chief Inspector enclosed the tiny, withered claw utterly in the spread of his palm. She was very small, the wavy brim of her picture hat level with the tip of his tie. Her raspberry smeared lips parted in a smile of great sweetness as she looked up at him through those preposterous eyelashes and said, 'I'm sure we shall work very well together.'

After she had left, he sat shaking his head for a moment in amused disbelief then took the stop off his calls. Immediately the phone rang and the workaday world engulfed him.

Chapter Two

Police Constable Perrot's beat, which he had now had for seven years, comprised three villages. Ferne Bassett, Martyr Longstaff and Fawcett Green. Of the three, he much preferred the last.

Ferne Bassett was overburdened with weekend cottages, holiday homes and London commuters. Most of the time it was as quiet as the grave. The quietude may have been skin-deep but, as long as what was festering underneath did not erupt and start acting illegally, Perrot regarded it as no concern of his. In Martyr Longstaff a long-running feud existed between a scrap metal merchant operating, contrary to all council regulations, a business from his home and a neighbour furiously determined to put a spanner in the works. Confrontations were loud, violent, monotonously regular and often took place in the middle of the night.

But Fawcett Green – ah, Fawcett Green! Constable Perrot sighed with pleasure as he gazed about him. Dozing in the sunshine the place looked remarkably unspoilt. A great deal of the surrounding land belonged to a stately home which had been bought by a Far Eastern conglomerate. They had planted rather a lot of beautiful and unusual trees, created a large lake and left the rest alone. And, with a couple of exceptions, local farmers had remained sturdily resistant to the brandished cheque books of Bovis and Wimpey. Over the last fifteen years the place had hardly changed at all.

PC Perrot had lifted his Honda on to its stand at the very edge of the village though his destination was a good ten minutes' walk away. Residents, quite rightly, expected to see 'their' bobby strolling about, stopping for a word, hearing complaints and generally making himself available. Consequently it took him nearly half an hour to reach Nightingales.

His brief was simple but open-ended. He could take the interview with Alan Hollingsworth as far or as deep as the occasion seemed to demand. The constable's own feelings were that some nosy neighbour with too much time on their hands had got a bit carried away. He had not been informed who the concerned party was and did not wish to know unless it became absolutely necessary.

PC Perrot had deliberately chosen mid-morning on Sunday for his visit. It was nearly eleven. Time for the man to have finished breakfast but too early presumably to have gone out to lunch.

The constable's approach to the front gates had been noted. Old Mrs Molfrey, cutting branches of orange blossom in her front garden, smiled and waved her secateurs. In the adjacent house a white poodle with its front paws up on the sill barked at him through the glass and was promptly yanked from view.

The approach to the front step and garage could do with a weed. Thistles were starting to show in a border of leggy pansies and tangled aubretia. The tobacco plants on the front doorstep looked a touch on the dry side.

Finding no bell, Constable Perrot tapped smartly with the brass mermaid's tail. Noticing the curtains were still drawn, he waited a few minutes in case Hollingsworth was still asleep then rapped again.

In the lane a woman went by dragging a bawling infant. She pointed out the constable, assuring the toddler that if he didn't shut his bleeding gob the big policeman would cart him off, lock him up and chuck the key down the lavvy. PC Perrot sighed. What was the point of all his primary school visits when there were parents like that to contend with? No wonder some kids ran a mile when they saw him coming.

Hot, even in his blue cotton summer issue, Perrot rolled up his shirt sleeves and wiped his forehead with a handkerchief. Then he crouched down to bring himself to the level of the letter box, lifted the flap and peered in.

He could see the stairs and the hall floor on which were lying some letters and a freebie newspaper. At the far end of the hall was a closed door which Perrot assumed belonged to the kitchen. A second door stood ajar. By screwing his head sideways and pressing his cheek hard against the cold metal, the policeman could see a section of carpeted floor, part of a table, the arm of a chair and a pair of fully occupied leather slippers.

Putting his mouth close to the slit he called, 'Mr Hollingsworth?' Then, feeling more than a little foolish, 'I can actually, um, see you, sir. If you could come to the door, please? Constable Perrot, Thames Valley Police.' PC Perrot straightened up and waited. A high-pitched whine nearby made him turn round. Next to the gate was a lad who looked to be about eight. He was leaning on a chopper bike and holding a dog on a piece of string. The policeman smiled and raised his hand. The dog yawned again, the boy stared back, unblinking.

PC Perrot once more agitated the mermaid then, feeling

even more self-conscious, wondered if he should take upon himself the responsibility of a forced entry. Nervously he recapped on the circumstances in which such a procedure could be justifiably carried out. Immediate pursuit of criminal. To prevent a breach of the peace or a person being harmed. Someone inside unconscious or in need of medical assistance. It seemed to him that the last might very well apply.

He made one final attempt at addressing the feet, which he presumed belonged to the owner of the property. This time, sharply aware of being awarded marks out of ten for entertainment value, he remained upright and spoke very loudly at the opaque glass panel.

'I am about to forcibly enter sir, by breaking the door down. If you are able to—'

There was a thud inside the house then a dark shape loomed behind the glass. The safety chain was struggled with in a frantic manner accompanied by swearing and cursing. Two bolts; a mortise. The door was flung open. Someone on the threshold shouted, 'For Christ's sake!' into the startled policeman's face then he was dragged forward and the front door slammed.

Inside, the air was chokingly oppressive; sour and heavy. Perrot felt immediately stifled and slightly nauseous. He tucked his helmet more firmly under his arm and tried not to breathe too deeply. The man was shouting at him again.

'What the hell are you doing here?'

'Mr Hollingsworth?'

The man said 'Christ' again then turned and stumbled away. For a moment Constable Perrot thought he was going to crash into the sitting-room architrave. He lurched a few steps towards an armchair. From its position Perrot supposed it to be the one in which Hollingsworth had been sitting when his slippers were visible through the letter box. The cushion was widely and deeply indented as if a large animal had been curled up there for some considerable time. Hollingsworth reached the chair, turned round vaguely once or twice as if unsure which was the right way to face and fell into it.

PC Perrot hesitated, looking around him. Very little light came through the drawn velvet curtains but a lamp, shaped like a golden pineapple, with an unlined cream linen shade, had been switched on. An unpleasant odour came from a vase of half dead roses, their leaves crisp and brown. It mingled with the smell of alcohol, cigarettes, garlic and something the policeman recognised but could not have named but which was monosodium glutamate. Dirty cutlery and several used foil containers were spread all over a handsome inlaid table on which there was no cloth. Some of the containers still had bones and bits of food in. There were a lot of flies about.

Realising he would probably wait a long time to be invited, PC Perrot pulled one of the narrow-backed dining chairs out and sat down, a healthy distance from the table. He placed his helmet on the floor and adjusted his radio which was digging into his slightly plump middle. Then, indicating with a polite nod the foil dishes, said, 'Catering for yourself, I see, sir.'

Alan Hollingsworth did not reply. He was glancing at the clock, a giant sunburst of crystal rays and gilded face and figures. He looked dreadful. Hair matted, hanging in greasy hanks around his face. He hadn't shaved for days and from the look – and smell – of him hadn't washed either. Dark full moons of sweat saturated the underarms of his shirt. The rims of his eyelids and the corners of his mouth were encrusted with whitish yellow flakes.

Perrot, deciding he would give six months of his pension to have the windows open, made so bold as to suggest it. At this Hollingsworth started shouting again, the gist this time being that Perrot should say what he'd come to say and get out.

'Very well, sir,' said Constable Perrot, waving away an especially bloated bluebottle. 'We've had one or two concerned . . . um . . .' About to say 'rumours', he decided the word sounded a bit gossipy. 'Inquiries regarding the whereabouts of your wife. As I'm sure you appreciate, this visit in no way implies any accusation or suspicions on our part as to the lady's wellbeing. But it is normal police procedure . . .'

At this point Hollingsworth buried his head in his hands. His shoulders started to twitch, then jerk about violently. Strange, hysterical sounds came from his throat. Coarse sobs. Or they could have been guffaws. Then he threw his head back so savagely one would have thought his neck might snap. Perrot saw the face, crisscrossed with tears, but was still not sure whether the man had been laughing or crying.

'Can I get you anything, Mr Hollingsworth? A cup of tea perhaps?'

'No.' The filthy, double cuffs of his shirt hung down loosely, covering the backs of his hands. He wiped his face and then his nose with one of them.

'You're plainly not very well, sir.'

'I'm pissed, you stupid idiot.'

Perversely, this insult, far from annoying Constable Perrot, produced in him a quiet confidence. To his mind the resident of this splendid property, by behaving no better than some rowdy council house layabout, had rejigged both the social and psychological balance of the encounter to his own benefit. The policeman unbuttoned the flap on the chest pocket of his shirt and produced a notebook and Biro.

Hollingsworth picked up the nearest bottle, which was uncapped, poured a stream of liquid into a smeary tumbler and sloshed it down. The smell of his sweat became more pronounced and the degree of acridity increased. It occurred to Constable Perrot for the first time that Hollingsworth was not only despairing but possibly afraid.

'Am I correct in understanding that Mrs Hollingsworth is visiting her mother?' No reply. Constable Perrot repeated the question with much the same result. He waited a few moments then said, 'If you refuse to help me here, sir, I'm afraid I must ask you to present yourself—'

'I'm not going out!' Hollingsworth jumped up. He braced himself against the chair as if in readiness against a forcible removal. 'I can't leave the house!'

'Please, calm yourself, Mr Hollingsworth. This really is just routine procedure. Nothing to get upset about.' Even Perrot, unimaginative almost to the point of stolidity, knew that this was unlikely. The procedure may well be routine but the situation, he felt certain, would prove to be most irregular. He flipped open his notebook, clicked his pen and smiled encouragingly. 'Am I right in thinking that your wife is visiting her mother?'

'Yes.'

'Could I have the address, please?'

'What for?'

'Just to satisfy ourselves as to her whereabouts, Mr Hollingsworth.'

'There's no need, I assure you.'

Constable Perrot waited, pen poised, patience on a monument. When it became plain that the proceedings would not continue until he gave a satisfactory reply,

Hollingsworth suddenly leaned closer towards the policeman who had to force himself not to lean back.

'Look, is this all confidential?'

'Certainly, sir. Even if I decide to file a report,' he hoped Hollingsworth did not realise this was inevitable, 'it would remain purely a police matter. Unless of course further circumstances dictated a different policy.'

'My wife doesn't have a mother. Actually, the vicar came round asking questions. He was quite persistent – you know what do-gooders are.'

PC Perrot, who inevitably had had rather more experience with the way do-badders were, nodded agreeably.

'I said the first thing that came into my head to get rid of him. But the truth is,' his voice cracked at this point and Perrot got the impression that he was struggling not to weep, 'she's left me.'

'I'm sorry to hear that, Mr Hollingsworth.' And he genuinely was. Colin Perrot, extremely contented with his own marital bargain – amiable, pretty wife, smashing teenage daughter and a pair of lively sons – briefly felt, by proxy, a touch of the anguish consuming the pathetic figure facing him. No wonder he was cursing and drinking and flailing around like one demented. Without realising they were doing so, the policeman's fingers strayed to the frame of his chair seat and pressed the wood.

'And before you ask, I don't have an address.'

'How long has Mrs Hollingsworth been gone?'

'I'm not sure.' Noticing Perrot's look of disbelief he added, 'Days and nights just seem to have run into each other. Three days, four maybe.'

'Couldn't you be a little more accurate, Mr Hollingsworth?'

'God, it's something I'm trying to forget, man! Not dwell on.'

'She hasn't been in touch?'

'No.'

'So you have no idea of her whereabouts?'

'Well, I wouldn't have, would I?'

'Did she leave a message?'

'On my answerphone. Wiped, before you ask.'

Very convenient, thought PC Perrot. He felt surprise at this sudden shift into cynicism and wondered what had provoked it. Perhaps the notion that, if Hollingsworth was all that desperately in love with his wife, he would have surely wished to retain the sound of her voice.

'What was her state of mind when you last saw her?'

'Just as usual.'

'Do you have any idea why she chose to leave?'

Hollingsworth shook his head. Or rather rocked it from side to side in his hands.

'Is there another man involved? An affair?'

'I find that hard to believe, and not just for reasons of vanity. Where would they have met? She never went anywhere except with me and the chances of secretly carrying on in a place this size are practically nil.'

'You're right there, sir.' It didn't seem kind to add, as he truthfully could, that he would have been one of the first to know about it. 'What did the message on your machine actually say?'

'Simply that she was going away and not coming back.'

'Did she go by car?'

'No. She doesn't drive.'

'Would she be staying with a friend, do you think?'

'I doubt it. She dropped them all when we got married.'

'Mutual friends?'

'We didn't socialise. I worked long hours – money was terribly important to Simone. I don't mean she was selfish or greedy, she wasn't. But she'd had a hard time before she met me. A very hard time. Both as a child and a young woman. I sometimes felt that, however much I put in the bank, she would never feel really secure.'

During this speech, the longest he had uttered, Hollingsworth seemed to have started to sober up. He was focusing now with a reasonable degree of accuracy on his interrogator and plainly gathering his wits. Perrot was unsure whether this would mean more intelligible information or a careful rein on the tongue. And, suspicious again, he asked himself why Hollingsworth might have any need to monitor his speech.

'You mentioned your bank, Mr Hollingsworth. Did your wife use the same one?'

'No.'

'Where was her account, please?'

There had been a brief pause before Hollingsworth answered and when he did it was with an air of improvisation. 'Lloyds.'

Perrot was convinced that Hollingsworth had seized on the first name that came into his head. Yet it seemed foolish to lie about something so unsinister, not to mention easily checkable. Why not just tell the truth?

'You're sure about that, sir?'

Hollingsworth was looking at the clock again, his eyes slipping and sliding over PC Perrot's shoulder. Then, belatedly aware that he had been spoken to, 'What?'

The constable let it go. But he made a note of his impression that Hollingsworth was being deliberately evasive. PC Perrot's reports were models of scrupulous recording, if a trifle long-winded. The comment had been made more than once at headquarters that here was another Perrot mini series, telling them more about whatever issue was in the air than any rational person would ever wish to know.

'So, Mr Hollingsworth, I suppose—'

'Look, I'm not interested in your suppositions. I've answered your questions to the best of my ability and I have nothing else to say.' He got out of his chair in one fairly smooth movement, standing upright with comparative ease.

Constable Perrot wondered if the man had been as drunk as he first appeared or if his apparent lack of sobriety was merely a ploy, a cover behind which he could reasonably be excused from understanding the questions put to him. But he had answered them all but the last, albeit in a somewhat dazed manner.

Perrot started to feel a little out of his depth. Naturally, being a policeman, he had a suspicious mind but it was not usually engaged on matters of much psychological complexity. He concluded that he would get no further with Hollingsworth in his present mood and decided to call it a day. Putting away his notebook and retrieving his helmet from beneath the chair, he too rose to his feet and moved towards the door.

'Thank you for being so cooperative, sir.'

'Yes, yes.'

Plainly the man couldn't wait to get rid of him. In the hall PC Perrot, about to don his helmet, halted and, with what even the most ungifted amateur would have recognised as stagily risible urgency said, 'Oh dear. Um, I wonder if I might use your toilet, sir?'

'Oh, well. I'd rather you . . . It's a bit of a mess.'

'No problem, Mr Hollingsworth.' Perrot had already set his foot on the stairs. 'This way, is it?'

'There's one in the hall.'

'Many thanks.' And up he went.

The bathroom opened off the master bedroom. PC Perrot lifted the lavatory seat making quite a clatter then checked the vanity unit, medicine cabinet and the jars and bottles standing on the rim of the bath, all the while congratulating himself on this spur-of-the-moment inspiration. He coughed loudly to show he was still in there and started to run the hot tap. Then, downstairs, the phone rang and was immediately answered.

Perrot seized his chance. Swift and silent, he stepped into the bedroom. He opened and closed drawers then checked out a large, white, fitted wardrobe decorated with gold. Then he returned to the bathroom, flushed the cistern and turned off the tap.

Halfway down the stairs he stopped and tried to listen to Hollingsworth's side of the telephone conversation. Unfortunately the noise from the pipes and reflooding cistern made this difficult. But, though Hollingsworth was speaking quietly, at one point the tone of his voice became quite ferocious, rising almost to a hiss.

'What problem? *For God's sake, Blakeley*. No, that won't do! I need all of it, I *told* you . . .' More vocal sounds of quiet desperation followed before the receiver was laid down with unexpectedly gentle precision.

Perrot reckoned this final gesture might have been in belated recollection that there was someone else in the house, perhaps presaging a foolish pretence that the call had never happened. He made a great deal of unnecessary noise running down the last half-dozen steps.

'Very good of you, sir.' He spoke in a bright, newly relieved manner. 'I'll be off now then.'

Hollingsworth was staring into space. The expression on

his face was dreadful, the skin stretched drum-tight across the cheekbones, the eyeballs bulging. His lips were drawn back in that savage grimace of anguish that, in the newspaper photographs of the victims of tragedy, seemed so cruelly to mimic radiant joy.

PC Perrot hesitated in the hallway. He said, 'Is there anything I can do?' and was relieved when there was no reply. Knowing that he should persist and that Hollingsworth was actually in quite a bad way, Perrot made an excuse to himself (the bloke really needed a doctor, not a copper) and left.

His Open Text report, as always, left nothing out. Facts aplenty; descriptive notes in almost Proustian detail. His opinions as to the truthfulness, or not, of the interviewee. Times of arrival and departure correct to the minute. The result, Perrot felt sure, would lead to further and much more stringent questioning of Alan Hollingsworth.

Unfortunately it was another forty-eight hours before the attention of anyone with enough authority to order such an investigation was drawn to the report, by which time the owner of Nightingales was in no condition to help anyone with their inquiries.

The following morning at eleven o'clock Sarah Lawson came to collect her eggs. Avis Jennings, the doctor's wife, had a cousin with a smallholding at Badger's Drift where he kept free-range chickens and several ducks.

Sarah had accepted an invitation to stay and have coffee which was rare, though Avis constantly asked, for she thought Sarah the most interesting person in the village by far and longed to know her better. But nearly always Sarah just paid for the eggs and with the exact money. It was as though being drawn even into the briefest of conversations over change was either a nuisance or a waste of time.

But today, intrigued, Avis assumed, by her opening gambit, 'You'll never guess what I just saw!' Sarah was sitting, gently rocking back and forth by the stone-cold Aga, in the Jennings' kitchen. She was wearing blue, as she nearly always did, a jerkin embroidered with peacock-coloured silks, a long, full skirt of washed-out indigo. And a necklace of cornflowers fitted together in the manner of a child's daisy chain.

'Easy to see what your favourite colour is,' said Avis. She wondered about quoting one of the few lines of poetry that still stuck in her mind from school. It was certainly appropriate. She cleared her throat. '"I never saw a man who looked with such a wistful eye—"'

'Don't!' Sarah stopped rocking, her feet coming down hard against the stone-flagged floor. 'I hate that poem.'

'I'm . . . sorry.' Instead of being satisfied that she had finally scratched Sarah's emotional surface, Avis felt awkward and uncouth. She was about to change the subject when Sarah spoke again.

'There's a painting by Van Gogh. A prison yard, mile-high walls. Almost circular, like a tower. The men trudge round and round, their heads down. Everything's grey and wretched. But then, right at the top of the picture and so small you could almost miss it, there's a butterfly.'

'I think I know the one you mean,' lied Avis. 'Isn't it in the National Gallery?'

'I'd go slowly mad if I couldn't see the sky.'

'Well, I shouldn't think you've much to worry about.' A jolly laugh which didn't really come off. 'It's not going to suddenly vanish. Not that there's anything to vanish, of course,' she stumbled on. 'Just emptiness, really. But . . . very, um, beautiful.'

'Yes. One understands why people who believe in heaven think it must be up there.'

Avis, glad to be occupied, bustled about getting the coffee. In honour of the occasion she took some beans out of the freezer. These were normally kept for Sunday morning when there was time for Dr Jim, as everyone in the village including his wife called him, actually to savour the breakfast tipple rather than just slosh it down and run. Without quite knowing why, Avis pushed the jar of Maxwell House behind her food mixer as she got the grinder out.

'This makes rather a noise, I'm afraid,' she screamed over the whizzing screech. She realised she should have spoken before switching on but the whole situation, no more than a storm in a teacup really, had got her flustered. Not that Sarah had appeared critical. Indeed she had never been known to voice, even obliquely, an unkind word about anybody. This was not because she was not interested – quite the contrary. Sarah seemed more completely interested in whoever she was with and in their mutual surroundings than anyone Avis had ever come across. The degree and quality of her attention, once she had deigned to bestow it, was remarkable. Yet though not entirely without warmth, there was something deeply impersonal about it.

Avis's husband, miles from being a fanciful man, once said that spending time with Sarah was like standing in front of a mirror, one was observed with such precision and clarity. Avis thought it was more like being looked at through a camera lens.

Pressing down the plunger of the cafetière she now said, 'Do you like milk or cream, Sarah?'

'Milk's fine.'

'And sugar?'

'No thanks.'

Avis got down her best cups. Sarah had moved to the old wooden table underneath the window and was transferring the eggs from their grey, cardboard stacking sheets to a blue and white mottled bowl. She paused a moment, holding a speckly, pale tan one in the palm of her hand. There was a small feather still sticking to it and the darker brown freckles were rough against her skin.

'Aren't they the most beautiful things?' She balanced the final egg carefully on top of the rest. 'I love looking at them. Why anyone ever puts them in a fridge is beyond me.'

'Absolutely,' agreed Avis, vowing silently that from that moment on she never would.

'Apart from anything else, they get so cold the shells crack when you boil them.'

'Is that right?' Avis poured the coffee. It was only Sainsbury's basic but it had a lovely oily sheen and smelled divine. 'Would you like anything with it? A biscuit or some cake?'

Sarah said 'No thanks' again and half smiled. She didn't rush to elaborate on or explain her brief refusal as most people of Avis's acquaintance would have done. Nor, which was much more surprising, did she ask what the unguessable exciting thing was that Avis had seen just before her own arrival. Avis found this most impressive. She admired Sarah's control enormously while at the same time, to a more modest degree, admiring her own, for she was dying for a slice of tipsy cake. Momentarily she wondered if Sarah might not be restraining her curiosity but was genuinely uninterested. Surely this could not be true. She probably wanted to appear a cut above ordinary human nosiness. Understandable.

Then, as if to confound such reasoning, Sarah said in a

tone of humorous indulgence, 'Well, go on then. Tell me all about it.'

'A car came to Nightingales about half an hour ago. A black Mercedes.'

'Simone's back?'

'No. It was a man with a briefcase. Alan let him in. He only stayed a few minutes but when he left *he wasn't carrying the case*.'

Sarah burst out laughing. 'I wouldn't like to try concealing anything in this place.'

'It was pure coincidence I happened to be passing.' Avis blushed defiantly. 'I was taking old Mrs Perkins' repeat arthritis prescription. Saves her walking to the surgery.'

'Did you get the car's number?'

'All right, all right.' Annoyed at being made to feel foolish, Avis stopped worrying about appearing undisciplined, got the tin down and cut herself a large chunk of cake. 'But you can't deny it's all very mysterious. For instance, Alan hasn't left the house since Simone disappeared. You'd think he'd be out looking for her.'

'Perhaps he doesn't know where to start.'

'What about his work?'

'What about his work?' repeated Sarah, her tranquil voice emphasising the second word.

'Everyone says he's going to pieces.'

'How do they know if he hasn't left the house?'

'Ohhh!' Avis's voice flared with irritation. She swallowed her cake and dropped the fork which clattered on to her plate. 'Why are you always so . . .' Thinking pedantic might offend, she chose rational.

'Because irrationality alarms me.'

The two women looked at each other. Avis swallowed again, this time from nervous excitement. Sarah had never before today offered even the smallest, most innocuous personal revelation. And now, two in succession. Avis seized on what she determined to regard as an invitation to friendship and her mind leaped into the future. They would tell each other the complete story of their lives and discuss everything both trivial and profound. Sarah would talk about her work and Avis would learn about art and music and literature. She saw her horizons stretching wider and wider, her plain old world transformed into something both complex and extraordinary. Her mind would open like a flower.

Sarah, having finished her coffee, was getting up to go in the same composed, unhurried way that she had arrived. Picking up her beautiful mottled bowl of eggs she moved towards the door.

'Shall I see you next week?' cried Avis, already looking forward to it.

'Doubt it. These will probably last me quite a while.'

'That batty old woman next door's been to the police.'

'How do you know?'

'Teddy Grimshaw saw her. He was talking about it in the pensions queue.' Reg had not himself been in the line-up. The Brockleys' joint pensions went straight into his bank account. But the post office also doubled as a newsagents and he was in there paying the monthly paper bill. The *Daily* and *Sunday Express, Radio Times* and, for Iris, the *Lady. Green Fingers*, the gardening journal taken for many years, had recently been cancelled after some female jobbing columnist had taken it upon herself to suggest that excessive neatness in a plot was not only bad for the plants but denoted a seriously neurotic personality in the plantsman.

'What on earth was Mr Grimshaw doing in the police station?'

'Making a formal complaint about that abandoned traffic cone.'

'The one leaning against the wall behind the phone box?'

'I hope you're not suggesting another has sprung up, Iris.'

'No wonder house prices are plummeting.'

The Brockleys were taking tea on the patio. Now Reg got up from his green plastic chair and walked down the steps. As he contemplated his lawn, close-shaven in lines straight as prison bars, his prim lips puckered into a smirk of satisfaction.

He walked down the path, his eyes swivelling, alert for alien seedlings or overconfident species that had ceased to know their place. Spotting a lacewing clinging to a violent orange floribunda, he broke off the leaf, squeezed it round the offending insect and dropped the shrouded corpse into the dustbin.

The Brockleys had no compost heap and could not understand those who did. To them the whole point of having a garden was to keep it contained, not encourage it to go burgeoning about all over the place.

Iris called out, 'Another finger dainty, dear?'

Receiving no reply, she picked up a sunray of bloater paste soldiers and made her way towards her husband, her stout little feet carefully avoiding the cracks in the crazy paving. No point in deliberately courting bad luck.

Reg had eased his way behind a ceanothus and was now peering into the Hollingsworths' unruly herbaceous border. In the early evening silence frogs plopped in and out of a tiny pond. What he was disturbed him greatly. As he wriggled back into his original position, Iris clicked her tongue.

'You've snagged your cardie.'

'Iris—'

'Your best Fair Isle.'

This garment was Reg's only concession to retirement. Beneath it he wore a crisp collared and cuffed shirt, a plain closely-knotted tie and a pair of dark trousers with creases so sharp they could have opened an oyster.

'He's digging, Iris.'

'*Digging?*'

'A hole.'

'But he never touches the garden. He hates gardening.'

'Nevertheless . . .'

'And the ground's like a rock.'

'He's turned the hose on it.'

After Iris had also craned round the ceanothus for a sight of the excavation they returned soberly to the house only just in time for the six o'clock news to which Reg, for the first time that either of them could remember, could hardly give his full attention.

Iris was distracted to such a degree that Shona was allowed to emerge from her basket and stand quietly in the centre of the room without being reprimanded. In gratitude she started to wag her tail.

'He must be burying something,' suggested Reg.

His wife, rinsing the crockery for the second time in clear running water, drew in her breath. One long, excited sibilation. 'You don't think . . . ?'

'What?'

'Nelson?' The cat had still not reappeared and Alan was no longer to be heard calling him. Iris added, with a trembly wince in her voice, 'How big's the hole?'

'Impossible to guess from that angle. I'd need to look out of Brenda's bedroom window.'

'Chance'd be a fine thing.' Iris laid the cloth and sat down to face her husband over the kitchen table. The discovery of the hole could well presage imminent upheaval and the Brockleys were torn between pleasure at the prospect of an exciting scandal and alarm at the thought that chaos could possibly ensue, chaos that might tip the precisely weighted balance of their world and introduce more than a touch of Iris's 'hurly burly'.

'I can't help thinking of that terrible business in Gloucester last year.'

'Ohhh!' cried Iris. Her hands, two little pink lumps of dough, flew together and became one large pink lump. Her features shimmered under a racing flood of emotion. Alarm, pleasure, titillation, dread. 'But it's been four days since she disappeared. Surely he would have . . .' Iris hesitated, unable to bring herself to utter the word 'buried'. Disposed of seemed demeaning, as if Simone was something less than human. Concealed suggested inefficiency on Alan's part. Hidden was rather lightweight and might be said to reduce the whole terrible business to no more than a macabre parlour game. Iris decided to pass, concluding tamely, 'by now.'

That was when Brenda arrived from work. After she had completed her ablutions and was sitting down letting a nice cup of tea get cold and picking the onion out of the pasty, Reg slipped away.

His daughter's door was ajar. He pushed it just as wide as he needed to get inside – fortunately it did not squeak. He tiptoed to the larger of the two windows which looked over the back garden. From here he could see the hole quite clearly. As far as he could judge it seemed to be about four feet round and two feet deep. Nowhere near big enough to accommodate a body even if tightly curled. On the other hand Hollingsworth had plainly not finished digging, for the spade was left jammed into the ground.

Reg, who always cleaned his tools with newspaper before hanging them on their clearly labelled hooks, gave a 'tsk' of censure. Though he would have been outraged if such a suggestion had been put to him, in truth Reg disapproved more of this example of slovenliness than if he had come across Alan actually interring his spouse.

And then the man himself appeared. Suddenly he was there, on the terrace. Reg jumped back out of sight. After a moment he heard the sound of the spade scraping and chopping at something and then repeated hard bangs as if the earth was being beaten level. He risked a peep round the curtain and saw that the hole was being filled in.

Reg hurried away, adjusting the door, as precisely as he could remember, to show exactly the same gap.

As he sat down again, Iris raised her finely pencilled brows, indicating the food still lying on the table.

'She's hardly eaten a thing.' She scraped the remains of Brenda's supper into a bowl marked DOG.

'Now, Iris. I've surveyed the—'

'I mentioned he'd been digging and how he never had before. She said, in that cold sort of way she's taken on lately, "A person can change, I hope, Mother." I thought, he's not the only one.'

'Are you listening to me?'

'Of course I am. Just because I'm talking doesn't mean I'm not listening.'

'I would say that hole was of a size to comfortably accommodate a medium-sized box file.'

'That's nice.'

'However, the situation has now changed somewhat . . .'

Brenda was sitting on the sofa in the lounge. Ostensibly

transfixed by *Watchdog*, she was in fact preoccupied entirely with her own private misery. She could hear her parents droning on but only remotely, like waves on a distant beach. Queasily swamped by thoughts of Alan Hollingsworth, she stared at the screen, not registering the everyday saga of crooked folk and their imaginative swindles.

Since that dreadful moment when their eyes had met through the glass of her bedroom window, he had not been out of her thoughts for an instant. Her work had suffered. Asked that morning to take one of the tills, a rare and unwished for honour, she had been so locked within a remorseful maze of argument and counter-argument that she had not even registered the sympathetic – or repelled – glances her appearance always provoked.

'If only' had been the gist of her anguished reasoning. If only she hadn't looked out precisely at that moment. If only he hadn't glanced up exactly when he did. But by now, a bare two days after the event, these feverish reflections had inflated the incident into a tragedy of Sophoclean weight and proportion.

Bearing the unbearable had brought her almost to the point of exhaustion. She had not slept and now, though so tired she could barely focus, knew she would sleep fitfully if at all the coming night.

Aware at one level that she was being ridiculous, Brenda had striven to see the incident as if from an outsider's point of view, to establish in her mind its essential triviality. But her exertions had seemed to make matters worse. Like a swimmer struggling against a powerful current, she had become more and more enmeshed. She realised now that, until matters had been put right between them, the black torment would continue. She saw herself becoming really ill.

Brenda got up quickly before fear could atrophy her limbs, hurried into the hall, grabbed her keys and put on her coat. Her mother's 'Where are you going?' was cut off by the door slam.

Brenda ran down the path, round to Nightingales' tall black and gold gates and wrenched them open. She could do it as long as she didn't stop to think. Opening gambits – I can't say how sorry. What you must think. I couldn't bear it if – floated to the surface of her mind, broke like bubbles and were straightaway replaced by more.

These remedial flourishes brought Brenda to the front door. On the point of dissolving into desperate tears, she knocked very loudly.

Immediately the door was opened. Alan Hollingsworth came out and moved forcefully forward. For one terrible moment Brenda thought he was going to push her off the step. Or even knock her down. He slammed the door behind him and started walking towards the garage.

Impossible as it might appear, Brenda was instantly convinced he hadn't seen her. His eyes appeared to be fixed on some distant point or object. He could almost have been in a trance. His face was ghastly; grey-white with little cuts on his cheeks and chin. One or two had tufts of cotton wool with traces of blood sticking to them. His movements were mechanistic and strangely concentrated.

Brenda, horrified, watched as the car was backed out. Surely he wasn't going to drive in that zombie-like state. He would have an accident and kill someone. Or, a million times worse, himself!

She ran across the gravel crying, 'Wait!' but the car was already reversing down the drive. Brenda waved her arms, crossing and recrossing them at the wrists as if signalling on a flight path.

Now he was turning. She saw his shoulder dip as he bent to change gear. She raced back to The Larches – blessing the key ring in her pocket – and flung herself into the Metro. The engine caught first time. Brenda, briefly aware of her parents' startled faces at the kitchen window, scraped a wing on the gatepost. Then she was out in the lane and away.

At the T-junction where St Chad's Lane ran into the main street Brenda stopped and looked anxiously both ways. On the outskirts of the right-hand exit from Fawcett Green the tarmac was being repaired and a set of traffic lights had been installed. They showed red. Two cars were waiting, neither of which belonged to Alan.

Guessing that he would not have had time to precede them and praying she was right, Brenda turned left and put her foot down. Usually a timid and decorous driver, she touched fifty while still in the village and sixty the second she was on the open road. Within minutes she had spotted the Audi.

It was moving along quite slowly. Brenda settled down to follow, keeping just one vehicle, an electrical van, between them. When this turned off, she remained unconcerned, reasoning that if Alan had not noticed her standing under his nose on Nightingales' doorstep he was hardly likely to spot her in the present circumstances.

He drove through Causton and Uxbridge before taking the road towards West Drayton. They passed the stately building of the Montessori School, half hidden behind tall trees, and the much less stately Crowne Plaza Holiday Inn. At one point a massive blue and white container lorry, Transports Frigorifigues European, roared by. When the driver pulled over to the inside lane, Brenda lost sight of

Alan and had to grip the wheel very tightly to stop the sudden trembling in her hands. Unable to overtake the lorry, she could do nothing but follow it and pray that the Audi would not suddenly enter the middle lane and speed off, for she was sure she would not have the skill or courage to follow.

Then came a nightmare four-lane intersection with signs to Heathrow, Central London and Slough. She saw Alan in the second stream. Gritting her teeth and screwing up her face with anxiety and effort, Brenda overtook the great pantechnicon, fleetingly aware of two great blue interlocking circles on its mile-long chassis. Several horns hooted so she knew she had done something wrong.

Alan was following the sign for Heathrow. Once more safely on his tail, Brenda relaxed slightly. She was starting to feel happy, or at least pleasurably excited, and realised that, for the first time in her life, she was having an adventure. She sat up straighter in the car, lifted her chin in a daredevil sort of way and briefly drove with one hand on the wheel. A huge white model of Concorde flashed by to her right and they were in the airport tunnel.

There was a great deal of noise, screaming whoops and wails as two police cars tore by closely followed by an ambulance. A Sheraton Heathrow bus blocked her view and, emerging into the light again, Brenda discovered that Alan was now in the nearside lane and aiming for the Short Stay Car Park. Confused, uncertain and desperate not to lose him, she signalled and simultaneously swung over directly in front of a black cab. The driver signalled viciously in return and further demonstrated his fury by a stream of rabidly picturesque sound bites as he passed.

Alan was reaching through his window for a ticket from the machine at the entrance. Brenda did the same then wondered how, having no purse, she would be able to pay for it. At least she had filled up with petrol on her way home from work. Alan drove to the higher level and Brenda followed. He got out carrying a small case and made his way towards the lifts.

Brenda crept out of her car using the door furthest away. Having parked with about a dozen vehicles between them, she sidled, half crouching, past several rear number plates ready to duck should her quarry decide to retrace his steps. As Alan pressed the lift button he glanced about him and Brenda remained very still, unaware that she was an object of humorous derision to a couple in a nearby Saab.

As soon as the lift doors closed, she ran forward and rested her finger on the descending arrow, burning with impatience. She had never been to an airport but her feverish imagination had already supplied a teeming concourse in which Alan would be swallowed up without trace the moment he set foot on it.

The second lift arrived and when she emerged at ground level Brenda's worst fears were realised. Tears of frustration welled as she dodged cars and mini buses and crossed two roads to gain the automatic swing door that was the entrance to the terminus.

Once inside, at once she knew herself defeated. Standing between the desks for Aer Lingus and British Midland she observed the vast hall where seemingly thousands of people queued, manipulated trolleys, grumbled, sweated, lugged cases, railed at children or just sat slumped, stuffing food into their mouths.

Now that secrecy was not an issue, Brenda moved boldly if miserably about, staring at the multicoloured computer screens above her head and the brightly lit shopping section. Austin Reed, Tie Rack, the Body Shop – it was like Uxbridge High Street.

If only she knew why Alan had come to Heathrow she'd have some idea where to look for him. He had carried a bag but it was such a small one, more of an attaché case really, that you couldn't count it as luggage. Which was why she had assumed he wasn't flying anywhere. But she could be wrong. If this was so then the situation was indeed hopeless for, without knowing his destination, there was no possible way to discover in which area he would be waiting.

Of course he could be meeting some— Brenda stood stock still then, her hand on her pounding heart, her cheeks icing over, understanding at last what an absolute fool she had been. No wonder he had raced out of the house, flung himself into the car, driven like the wind. Simone was coming back!

Oh God, she might bump into them. Hand in hand, laughing and kissing, arms round each other. Making up for lost time. True, they wouldn't guess why she was here but Brenda knew she would not be able to bear it. She hurried away from the drift towards the main entrance. She passed a burger bar and more shops, not even looking where she was going, anxious only to find a hiding place.

Which is how she almost came to miss him.

Alan was standing in line with several other people on some steps going down to a lower level. Brenda, stepping quickly back, glanced at the brightly illuminated amber and black sign over her head. Left Luggage.

The steps doubled back on themselves so, once Alan had disappeared on to the underneath shelf, as it were, she was able to join the queue without risk of discovery. There were seven people between them.

When she entered the baggage area, she stood to one side

near the back wall, as if waiting for someone. From this position she was able to observe Alan queuing for the X-ray machine. The first thing she observed was that, if such a thing were possible, he looked even more ill than he had when she had first seen him.

He was staring at a woman who was wearing a bright sombrero. She had been asked to open her luggage which was then thoroughly examined. Unaware that a one in ten search was normal procedure, Brenda marvelled at the shrewdness of the staff, for the woman looked just like an ordinary holidaymaker. She had even thought to bring along two small children.

Alan put his case on the moving track; a dark outline enclosing a mass of grey scrawl slid by on the screen. Brenda, noticing an *Evening Standard* sticking out of a waste bin, picked it up. When Alan handed in the case, received a yellow ticket and turned to leave, she hid behind the paper until the scruffy, unpolished shoes had climbed above her head and disappeared.

Brenda hurried after, determined not to lose him again. He didn't go far. Just a few yards away, high above the crowd, was a pub and several eateries. She watched Alan climb the stairs then, knowing him to be safely contained at least for the next few minutes, relaxed for the first time since she had left the house.

Immediately she thought about her parents and how worried they would be at her sudden, wild departure. There were a few loose coins in her coat pocket and a bank of telephones close by. Brenda put in ten pence, rang home and just had time to gabble some sort of made-up story before she was cut off.

Then, cautiously, she made her way to the foot of the steps. She was standing next to some computer war games, one of which was being ferociously manipulated by a dark-skinned young man in a baggy T-shirt. He kept shouting 'Yes!! Yes!!' and banging on the machine with his fist. Every few seconds he drank from a water bottle and pulled his T-shirt away from his skinny body, agitating it to let the air circulate, sweating in the heat of his vicarious battle.

Brenda crept slowly upwards. She wasn't too afraid of meeting Alan coming down, reckoning that, as he was presumably visiting one of the watering holes, he would by now be safely sitting with a plate of something or, at the very least, a drink. Hesitantly she peered over the parapet.

The set-up was open plan. The frontage of a pub, Garfunkel's café, a Häagen-Dazs, and Harry Ramsden's fish and chip restaurant simply ran into each other, without dividing walls.

Brenda looked around the spread of tables in the ice-cream parlour. Some were black with matching chairs, others, speckled malachite, stood on one leg surrounded by camel-coloured plastic stools. There were lots of potted palms. Alan was at the counter buying a cup of coffee.

Concealed behind a large sign suggesting that customers requiring the Häagen-Dazs Table Service Queue Here, she watched him go into the dining area. He sat close to a huge black and white photograph of a lascivious couple radiant with gluttony. Even from where she stood Brenda could see they were licking each other's lips, if not actually devouring each other's tongues. She crossed over to the entrance of Harry Ramsden's and pretended to read all about the good things they had to offer. When she looked over her shoulder, mere seconds later, Alan had gone.

Wildly now, not caring at all whether she was discovered or not, Brenda flew down the stairs in pursuit. At the bottom of the steps someone barred her way.

'Excuse me.' It was the boy from the war machines. 'You got any change, love?'

'What?' Disorientated, she stared at him in bewilderment. 'No. No, I haven't.' She pushed him out of the way and stood staring crazily about her. Then ran back up the steps to get a better view. But it was hopeless. Just a massive, heaving swarm of unidentifiable people.

'What shall I do? Oh, what shall I do?'

Brenda did not realise she had spoken aloud. The boy from the war games machine started to laugh but she did not hear.

Was Alan going home? Should she run back to the car park and try to catch him there?

But surely, if he had checked in his luggage he would later need to reclaim it. In which case he must still be somewhere on the concourse. Unless . . . unless . . .

Brenda screwed up her tense, white face trying to come to a decision.

Behind her back someone else now stood beneath the gobbling, slobbering black and white lovers. Someone whose eyes were suddenly sharp with recognition. And not a little alarm.

Chapter Three

PC Perrot, savagely plucked from his natural habitat, sat uneasily in the reception office at Causton police station. Mulling over what he had heard of DCI Tom Barnaby, Perrot was not a happy man.

Fair, they said, but with a sharp edge to his tongue. Stood square behind his team but had been known to fall on it from a great height should its attention be wandering. Never backward in coming forward to claim credit – pretty common – he was also known for never passing the buck. Could be amiability itself but catch him on an off day and – here Perrot's confidant had grinned and drawn his thumbnail graphically across his throat.

Of course, Perrot was presently telling himself while shifting uneasily on a hard wooden chair, a lot of this was probably hearsay. You had to allow for the temptation to exaggerate any macho tendencies. The inclination to admire, even revere hard men was strong.

In his mind Perrot went over his report on Alan Hollingsworth in as much detail as he could recall. It had seemed to him as brief and as scrupulous as accuracy would allow and waffle-free, which is what he had been led to understand was required. He wondered now if perhaps he had overstepped the mark when summing up by suggesting that further investigation of the subject under inquiry was probably advisable. If he'd realised it was going to end up on the desk of some bigwig in the CID . . .

PC Perrot produced a snowy handkerchief, passed it over the droplets of moisture on his brow and tucked it away again. As he did so a fair-haired, very pretty police sergeant put her head round the door. One look and she gave him the sort of smile usually seen on the faces of dental receptionists approaching intensely nervous patients.

'Constable Perrot?'

He followed her along a lengthy corridor past a series of gun-metal doors, all showing neatly typed cards slotted into metal frames, down some uncarpeted stone stairs, along another seemingly endless corridor then two right turns in quick succession. He thought, I'll never get out of this alive.

'Someone will take you back.'

'Oh. Thank you.'

Just as he started to feel they must have walked at least twice round the entire building, they turned into a much shorter corridor with a glassed-in door at the end. Sergeant Brierley rapped on this. As they waited, she smiled at him again.

'You'll be all right. He's a pussycat.'

Constable Perrot was not consoled. There were pussycats and pussycats in his opinion. Tigers were pussycats. And lions.

From inside the room came a raucous sound. More of a bark than a roar but still not very pleasant. Sergeant Brierley opened the door.

'Constable Perrot, sir.'

The big man behind the desk was scanning something that Perrot recognised as his Open Text report, riffling through the pages – there now seemed to be an awful lot of them – and frowning.

In the corner of the room, perched on a wide windowsill, was a thin, youngish bloke. Pale and ferrety-faced. Red hair. A mean mouth.

The air was like warm soup. A large fan swirled it round in sluggish circles. Perrot was not asked to sit down. Eventually the DCI said, without looking up, 'Ever thought of writing a novel, Constable?'

'Sir?'

'With your eye for detail and feeling for suspense you should make a fortune.'

Unsure whether this was an insult, a compliment or a joke, Perrot remained silent. He kept his gaze forward and slightly cast down, avoiding the eye of the younger officer who he had already decided would give a coldly unsympathetic reception to anything he might say or do.

Next to a stack of trays full of assorted paper on the big bloke's desk, Perrot noticed a photograph in a silver frame of an attractive woman with curly hair, holding on her lap a little girl of quite remarkable beauty. Like a Pears advert, she was. Perrot, slightly comforted by this sign of domestic normalcy, kept it in his line of vision until one or the other of his superiors saw fit to break the silence.

'Why wasn't this report marked urgent?'

'Well . . . I . . .'

'We've got a man here whose wife has disappeared. He refuses to answer the door until you threaten to break it down. You find him drunk and in an extremely unbalanced mental state. He lies to you about why she's left, contradicts himself, refuses to give the name of a single friend or relative who might confirm her whereabouts. He can't produce any note or communication from her. After looking around upstairs – the only moment, incidentally, when you seem to have displayed a single shred of intelligence, let alone initiative – you find Mrs Hollingsworth has gone without taking any of her clothing or personal effects.' Barnaby broke off here and threw the stack of paper into a wire tray. 'Would you say that was an accurate summary of what I've just ploughed through?'

'Yes, sir.'

'Cellar floors have been torn apart for less.'

'Sir.'

'I can't think of a single officer in my nick who wouldn't have had something like this,' Barnaby swiped the basket vigorously with the flat of his hand, 'on a senior man's desk within half an hour of completing it. And a good proportion of them would have brought Hollingsworth in for further questioning.'

Scarlet-faced with shame and humiliation, Constable Perrot hung on to his helmet and dropped his eyes to the carpet. He yearned for it to split apart and reveal gaping floorboards through which he could crawl away and die. The dreadful pause continued.

'Well, what's done is done, I suppose. Tell me what you've found out since.'

'Pardon, sir?'

'This is dated Sunday. I presume you've had time to make inquiries in the village? Did Mrs Hollingsworth talk to anyone about going away? What did people think of her marriage? Does anyone know who this Blakeley you overheard her husband speaking to might be? How were the couple regarded? The usual stuff.' Barnaby paused for Perrot to reply. He stared at the policeman who still did not look up. His colour had deepened to a roguish violet and the perspiration pouring down his face and neck increased.

He adjusted his helmet, leaving sweat marks on the navy blue nap.

'This beggars belief,' said the Chief Inspector. 'Have you done anything, Perrot, anything at all, since you talked to Hollingsworth?'

'Yes, sir.'

'Let's have it then.'

'And keep it short,' said the man on the windowsill. 'Our annual leave starts next month.'

'I was concerned about Mr Hollingsworth's physical condition.' The policeman spoke in the manner of someone coerced into public address much against their will. 'So I rang Dr Jennings the local GP and suggested he call round. Which he did. But there was no reply.'

'Was Hollingsworth one of his patients?'

'Yes.' Here Perrot, feeling he was creating a sorry enough impression without cringing, braced himself, raised his head and looked directly into the fierce heat of the Chief Inspector's regard. An unsmiling countenance. Fierce eyebrows like little black horsehair rugs. High colour. Eyes brown. Perrot had always thought brown eyes could never look anything but warm. Ah well, you live and learn. 'Both Alan and his wife were registered but I think Dr Jim had only actually met Simone.'

'Dr Jim?' The red-haired man sniggered. 'Jesus.'

'You've nothing else to add to this pathetic story?'

'No, sir.'

'You've been buried in the sticks too long, man. Right, I shall be at Fawcett Green within the next hour or so. Make sure you are as well.'

'Yes, sir.' Silently Perrot prayed that this would be the end of his ordeal. And vowed to make up for his foolish mishandling of matters so far. To be crisp, alert, observant.

To show them that a country copper was not necessarily a dud copper.

'You certainly know how to play it by the book.' Barnaby nodded once more at the exuberantly detailed report and rose. Perrot gulped as he got the measure of the man. 'But if you want to get anywhere in this business you'll have to learn to play it by ear as well.'

Perrot, deeply contented where he was and with no ambition even to make sergeant, especially if it meant mixing with mean-lipped bastards with eyes like hailstones, mumbled, 'Thank you very much, sir.'

'It was a reprimand, Perrot, not a compliment.'

The man on the windowsill burst out laughing then falsely pretended to disguise it as a cough.

'How long have you been in the force?'

'Thirteen years.'

'And your present posting?'

'Seven, sir.'

Yes, far too long, thought Barnaby. They got settled and over-comfortable staffing these rural outposts. A little sortie from time to time for a refresher course or an update on legal or ethnic matters then back under their security blanket. You couldn't blame them. Their brief, after all, was to get really dug into the community. Frequently they got so well dug in that there was hell to pay when they were moved on. Especially if the locals had taken a shine. It was certainly about time they got this one shifted. Barnaby could imagine the style of policing employed by Perrot. Paternalistic, kind but firm. Caring – whatever that devalued word now meant. All well and good, but not if it left him incompetent to handle anything but the simplest of misdemeanours. The man appeared to be about as useful as a cat flap in a submarine.

Perrot read his senior officer's mind and his heart turned over.

'Right, Perrot. You can go.'

'Sir.'

Somehow Perrot's feet covered the carpet as far as the door. The knob slipped in his sweaty fingers as he tried to turn it. The tighter he gripped it the more it slipped. He used his handkerchief. A hundred years passed before he found himself once more outside in the corridor. He stood for a moment braced to hear derisive chuckles from the room he had just left but there was only silence.

Troy was still enjoyably reflecting on Perrot's interview as he drove Barnaby's Rover Four Hundred swiftly along the A4020 towards Chalfont St Peter, the windows wide open against the warm, pressing air. Nothing entertained him more than another's discomfiture. It had been good, the chief's crack about writing a novel. Troy only thought of smart remarks and snappy put-downs hours, sometimes days, after their natural insertion point into the dialogue had passed.

'He's a throwback, if you like,' he said. 'I bet that bloke on telly years ago was like Perrot. Apparently he'd pat the villains on the head, give them a stern talking to and a lollipop to make it better. My nan's for ever on about it.'

'Dixon of Dock Green.'

'That's him. A right anachronism.'

Every now and again Troy, who was always coming across words he didn't understand, took the trouble to look them up in his daughter's dictionary. Once aware of the meaning, he would flaunt them till he got bored or until the next enigma turned up. Last month it had been cognisance. Before that, pachyderm.

Barnaby rolled an ice-cold can of Orange Fanta, snatched from the Automat just before leaving, against his cheeks, hoping to cool them down.

'I trust you know where you're going.'

'Roughly. It's not far from Compton Dando.'

'Never heard of it.'

'Course you have,' said Sergeant Troy. 'That manor house full of New Age weirdoes. Where the old geezer in the long nightie got stabbed.'

'Oh. Yes.'

'I'd go mad living out here.' Troy looked out of the open window and down his nose. It was a pale, narrow nose. Jutting out only slightly, it descended in an elegant straight line, like the nosepiece on a Roman helmet. 'I mean, look at that.'

'That' was a thatched cottage of such dreamlike perfection that it was almost impossible to believe it was occupied by credit-carded, telly-watching, bar-coded human beings. A gingerbread family might have been more appropriate. Or a painted weather man and his wife, trundling in and out at regular intervals, as immaculately inexpressive as their storybook setting.

'Who'd want to live in a house with a wig on?' Troy's remark was laced with baffled resentment. He hated being presented with the spoils of people with immeasurably more money than himself, especially when they chose to chuck it about on such incomprehensible trifles.

The sergeant was urban spirit incarnate, weaned on exhaust fumes, addicted to multi-storey car parks and multiplex cinemas carpeted with popcorn, to ziggurating shopping malls studded with zooming glass lifts and throbbing to the beat of hard rock, to space-invaded pubs.

'Might as well be dead,' he added, never averse to

ramming home a point already more than adequately made.

They were coming into Fawcett Green and Barnaby pointed out that St Chad's Lane was the narrow turning on the right. Troy forbore to ask what else could the turning be in a two-street, one-horse dump like this?

He was delightedly vindicated when, a moment later, the horse itself appeared, sedately clopping along. A small child, wearing a velvet riding hat and jodhpurs, bobbed on the vast leather saddle. Troy, father of one and daily exposed to the world's wickedness, immediately wondered where its mother was.

Becoming aware of the car, the little girl skilfully eased her mount on to the grass verge and gestured with calm authority for them to pass. Troy, who would have much preferred flustered anxiety that he could have authoritatively soothed, muttered, 'Kids today.'

'Over there,' the Chief Inspector pointed. 'Where the bike is.'

Perrot's Honda motorcycle was standing inside the gates of Nightingales, which were wide open. His yellow safety jerkin and white helmet marked POLICE rested on the seat. The constable himself was nowhere to be seen.

Troy drove in and the two men got out of the car. In spite of the heat, the sergeant then put on his immaculately pressed, silver-grey flecked cotton jacket after giving the collar a quick once over and removing a stray red hair.

Barnaby rapped sharply on the front door but no one answered. The house had a desolate air as if recently abandoned, though vases and ornaments could still be seen on the windowsills between the glass and half-drawn curtains.

'Tray posh,' said Sergeant Troy, peering through the glass.

A narrow shingle path ran down the side of the garage to the rear of the house. Barnaby and Troy crunched along it and entered a somewhat neglected garden. This was encroaching on to the patio, a pleasant if unimaginative arrangement of multicoloured slabs. It held parched begonias in smart Chinese pots, a barbecue, still full of ashes, and a large, blue and white daisy-patterned hammock.

Barnaby, a gardener to his fingertips, climbed down the steps and stared with irritation. There were some beautiful day lilies surrounded by couch grass, a newly planted but unwatered rhododendron, 'George Reynolds' and a sad old hebe which also looked as if it could do with a drink. But there was one patch that caught his eye. Not far away was a small section of ground which looked slightly softer than the rest and had been freshly turned over. Perhaps Hollingsworth had decided to start tidying up but that was as far as he'd got. Given the man's state of mind as described by Perrot, it seemed unlikely.

'Sir! Over here!'

Barnaby heard his sergeant rattle and shake the French windows. Before he could scramble back up, Troy had run over to the barbecue, seized the metal tongs and smashed the glass. He put his hand in and turned the key then broke two more panes to release the bolts. By the time Barnaby reached him the windows stood wide open.

A man was lying on a brightly patterned rug in front of an empty fireplace. Barnaby crossed quickly over and knelt beside him. Troy stood on the threshold, his fastidious nature affronted by the mixture of stale offensive odours about the place, not least of which came from the pool of urine beneath the recumbent figure. Troy noticed a tumbler lying on its side a short distance from the man's right hand.

'Is he a goner?'

'Yes. Get hold of the FME, would you?'

'Righty-oh.' Troy crossed over to a fussy gilt table holding a mock Edwardian telephone.

'Don't touch that,' said the Chief Inspector sharply. 'Use the car radio. Ask them to send a photographer. And a round-the-clock watch.'

'OK, OK.' Keep your hair on, a phrase that Troy would never have dared utter, provided the subtext. At the French windows he hesitated. 'You don't think he's just . . . conked out then – Hollingsworth?'

'We don't know yet that it is Hollingsworth. Try and find out what's happened to Sniffer of the Yard. If he's good for nothing else, at least he can identify the body, pro tem.'

When his sergeant had disappeared, Barnaby straightened up and looked about him. He would have recognised the place anywhere, thanks to Constable Perrot's eye for detail. What a loss to the airport bookstalls that man was. Not necessarily, however, a permanent one. Should he carry on with the staggering lack of acumen and foresight that he had shown so far, a career change might well be in the offing. And sooner rather than later.

Barnaby worked his way once round the room, keeping as near the edge as possible, protecting the scene as severely as if the man had been found with his head bashed in. Why precisely, he would have been hard put to say. Though this was clearly an unexplained death, there was nothing at this stage to suggest it was suspicious. Perhaps thirty years' exposure to dirty work had given him a nose for it.

The Chief Inspector looked into cabinets of china, along shelves of books, at pictures and photographs. He carried his hands loosely at his sides. Years and years ago he would have held them away from his body, maybe even slightly in the air to remind him not to reach out or handle anything.

As a young constable he had been seconded to a fire-eating DCI who had simply terrified him. Once, arriving at the scene of a murder and finding the body, a wretched half-naked young woman lying face down in a muddy ditch, Barnaby, unthinking, jumped into it and pulled her dress down. He had received a tongue-lashing that almost brought tears to his eyes. (What do you think she wants? Her arse covered or the shithead who did this put away?) For months afterwards he had been made to keep his hands in his pockets until the first stage of any investigation was completed. Jeeringly called 'Tommy Billiards' by the rest of the team, the humiliation paid off, for he never did it again.

At the front of the house his own bag carrier, having made the necessary calls, was getting out of the car. Aware that the local talent was huffing and puffing down the lane, Troy waited until Perrot was a few yards away then turned and walked briskly off. The constable, scarlet-faced and perspiring heavily, caught up with him on the patio.

'Um, good morning, Sergeant.'

'Well, hullo, Polly.'

Perrot eyed the smashed windows with dismay. 'What's happened?'

Troy grinned, shrugged, and said, 'We thought you'd taken the day off.'

'Call of nature, Sergeant,' said Perrot.

In truth, after standing sentry for over two hours and finding himself absolutely ravenous, he had popped up to Ostlers for a double Twix and a cold drink. The chocolate was now melting in his pocket, the aluminium can thrown into some bushes when he spotted the DCI's car.

'What'd you think that's for then?' Troy jerked his head towards the Hollingsworths' charming little fish pond then said, 'You're in deep do-do, Poll. And not just for leaving this place unguarded.'

Unsure how to respond but already resigned to the prospect of endless parrot jokes, the policeman remained silent. Troy crossed to the French windows. As his black shadow fell across the creamy carpet, Barnaby looked up.

'He's just drifted back, sir.' Standing aside, Sergeant Troy indicated to Perrot that he should enter the room.

PC Perrot stepped over the threshold and stopped dead. He stared at the body on the hearth rug. Barnaby watched the colour drain from his face and saw that there was no need to spell out the seriousness of the policeman's position.

'Is this the man you know as Alan Hollingsworth, Perrot?'

The constable moved a few steps to the left and slightly forward so that the dead man's profile was in his line of vision.

'Yes, sir.'

Perrot hadn't fainted since he was twelve years old. A scorching day very much like this when he had had to have a tetanus jab after scraping his leg on a rusty fence. Standing waiting, dizzy in the heat, afraid of the needle, he had passed out cold. He must not do that now even though he felt a thousand times worse. Not with the sneering sergeant at his back and cold condemnation flowing across the carpet to his face.

How was he even to handle, let alone survive, this appalling situation? What sort of fool, the foolish Perrot now asked himself, would stand for hours in front of a building simply because his knock had been unanswered? Surely a quick check around the place would be the next step? Then the dead man would have been found. Or, unspeakably harder to bear, a man who might not have been quite dead. A dying man whose life could have been saved.

Scourging deeper, Perrot recalled the report that he had not marked urgent or put directly on some senior officer's desk. Would doing so have made a difference? Immediately Perrot convinced himself that it would. After all, hadn't the CID heavy mob come over to Fawcett Green almost straightaway?

His offence was indeed monstrous. Perrot tried to stiffen his face muscles lest they should quiver and hung his head. His ears hummed. The foetid air was rank with accusation.

Just as he felt he would not be able to remain upright another minute, the Chief Inspector said, 'Outside, you. The less trampling about the better.'

'Sir.'

A car drew up at the main gates. Two doors slammed, two sets of footsteps crossed the gravel. Someone rapped the front door and Sergeant Troy shouted, 'Round this way!'

Police Surgeon for years, now mysteriously restyled Force Medical Examiner, Dr George Bullard had noted wryly when so informed that, though the designation might change, the raw material showed a tendency to remain as unprepossessing as ever. He was accompanied by a young man in a Stone Roses T-shirt, jeans and filthy sneakers with a camera round his neck, one under his arm, assorted lenses and a light meter.

As the photographer worked taking shots from all angles, balancing on his toes at one point on the very edge of the fireplace, Perrot, as instructed, retreated to the patio and further persecution. Barnaby and George, old friends as well as old colleagues, stood to one side passing on the latest station gossip, putting the world to rights, talking about their families. Doc Bullard had just had his first grandchild. Barnaby and his wife longed to be in the same position but did not hold out much hope. Recently their daughter Cully had pointed out that Juliet Stevenson, an actor she greatly admired, had just had her first baby at thirty-eight. A mere thirteen years to go, her parents noted sadly when Cully and Nicholas, her husband, had left. We'll be too old to pick it up, Joyce said. And she was only half joking.

'Just the stiffy, is it?' asked the photographer, indicating that he was through.

'For now,' said the Chief Inspector.

If he sounded confident, that was because he was confident. Perhaps because Nightingales already appeared to be at the centre of a mystery, Barnaby felt certain that Alan Hollingsworth had not succumbed to a stroke or heart attack. Or alcohol poisoning even though, according to Perrot, he'd been lowering gallons of the stuff for days.

Even so, Barnaby felt it would be prudent to wait until the postmortem before getting Scenes of Crime out. Cuts and more cuts were the order of the day and even a straightforward investigation with a modest team cost money. Though a mere droplet in the ocean which formed the Thames Valley budget, he would nevertheless be, quite rightly, reprimanded should it be spent unnecessarily.

On the other hand if murder was eventually proven and evidence had been lost or damaged under the day-to-day business of cleaning and tidying up the house and Hollingsworth's effects and sorting out his affairs then he would be in much deeper trouble. The worst, in fact, for such an error could well result in a killer getting clean away.

The Chief Inspector suddenly became aware he was being spoken to.

'Sorry, George.'

Dr Bullard was kneeling on the hearth rug, having unpacked his bag, spread out the tools of his trade and pulled on thin latex gloves. Obligingly he repeated himself.

'I'd say, from the look of the pupils, he took a whacking great overdose.' He loosened the waistband and undid the flies of the dead man's trousers. When he picked up the rectal thermometer Barnaby, out of respect, turned away.

He caught sight of his sergeant, swinging in the daisy hammock, smoking, his face turned to the sun. He knew that Troy would be bewildered by this attitude. Respect for the dead had always struck the sergeant as pointless. Barnaby wondered if this was a generation thing or a question of individual temperament and decided probably the latter.

He pondered on the division between people with imagination, those able to put themselves in another's place, and people without. This had always struck him as perhaps the most unbridgeable gap of all. All other differences, given willing hearts and minds, could be reconciled. But how to bestow a gift that nature had unkindly (or, some might argue, kindly) withheld?

'I'd say he's been dead a couple of days. Perhaps a bit less.'

The doctor was unfastening the dead man's shirt. Suddenly bored with the dismal ritual, the Chief Inspector went outside. It occurred to him to pass this consoling piece of information on to PC Perrot but the man had, once again, disappeared. Sergeant Troy stopped swinging and attempted to look more alert while still plainly relishing the sunshine.

'This is the life, eh, guv?'

Barnaby marvelled at such detachment. Shortly after discovering a human being who would never again see the sunrise this was, apparently, the life. Very occasionally and for barely a heartbeat the Chief Inspector would envy his sergeant. This was not one of those occasions.

After ten minutes or so, George Bullard joined them. Although he did not actually say this is the life, there was tremendous relish in his inhalation and exhalation of the fragrant summer air. Barnaby began to feel rather out of things.

'The van should be along any minute, Tom.'

'Any chance of a PM fairly soon?'

'Every chance. I'm clear, actually, for the rest of the day.'

'That's what we like to hear.' The Chief Inspector looked around. 'Where's our plod, Gavin?'

'I put him out front to move people along. Last time I checked he was admiring some little kid's drawing.'

Barnaby gave a groaning laugh.

The doctor said, 'He's all right, Colin Perrot. I used to live on his patch. He always had time for you.'

'I'm sure he's a warm and richly loveable human being,' said Barnaby. 'But I'm starting to think he's a bloody useless copper.'

The investigation into Alan Hollingsworth's death being necessarily delayed until the PM report, it was Simone's disappearance that now absorbed Barnaby's attention.

Half an hour had passed since the mortuary van departed. A uniformed police presence was now stationed at the front and rear of the house.

The time was one thirty. What better place, suggested Barnaby, both to eat and glean information than the village pub? Walking there, they were overtaken by Constable Perrot. He halted briefly near the crossroad and was seen to reach into the hedge and pick up an aluminium can.

'Little Miss Tidy,' said Sergeant Troy.

The Goat and Whistle, awaiting its hundred and fiftieth birthday, had recently been transformed by the brewers. Its ceiling, kippered by years of tobacco fumes to a rich yellowy brown, had been stripped and repainted with dark, yellowy brown varnish. Its scarred counters, well-worn quarry-tiled floor and old fire grate had been ripped out and replaced by artificially distressed counters, creatively cracked stone flags scattered with fake sawdust and a chipboard Elizabethan inglenook. The ancient dartboard disappeared and an Astaroth v. the Dark Hellhounds of Erewhon space invader arrived.

This imaginative transformation, unasked for and unwanted by both mine host and his customers, had cost thirty thousand pounds. The landlord was assured that, once the word of such startling refurbishments got about, his takings would be going through the roof. So far there was no sign of this. He had replaced the dartboard out of his own pocket.

Half a dozen heads turned as Barnaby and Troy came in and conversation ceased. The Chief Inspector ordered a ham salad and some Guinness, Troy a corned beef and Branston pickle baguette and a half of bitter. He took them to a table near the space machine and started to play.

Waiting for his meal, Barnaby was soon engaged in conversation, the landlord, Daniel Carter, opening.

'Yours, is it? That Rover down the lane?'

Barnaby admitted that it was.

'Everything all right?' The question was put by an elderly woman who had come up to the counter for a refill of her gin and peppermint. Although no one else moved, Barnaby was aware of a general gathering of attention keenly focused on his reply.

'Actually we're looking into the disappearance of Mrs Simone Hollingsworth.'

'What did I tell you, Elsie?' said the gin and pep over her shoulder.

'Thanks, Bet. I'll have a drain of White Satin.'

'Deaf as a beadle,' said Bet, swivelling back. 'You've taken long enough about it.'

'Did you know the couple?' asked Barnaby. Addressing the old lady, he also glanced around the room. The floodgates opened.

By the time he had finished his tired undressed salad and near transparent shavings of ham he had discovered that Mr H worked all the hours God made, Mrs H was always done up like a dog's dinner. He never mixed, she mixed but got bored with you after five minutes. They'd give at the door but not what you'd expect, taking the property into account. The last anyone had seen of poor Simone was on the Causton bus. And, rounded off Elsie, don't tell me anyone leaves their old man with no more than a handbag and a thin jacket. Specially when he's loaded.

So far, so familiar. Barnaby became resigned. But then Daniel Carter leaned forward. He looked left to right as if about to cross a busy road and seemed on the point of tapping the side of his shiny red nose.

'Now if it was Alan who had disappeared, you wouldn't have to look far.'

'Really? Why is that?' countered the Chief Inspector.

'You should know,' said Elsie. 'You're the fuzz.'

'He was had up for it?'

'Gray Patterson.'

'GBH.'

'Common assault, weren't it?'

'Same difference.'

'All over some theft or other,' said the landlord. 'They worked together, see, him and Hollingsworth. Partners supposedly, in this computer business. Pen something.'

'Penstemon,' shouted deaf Elsie.

'That's it. Then, according to the report at the magistrates' hearing, Patterson designed some new programme or whatever they reckon to call it. Something really special that should have made him thousands. And Alan ripped him off.'

'Stole it like.' A fat man, having finished his steak and kidney pie, chipped in for the first time.

'I don't know all the ins and outs,' continued Daniel Carter, 'but there weren't half a ruckus. Ended with Patterson blowing his top.'

'Is that right?' asked Barnaby.

'Beat the shit out of Mr H,' said the old lady, daintily tipping back her glass.

'Now he's stony-broke, Gray. Owes money on the house, can't sell it, can't move. In schtuck, as the saying goes.'

'I heard he was trying to let.'

Barnaby finished his drink. He would have thought it excellent had he never been exposed to the velvety soft bitter sweetness of the Irish version. A year ago he and Joyce had been in Sligo for the Music Festival and the Guinness had been a revelation. The difference, they told him, lay in the water.

Troy, having finished banging and thumping and cursing Astaroth and Co. was now leaning up against the machine chatting to a youth who was banging, thumping and cursing in his turn. Now, catching the boss's eye, he murmured, 'Cheers, mate,' and moved towards the door.

'Get anything?' said the Chief Inspector as they walked back down the lane.

'Only that Mrs Hollingsworth was a great looker but seemingly kept it all for her husband. Bloke I was talking to's the brother of the bird who cleans for that old woman.'

'Which old woman? This place is swarming with them.'

'That daft one who came in to see you.'

'Not so daft, as things are turning out.'

Since the event of Perrot's Open Text report, Barnaby had thought more than once of the eccentrically dressed and supersonically bewigged Mrs Molfrey. His memory of their recent meeting had become imbued with a charming piquancy which he feared had not been present at the time. He didn't really want to talk to her again, suspecting she might well turn out simply to be a chaotic-minded and garrulous old bore.

'What about you, chief?' said Troy. 'Any luck?'

'If it turns out we're looking at murder, I've a nice juicy suspect. Someone who beat up Hollingsworth after the man had apparently swindled him out of a lot of money.'

Troy whistled. 'No longer Mr Nice Guy then, our Alan.'

'If he ever was.'

They had reached Nightingales. There were a handful of people outside but, as the gates were closed and the constable on the front doorstep was a silent and unforthcoming stranger, no one lingered.

'Got a message for you, sir,' said the constable. 'Lady next door, to the left, wanted a word with a senior person.'

PC Ramsey had got this information from his colleague guarding the rear of the house. Apparently Kevin, hearing a rustle just beyond the fence, had gone to investigate and found a face peering at him through a tangle of green stuff. The whispered request having been delivered, the face vanished, as if its owner had been sharply pulled away.

Barnaby, wrongly assuming a prurient interest in the

goings-on at the Hollingsworths', made his way to The Larches. Troy rapped on the fruit-gum panels. They moved inwards, as if by magic.

Barnaby called out, 'Hullo?'

'Come in.'

The words, whispered from directly behind the door, were barely audible. The two detectives stepped inside.

Ten minutes later, though the tension in the room twanged like a harp, Barnaby had still not been told exactly why they were there. He sat on a sofa eating a sandwich so fine it dissolved on the tongue like a Communion wafer. It was thinly filled with bland, almost tasteless cheese and had a droopy fringe of cress. It was also ice-cold. Mrs Brockley obviously kept her bread in the fridge. Barnaby's teeth had started to ache and he drank some tea hoping to warm them up.

The Brockleys were looking at each other. Not the silent 'You', 'No, you' matey joshing that couples sometimes go in for. Their glances did not quite meet. His seemed to say, don't you dare. Hers was harder to read. She was plainly distressed and under a lot of strain but she was also angry. Her eyes glittered.

'You asked us to come round, Mrs Brockley?' said the Chief Inspector, not for the first time.

'Yes.' She looked directly at him and he realised that her eyes were glittering not with anger but with tears. 'Something very—'

'Iris!'

'We'll have to talk to them sooner or later.'

'You needn't have asked them here. The whole place will know.'

Barnaby, becoming impatient with all this prevarication,

attempted reassurance. 'Mr Brockley, we are going to be carrying out a house-to-house inquiry shortly regarding Mrs Hollingsworth's—'

'What's that? House to . . . ?'

'It means everyone in the village will be visited. I'm sure, once this gets underway, people will simply think we happened to start here.'

'You see,' cried Iris.

Reg seemed unconvinced. Looking at them both, the word 'corseted' entered Barnaby's mind. Practically obsolete in these days of teddys and bodys, Lycra and Spandex, but a word surely made flesh by these two rigorously constrained people. Tightly-laced, pushed and pulled and whaleboned into a respectably shaped life that was beyond reproach. A life that surely could not properly breathe.

'Our daughter's disappeared.'

It was Iris who had spoken. Reg covered his face with his hands as if suddenly exposed to public shame.

'Brenda went out on Monday evening in the car. Rather suddenly, actually. When she wasn't back by ten—'

'She did ring up, Inspector,' interrupted her husband.

'That was two days ago,' shouted Iris.

Sergeant Troy, sussing that he was about to partake in the most boring non-event in the history of mankind, polished off his fourth scone, scooped up a couple of chocolate biscuits and let his attention wander. He glanced at the clock yet again.

It was hard to miss this splendid timepiece. Wherever one looked in the room its movement caught the eye. Diamanté numerals on a black velvet face and golden hands. On the tip of the minute hand perched a large pink and yellow butterfly with sequinned wings and long wobbly antennae. Every sixty seconds it jumped forward and Troy's nerves were starting to jump with it.

'Is she usually back by ten, Mrs Brockley?' asked Barnaby.

'No,' said Reg. 'She doesn't go out, you see.'

'I'm sorry?'

'Well, to work of course. And occasionally shopping.'

'But not at night.'

'How old is Brenda?'

'Twenty-nine.' Though Barnaby's face remained expressionless, Iris must have sensed incredulity, for she added, 'I realise she's not a child but she's never, ever done anything like this before.'

'In her entire life,' said Reg.

'So when did she telephone?'

'About nine o'clock. Said she was staying with a friend.'

'Not staying with,' Reg corrected his wife. 'Just with. As in being with. Talking to.'

'We didn't even know she had a friend,' said Iris with unconscious pathos.

Even if she had not been twenty-nine, Troy, having glanced at the elaborately framed studio portrait on the sideboard, would not have given her as much as the wax from his ears. Talk about a dog. Worst in show at Crufts and then you were insulting the canines. No point tuning up your whanger for that one.

'It's all very well her saying not to worry,' said Iris. 'But of course we did.'

'All night long.'

'And in the morning . . .'

They had argued for nearly two hours about ringing Brenda's office. Iris, black shadows round her eyes, was a thousand per cent for, Reg totally against at first then wavering in the face of his wife's extreme agitation. They had faced each other over the unlaid kitchen table – breakfast would have choked them – torn between doing what was socially acceptable and correct and easing the sick uncertainty in their hearts.

'What on earth will they think?'

'Fiddle to what they think.'

'It's not business etiquette, Iris.'

'I don't *care*.'

'Personal calls are frowned on. Brenda's always been very hot on that.'

'You don't have to talk to—'

'We'll get her into trouble.'

'Just ask if she's there. Say it's business. Pretend to be a customer.'

'She'll be home at half past six.'

'I can't wait nine hours,' screamed Iris.

So, to the accompaniment of his wife wailing and the poodle barking, Reg had rung the Coalport and National Building Society. He had been put on hold and exposed to a bagpipe and electric organ rendering of 'Ye Banks and Braes', a tune that, for the rest of his life, he could never listen to without a cold and nauseous upsurge of reminiscent dread.

Eventually he was transferred to Personnel to be told that Miss Brockley had not arrived for work that morning and that there was no message. After Reg put the phone down, he and Iris had sat very quietly for a long time. Even Shona crept back to her basket uninstructed.

The next twenty-four hours crawled by. The Brockleys couldn't eat. Cups of tea were made and stood around, uncoastered, on various pieces of furniture until they were stone cold.

It was Iris, by Wednesday morning nearly demented,

who had seen the policeman in the Hollingsworths' back garden and impulsively spoken to him. Reg had hurried to stop her, a second too late.

'Do you think,' Barnaby was asking now, 'that this was a boyfriend she was referring to?'

The Brockleys opposed this suggestion with what the Chief Inspector could not help thinking was a ridiculous degree of certainty. After all their daughter was nearly thirty and, even if her social life was somewhat limited, must have met plenty of men in the course of her work. Brenda's photograph was on the edge of Barnaby's sightlines and registered only as part of the background.

'Nothing like that,' Reg was saying.

'Brenda's a most particular girl.'

'We've brought her up to be very choosy.'

'Tell me again if you would,' said Barnaby, 'about the phone call. Her actual words, if you remember them.'

If they remembered them! The eager, breathless sentences were engraved on both their hearts.

'Daddy, I might not be home for a little while. I've run into a friend. We're going for something to eat. Don't worry if I'm a bit late. See you soon. Bye.'

'The strange thing was –'

'Apart from getting such a message in the first place,' Iris interjected.

'– she seemed to be speaking from a railway station.'

'Oh yes?' said Barnaby.

Troy glanced covertly at his watch and yawned inwardly, stretching his lips without parting them and lifting the roof of his mouth. He glanced covetously at the rest of the chocolate wafers. Amazing, no matter what state people were in they always made some tea and prised open the biccy box.

'There was a lot of background noise,' explained Reg. 'Announcements.'

'Well, Mr Brockley,' Barnaby got up, his large frame blocking half the light from the window, 'I suggest the best thing to do, if you haven't heard from Brenda by tomorrow, is to come into the station and register her as a missing person.'

'The *police* station?'

'That's right.'

'Couldn't you do that for us now, Mr Barnaby?' said Iris.

'I'm afraid not. There are certain procedures to be followed. Forms to be completed.' Barnaby did not add, as many of his colleagues seemed so easily able to do, I'm sure everything will be all right. He had knocked on too many doors and had to tell too many distraught families that the situation regarding their children was very much not all right.

They were shown out through the kitchen. Troy stopped at the poodle's basket, bent down and patted the dog. Fondled its dejected ears.

'She'll be back soon,' he said cheerily. 'Keep your tail up.'

The preliminary stages of the postmortem were completed by six o'clock. The full report would not be on the Chief Inspector's desk until the following afternoon but George Bullard rang the results through straightaway.

Alan Hollingsworth had died from an overdose of the tranquilliser Haloperidol in a solution of whisky. There was no food in the stomach. The drug was available only by prescription under various brand names usually in 0.5 milligram capsules. As near as could be reasonably assessed, around six or seven milligrams had been taken. No capsule casings appeared to have been swallowed. There were no unexplained marks on the body. The heart, lungs and other internal organs were sound.

'Good for another forty years,' concluded Dr Bullard.

'What about times?'

'Late Monday night, I'd say. Or early Tuesday. It's hard to be more precise after forty-eight hours.'

'Oh, come on, George.' Silently he cursed Constable Perrot.

'Sorry.'

Barnaby sighed then said, 'Would such a dosage be enough to kill someone?'

'Probably. Especially with all that booze. From the way he was lying I'd say he took the stuff sitting on the sofa then, when he became unconscious, just rolled off. The rug was very thick and, let's face it, dying is about as physically relaxed as you can get. Which was why he wasn't bruised.'

'And what's this about "no casings"? Are you saying he took the stuff in tablet form?'

'Couldn't have. Only made up in capsules.'

'Hang on.' Barnaby paused and felt again that strange and unsubstantiated conviction which had visited him when he first saw Alan Hollingsworth's body. 'Isn't it bitter? The stuff in these tranquillisers?'

'Sometimes. Not in this case. Haloperidol's pretty tasteless.'

'Wouldn't the casings have dissolved anyway?'

'Perhaps. But there'd still be traces of gelatin in the stomach.'

'Right. Thanks, George.'

So there it was. A straightforward enough story. A man's wife has left him. He tries to drown his sorrow in drink. But drink wears off. More must be taken, which in its turn will also wear off. And so on and wretchedly on. Much better to end it once and for all.

So, having been driven to this miserable conclusion, what does Hollingsworth do? Chuck the tablets in his mouth, wash them down with hooch and get it over with? No, he sits on the settee, carefully pulls the sixteen or so gelatin capsules apart, tips the contents into his glass and stirs till dissolved. Then disposes neatly of the cases. It was possible, of course. Some people would behave with such neatness and precision even *in extremis* – the Brockleys for example. But that was not how the dead man had acted so far. He had shown nothing but shambolic desperation.

Though still wary of setting a full-scale investigation in motion, Barnaby now saw his next step as unavoidable. And so it was that early the next morning a Sherpa van turned into St Chad's Lane. Shortly afterwards, Scenes of Crime, to the intense excitement and satisfaction of the village, unloaded their stuff and set in motion the austere and impersonal machinery of investigation.

Chapter Four

Notified that his car was ready, Barnaby, rejecting the lift, made his way downstairs. Huffing and puffing to and from the car park to his room was practically the only regular exercise he got these days. He discounted gardening which was necessarily intermittent and, as his plot was now so old and well-established, involved very little in the way of hard digging.

He had quite a distance to huff and puff. In common with the headquarters of many civil businesses, the higher a person's rank in the police force the further away from the ground floor his or her office would usually be found. The Chief Super was rumoured to reside in the crow's nest, a steel and plastic anti-lightning device screwed halfway up the radio mast on the roof of the main building.

Passing through reception Barnaby noticed the Brockleys and could see straightaway that the stays of their lives had loosened further. They were sitting side by side in comfortless polystyrene shells. Plainly their daughter had not returned. There was a sad reversal in the manner of their appearance. Reg now looked as ill and distraught as had his wife the previous day. Iris sat like a rock. Her tightly folded arms pressed a framed photograph hard against her chest. Her face, though expressionless, was savagely compressed, appearing to spread outwards. She looked like the lemon on the old squash advertisement: Idris When I's Dry.

They had indeed waited, as Barnaby suggested, almost another whole day before reporting Brenda missing. Such subjection to authority in a situation like this seemed to him almost unbelievable. Ridiculous even. He was about to go over when a policewoman came out from behind the desk and approached them.

The heatwave, promised for some days by the weather forecasters, was now well on the way. The car was like an oven. All the windows were open but Barnaby could still feel the leather burning his legs. His shirt was limp and already glued to his back. Troy, in a crisp, apple-green Lacoste sports top (genuine Alligator motif, three pounds from a car boot) looked as if he had just stepped out of a fridge, not a trickle of sweat anywhere. He was moaning, as always, this time about his sex life.

'I mean, if I'd wanted to screw a marble statue I'd've got a job in the British Museum.'

Barnaby opened all the windows.

'Eventually I said to her, don't wake up if it's too much trouble.'

'And did she?'

'Hard to tell. She don't give much away, Maureen.'

The Chief Inspector, pausing only to reflect that whatever his sergeant's sword did in his hand it certainly wasn't sleep, turned his thoughts to the Brockleys' only child.

Until now Brenda had hardly impinged on his consciousness. With both a dead body and a missing person on his plate, he had more than enough to be going on with. The fact that her parents had received a reassuring phone call also mitigated against any sort of concerned action. But, over forty-eight hours later, she had still not returned. And however resolutely they insisted on a complete lack of involvement in Alan and Simone Hollingsworth's affairs, there was no denying that the Brockleys lived virtually on the couple's doorstep. Could Brenda have seen or heard something that might have put her at risk? The more he thought along these lines, the less easy Barnaby became in his mind.

Troy was still droning on. As they were on the point of entering Fawcett Green, Barnaby tuned back in. This time the subject under the hammer was Mrs Milburn, Troy's mother-in-law.

'Lethal, that woman, She's got a donor card saying on no account use any of this person's organs after her death. They are bloody toxic.'

'Rubbish.'

'I've seen it. Got a skull and crossbones on.'

Troy parked on the pub forecourt at ten minutes to eleven. Barnaby had an appointment on the hour with Dr Jennings. Troy was detailed to chase up the address and telephone number of the mobile hairdresser, Becky Latimer. And also Sarah Lawson, the other person mentioned during Mrs Molfrey's earlier visit to Causton police station. The two men would meet up at Nightingales.

Already the lane was choked with people, as was the small field which backed on to the Hollingsworths' rear garden. An exasperated Perrot, rosy with ill temper, guilt and apprehension as to how this blatant example of his inability to keep any sort of control might persuade the force to deal with him, was trying to clear a way through for a muddy Landrover. The driver leaned pointlessly on his horn, underscoring the hysterical barking of his two golden retrievers. No sooner had the vehicle squeezed by than the passage closed up again.

Barnaby missed most of this, needing to cut through the churchyard to find the doctor's house. Troy decided, before going to the post office, to have a little fun at Perrot's expense. He pushed through the crowd largely by exercising sharp elbows and brute determination.

'I should move this lot along, Polly.'

'Yes, Sergeant.'

'Where's the barrier?'

'On its way.'

'Here.' Troy jerked his head indicating a wish for intimacy.

Perrot, his heart in his boots and his stomach twisted into knots of anxiety, moved closer.

'Just thought you might like to know the PM results. Died about ten minutes before me and the chief got to him. Close as that. Sad, ain't it?'

He strode on, leaving the ashen-faced policeman staring, in utter devastation, after him.

In the churchyard, having world enough and time, Barnaby dawdled, read the gravestones scabbed with green and yellow lichen, admired equally a simply inscribed slab and a grand mausoleum enclosed by ornate railings. One unadorned plot had a glass jar of wild flowers jammed into the ground; another green granite chippings and an empty metal vase. Grand monument or homemade wooden cross, what did it ultimately matter? Passing show. And all for the benefit and comfort of the bereft. The lonely bones beneath couldn't give a damn. In the elms around and about, rooks croaked and cawed their aggressive hearts out.

The Reverend Bream appeared, closing the vestry door

behind him and making his way down the path with a swish of armazine. Although walking with his hands demurely clasped across his richly curved front and his eyes cast down, Barnaby sensed something rather worldly about the vicar. His face was highly coloured and surrounded by a lot of crisply waving chestnut hair just long enough to touch his collar. He could have stepped straight out of one of those bibulous nineteenth-century paintings featuring two jolly cardinals.

'Hullo,' said the Reverend Bream. He smiled, revealing a lot of glistening white teeth. 'Are you part of our excellent constabulary?'

'That's right, sir. Detective Chief Inspector Barnaby.'

'To do with Nightingales, is it?' Then, when Barnaby nodded, 'A sad business. Poor Alan.'

'Did you know the Hollingsworths at all?'

'Simone slightly. She was in my bell-ringing team. The only time I spoke to her husband was the day she disappeared. She didn't turn up for practice so I popped round to see if things were all right.'

'Look,' Barnaby indicated a rustic bench, 'd'you think we might sit down?'

'Well, I'm just off to Hellions Wychwood for a christening.'

'It won't take a moment. Or we could meet later.'

'Oh, I expect it'll be all right.' The vicar glanced at his watch. 'I'm usually fifteen minutes early and they're bound to be late. People always are at weddings and christenings. Never at funerals. Can't wait to see them off and get back to the booze.'

'Did you know Mrs Hollingsworth well?' asked the Chief Inspector when they were sitting down.

'Not really. She came to a few meetings, missed a couple,

wandered half-heartedly back. Just looking for something to do, I think.'

'You didn't meet or talk for any reason? Apart from bell-ringing?'

'Good heavens no.' He laughed then glanced briefly upwards as though asking post-clearance on this innocent exclamation. 'Neither of the Hollingsworths were churchgoers. But then who is these days? Till it comes to needing a setting for the bridal video.'

The Reverend Bream did not speak in acid tones. He seemed cheerfully resigned to the scale of his neglect. Perhaps, as his high complexion indicated, he found solace in the occasional cup of claret. A little wine for his stomach's sake. Barnaby warmed to him.

'What did you think of her?'

'Simone? A bit dim – no, sorry. That's unkind. A better word, I think, would be guileless. And rather gullible. One got the impression that she would believe anything you said. Sweet-natured, as far as it's possible to judge. Tiny, just about five feet, I'd say, and very slender. Little hands and feet. Fair haired with a lovely skin. Astonishingly pretty.'

Another novelist. They were everywhere. Barnaby asked if the vicar remembered what time he had called at the house.

'Around six, directly we'd finished. I knocked several times, persisting because Alan's car was there. Eventually he opened the door looking quite dreadful.'

'You mean ill?' The Chief Inspector recalled Perrot's mention of a goodbye message on Hollingsworth's answerphone. This sounded as if he had already discovered it.

'Wildly distressed is how I'd put it. Almost incoherent. I stepped inside – uninvited but there are times when good manners must take a back seat. Asked if there was anything I could do. If Mrs Hollingsworth was all right. He said she'd gone to look after her mother who'd had a stroke. Almost before he'd finished speaking I found myself back on the doorstep.'

'You didn't call again?'

'There seemed little point when he so obviously hadn't wanted me there in the first place. I told Evadne and she got the village support system going – to poor effect, I'm afraid. I feel quite ashamed now. If perhaps I'd been more persistent—'

'I doubt it would have made any difference.'

The Reverend Bream got up, smoothing his cassock. Barnaby noticed that, in the bright sunlight, it had something of a greenish tinge.

'I suppose you couldn't tell me how exactly . . .' The vicar trailed off delicately.

'I'm afraid not, sir. We're still pursuing our inquiries.'

The Reverend Bream went off to wet the baby's head and Barnaby continued on his way to Dr Jennings' house. This turned out to be a very attractive two-storey building of golden stone with a much less attractive breeze block surgery bulging from one side.

Mrs Jennings showed him into a comfortable sitting room and went off to make some coffee. Barnaby employed the time waiting for her return in wandering around enjoying the books and family photographs. Happy snaps, school pictures – gold-rimmed ovals on dark brown mounts, two boys and a girl. Middle-aged people, old people. A girl of around eighteen with a roly-poly baby, both laughing fit to bust. A paterfamilias with muttonchop whiskers.

'Quite a family, Mrs Jennings,' he said, moving to help her as she entered the room. The tray looked very heavy.

'I wish they'd go away,' said Avis. 'Not for good, of course. Or even for long. Just sometimes.'

'Mine's gone,' said the Chief Inspector. 'I don't entirely recommend it.'

'It's different for men.' She was attacking the cake with a fearsome knife, long and curved like a Malayan kris.

Barnaby said, 'None for me, thank—'

'I mean, you're not so constrained by their presence.' She poured from a round-bellied pot then, pulling apart a little nest of tables, warmed to her theme. 'How many times, for instance, have you been chasing a criminal along the motorway and lost him because you've had to go and pick somebody up from netball?'

'Not often.' He thanked her for the table and then for the coffee. 'Well, never actually.'

'Exactly.' She placed the cake, a silver fork and a pretty starched napkin alongside. 'I'm renowned for my squidgy mousseline. This one's coffee. What d'you think?'

Barnaby thought a morsel wouldn't hurt. Only common courtesy after all. And he needn't eat it all.

A grave miscalculation. It was food for angels. He took a second loaded forkful, swallowed then smiled across at the woman who had engaged him in conversation with such ingenuous bluntness. There were people to whom it never seemed to occur that speaking from the heart could cause embarrassment and Avis Jennings, like Mrs Molfrey, was plainly one of them. Perhaps they were a speciality of Fawcett Green, which would be excellent news from an investigative point of view.

'So,' she took a long drink of her own coffee. 'I suppose it's about Alan.'

'We're also inquiring into Mrs Hollingsworth's disappearance.'

'Oh?'

'How well did you know her?'

'Hardly at all. She came to the WI for a bit. And bell-ringing. We had the odd chat.'

'What about?'

'Oh, this and that.'

Barnaby curbed his impatience. It was not difficult as the divine centre filling of the cake melted on his tongue. Bitter chocolate, almonds, burnt sugar, a trace of orange flower water.

'Did she tell you anything about her life before she was married?' He produced a notebook and pen.

'A bit. She seemed to have drifted rather. You know, all sorts of jobs, none with any real future.'

'For instance?'

'Served in a flower shop, did a course in make-up, demonstrated food mixers.' Avis, rummaging in her mind for accurate recall, frowned. 'Um, worked in television for a bit. Was a cashier in some sort of club. She rather skirted round that one. I wondered if it might have been a bit Soho. Sparkle and feathers and sad old men in waistcoats.'

Presumably she meant raincoats. 'In London, was this?'

'I got that impression.' Avis rummaged a bit more but came up with nothing new. Barnaby asked if she knew of anyone else that Mrs Hollingsworth was especially friendly with.

Avis shook her head. 'Simone wasn't into all girls together stuff. She's what was called years ago a man's woman.' Air quotes were hooked round the last three words. 'She might have talked to Sarah Lawson more. Was in her art class for a bit.'

That might be useful, thought the Chief Inspector as a distant buzzer went off.

'That's the last patient gone,' said Mrs Jennings. 'Come along, Inspector. I'll take you through.'

Dr Jennings, washing his hands, smiled cheerfully over his shoulder. The smell of soap and antiseptic filled the room. He waved at a chair placed close to the side of his vast, well-cluttered desk. His visitor sat in it.

'I don't like a great expanse of wood between myself and the patient,' said Dr Jim, taking his own seat. 'It creates too great a distance. Turns me into a figure of superior authority.'

The Chief Inspector, in common, he suspected, with the majority, liked to think his GP did have a certain amount of superior authority. At least in matters medical. Jennings swung his padded leather chair round and the two men sat cosily, almost knee to knee. Barnaby adjusted his position slightly to avoid a Well Woman poster listing, in detail, all the ills to which female flesh was likely to succumb.

'I believe both the Hollingsworths were on your list, Dr Jennings.'

'That's right.'

'I'm afraid Mr Hollingsworth died of a drug overdose—'

'Ah, that's it then. So much for the rumours. Which, I might tell you, have been fairly wild.'

'I understand, acting on a suggestion from Constable Perrot, that you called on him the other day.'

'Monday lunchtime, yes. Banged on the front door for a bit but no reply. What did he take?'

'Haloperidol. Have you ever prescribed medication containing this for either of them?'

'As a matter of fact I have.' He drew a largish, stiff brown folder towards him saying, 'I got this out in readiness, when you rang.' And pulled out a wad of notes.

'Mrs Hollingsworth – I never actually met her husband – came into surgery a couple of months ago.'

'When exactly?'

'March the ninth, if it matters. She was complaining of sleeplessness. Now I'm not the sort to hand out tablets on request, Inspector, because, quite often, the simple thing the patient is describing can conceal something much more complex. So I put one or two questions and, though I was not at all persistent, she got quite upset. Admitted she was lonely and unhappy. Missing "the Smoke".

'Then I asked if everything was all right at home. There was a very long pause and I began to think either she hadn't heard me or was not going to reply. Then quickly, as if suddenly making up her mind, she took her jacket off. Her arms were covered in ugly bruises. She shrank away when I tried to examine her and burst into tears. I could see straightaway she regretted the impulse. She wouldn't expand on the matter at all so rather than push and perhaps risk her not coming back if she needed to, I let it go.'

'And did she come back, Dr Jennings?' asked the Chief Inspector, jotting away and hoping his Biro would hold out.

'Yes. I'd given her a month's supply.'

'When was that? And how much would the dosage be?'

Dr Jennings glanced at his notes. 'Thirty tablets at half a milligram.'

'And she returned . . . ?'

'On the seventeenth of April. Said the tablets had helped her a lot, which I must say surprised me as she still looked really washed out. And even more unhappy. I gave her another prescription.'

'For the same amount?'

'Yes, but warned her I wouldn't be giving repeats ad

infinitum and that it was not in her interest that I should. So when she came back a week later—'

'A *week*?'

'With some story about the tablets disappearing, just vanished out of the bathroom cabinet, I didn't accept that for a minute.'

'What did you think had happened?'

'To be honest I was afraid she was on the verge of doing something silly and wanted another bottle to make sure she made a proper job of it.'

'So you refused to give her another prescription?'

'That's right. She became very distressed. Started to cry. I must say I did wonder then, briefly, if she might be telling the truth. Working on this principle I gave her half a dozen low dosage tranquillisers just to tide her over. Also the phone number of the Samaritans. And Relate.'

'What's that?'

'Marriage guidance, as used to be. I urged her to discuss her problems with someone. And explained, of course, that she could always come to the surgery and talk to me.'

Barnaby, pausing briefly to wonder at the fact that a doctor still existed who encouraged his patients to simply come and talk to him, asked what happened next.

'Nothing. She went away. I never saw her again.'

'Were you surprised when she left her husband?'

'I must admit I was. I hate to use sociological jargon, Inspector, but that girl struck me from the first as a born victim. It wasn't just that she was small and fragile, there was something so submissive about her. She was like a child on its first day at school, you know? Standing around waiting for someone to tell her what to do.'

'Was her general health reasonably sound?'

'Excellent, I assume. In fact the two visits I've just

described were the only times she came to the surgery.'

'Well, thank you for your time, Dr Jennings.' Barnaby got up as the doctor repacked the envelope file. 'There's just one last thing: what colour would these capsules have been?'

'The half milligram?' He looked both interested and puzzled. 'Turquoise and yellow. Why do you ask?'

'Just general background.'

'I don't see, if he committed suicide, what difference—'

But he was talking to space. A further courteous murmur of thanks and the Chief Inspector had departed.

Down the lane things were now a bit more orderly. SOCO were working entirely inside so there was not a lot to see. Quite a few people had given up and those that were left looked as if they were in half a mind to.

Perrot, his face grey with misery which he was plainly only just managing to control, stood just inside the wrought-iron gates. He sprang to open them as the Chief Inspector approached. Glancing at the constable's frozen features, Barnaby was surprised to see such absolute despair. If Perrot had taken a minor dressing down this much to heart, how the hell was he ever going to cope if he found himself in real trouble?

'What's the matter with you?'

'Nothing, sir. Thank you.'

'You look like a dying duck in a thunderstorm.'

'Yes, sir.'

'Out with it, man.' Silence. 'D'you think I've got all bloody day to hang about?'

'No, Chief Inspector.' Perrot came out with it. How Hollingsworth had been alive all the time he, the not merely foolish but criminally negligent Perrot, had been standing on the front doorstep. How the man's life might have been saved if only.

'You've been misinformed, Constable.' No need to ask who had delivered the good news. 'He died Monday night.'

'Ohhh!' cried Perrot. 'But . . .'

An expression of utter disbelief rinsed the misery from the policeman's features. Disbelief, Barnaby suspected, not so much at this new piece of information but at the discovery that such deliberate malice could be directed against him by one supposedly on his own side. It was a wicked old life, thought the Chief Inspector, and no mistake.

Troy was standing just outside the newly secured French windows, smoking. Inside, two people wearing transparent overalls and boots were about their business. The boots were like old-fashioned galoshes, the front flap folded over and fastened with poppers down the side. The air was close and smelt rather metallic.

One of the officers, a woman, was new to Barnaby. She was tweezering something from the rug where Hollingsworth had, presumably, breathed his last. As Barnaby watched, she slipped it into a clear plastic sachet with a tag already attached.

Aubrey Marine, twenty years in the business, having run a hand-held Hoover up and down every fold of the apricot velvet curtains, was now starting on the lining. He called out, 'Hullo, Tom. Here we are again.'

'How's it going?'

'No startling surprises, as yet. We looking for anything special?'

'One or perhaps two small prescription bottles labelled Simone Hollingsworth, probably empty. And thirty or so turquoise and yellow capsule casings, also empty.'

'How do you . . .' Aubrey pondered briefly then said,

'Ah, with you. Those torpedo-shaped things you can pull apart.'

'That's it.'

'Not like you to invite us to a suicide's party.'

'I'm not at all sure it is.'

'Farewell note says you're wrong.'

'What?'

'Goodbye, cruel world,' moaned Aubrey. 'First on the left on the landing.'

'Bugger!'

Barnaby jerked his thumb at Sergeant Troy. The two ascended the stairs avoiding the banister which was already thickly coated with aluminium powder. Troy, neurotically averse to the slightest smudge or stain either on his person or raiment, was excessively painstaking.

The room in question was small, awash with bright white light and crammed with electronic equipment. All the machinery was plugged in and gently humming to itself. Every screen but one was blank. On this, even beneath the silvery bloom of SOCO's dust, emerald letters gleamed. The photographer from yesterday, now wearing a Blur/Parklife T-shirt, tattered white shorts and the same filthy shoes, bent over the keyboard. A middle-aged woman, removing soft brushes from a steel case, addressed Barnaby.

'We're having to settle for pictures here, as you can see.' She sounded cheerful and friendly and appeared to think such information would be a delightful surprise. 'Blow them up nice and big and we should get some good results.'

'Not much use in evidence.' Barnaby was surly and morose.

'Best we can do, I'm afraid. The computer keys are quite deeply indented so there's no way we could lift a clear print with tape. It would just pleat and tucker.'

'I have attended a scenes of crime investigation before, thank you.'

The woman flushed, snapped her case shut and left, calling over her shoulder, 'I'll come back later, Barry. When the room is free.'

Barry winked at the two policemen then hefted himself and his tripod to one side so they could read Alan Hollingsworth's final message.

> To whom it may concern. I can no longer bear to go on living and plan to take my own life. I am of sound mind and fully aware of my actions.
>
> Alan Hollingsworth.

Staring uncertainly at the screen, Barnaby silently ran through every expletive and curse with which he was familiar then invented several more.

Troy, well experienced in assessing his chief's moods, saw that matters were presently in a state of flux. Could swing either way, as the man said when asked for his views on capital punishment.

'What's wrong with a pen and notepad all of a sudden?'

'They don't agree with paper. Cyber freaks.' Troy spoke with feeling and some distaste. His cousin Colin, who jeered at everything the police held most dear, was heavily into what he called 'Surfing the Net, flamming and spamming'. Tactically excluded by such specialist lingo, Troy reacted by murmuring 'Pathetic', sighing with boredom, looking constantly at his watch and telling Col to get a life.

Barnaby was likewise computer ignorant. Like a lot of middle-aged people, every time he came across the word modem in a newspaper or magazine, he assumed it to be a misprint for modern. He had picked up as much as he needed to file, bring up and cross-reference information. Anything more complicated and someone else took over.

Still, you didn't need to be a compugenius to see that tapping out a death note, complete with what by no stretch of the imagination could be called a signature, was an absolute doddle compared to forging a man's handwriting. And even if his sergeant was right and cyber freaks despised the use of paper, surely, in such extreme circumstances, Hollingsworth would have at least printed out his last message and signed it, if only to authenticate matters for his executors.

The more he thought about this, the more cheerful did the Chief Inspector become. The words on the screen now had the air to him not of bleak, resigned finality but of hasty improvisation. Mustn't get too cocky though. Best to wait till the pictures came out. They would show if Hollingsworth was the last person to use the keyboard.

'My daughter's learning to read with one of these. At playgroup,' Troy remarked.

'Good grief. Haven't they got any books?'

'Oh yeah. But the kids prefer this.'

Leaving, Barnaby looked back. The machine squatted there, passive, self-contained and, to his irritated fancy, with a will of its own. Running with this humanoid notion, he wondered how long it would be before they cut humans right out. Machine calling to machine, ripe with mechanical malice. Organising – or, more likely, disorganising – their owners' lives.

'Well, you won't get the better of me,' he muttered, closing the door behind him. 'You boss-eyed little Cyclops.'

The unhinged gate of Bay Tree Cottage had been pushed to one side leaving a narrow gap. Sergeant Troy, slim as a shark's fin but minus that creature's affectionate nature, slid through with ease.

He lifted the gate, put it to one side so that his chief could follow and knocked on the front door.

'Do with a new coat, this,' said Troy. He had given it five and was now rapping much more firmly on the narrow wooden panels, dislodging several flakes of Della Robbia blue.

Barnaby moved to the nearest window, the type with lots of small panes framed in white painted zinc. He glanced inside. No sign of human habitation.

There was no garage but on a roughish piece of grass next to the house were tyre marks and a small puddle of oil. Presumably Sarah Lawson's parking space. The drumming on the door had intensified.

'For God's sake, Gavin! Anyone'd think we were on a drug bust.' Barnaby watched as his sergeant reluctantly lowered his fists. The trouble with Troy was that he could never observe and assess a situation simply for what it was worth. If drama was naturally absent, it had to be created, an opportunity made for him to play the toughie. It got rather tiresome at times.

'Back to the ranch is it then, chief?'

'No. It's half twelve and I'm parched. Let's get a bite to eat.'

This time they sat in the garden at the Goat and Whistle. Geraniums blazed in window boxes. There was a sandpit with some buckets and spades and a Rockabilly giraffe which would agitate itself for up to five minutes on receipt of a fifty pence piece. Mercifully, at the moment there were no takers.

There was also an old tyre suspended by chains from a walnut tree. On it Troy, munching on pork scratchings, swung idly back and forth, a lager and black on the grass beside him.

Barnaby was struggling to finish his sausage roll. The pastry was hard and the filling, which in no way resembled sausage, tasted faintly of soap. He decided to leave the pickled egg, a strange shade of greenish fawn. Bravely, the Chief Inspector took a sip of his drink.

Last year his daughter and her husband had toured Eastern Europe with an Arts Council production of *Much Ado About Nothing*. Cully had sent her parents a copy of a Polish menu, woefully mistranslated. Joyce's favourite line had been: 'Our wines leave you nothing to hope for.' Barnaby had thought this merely an interpretive hiccup until he tasted Fawcett Green's Liebfraumilch.

'If this is going to run,' he said, 'we'll have to find somewhere else to eat.'

'Oh yes?' Troy was puzzled. A bag of crisps was a bag of crisps was a bag of . . . 'Do you want the rest of that roll, chief?' He got off his tyre and wandered over.

'God, no.'

'What's the plonk like?'

'Indescribable.' He pushed the nearly full glass, the roll and the egg across.

'Brilliant.' Troy sat down and tucked in. Then, with a mouth full of mumble, 'Thank you.'

'Your insides must be made of galvanised steel.'

'He knows how to make pastry, this bloke. I'll give him that.'

Troy munched happily while keeping an ear cocked should any input be needed. But the gaffer was silent. He wore his folded-in expression. Inscrutable, like those Oriental masters who train the heroes of comic books to be Masters of the Universe. Presently he produced a silver foil strip of antacid tablets, popped two into his mouth and crunched them up.

Eventually Troy said, 'You're very quiet, guv.'

'I'm thinking.'

Fair enough. Troy's egg vanished in two bites. A dirty job but someone had to do it.

'About this hair appointment,' continued the Chief Inspector, 'Mrs Hollingsworth had on the day she disappeared.'

'Right.'

'Made for round about the same time Sarah Lawson was invited for tea. Don't you think it's an odd thing to do?'

'No, no.' Sergeant Troy masticated, swallowed then said, with confident authority, 'They're like that, women.'

Women, like foreigners, the pigmentally challenged or differentially abled, like anyone in fact who did not fall into the lower middle to working class white male aggressively heterosexual brotherhood were diminished, in Troy's categorisation, to 'they'.

'Came home one night last week,' he expanded. 'Maureen's mate was giving her a home perm. Plus all her sisters were there. Everybody sitting round the kitchen table with their feet up guzzling chips and swigging Coke. Screaming, laughing, telling mucky jokes. Whole place stank of fag smoke and vinegar.'

Barnaby somehow did not feel that Simone Hollingsworth's sessions with the girl Mrs Molfrey had described as Maison Becky would follow a similar pattern but it seemed a touch snobbish to say so.

'When you talk to the hairdresser, find out if it's happened before. Someone else being around, I mean, when she's had to work on Mrs Hollingsworth.'

'Okey doke.'

'I wonder,' mused the Chief Inspector, 'why she didn't cancel when she realised she wouldn't be there.'

'They don't bother, rich people,' said Troy. 'They couldn't care less about putting you out.'

Barnaby felt his sergeant was probably right, in a general sense. And maybe it was as simple as that. But what he had heard so far of Simone did not tie in with that particular sort of arrogance. Quite the contrary.

'We going back to the house now?' Troy asked.

'No. Aubrey said it might be another couple of hours before they're through. I'd like to visit Hollingsworth's office or factory unit – or whatever these industrial set-ups are called. See what the background really is to this Gray Patterson fracas.'

'He's number one in the frame though, chief, wouldn't you say? Hates Hollingsworth, already known to be violent.' Troy hesitated before adding, 'Perhaps we should nip round to his place first? Before he has a chance to scarper.'

'He'll have scarpered by now if that's his intention.'

'Yeah, I guess so.'

'And we'll only get one version of the truth. I'd like to have something to compare it with.' Barnaby heaved himself up from the much stained wooden bench. It was one of two bolted to either side of the table and he had to scramble awkwardly backwards, being unable to move it aside. His temper was not improved by the discovery that he had a piece of chewing gum stuck to his trousers.

Sergeant Troy climbed into the driving seat and opened all the windows. 'It'll cool down once we get going.'

'God, I hope so.' Barnaby got Directory Enquiries on his mobile and asked for Penstemon's number. He rang it and told reception he would like to come over and talk to someone about Alan Hollingsworth.

'I'm afraid Mr Hollingsworth isn't in at the moment.' The young, slightly shrill female voice added, with breath-taking understatement, 'He's not very well.'

Though the police had, as yet, given out no official statement regarding the tragedy at Nightingales, Barnaby was surprised no one at Fawcett Green had thought to inform his office.

Speaking as he thought gently, he informed the girl in reception just how very unwell Alan Hollingsworth presently was. There was a lengthy pause, a sharp cry then a thud, as of a heavy object hitting something soft.

Listening, the Chief Inspector heard a confused hum of sound. Questioning voices were raised. Someone started to laugh in a high-pitched manner. The line went dead.

The company turned out to be based on one of those very large industrial estates which spawn on the outskirts of country towns. This one was about seven miles from Amersham.

Although, eventually, someone had given them precise instructions which Troy had carefully written down, he now found himself passing Texas Homecare and Allied Carpets for the third time. Previously he had come to a dead end in a builders' merchant's timber yard. There had been no verbal rebuke but the chief had started to drum his fingers on the rim of the wound-down window and glare about him.

Troy drove slowly, leaning into the windscreen, looking from left to right. It wasn't like finding MFI or Do It All which were not only hugely visible but had their own flags. Penstemon would no doubt be some little prefabricated Portakabin well off the main circuit. The heat from the windscreen was burning his forehead.

'Stop!'

'Sir?'

'There's a signpost.'

Troy, who had already spotted the signpost, murmured, 'Well, I never,' and drove as close to it as he was able. Penstemon was back the way they'd just come. Barnaby sighed and rapped rather more firmly. Troy reversed and a few minutes later spotted the long, low building. It, too, was displaying an emblem. An azure blue flower on a yellow background. The flag was flying at half mast.

The reception area was boringly conventional. Tubular steel furniture, low tables holding neat stacks of technical journals and a great many artificial plants emerging from pots of simulated earth. On the hessian walls were mounted several brilliantly luminous computer graphics in brushed aluminium frames.

As Troy closed the glass entrance door a young man wearing a pale, stylishly crumpled linen suit came forward to greet them.

'You're the police?' He barely glanced at the warrant cards. 'What absolutely terrible news. Verity's lying down,' he added, as if they had asked for her by name. 'She's the person usually on reception. I'm Clive Merriman.'

'I'm sorry to be the bearer of such bad news, Mr Merriman.' Barnaby undid his jacket the better to revel in the air conditioning. 'Do you think we might have a word with whoever has been in charge during Alan Hollingsworth's absence?'

'That's our accountant, Ted Burbage. I told him you'd be coming.'

Mr Burbage's office was not far. In fact nothing was. They passed only three other rooms. One held several people sitting at keyboards. The second held several monitors and had Alan Hollingsworth's name in gilded letters on the door. The third was labelled '*loos.mail@ femail*'.

'Causton CID?' Mr Burbage, a man not so much deeply tanned as caramelised, was giving Barnaby's card a much closer inspection. 'What on earth's going on? Is it something to do with Alan?'

'That's right, Mr Burbage.'

'Sorry, please sit down.' Then, as the two policemen did so, 'Will this take long?'

'Hard to say, sir.'

'Better sort out some tea, Clive. Or,' he looked inquiringly across the room, 'perhaps you'd rather have something cooler? We have a Coke machine.'

'That would really hit the spot. Thanks very much.'

After the cold drinks had turned up and instructions given for his calls to be held, the accountant got up from his chair and stood facing his visitors. There was something rather defensive about the movement. And about the way he leaned forward, balanced by fingertips resting on the edge of his desk. He looked a bit like a goalie bracing himself for a deceitful kick from a sharp left-winger.

'So.' A deep breath. 'Found dead was all we could get out of Verity. Once we'd brought her round, of course.'

'Mr Hollingsworth's body was discovered mid-morning yesterday but we think he died late Monday evening.'

'Good God.'

'An overdose.'

'Suicide?' It was one long groan. He put his head in his hands. The burnished bald spot glowed less emphatically. 'The insurance'll never pay out. God, what a mess.'

'There'll be an inquest when our preliminary inquiries are complete, Mr Burbage. I should wait for the coroner's verdict before rushing to conclusions.'

'There are several full-time workers here, you know.' Burbage had rushed on well before the Chief Inspector finished speaking. 'People with mortgages, families, dependants. What is going to happen to us if the business folds?'

This lack of distress at an employer's demise was to be found in all the interviews carried out at Penstemon. Alan Hollingsworth, while not actually disliked, certainly did not seem to evoke much warmth of feeling amongst his staff.

A second later, when Mr Burbage had caught up with Barnaby's suggestion about the coroner's verdict, an amazed questioning possessed him. The Chief Inspector wasted several minutes getting the interview back on the rails.

'I assume Mr Hollingsworth was in touch with the office while he was away?'

'Yes, of course.'

'What reason did he give for his absence?'

'Summer flu.'

'Was that like him?'

'Absolutely not. Never had five minutes off since I've been here.'

'Did you speak to him yourself?'

'Naturally. There were various things to discuss. Ongoing problems.'

'Money problems?'

All expression vanished from Mr Burbage's cool, pale eyes. 'I really couldn't say.'

'How did he sound?'

'Not well at all. And he was also rather . . . wound up. If I didn't grasp what he was saying straightaway he started to shout, which was also unlike him. He was usually very courteous.'

'Was there anything untoward about his last day here?'

'Only that he went home early. Around five fifteen.'

'Did he say why?'

'It may have been something to do with a phone call Verity put through. She said it was from his wife.'

'I see. You appear to be a small concern,' said the Chief Inspector, looking round. 'Or is this perhaps not the only branch?'

'No, wysiwyg.' Faced with bewilderment, he elaborated. 'Computer speak. What you see is what you get. As to your question . . .'

Ted Burbage hesitated. Barnaby recognised the wish to be helpful struggling with the professional money man's ingrained habit of close-mouthed caution. 'Small but stable. This is a thriving time in the industry. We can't all be Bill Gates but when the big boys thrive there's always a nice helping of crumbs for the little boys.'

As an example of appearing to say something while in fact saying nothing it was pretty neat. Barnaby nodded. Even he had heard of Bill Gates.

Troy also nodded, in accord. Not that Burbage would have noticed. The sergeant was sitting in a wide leather armchair, the position of which, slightly behind and well to the left of the accountant, had been chosen deliberately. Though Troy's note-taking was both rapid and discreet – often he would cover several pages while hardly seeming to glance at his book at all – he was aware that seeing their spoken words written down could really throw some people, even cause them to dry up. Hence, whenever possible, he would play the invisible man.

The chief was asking now how well Burbage knew the firm's late owner.

'That's difficult. I didn't know all that much about him

but whether that was because he chose to conceal things or because there wasn't much to know I couldn't tell you. He talked about work all the time but men do of course. And those who are hooked on computers are the worst of the lot. I felt sorry for his wife.'

'Did you ever meet her?'

'No. She didn't come here and Alan didn't go in for socialising. At least not within the firm.'

'You're not aware then that she left home several days ago?'

'Left . . . ? No, I certainly wasn't.'

'Did he ever indicate—'

'Look, you'd be far better off putting questions about Alan to . . .' Burbage floundered into silence and stared out of his picture window at the double-glazing company's fascia across the road. Barnaby could not have asked for a sweeter segue.

'We shall be talking to Gray Patterson later, Mr Burbage.'

'Sorry?' The accountant frowned now as if trying to remember where he had heard the name before. Barnaby did not help him out. 'Ah, Gray, of course, yes. He'd perhaps know more about it.'

'Perhaps you can fill me in with a bit of background regarding the trouble between the two men.'

'Ohhh, that.' Pause. 'Rather technical, I'm afraid.' Mr Burbage spoke with crisp, dismissive brevity, plainly regretting his earlier slip of the tongue. From now on Barnaby judged the interview would be unembellished by any bits of gossip or private opinion as to the personalities involved. Never mind. With a bit of luck there would be some gleanings along those lines in the outer office. Wearing an expectant, interested expression he waited, maintaining eye contact. He was good at that.

'Something to do with creating a new language,' said Mr Burbage so grudgingly one would think he was giving away a shameful secret. 'One where you can write an application, run it on any machine and also transfer stuff straight from the Internet on to your own computer.'

'I understand,' fibbed the Chief Inspector. 'Did they found Penstemon together – Hollingsworth and Patterson?'

'I'm not sure about that. But Gray has certainly been involved from the very beginning.'

'What was their relationship?'

'How do you mean?'

'Were they friends?'

'I've no idea.'

'Oh, come on, Mr Burbage.' Barnaby allowed himself a flare of irritation. 'Half a dozen people work here at very close quarters. You must—'

'As far as I know it was just business.'

'So how did all this drama come about?'

'You should ask Patterson.'

'There's always more than one side to any story. And I'm never going to hear Hollingsworth's.'

'That's true.' A respect for balance, a proper equilibrium, prompted him to continue. 'Well, as I've already explained, they'd got this new micro system going. And after almost a year things had got to the stage where Gray felt they were ready to talk about marketing. Alan said he wanted to develop the package a stage further feeling that this would push it into the really big league. 'Worldwide' was what he actually said. Gray had come to a full stop on it and naturally asked what direction Alan thought this further stage would take. Alan was evasive, saying he needed more time to clarify his ideas. About a month went by—'

'Bringing us to?'

'Oh, early March, I suppose. Anyway, Gray started pressing him again. You must understand, Inspector, that this world is intensely competitive. With everyone always desperately looking for an inventive edge, time is absolutely of the essence. Days, even hours sometimes, can count. Though he trusted his colleague, never having had cause to do otherwise, Gray's anxiety about this evasiveness led him to try and access the file. You understand what I mean by this, Chief Inspector?'

'Vaguely,' replied Barnaby. He certainly knew it had nothing to do with filing cabinets, those cumbersome metal objects without which no office had once seemed complete.

'It couldn't be found. Gray checked twice then looked for the back-up. But the floppy had also gone. Alan professed puzzlement. He appeared upset but not nearly as upset as Gray who was absolutely distraught. We're talking about months of very hard, creative work here. Not devastatingly original perhaps – most of the new stuff is designed on the shoulders of what's gone before – but, as far as they knew, well ahead of the race.

'There was a certain amount of acrimonious exchange which ended with nothing resolved then things seemed to settle down somewhat. We thought Gray had simply accepted the fact that, due to some dreadful carelessness on someone's part, Celandine – that was the project's code name – had been accidentally wiped. But we were wrong. The mildness of Alan's reaction to the disaster had made Gray suspicious. He borrowed Alan's keys on some pretext or other and got the one for Nightingales copied. One afternoon, when Mrs Hollingsworth was presumably known to be elsewhere, he got into the house, plugged in to Alan's personal computer and discovered that Celandine had been sold to a company called Patellus for two hundred thousand pounds.'

Barnaby allowed himself to look impressed, which wasn't difficult. He said, 'Are Patellus one of the big boys you mentioned earlier?'

'Ish. Not in the league of Lotus or Novell but on the way. Gray drove straight back here, stormed into Alan's office, locked the door and set about him. It was appalling. The noise . . .' Mr Burbage shuddered with distaste. 'I called the police. I had to. I thought they were killing each other. Gray got a suspended sentence, as I expect you know.'

'Indeed. But he won't leave the matter there surely?'

'Oh, no. He's taking us to court for loss of earnings. Although—' Burbage broke off, looking quite put out. Plainly, for the duration of his narrative, he had forgotten that the owner of Penstemon was no more. 'What will happen now I don't know.'

'I assume the company can still be sued?'

'Alan *was* the company. We're not Plc. There are no shareholders. And I can tell you that there is no way we could find two hundred thousand pounds, let alone court costs. That is,' he added hastily, 'in the strictest confidence.'

'So one could say that Hollingsworth's death was very much to Gray Patterson's disadvantage?'

'I suppose so. Yes.'

'Do you have any idea how much of the work on Celandine each man put in?'

'Not really. I doubt if even they did to any precise degree. These things are very difficult to quantify.'

'Or why Hollingsworth should suddenly have needed such a large amount of money?'

'None at all.'

'Could I ask if the name Blakeley means anything to you?'

'Freddie Blakeley? He's our bank manager. At Nat West.'

'Thank you. And, I wonder, do you have the name of the Hollingsworth family solicitor?'

'Jill Gamble at Fanshawe and Clay. They are Penstemon's solicitors also.'

'And, one last question. Someone should be notified that Hollingsworth has died. In the absence of his wife, who is presumably his next of kin, do you know of any close relation?'

'He has a brother in Scotland. Alan described him once as a very pious man, full of rectitude and a pillar of the community. I'm not sure that he's not a minister.' Mr Burbage allowed himself a smile of wintry satisfaction. 'They weren't close.'

'Well, thank you, Mr Burbage.' Barnaby got up.

The accountant, with a wheeze of relief, did the same.

'If we could have a word now with the rest of the staff?'

Gamely Mr Burbage escorted them into the outer offices where he stayed, as chaperon, for the duration of their inquiries. He even gave up the keys to Alan's office without demur and stood by as it was locked. Plainly an unhappy man, he then went outside to wave them off.

Chapter Five

'I need some smokes,' said Sergeant Troy. Walking down the lane on the way back to Nightingales, they were just passing Ostlers. 'Do you want anything, chief?'

Barnaby was ravenous. It was now nearly four o'clock. Seven hours since he had eaten – for no reasonable person could describe the mess of pottage dished up in the Goat and Whistle as food.

He followed Troy into the cool whitewashed interior, ducking his head to avoid the beams and looking eagerly about him. He needed something filling and tasty which did not have to be irradiated by way of making it edible.

The choice was not uplifting. Fruit, chocolate, cheap biscuits of an unfamiliar brand. A baker's tray lined with grease-spotted paper held a few tired buns and several strange-looking domed tarts covered with shreds of coconut. Next to these was a single sausage roll which, in style and finish, looked morbidly familiar.

'Hey,' beckoned Troy. 'Look at these.'

Lying across the ice-cream unit was a wooden board supporting several small, wheyey cheeses, each placed carefully on individual mats of slatted straw surrounded by laurel leaves. One of the cheeses was concealed beneath a charming hinged pewter mould shaped like a hedgehog.

'Isn't it cute?' There was a metal loop in the centre of the creature's back. Troy slipped his little finger through and lifted up the mould. 'My mum'd love one of them.'

Unsupported, the cheese slowly collapsed, spreading downwards and outwards into a lumpy, cream-coloured puddle.

At that moment the multicoloured strips of plastic at the rear of the shop slapped and fluttered and an extraordinary figure appeared.

A large woman in a long, dun-coloured dress. The soft pieces of leather wrapped round her feet were secured by narrow thongs. Her brown, hirsute legs were bare. She had on a cotton bonnet of the type worn by milkmaids in musical comedies and a wide white ruff of the type worn by the aristocracy in Holbein portraits. She moved smoothly, as actors sometimes do in Victorian drama on television, as if on concealed roller skates.

Weird, decided Sergeant Troy. He did not relish the idiosyncratic.

'So, gentles all.' She sat behind the till with a bestowing air, as if her customers had just been accorded a rare treat. 'How can I assist you?'

Troy, who had positioned himself in such a manner as to conceal the collapsing cheese, said, 'Forty Rothmans, please.'

'Sir Walter's friend?' She took down the cigarettes. 'Virginia's finest.'

'Thank you.' Troy couldn't stop staring. Awkwardly placed for handing over the money, he gazed around him, pretending interest. 'Unusual place.'

'You admire the Tudor period?'

'Oh yeah.' The sergeant was fervent in agreement. He struggled to recall a single relative fact without success, settling for, 'Been to Windsor Castle.'

'But that's ancient. Hardly sixteenth century.'

'That a fact?' Troy changed the subject. 'Lovely day.'

'Peradventure. That will be two ninety-five, please.'

The sergeant looked around for his chief who was polishing an apple on his sleeve and sussing the cold drinks layout.

'No doubt you're intrigued as to the manner of my appearance?'

'You could say that,' agreed Sergeant Troy.

'I'm off shortly to give an illustrated talk to the Townswomen's Guild on the making of cheese in Elizabethan times, hence the garb. Look behind you and you'll see my samples.'

The words had a ring of bright confidence. Touching really, thought Troy as he duly turned and looked behind him. The runny stuff had been almost totally absorbed by the straw mat. Turning his back and hoping to conceal the precise details of his move, the sergeant replaced the mould in its original position.

'Ah, ah!' cried Mrs Boast. 'Mustn't touch. They may not be quite set.'

'Sorry.' At ease now that the moment of hazard was past, Troy smiled, sauntering over to pay for his ciggies. 'Do a lot of this sort of thing?'

'Oh yes. Schools, clubs, institutes. My specialties are still-room receipts, baking and dairy crafts. Hubby lectures on flag-wagging and mediaeval armour. Martial swashing on demand.'

'Is that a fact?'

'At weekends we fight.'

Tell me about it, thought Sergeant Troy.

'With the Civil War Society. I could give you details.'

But Troy was saved as his boss came alongside, laying a

blister pack of cherry Genoa, an apple and a Lion bar on the counter and wondering aloud if there was such a thing to be had as a can of Seven-Up.

'We say "tin" at Ostlers,' chided Mrs Boast. 'It's a little way we have. A little discipline. Perpetuating classical English.'

'Do you have a tin of Seven-Up?' asked the Chief Inspector politely.

'Never stock it.'

Barnaby added a Diet Coke to his pile and offered a ten pound note. Mrs Boast, no doubt already in character and only truly at home with the doubloon, appeared put out.

'Haven't you anything smaller?'

'I've got some change, chief.'

As his Sergeant paid, Barnaby fished out his warrant card and explained what their business was in the village. He asked the shopkeeper what she knew of the Hollingsworths.

Mrs Boast stretched her neck like a rooster then settled back into her ruff. This was necessary from time to time as it was rather prickly. Her head, resting atop the concertinaed white pleats, reminded Barnaby of a certain sort of religious painting, the ones where, at the end of a banquet, the head of a malcontent is borne in on a platter along with the fruit and nuts.

'I never met Alan. He ordered a stack of frozen individual meals just after she walked out but that was by telephone. Used his credit card and hubby delivered. Simone would come in from time to time or I'd see her occasionally ringing someone from across the way.' She nodded at the plate-glass window through which the British Telecom box was clearly visible.

'Surely they had a phone at home?' asked Troy.

'Always having trouble on the line. Or so she told me.'

Barnaby said, 'What was your impression of Mrs Hollingsworth?'

'A pampered jade,' declared Mrs Boast, slipping once more into Shakespeak.

Several people had by then come into the shop and one of them was waiting to pay. Barnaby left it there, knowing that, should a full investigation be set in motion, house to house would also be putting questions.

Outside Nightingales the SOCO van shimmered in the heat. The honest burghers of Fawcett Green, though now restrained by barriers, showed no signs of resentment. Rather, there was an air about the place of a good day out. People were standing around or sitting on the grass verges chatting amongst themselves, savouring, with unself-conscious jollity, the presence of death. A family group, complete with dog, devoured sandwiches and sucked drinks through straws. The woman's hair had been elaborately waved and she wore a lot of make-up, possibly anticipating television cameras.

Perrot, just back from a short lunch break and full of his wife's delicious home cooking, opened the gates. Barnaby and Troy eased their way through, the latter contenting himself this time with a couple of sotto voce squawks. The constable remained aloof, gazing coldly into the middle distance until addressed by the Chief Inspector.

'In the house, Perrot. Ask the man on the front door to take over here.'

'Sir.'

They found Aubrey Marine at the kitchen table surrounded by stained mugs and plates, an overflowing pedal bin and a cardboard Baked Beans box, also crammed with debris. On the dirty ceramic hob stood a frying pan smelling of rancid fat and a burnt saucepan. The sink was stacked with dirty cutlery. Flies were everywhere. Barnaby was reminded of the set for the Causton amateur dramatic society's last production, *The Caretaker*, which his wife had, very successfully, directed.

'What on earth's that smell?'

'Whisky. The sink reeks of it.'

'Did you find the pill bottles?'

'Nope.'

'What about the capsule casings?'

'Zilch. We've been through all this lot and the wheelie bin. Might turn them up in the long grass.'

'I don't think so.'

'Maybe he put them down the toilet.' Troy looked about him, metaphorically holding his nose.

'It's possible,' said Aubrey. 'But they weigh nothing. I think we'd have found at least one or two still floating.'

'I'm going aloft. Have a look round down here, Sergeant. Check out that bureau with the glass front and the desk. See if you can lay your hands on a phone bill.'

'Right, guv.'

Barnaby entered the hall where Perrot waited awkward, uncertain, anxious to please. Together they climbed the stairs. Barnaby paused on the bend to admire a print of 'Peupliers au bord de l'epte'. Framed in transparent Perspex, its serene beauty charmed the eye and soothed the heart. What do you want, the Chief Inspector entertained himself by musing, if you don't want Monet?

On the landing he asked Perrot to check the three smaller bedrooms.

'What am I looking for, sir?'

'Anything that might shed light on Mrs Hollingsworth's

disappearance or her husband's death. Surely I don't have to draw you a picture?'

'No, sir.'

The master bedroom was directly facing Barnaby. He opened the door and found himself facing another theatrical backdrop, cleaner and vastly more frivolous than the kitchen. Perfect, in fact, for the Merry Widow.

A king-sized bed was surrounded by cloudy draperies which had been gathered up and fastened into a gilded metal crown attached to the ceiling. The ivory headboard was enlivened by pastoral scenes in delicate pastel shades. Nymphs and shepherds cavorted in meadows of spring flowers beneath the eye of their Olympian overlords. Centaurs lapped from a rippling stream.

A wedding photograph stood on the bedside table. Barnaby picked it up to study it more closely. There was that about the groom that the Chief Inspector recognised. His son-in-law, Nicholas, had shown just such a combination of emotions on his nuptial day. Pride, deep satisfaction, elation even. The look of the hunter-gatherer who has not only come across a species thought to be extinct but has brought back a specimen for all the world to wonder at. Yet the strain showed. The wonder of being chosen was clearly grazed over by anxiety, for would not every man be seeking such a rare prize? Poor Nico. He was still hanging on in there but Barnaby sometimes wondered for how much longer. He turned his attention to Hollingsworth's bride who looked traditionally radiant.

The vicar, he decided, had been spot on. Simone Hollingsworth really was astonishingly pretty, if a trifle artificial-looking for his own taste. Smiling brilliantly from beneath a tumbling froth of veiling, she looked rather like one of those skilfully lacquered creatures who swan around the cosmetic sections of department stores spraying unwary women – and men too if they weren't sharp about it – with perfumed atomisers.

Barnaby took the picture to the window for better light and stood silently appreciating the rosy, glistening mouth. Nearly always the two halves of a top lip are imperfectly matched but here was absolute symmetry even to the perfect cupid's bow. The bottom lip was fuller than he would have expected, giving an impression of sensual generosity. She had wide set greyish-green eyes with long curling lashes and warm, blushing apricot cheeks. Looking more closely, he realised the shape of her mouth had been very skilfully realised by a pencil and he thought he could discern, beneath its lush contours, a narrower and rather less seductive outline. Her hair, curling round ears as delicate and translucent as little shells, was so fair as to be almost white.

She was holding a spray of ivory rosebuds bound with silver ribbons and wore not only a wedding ring but an extremely large diamond solitaire. No wonder she looked bloody radiant. As quickly as he came to this conclusion so Barnaby chided himself for such chauvinistic cynicism. Lucky the family were not present to read his mind. Cully would have really sharpened her claws on that one.

The Chief Inspector was no great believer in physiognomy and so drew no conclusions regarding Mrs Hollingsworth's character from such external comeliness. He had come across too much vicious behaviour by human beings who might have modelled for Botticelli. And acts of great charity and kindness from those who could have climbed out of a pit dug by Hieronymus Bosch.

He put the picture back and wandered into the bathroom. More schlock. False marble floor and starry ceiling, copper-coloured mirror glass walls – the whole place shimmered in bronze light. There was a vast triangular forget-me-not blue bath with high arched golden taps, the handles made to resemble multi-petalled chrysanthemums. Every possible flat surface in the room was covered with jars and bottles and tubes and aerosols. As Constable Perrot had surmised, she couldn't have taken even a single pot of cream, for there was not an empty space anywhere.

Barnaby opened a drawer in the appropriately named vanity unit. Rows and rows of neatly arranged lipsticks. Annoyed with himself for time-wasting, he surrendered to a compulsion and counted them. Seventy-three. Dear God, *seventy-three*. He recalled Joyce's modest collection and no longer wondered what Simone Hollingsworth did all day. Just laboratory testing this lot could prove a lifetime's occupation.

There were around a dozen boxes of perfume. One had the lid open and the atomiser had been taken out and was standing by the washbasin. Barnaby thought it likely this meant she had been wearing the perfume, called Joy, when she left the house. He took a tissue and sprayed it. The scent was very rich and flowery, quite beautiful in fact. The Chief Inspector thought he might get some for his wife's birthday which was in three weeks' time and slipped the tissue into his pocket.

He drifted out again, crossing into the white and gold fitted wardrobes that ran all down the facing wall, sliding the nearest open. Troy came in, sniffing the air.

'Bet you can't get that at Superdrug.'

'Any luck with the phone bill?'

'No, chief. Sorry.'

'Doesn't matter. We'll contact British Tel.'

'In relation to what?'

'Think about it.'

Troy had a go this time but was quickly defeated. His introspection was not of a constructive or perceptive nature. It involved kick-starting a few hardy old perennials, whirling them vigorously around like salad in a basket and letting them settle.

Resigned to passing on this one, he joined his chief who was now opening another section. The ball bearings rumbled sweetly. Soft falls of velvet and lace, drifts of sparkling georgette, neat outlines of wool and linen and tweed were conjured, concealed, revealed again. Systematically Barnaby checked all the pockets. The clothes were so tightly packed you could not have slid a cat's whisker between any of them let alone a Gold Card from Harvey Nicks.

'Wouldn't mind a slice of that with my bedtime cocoa,' said Sergeant Troy who had also clocked the wedding picture. Then, receiving no response to this jaunty lubricity, 'Do we know if she went off with that gobstopper on her finger?'

'Not yet.'

'Might explain why nothing else is missing. That'd keep her going till the end of the century.'

'Check these handbags, would you? Then the shoes. There might be something in one of the toes.'

'Won't be a sec.' Troy disappeared into the bathroom. He used the toilet calling out over the flush, 'I've always wanted to have it off in a jacuzzi.'

Barnaby worked his way through the first of two chests of drawers. Cashmere sweaters all in pastel shades, filmy underwear and scarves, a Paisley shawl. There were also dozens of unsealed packets containing prettily flowered leggings, pale tights and stockings with black or cream lace tops. Nowhere could he find clean, used hosiery. Perhaps she never wore anything twice. There was a leather jewel case full of quite dazzling costume jewellery but minus the rock of ages.

'Maureen says,' Troy came back in, 'you can come off in one of those if you sit in the right place for long enough.' He sounded both dubious and miffed. There seemed to be more and more things women were doing without the need of male assistance. Pretty soon, he decided, we'll need a preservation order to stop us dying out from lack of use.

Mrs Hollingsworth had a positively Marcosian relish for footwear. Troy slid his fingers inside strappy numbers with slender heels, brightly coloured slip-ons in glove-soft leather, court shoes, suede flatties with thin gilt chains looped across the tongues, pearly evening sandals sparkling with rhinestones. There were some Filo sneakers but no serious walking boots or Wellingtons. Presumably, though living in the heart of the country, Mrs Hollingsworth was not much of a one for getting close to nature. He started on the bags.

Barnaby, standing by the bed which was neatly and cleanly made, wondered why Hollingsworth had not been sleeping in it. Perhaps he had rejected the idea for superstitious reasons fearing such a surrender might seem to be bowing his head to the fates. Acknowledgement not only of the fact of her leaving but that she would never return. Perhaps he'd wanted to stay close to the telephone. Perhaps he'd simply been too drunk to climb the stairs.

'Well,' said Sergeant Troy, snapping the final clasp, 'nobody could say he kept her short.'

Barnaby could not agree. Recapping on what he had heard so far about Simone – the aimless wanderings about the village, her vague, brief membership of this group or that, shallow time-filling conversations in place of real friendship and the harsh treatment meted out possibly because she had attempted to fly a little further afield – it seemed to the Chief Inspector that she had been kept short of the one quality above all others that made life worth living. Namely freedom.

'Be turning up any minute now, once she knows he's snuffed it.'

'Why d'you say that?'

'Rich widow. She'll want to collect.'

'I hope you're right.'

'Course I'm right. Stands to reason.' The most unreasonable things stood to reason with Sergeant Troy, provided they supported his prejudices.

Outside on the landing, Perrot cleared his throat then knocked as if Barnaby had been in his office at the station.

'Find anything, Constable?'

'Nothing relevant, sir. Mr Hollingsworth's clothes, shirts and so on. I checked all the pockets and turn-ups. Two piles of fashion magazines but no notes or bits of paper concealed although one magazine had a page torn out. Several suitcases and lightweight travel bags, all empty. Sheets and duvet covers, blankets, towels, pillowcases—'

'Yes, yes, all right, Perrot. It's not the first day of Harrods' sale.'

'No, sir.'

By now everyone was on the landing. Troy led the way down the stairs, running lightly on the balls of his feet, slyly savouring the contrast between his own slender athleticism and Perrot's barrel-chested, oaken-thighed stolidity. Not to mention that bulky pachyderm bringing up the rear.

* * *

As the two policemen made their way towards Gray Patterson's place, Barnaby mentally ran over his conversation with Penstemon's accountant and the description of the magistrates' hearing in the *Causton Echo*, a cutting of which had been sent to his office.

A man more sinned against than sinning, by all accounts, Hollingsworth's former colleague. Betrayed, swindled out of a great deal of money then sacked. Was it likely that a brisk punch-up would satisfy Patterson's quite justified rage? And what was the truth about the relationship that 'went back a long way'?

Barnaby looked forward to having these questions answered and had no doubt that, once he met the man, a whole new whatever was the collective noun of questions would arise. He whiled away the next few minutes trying to think of what that noun might be. A poser, a quiz, a snoop. A speculation, a viva. A nosey. A grill . . .

Number 17, the Street, was situated on the outskirts of the village several yards from its nearest neighbour and almost totally concealed from passers-by behind a belt of blue piceas. A green painted board declared that the property was To Let. The place itself was a low, whitewashed, double-fronted building in the style that estate agents and people who know little of real country living call 'farmhouse'.

As soon as Barnaby opened the gate a black and white Border collie rushed towards them. Plainly confused about what constituted guard duties, it was not only barking loudly but vigorously wagging its tail.

It jumped up at Troy who, torn between his love of dogs and a passion for immaculate attire, demonstrated both by clicking his tongue at the animal and asking its name, then brushing the knees of his trousers with his handkerchief. By this time the collie was dancing away over a large expanse of roughly mown, extremely weedy grass, looking back occasionally to make sure they were following.

By a far hedge a man was tossing clippings into an old oil drum. Barnaby hoped, in this burning drought, he was not going to attempt to set fire to the stuff. One spark and half the village would go up.

Patterson stuck his fork in the ground and came forward to meet them. The vociferous dog, having delivered her charges safely, was now looking back and forth between the visitors and her master, nudging his attention towards this successful feat.

Patterson said, 'Shut up, Bess.'

Barnaby presented his warrant card. Troy bent down, patted the dog's sharp, intelligent face and said, 'Good girl.'

'I've been expecting you. Verity rang. From the office.'

Barnaby's imagination, lazily working from a received scenario, had conjured a well-built, bellicose type. Gray Patterson was slender and quite tall. His shoulders curved slightly forwards. A donnish stoop, decided the Chief Inspector, before remembering the man had spent probably the last twenty years crouched over a keyboard. He had red-gold hair, curly and tight against his head, greenish-grey eyes and a clear skin, still scarcely tanned in spite of his outdoor labours.

'Let's get away from all this rubbish.'

He ploughed through a heap of conifer branches, kicking them aside, and waved his visitors in the direction of a couple of shabby deck-chairs. Barnaby, already picturing the vast, ungainly struggle when he tried to extricate himself, declined the offer. Troy folded himself into the striped canvas sling with a single movement of great elegance.

Staring severely at his subordinate, the Chief Inspector lumbered over to an ancient wooden stool which lay on its side under an apple tree. He righted it and sat down in the shade. Patterson perched on the rim of an old water-wheel. Bess immediately ran to his side and lay down, half hidden by a drift of moon daisies, panting in the heat.

'You lot are playing all this very close.'

'Is that right, Mr Patterson?'

'No one seems to know whether Alan topped himself, swallowed the stuff by accident or was done in.'

'We're simply making a few inquiries at this stage.' Smoothly Barnaby sidestepped the invitation to reveal all. 'I understand you knew Mr Hollingsworth quite well.'

'Not as well as I thought, obviously.'

'You refer to the trouble at Penstemon?'

'What else?'

'Perhaps you'd like to give me your version of what happened, sir?' said the Chief Inspector.

'I doubt it'll vary much from what you've heard already.'

In this Patterson was not quite correct. Although the running order of events and the events themselves departed hardly at all from Burbage's account, having the background fleshed out added a slightly different gloss. For a start there were an awful lot of 'I's' and 'my's' scattered through the narrative.

'Am I to understand,' asked Barnaby, 'that this project was not a joint effort between yourself and Mr Hollingsworth?'

'It certainly wasn't. I had the idea and I did all the groundwork. Alan's input was minimal. Naturally the work was financially backed by the company and I was drawing a decent salary. On the other hand, if Celandine took off, the business stood to do very well. And I'd been promised fifty per cent of any money the program brought in.'

'In writing, sir?'

'Hah!' It was a savage shout. Bess, alert and concerned, pricked up her soft, black and white triangular ears. 'I'd known him for ten years and worked with him for nearly that long. It never occurred to me such a thing would be necessary.'

'So, morally, you feel that you're entitled to at least half of the two hundred—'

'Too bloody right I am!' Patterson's long, narrow hands were locked together in his lap. He pulled on them savagely, cracking the knuckles. He swallowed hard as if forcing down some galloping sickness. It was some time before he could speak again.

'I've taken legal advice. Did you know, if you're on your uppers, you're allowed one free session at the CAB?'

'Broke, are you, Mr Patterson?' asked Sergeant Troy.

'Worse. I was committed to my financial limit before all this happened. Now I'm up to my ears in debt. Not to mention negative equity.'

'What advice did they give you?' asked Barnaby. 'The CAB?'

'To sue. Especially as I'm entitled to legal aid so don't risk losing lots of money in costs. What will happen now he's dead, though, I'm not sure.'

'Do you have any idea why he should suddenly need such a large amount of cash?'

'None at all.'

'When did you last see him?'

'At the magistrates' hearing.'

'But that's weeks ago,' said Sergeant Troy. 'Surely, in a little place like this—'

'He's not difficult to avoid. Never walks anywhere. Doesn't use the pub.'

156

'What about Mrs Hollingsworth?'

'Oh yes, I saw her. About a day or two before she sloped off.' He picked one of the daisies and started tickling the dog with it. Bess rolled on to her back and kicked her legs in the air with happiness.

'I was on my way to call on Sarah Lawson – have you met her yet?' Barnaby shook his head. 'And Simone was using the phone, which is just outside Bay Tree Cottage.'

'You didn't happen to overhear any of the conversation?'

'I'm afraid not. Does it matter? I mean, there's no mystery about her leaving, is there?'

'What day would that be, Mr Patterson?'

'Let's see.' He closed his eyes. 'Sarah wasn't teaching so it couldn't have been Wednesday. Monday I didn't go out, so that makes it Tuesday.'

'Mrs Hollingsworth still there when you left the cottage, sir?' asked Sergeant Troy.

'No. Though it was a very brief visit. Sarah was working and didn't want to be disturbed. I may as well tell you,' Patterson said wryly, 'because I'm sure you'll be told by some village busybody soon enough, that I have serious designs on the lady. Not getting very far though, am I, Bess?'

Directly addressed, the dog trembled with pleasure. She sprang up looking excited, as if some great adventure was afoot. She tried to put her head on his knee and Patterson called her a stupid animal.

'You're divorced then, are you, sir?' asked the Chief Inspector.

When Patterson did not immediately reply, Sergeant Troy, with a smirk, man to man, suggested that perhaps he had just been dead lucky and got away with it all these years.

'I'm sorry?'

'Stayed single, like.'

'I think that's my business, don't you?' There was something slightly vexed in his voice, as if he was being forced into evasion against his will.

'How well did you know Mrs Hollingsworth?' asked Barnaby after a pause into which he managed to inject mild surprise that Patterson should find answering such a harmless question problematical.

'Hardly at all. Alan and I didn't mix socially. She struck me as a bit of a ninny, to tell you the truth. The silly frilly sort.'

'But good-looking?'

'Oh, yes. Lovely.'

'Were you surprised when she left?'

'We all were. Kept the village speculating for days.'

'Did Alan ever talk to you about his marriage?'

'No. I'd known him during his first – best man at the wedding and all that. Perhaps he thought I was bad luck.'

'I didn't realise he'd been married before.' Barnaby sat upright on his mossy perch.

'They both had. Miriam, the first Mrs Hollingsworth, was terrific. Intelligent, forthright, full of go. Completely wrong for him. Alan's ideas of how to treat a woman were those of a man twice his age. Buy them a nice little house, dress them in pretty clothes and jewellery, give them a few flashy toys to play with and they'll be happy as the day is long.'

What's wrong with that? Troy argued silently. I wish I could find some wealthy middle-aged nympho to set me up with a few flashy toys.

'She'd just qualified from medical school when they met and naturally wanted to practise. There were rows about that but when Miriam threatened to leave, he gave way.

Once she was working, things got worse. Sometimes the house was empty when he got home. Naturally she'd be called out occasionally. It all came to a head at three o'clock one morning after a phone call. Alan accused her of having an affair, though where the poor girl would have found the time or energy ... Apparently he followed her to this house, banged on the door and forced his way in. She was upstairs with a dying patient. Well, that was it. Next day she packed her stuff and left. They divorced a year later. By then Miriam had joined a medical centre at Birkenhead. Still there, as far as I know.'

'D'you think she'd have reverted to her maiden name?' asked Troy, pen flying.

'Shouldn't be surprised.'

'Do you know what it was, sir?'

'Kenton.'

'He seemed to have chosen more wisely this time,' suggested Barnaby.

'The thing you have to understand about Alan is that he was ferociously insecure. Always thinking someone's stealing a march. That's why he put in far more hours than was necessary at work. The firm was at least as stable as any other small business in these dodgy times. And why he was for ever ringing home to check that Simone was safely tethered.'

'Hadn't learned his lesson from the first time then?' said Troy. He was watching the dog who was once more lying on her stomach and staring hard at a clump of bamboo. Her nostrils twitched as if sensing the passage of something small and vulnerable.

'Obsessives can't "learn lessons" any more than the mentally deranged can pull themselves together.'

'You said they'd both been married before,' said the

Chief Inspector. 'Do you know anything about Simone's first husband?'

'Not much. Alan just said it didn't last long and the bloke was a bad lot.'

'Do you know what his name was?'

'Sorry.'

No matter. It could soon be checked. Barnaby was not displeased with this interview which was proving satisfyingly fruitful. He just wished it wasn't so hot. Everything was sticking to him and he was sticking to the wood. Round globules of sweat ran from his forehead into his eyes. As he fumbled for a handkerchief an apple fell, bumping softly on the feathery grass. The dog sprang forward and Patterson shouted, 'Leave it, Bess!' He got up and kicked the apple, which was then seen to be crawling with wasps, out of the dog's way.

The lengthy pause encouraged Patterson not to reseat himself. He said, 'Is that it then?'

'Almost, sir. We would like to know where you were on Monday evening and the early part of Tuesday morning.'

'Is that when . . . ?'

Barnaby's deeply tangled, shaggy eyebrows rose intimidatingly. They were amazing, those brows, reflected Troy. The texture of horsehair and so exuberant you could have stuffed a sofa with them.

Barnaby said, 'If you could just answer the question please, Mr Patterson.'

'Oh, here. I was here.'

'Alone?'

'To my sorrow. I did pop round to Sarah's around eightish but she'd gone out.'

'No one called round?'

'What, in the middle of the night?'

'Phone calls?'

Patterson shook his head.

'Do you still have the key you had cut for Nightingales' front door?'

'No. Threw it away.'

'Where?'

'God, I don't know. Waste bin, wherever.'

'Did you wear gloves when you were in there?'

'Of course not. I wasn't trying to conceal the fact that I'd been. Only the fact that I was going.'

'We'll need your fingerprints, Mr Patterson. Purely for purposes of elimination. Could you come into the station, perhaps tomorrow?'

'I can come tonight. I've got to go into Causton for some dog food.'

'Could I just get your full address and phone number, sir?' Troy inscribed these carefully. 'And Gray – short for Graham, is it?'

'No. My mother's maiden name.'

Well, la di frigging da. Troy snapped a rubber band sharply round the notebook and slipped it into his jacket pocket. Then, irritated when it spoiled the line, took it out again. He thought about his own mother's maiden name which was Titchboot and was bloody glad she hadn't been of the same mind.

They were walking towards the front of the house now, the dog frolicking alongside. Burs and seeds were clinging to her coat and her belly was streaked with pollen. Barnaby was reminded of the Brockleys' poodle and wondered if the girl had turned up.

As Patterson opened the gate, the Chief Inspector indicated the notice-board. 'You'll let us know, Mr Patterson, if you move out?'

'Chance'd be a fine thing. Six hundred a month, the agent's asking. The plan is to let this and rent somewhere dirt cheap for myself. One way to cope till the market picks up. If it ever does.'

'Any takers?'

'Not really. So many people seem to be in the same boat. A woman did turn up last week. Described herself on the phone as a disenchanted Londoner. Loved the house. Didn't like the outlook.'

All three men turned and gazed out over the shimmering sea of tawny wheat stretching almost to the horizon. Occasionally there were poppies. Though nothing had yet been cut, the ripe air smelled of hay. Above their heads, so high as to be almost invisible, a skylark sang its heart out.

'What didn't she like about it?' asked the Chief Inspector.

'Said it was boring.'

Longing for another cold drink but unwilling to engage in more prithee gadzookery, Barnaby plodded back to Nightingales where he planned to settle for a gallon of tap water, hopefully tricked out with an ice cube or two. Baking in the heat, the surface of the lane released a rich, tarry smell reminding him of his childhood when he would crouch on the kerb, popping bubbles with a stick.

By now the onlookers were in the grip of a deeply satisfied silence. SOCO, having finished in the house, were to be seen in full view systematically working over the front and back gardens. As the two policemen were climbing over the barrier, the woman in the straw hat caught hold of Barnaby's sleeve.

'Are you in charge?'

'What is it?' Barnaby was at his crispest, which could be very crisp indeed.

'No need to get all aereated,' snapped the woman. 'I'm only passing a message on.'

'They don't care, do they?' said her friend.

'He came out looking for you.' The first woman pointed to Arcadia. At the far end of the garden a man, outlined very clearly in the blazing afternoon light, was working the ground with a long-handled hoe. When he saw them looking, he waved a large red and white spotted handkerchief in the air. Barnaby thanked his informant, who shot back 'Better late then never', and made his way over.

The Chief Inspector's heart lifted with pleasure the minute he stepped through the gate to set foot on an old brick herringbone path. It ran between two deep herbaceous borders crammed with lilies and pinks, wallflowers and candytuft, lupins – every variety possible of cottage plant. These were backed by tall mallows and hollyhocks; by sunflowers and blowsy, powerfully scented roses. Over all hovered a great profusion of bees and butterflies. The scene was so reminiscent of a romanticised illustration that Barnaby half expected to find his way edged with cockleshells.

He continued happily towards the back of the house and wondered if the person coming towards him was Cubby, Mrs Molfrey's *innamorato*. The man in thrall to his embroidery frame and faggot making and too old for any arsy-varsy. Old he might be but, straightened up now and smiling, he certainly seemed in excellent fettle. Short and rotund, fresh-faced and with very bright clear eyes and rosy cheeks, he would have fitted a treat into Snow White's entourage. Happy, the Chief Inspector would have said, if asked to name the one he most resembled.

They met on the edge of the vegetable garden which was

punctuated by several wigwams of runner beans and an obelisk, almost invisible beneath a torrent of cream and lilac sweet peas. As Barnaby introduced himself and Troy, his eyes strayed to a row of the most superb onions he had ever seen. Like the domes of Brighton Pavilion tightly wrapped in stripy brown paper.

The gardener, wiping his hand on his dungarees before holding it out, said that he was Mr Dawlish and he was sorry to trouble them. Barnaby commented on the onions and Cubby, recognising a kindred spirit, immediately started a discourse on the relative methods of feeding and pest control.

Sergeant Troy, bored, fired a Rothmans and slipped into the greenhouse for a crafty drag. There was a strange niff in the air, hot and earthy. Exposed only to the hard, tasteless spheroids watering under wraps in supermarkets, he failed to recognise the smell of ripening tomatoes.

Looking around, his tedium intensified. Troy was not an enthusiast of your average ferny grot. What were gardens good for anyway? Hanging washing. Getting out the barbie and ghetto blaster then popping some nice cold tubes at the weekends. Plus running about screaming if you were three and your mates came round for a skip and a jump. Any backyard would do as well and all the wife had to do with that was hose it down. Through a greenish pane of glass he noticed that the chief and the little tubby guy were sauntering towards the house. Hurriedly he set about catching them up.

As they approached the back door, Troy tossed his cigarette away. It landed in a clump of pinks. Cubby gave a small involuntary cry as if struck by a sudden pain.

'Are you all right, sir?' asked Sergeant Troy. For once the concern in his voice was genuine. His grandfather, roughly

164

the same age as this venerable relic, had recently and very suddenly passed away. One minute he was in the chip queue, right as a trivet and wondering if there'd be any spare batter bits, the next out cold under the wrestling poster. It made you think.

'Yes, oh yes. Thank you.' Cubby took a last look at the Rothmans burning Mrs Sinkins' eye out. 'Do come in.'

Mrs Molfrey was dozing in her wing chair. Waking in a trice, she started to struggle to her feet.

'Please, Mrs Molfrey,' urged the Chief Inspector. 'Don't get up.'

'I'm not getting up,' said Mrs Molfrey. 'I'm re-arranging my pantaloons.'

These were quite splendid. Panne velvet in rich crimson, gaucho style. With them she had on black lace stockings and suede shoes with high filigreed tongues and silver buckles, like those worn by principal boys in pantomime. Over her shoulders was draped a pale sea-green shawl, cobweb fine and glittering with brilliants.

'Welcome, Inspector, welcome. Do sit down. And your accomplice too. Now,' she tapped the little box resting on her bony chest. It whistled back. 'What's afoot?'

Troy had perched on an old chaise longue which prickled his thighs. Barnaby chose a saggy but comfortable-looking armchair. Cubby hovered.

'I understood that Mr Dawlish had something to tell us.'

'Both of us have,' asserted Mrs Molfrey. 'Trouble is, I've forgotten my bit. Off you go then, honey dumpling.'

'Well . . .' Cubby blushed to find himself thus publicly addressed. He stood awkwardly as if he wished he wasn't there. Like a child hiding a gift behind its back and unsure whether it will be appreciated.

'Building up a picture of the deceased's final hours is

terribly important, Cubs. They all do it.' Mrs Molfrey jerked her thumb over her shoulder at some tightly packed bookshelves. One was entirely green and white. 'Dalgleish, Wexford. That one who drinks—'

'Is this something to do with Alan Hollingsworth, Mr Dawlish?'

'Yes.' Cubby took a deep breath. 'I'd just opened the kitchen door to pull a bit of mint for the potatoes when I heard him open the garage—'

'When was this, sir?' Sergeant Troy prepared to make a note.

'Around seven thirty Monday evening.'

'You say "heard" Mr Dawlish,' said Barnaby. 'Didn't you see Mr Hollingsworth?'

'No. The hedge is in the way. But I can't imagine who else it could have been.'

'And he drove off?'

'I'm afraid I can't tell you that. I came straight back in. Elfrida had the television on without her earpiece and it was very loud.'

'I see. Did you hear anyone come back?'

'Well, you know I believe I did. I wouldn't like to swear to this because at night sounds have a strange habit of misplacing themselves. One is never quite sure where they originate. But I was just falling asleep when I heard a car drive up – I'm pretty sure it was next door. And then a door slam.'

'The car door?'

Cubby hesitated. 'I couldn't swear to that. The sound was . . . muted. I think the car must have been in the garage by then. It would still be open I should imagine, as he drove off in such a hurry.'

'It wasn't the front door?'

'I don't think so. But, as I say, I was just dropping off so I can't really be sure. But the kitchen opens directly off the garage. It might have been that which I heard.'

'Did you hear voices?'

'No.'

'Or the garage being closed?'

'That, yes.'

'You're quite sure?'

'Positive. It makes a peculiar wheezing sound. One of those remote control radar things.'

'And have you got a time on this, Mr Dawlish?' asked Sergeant Troy.

'Let's see, I have my wash at ten thirty, make some cocoa and read a little while I drink it. Then I say my prayers and get into bed. So I'd say it was somewhere between eleven and eleven thirty p.m. I usually drop off very quickly.'

As well you might, thought the Chief Inspector, reflecting on the gentle, harmless pattern of this sweet old man's life and comparing it to the smash and grab maelstrom in which he was compelled to live such a large portion of his own. No wonder he usually dropped off very slowly and then only when aided by a couple of Mogadons or a slug of something forty per cent proof.

'So you heard nothing else from the direction of Nightingales after that, sir? The front doorbell, for instance?'

It was a lot to hope for and, of course, he didn't get it. Still, this was meaty stuff. Hollingsworth, who by all accounts had not left the house once since his wife disappeared, had been away for something like three hours on the night he died. And the time of his death could now be narrowed down a little more, for the man had not been quickly and violently killed the minute he re-entered the house. There would have been conversation, drinks offered, drinks poured. Certainly the stuff had not been forced down his throat. He must have sat there talking with, if not someone he trusted, at least someone he believed he had no cause to fear.

Of course Dawlish's comments would be useless as evidence. It could have been anyone driving away and driving back. Anyone closing the garage door. But for now and because, so far, it was all he had, Barnaby chose to believe the obvious. And, after all, the obvious was so very often true.

Sergeant Troy was asking Mrs Molfrey if she could confirm any of Mr Dawlish's comments.

'Alas, no. I was watching television, Taggart actually. I can't stand the suspense between episodes so Cubby tapes all three then I have a good wallow.'

His tale told, Cubby was despatched to produce some refreshments. Barnaby directed his attention to Mrs Molfrey who was regarding him with lively interest. Today her complexion was the soft vivid pink of Turkish Delight. Her dark eyes shone. He decided, finding himself on the spot, as it were, to remind her of their earlier conversation.

'We'll be talking to your hairdresser later on today, Mrs Molfrey. About her appointment with Mrs Hollingsworth. And also to the girl who cleans for you.'

'Heather? You'll find her in a council bungalow behind the hostelry,' explained Mrs Molfrey. 'With her boyfriend and assorted infants. He plays a Harley Davidson.'

Troy stopped writing and started at Mrs Molfrey, open-mouthed.

'It's a guitar,' said Cubby, chiming in from the kitchen.

'The sergeant would know that,' called back Mrs Molfrey. 'A young blood like himself.'

The kettle bubbled and spat and Cubby raced about.

'He's a giddy boy,' said Mrs Molfrey. Then, 'I'm so glad you're taking the matter of Simone's disappearance seriously, Chief Inspector. Next door thought I was quite overstepping the mark, coming to see you. But then they'd sit tight if the house was burning down rather than run outside and draw attention to themselves.'

She did not mention Brenda. Did that mean the Brockleys' daughter had returned? Or merely that Mrs Molfrey knew nothing of her absence. In either case, bearing in mind her neighbours' desperate wish to keep the news to themselves, Barnaby saw no reason to comment.

'I couldn't help wondering if Alan's death was connected in some way with his wife's disappearance. Do you have any spin on that, Chief Inspector? Or are you waiting on the results from the PM?'

These crime buffs, they made you laugh. Troy snatched at his notebook which was slipping off his knee. He was delighted to have come across this barmy old trotter again and couldn't keep his eyes off her. She seemed to him like some magical character from a panto or fairy tale. There ought to be a black cat around the place. And one of those broomsticks with twigs tied round the handle. Troy really looked forward to describing Elfrida Molfrey to his daughter at bedtime. Even now he composed the opening sentence: 'Once upon a time, in the middle of a dark wood, there was a higgledy-piggledy cottage . . .'

Mrs Molfrey shouted, 'Don't forget the pecan and marmalade yum-yums.'

And Cubby called back, 'Hey ho.'

Mrs Molfrey reached out and drew a two-tier trolley up to her chair. On the bottom level were some lorgnettes attached to a gold and tortoiseshell holder, a cigar box with pens and pencils, a glue pot and scissors, writing paper and envelopes, some mineral water, a clean glass and today's copy of *The Times*. There was also a strip of folded white card resembling the brass Toblerone on a bank manager's desk on which her name was written, in exquisite copperplate.

'It's to remind me of who I am,' explained Mrs Molfrey, noticing Barnaby's surprised glance. 'One so easily forgets, don't you find?'

Cubby came in then with a heavy tray. He looked after Elfrida first. Swinging the hinged top of her trolley over her lap, he unrolled a richly embroidered tray cloth and matching napkin and laid out her tea, a plate of cake with a little silver fork and a crystal vase hardly bigger than an egg cup. This held a wisp of asparagus fern and three pale yellow rose buds.

Troy spent the next quarter of an hour trying to prise his jaws, locked on the delicious ticky-tacky, apart and avoiding the large and extremely hard nuts. A single sip and he nudged his dish of tea under the chaise longue with the heel of his shoe. Barnaby gently prodded Cubby and Elfrida further on the lives and general behaviour of their nearest neighbours. He asked if either of them had ever heard signs of a serious disagreement.

'A rumpus?' asked Mrs Molfrey. 'Good gracious, no. Did you, sweeting?'

'Not at all,' said Cubby.

'Did she ever express unhappiness when talking to you?'

'Never. Ennui, but that was to be expected. Shut up in that dreary, tasteless house.'

'Sounds as if he couldn't trust her.' The words were spoken unclearly but with much sympathy and understanding. Troy had never met a woman he would trust further than the nearest lamp post. Or a man either, come to that. He did not have a very rosy view of human nature. And human nature, unsurprisingly, did not have a very rosy view of him.

'I do feel,' said Cubby, 'that Alan must have been rather lacking in confidence in that respect. After all, most couples mix constantly with members of the opposite sex without running off with them.' As he spoke, Cubby looked across at Elfrida in a calm, relying sort of way. The implication was that, even if a stream of handsome gallants should come thundering up her garden path, he knew that not one would be allowed admission.

To Barnaby's surprise, rather than treating this preposterous suggestion as a huge giggle, Elfrida raised her right hand, afire with several magnificent rings, lowered her crepey violet eyelids and inclined her head with an elegant, accepting grace.

The two policemen caught each other's eye. Troy winked in joyous disbelief. Barnaby spent a moment silently admiring this breathtaking chutzpath before steering the conversation back to the subject that really interested him.

'Did Mrs Hollingsworth ever suggest to you that her husband was violent?'

'Alan? Nonsense!'

'Quite impossible,' said Cubby. 'He adored her.'

Barnaby took this with a lorry load of salt. He had attended too many domestics where the husband had adored his wife before knocking her senseless, sometimes permanently. On a more trivial level he asked if the Hollingsworths had been having problems with their telephone.

'Simone never mentioned it to us.'

For a short while everyone ate and drank with relish. Cubby's socks, blobbed with many beautifully woven darns, were clearly visible inside his open leather sandals and Barnaby wondered if he mended them himself. Having finished his cake and tea, he said, 'Mrs Molfrey, when we first arrived you suggested you also had something to tell us but it had slipped your mind. Have you remembered what it was?'

'I'm afraid not, Chief Inspector. I can tell you that it was something auditory. An unexpected or wrong sound. Or perhaps a lack of sound where one might have expected such a thing to exist. I wouldn't dwell on it, you see, but it happened on the day Simone disappeared.'

'Well, if it comes back to you, perhaps you'll let me know.' Barnaby produced a card from his wallet and gave it to her. 'This number gets straight through to me.'

'Ohh, thank you.' Mrs Molfrey glowed with delight. 'Rest assured I shall not abuse the privilege.' She studied the slip of pasteboard through a magnifying glass.

Troy didn't get it. Seemed to him the chief was asking for trouble. The old trout would be on the blower every five minutes.

As Cubby got up to see them off, there was a bone-cracking snap. Barnaby assumed it was an elderly joint giving way until he saw his sergeant wince and rub his jaw.

As the Chief Inspector turned to go, he noticed for the first time on the wall behind him a large sepia photograph of one of the loveliest creatures he had ever seen in all his life. A girl of perhaps eighteen with the sweetest expression on her perfect features. A great cloud of dark hair banded with strings of pearls; huge dreaming eyes. Her slender neck rose from clouds of tulle pinned here and there with gardenias and her small, exquisite hands were crossed at her breast. Encircling the picture were several theatrical posters.

Although there was no longer even the memory of resemblance between this heavenly beauty and the withered old lady in the wing chair, Barnaby knew at once that they were the same person. And he wondered how Mrs Molfrey could bear to contemplate daily such a cruel comparison.

'You know who she is, of course?' Cubby said shyly when they were once again walking down the worn brick path.

'I'm afraid I don't,' said the Chief Inspector.

'Elsie Romano.' Then, when Barnaby appeared puzzled, 'A star of the Edwardian theatre. And one of the great beauties of this, or any other century.'

Troy, bringing up the rear, winked again, this time winding his index finger round and round close to his forehead.

'She was the toast of the Ivy and the Trocadero. And the Café d'Angleterre. When she and Jack went dancing there, after the show, people would climb on to the banquettes and even the tables to catch a glimpse of her.'

'Is that a fact, Mr Dawlish?' Barnaby, born in 1941, three years after the Café d'Angleterre had been bombed to bits, could think of nothing else to say.

'So you see how privileged I am. Just an ordinary chap, never been anywhere, never done anything. Yet here I am, practically at the end of my days, with this sudden ... honour, as you might say. This opportunity to care for a most rare and lovely ...' Greatly moved Cubby pressed the red and white kerchief to his brimming eyes.

Troy, face averted, shoulders twitching, opened the garden gate.

'I'm sure, if you caught her at the right moment, Elfrida would show you the photograph of herself and Jack on the steps of the Gaiety.'

'That was her husband – Jack?'

'Good heavens, no.' Courteously Cubby attempted to conceal his amazement at such ignorance. 'Jack was Jack Buchanan.'

Barnaby had planned to call on the Brockleys next. Not only to see if Brenda had returned but also because, as the only other inhabitants of the cul-de-sac, they were uniquely placed to support Cubby Dawlish's statement. Indeed, up late and no doubt anxiously looking out for the lights of their daughter's car, they might even be able to add to it.

But now, just as they approached The Larches, Perrot came running towards them. He cried out, 'Sir! Sir!'

'What is it? What's happened?'

'Mr Marine said to tell you they've found her!'

'Found who?'

'Why, Mrs Hollingsworth, sir.'

'I'd forgotten what a funster you are, Aubrey.' Barnaby's heart, which had started to bang wildly in his chest when he raced down the lane, along the side of the house and into the back garden, was slowly returning to normal.

'Sorry,' said Aubrey Marine. 'I've always had this feeling for drama, I'm afraid. Can't seem to control it.'

Barnaby had flopped into a chair on the patio a few feet away from a small, newly turned heap of earth. He was mopping his scarlet face with a handkerchief and making a strange noise. Half pant, half snarl.

'Are you all right, Tom?'

'No thanks to you.'

'I should have said a reasonable facsimile of Mrs H. Although reasonable is hardly the word, as you will see.' He was moving towards the French windows which stood wide open. 'Come and have a look.'

All the SOCO team were present in the sitting room, as was Sergeant Troy. They had gathered round a table on which lay an Asda carrier bag covered with dirt and a small, semi-transparent envelope file. Still wearing his gloves, Aubrey turned back the flap and, using a fine pair of tweezers, pulled out what appeared to be a single Polaroid photograph about five centimetres square. He laid it on the table. Barnaby bent down to look more closely.

It was the woman in the wedding portrait. Recognisable, even without her make-up and despite the expression on her face which was piteous in the extreme. Her features were distorted; her lips so tightly clamped together that the luscious cupid's bow had quite disappeared. Her skin had a greyish white pallor but this, Barnaby told himself, could have been due to the harshness of the flash. She was holding across her chest a copy of the *Evening Standard* dated Thursday, 6 June.

About to speak, the Chief Inspector was silenced by Aubrey who held up his hand, saying simply, 'Wait.'

In spite of the folder, it seemed that damp had affected the contents of the plastic bag. Slipping the tweezers beneath the left-hand corner of the picture, Aubrey had to peel it away. There was another underneath.

Now her eyes, darker and much larger, were puffy and swollen with weeping. There were bruise-like shadows on her forehead and just beneath her jaw. The fingers of the hand gripping the newspaper were filthy and covered with some sort of stain. The date this time was 7 June.

The last one was the worst. Mrs Hollingsworth's pretty mouth was a real mess. Her bottom lip appeared to have been split and the blood flowing from it had been left to dry on her neck and chin. There was a savage mark across her right cheekbone and her right eye had been severely blackened. She no longer looked frightened. Just sat, her head hanging, expressionless. Beaten, in every sense of the word. Her hair had been savagely chopped and in one or two places, where the skin showed through, looked as if it had been pulled out. A wodge of newspaper had been jammed in her mouth. Her blouse had been torn open and a complete page of the *Sun* dated Saturday, 8 June, was pinned to the front of her brassiere.

Troy said, '*Jesus.*'

Barnaby stared at the escalating misery spread out in front of him. Inevitably, given his length of time in the force, he'd seen much worse and the shock he now felt was not simply a natural one of pity and revulsion. Mingling with these emotions was exhilaration at the suddern and dramatic turn the case had now taken. He had long ago accepted that this excitement, even in the face of another's anguish, was an aspect of his personality that the job seemed to encourage if not actually demand. It had been many years since he had chided himself for callousness.

'Whole new can of worms here, guv,' said Sergeant Troy, master, as ever, of the original one-liner.

Barnaby, his mind swarming with fresh possibilities, did not reply. Using the tweezers, he was turning the photographs over and studying the backs, unmarked except for splotches of moisture.

'Envelopes?'

'I certainly don't recall seeing any earlier but we'll have another look.'

'Try your best.' With a saliva test they could be halfway there. 'Don't think much of their choice in wallpaper.' This was thinly striped and covered with sentimental drawings of puppies going about their natural business in many archly contrived ways.

'It was everywhere, that,' said Aubrey. 'A few years ago.'

'Could you give it priority, please?'

'OK.' Aubrey Marine dropped the carrier into a labelled transparent bag. 'Why d'you think he buried this?'

Barnaby shrugged. 'Couldn't bear to have the pictures in the house?'

'Why not just burn them then? Or chuck 'em in the dustbin?'

'Because if they don't deliver the goods when he hands over whatever it is they're after, this may be all he's got to take to the police.'

'A shakedown, then?'

'Looks like it.'

'Timing's a bit close, isn't it, sir?' asked Sergeant Troy. 'I don't mean for taking the snaps. If they pinched her on the Thursday afternoon they could well have taken the first one that evening. But posting them?'

'A bit tight, yes.'

'I mean, all three must have been here by Monday, latest. Risky, even sending them first class.'

'The Post Office have a special service that guarantees next day delivery,' said Aubrey. 'Only a couple of quid but you have to fill a form in. Which I doubt these people would want to do. Of course they could have just been stuffed through the letter box.'

'Bloody hell,' said Sergeant Troy. 'That's a bit chancy, isn't it?'

'Not necessarily. Middle of the night, everyone asleep.' Aubrey Marine, after asking if Barnaby was through with the snaps for now, tweezered them back into their plastic sheath.

'I must say this throws a new light on Perrot's interview.' Barnaby was walking away, stepping once more out of the French windows. 'No wonder Hollingsworth couldn't wait to get him out of the house.'

'Explain why he yanked him in off the doorstep as well, chief,' said Troy. 'First thing these bastards do is threaten to kill the victim if the other party goes to the police.' He added, 'Tell you what.'

Barnaby grunted. It was not a sound to encourage a confidence.

'I reckon this is proof positive he topped himself. Paid over the money – which is what he dashed off for on Monday night – then they got in touch and told him she's had the chop. Nothing else to live for so he goes and does the business. What do you think?'

Barnaby thought it went totally against his deepest instincts so far concerning the case and that it sounded very likely indeed. Having no wish to dwell on such an exasperating insight, he stifled it by the thought that, as they now had a kidnapping and perhaps some mortal remains to search for, he would be able to commandeer a decent team and some sort of realistic budget.

Perrot, once more on duty in the lane, braced himself as the two men emerged. But Troy was satisfied this time with a rude gesture engaging his thumb and first finger and a murmur of 'Panty wanker'.

Barnaby looked across at the Brockleys. Once more the poodle was up on its hind legs and staring out of the window. Behind the dog stood Iris, white-faced and motionless. Although she also faced the outside world, it was in the alert yet only partly comprehending manner of the blind person. She appeared deeply puzzled and much smaller than when he had last seen her.

It was now nearly seven. The Chief Inspector felt a strong disinclination at the thought of adding yet more misery to the already deeply miserable content of his day. Someone else could go and talk to the family. He'd had enough.

'Oh, Constable.'

'Sir.' PC Perrot, as steely upright as a guardsman, stiffened his sinews even further.

'Any post at Nightingales – my desk. Got that?'

'I'll bring it in personally, Chief Inspector. On the bike.'

'No need to go mad, Perrot.'

'Very good, sir.'

Colin Perrot watched the two policemen walk away. His shoulders loosened slightly. He walked up and down the grass verge for a while then let himself through the black and gold iron gates and walked up and down the gravel path. He stood on the step for a bit. A police presence.

There was not much in the way of spectators to attend the departure of the SOCO team some little time later. Perrot looked at his watch – seven thirty. That explained matters. It took more than a handful of plainclothes investigators to keep Fawcett Green from viewing *EastEnders*.

Perrot sighed and wondered, as he was unobserved by anyone with the slightest degree of authority, whether he could perhaps bring one of the patio chairs round to the front of the house and sit down. He'd now been on the go for nine hours and his feet and back ached.

The overtime was nice though. It was his son's birthday in a month's time and Robby wanted a mountain bike. The boy had already accepted that it would probably be second-hand – so many of the children's presents were – though polished up and looking as smart as his dad could make it. But it would be great to surprise him with a new one.

Perrot wandered round to the rear of the house at this point, reasoning that this aspect needed just as much surveillance as the front. More, probably, being concealed from public view.

It was very still and quiet in the garden, the shrubs and trees bathed in a pale, golden light. The only sounds came from a few bees ferreting around in submissive blossoms, frogs jumping in and out of the pond and a dog fox barking, way across the fields.

Perrot sat in the daisy hammock and relished the silence. He breathed slowly and deeply, savouring the fragrant, musky scents. It seemed impossible that only a short time ago the place had been swarming with men and women extracting ugly disturbing evidence from the sweet-smelling earth.

Gradually, in the warm soft air, Perrot's wounded pride began to heal. He had smarted dreadfully after the DCI had so contemptuously dismissed him at Causton station. But over and above his shame at failing so miserably to act in a prompt and intelligent manner was a far greater fear. He was now permanently haunted by the words, 'buried in the sticks too long'.

Perrot was a country man. Transplanted, he felt he would shrivel up and die. Not true, of course. Trixie would tell him not to be so silly. They would be all right, she had said when he voiced his anxiety. As long as they were together.

But it wasn't as simple as that. Places changed people. Occasionally Perrot had been away on update courses and some of the townee coppers he had met there – well. The way they spoke to each other, their attitude to the public.

Talk about cynical. They sounded as if they were at war half the time. The words 'cutting edge' had been bandied around a lot. Perrot had felt really out of place.

He had made no attempt to talk about his own work, recognising the scorn with which such a description would almost certainly have been received. No one was interested in hearing about the three villages under his care. About the boisterous children, including his own, running noisily out of the brand-new primary school at half past three, clutching paste and paper models or exuberantly painted daubs. Or of how relieved the anxious elderly were to hear his knock on the door. His spare-time activities, refereeing on the football field and supervision of the Infant Cyclists' Time Trials, also remained unmentioned.

Naturally there was a downside to the job. Burglaries, an occasional case of child abuse (quickly known about and dealt with in a small community), drunken fights, the odd domestic. But nothing at what you could honestly call the cutting edge. Nevertheless, no one would ever convince Perrot that his daily duties were of no importance. Certainly not that spiteful, foul-mouthed, red-headed, toe rag of a sergeant from the town nick. When Perrot had told his wife about the trick played on him, she could hardly believe it. Tried to suggest that her husband had misheard what Troy had said. That no one could be so deliberately mean. That was when Perrot had said that if he was transferred to Causton he would leave the force.

Leaning back now he closed his eyes and tried to put such thoughts from his mind. No point in jumping the gun. By now the DCI might well have forgotten he ever had such a thought. And if he (Perrot) remained crisp, alert and totally on the ball, there would be nothing to remind the powers that be that he had ever been anything else.

That was the way to do it. Perrot adjusted a cushion to make himself more comfortable and swung his legs up. A quarter of an hour passed in pleasant contemplation of a tumbling clematis, the Chinese pots and Hollingsworth's barbecue. The sky became streaked with lavender and pale yellow as the evening came on.

What would be really good, thought Perrot dreamily, now barely registering the aquatic frogs, what would be really totally excellent would be for him to find some vital clue, or discover someone, someone totally unexpected, in a compromising situation . . . that would bring the case . . . that would solve . . . a successful . . . conclusion . . . so impressed . . . all of us here . . . well done, Constable . . . no question now of . . .

Perrot slept.

Chapter Six

A woman who appears to have walked out on her husband, and that husband's consequent death, possibly by his own hand, is one thing. The holding of a human being to ransom and their consequent cruel mistreatment is quite another. By lunchtime the following day, an official inquiry into the disappearance of Simone Hollingsworth was up and running.

Detective Chief Inspector Barnaby had been allocated a team smaller than he would have liked but that was nothing new. They had received as detailed a briefing as he was able to give and had now gone about their business. Every inhabitant of Fawcett Green would be asked what they knew of the dead man and his missing wife in an attempt to obtain feedback on the marriage and the general pattern of their lives.

The police would hope to come across someone on the market run who had noticed Simone's movements after she got off the bus; had perhaps even talked to her on the journey. Also they would be checking on possible sightings of strange vehicles in the village on the night of Alan's death.

Barnaby composed a fax to be circulated to every estate agency within a ten-mile radius of Causton asking for details of any property let within the last couple of months; this to include shops, offices and even lockups. He also asked for a list of empty properties. It wasn't very likely that the kidnapper had presented himself at an estate agent's in the proper manner, signed a contract and written an appropriate cheque. But the possibility could not be overlooked. After all, Simone had to be hidden somewhere.

His team included Sergeant Brierley whom Barnaby had chosen especially to call on the Brockleys. She was sensitive, intelligent and well able to pick up things a more prosaic interviewer might miss.

Three people remained in the station trying to flesh out what was already known of Alan and Simone's background, starting with an attempted trace of their ex-partners. The fact that Simone's previous husband had already been described as a bad lot sounded mildly promising. Was he perhaps connected with the club, described by Avis Jennings as 'very Soho', where Simone used to work?

The Chief Inspector's first inclination was to bring Gray Patterson in immediately for further questioning. There was no doubt that the kidnapping, and probable ransom of Mrs Hollingsworth, would constitute for him a sweet revenge. It would offer not only a certain amount of financial recompense for the theft of his work but the pleasure of knowing that the man responsible had been sweating his days away in a drunken fever of fearful anticipation. Couldn't improve much on that as a dish best eaten cold.

But then, thinking it over, he had decided to put off seeing Hollingsworth's former colleague until after the fingerprint comparisons came back from the laboratory. These had been promised by mid-afternoon, at which time he would be interviewing Freddie Blakeley, Penstemon's bank manager. Barnaby was hoping to learn more about the company's financial affairs and also the details of how the ransom money was raised.

The preliminary inquest had been held on Alan Hollingsworth and adjourned pending further police investigation. The body had been formally identified by Ted Burbage. Hollingsworth's solicitor Jill Gamble had been able to supply the address and telephone number of the dead man's brother and the station in central Aberdeen had sent someone to break the news.

The postmortem report added little to George Bullard's telephone call. Barnaby, skimming through it, felt his attention wandering and sent out his minion for a caffeine shot.

'And not that stale stuff that's been sitting there since . . .' Barnaby was distracted. Now standing by the window, his eye had been caught by a messenger from Forensic crossing the forecourt towards the main building.

'Since Madonna was a virgin?'

'Ay?'

'"In love for the very first time,"' croaked Sergeant Troy. Music was a closed book to him.

'Fresh.'

By the time his sergeant returned with two cups of excellent smooth Brazilian, Barnaby was engrossed in the SOCO report forms, pulling out from the mass of information the most immediately relevant. The report covered Nightingales and its contents plus the buried photographs. Those for the gardens, garage, car and Hollingsworth's clothes would follow, piecemeal, over the next few days.

As was to be expected, there were several unexplained prints around the place. Some would naturally have been made by Simone. Others by Perrot and the vicar. Only Hollingsworth's were found on the keyboard connected to the monitor displaying the dead man's final words.

Barnaby was not cast down by this, for alternative methods of getting the message on to the screen had already been put forward. These included feeding it into the machine by floppy disk. Swapping the keyboards round – there had been two more in the room. Or shielding the one that was used by a thin plastic cover, rather like those used in shops to keep the till clean.

The report on the photographs of Simone and the plastic envelope file showed several tiny pressure points in the top right-hand corner of the Polaroids, indicating that they had been handled by more than just SOCO's tweezers. The only fingerprints present were Alan's. This was also the case with the glass found on the rug.

The glass contained traces of Haloperidol, as Barnaby had been sure it would. Someone had shaken the drug into the tumbler – none was found in the bottle itself – added the whisky and, presumably, offered the result to the victim, all without leaving a single mark.

But how had the powder been put in? Bold sleight of hand with the perpetrator simply turning their back? Or in another room with the tumbler then placed on a tray and handed directly to the victim?

Another possibility was that the murderer could have wiped the glass clean after Hollingsworth became unconscious then simply pressed his fingers round it. This was never as satisfactory as those who tried it seemed to think. Nearly always anxious to make a good impression (so to speak), they used too much force and unnaturally even marks resulted.

Barnaby closed his eyes and thought himself back into

Nightingales' sitting room at eleven o'clock last Monday evening. He often did this sort of thing and did it rather well. And, as his imagination was vivid but not especially original, he was able to avoid the sort of wild scenarios a more creative person might have dreamed up.

Here was the room, stale and frowsty, curtains drawn. And here came Alan – Barnaby heard the car door slam – fresh from delivering the ransom. What had they told him? The oldest chestnut in the book, perhaps. That she'd be waiting there when he got home. In which case he would be running through the empty house, upstairs and downstairs, in and out of all the rooms, calling her name, Simone! Simone!

Poor bastard.

But what if Nightingales proved not to be empty after all. Perhaps the murderer was already *in situ*. Or did he – or she – enter surreptitiously, unaware to Hollingsworth? The latter struck Barnaby as rather unlikely. If this was someone the dead man was prepared to sit down and have a drink with, there would be no need for such a furtive approach.

The temptation was to see some connection between the kidnapping and Hollingsworth's death, paradoxical though this might at first appear. After all, why kill a goose which has just produced a presumably quite substantial golden egg? And who might well be persuaded to lay a few more.

One fairly obvious reason was that Hollingsworth had become dangerous. What if, instead of driving away straight after the drop, he had hung around to see who picked the money up? Perhaps even attempted to follow. Spotted, his life wouldn't be worth twopence. Especially if, as Barnaby's instincts were strongly telling him, Mrs Hollingsworth had already been done away with.

His thick fingers riffled through the report. He noticed there had been no forced entry. As the house had been secure when the body was found, this meant either someone owned a key or they had knocked and been admitted.

Gray Patterson had had a key. Thrown away, according to him, but then he would say that, wouldn't he? And, even if this was the case, might there not be circumstances when Hollingsworth would let the man he had betrayed into his house? What if Patterson had appeared on the doorstep with some cock and bull story about catching sight of Simone somewhere – on a bus perhaps, or in a café? Highly unlikely, given the true circumstances, but Alan wouldn't have reasoned like that. Desperate men clutch at any straw.

Then there was Simone's key. Presumably in her handbag when she'd boarded the Causton bus, it could by now be in the hands of a very dodgy lot indeed.

Barnaby pulled back his damp shirt cuff. All these musings, mind-clearing rather than genuinely fruitful, had brought him up to one o'clock. He picked up his crumpled fawn cotton jacket and left his office for the staff canteen and a brief lunch before his meeting at the Nat West.

Drearily mindful of his weight, the Chief Inspector chose a dish of grated carrots, raisins and almond flakes with a wedge of lemon and two slices of smoked turkey breast. Squeezing the lemon over his salad, he thought the one thing you could say in favour of this sweltering heat was that at least it killed off an inclination to gluttony.

The station cat, Craig, strolled up. Pressed upon the force under the guise of a great mouser by a telephonist moving house, he immediately circumvented any onerous duties in this direction by moving more or less permanently into the canteen. Here, in spite of constant titbits from gullible diners and doubling his weight in the first week, he strove successfully to give an impression of fragility and despairing hunger that melted nearly every heart. He would have made a fortune as an actor.

'Go away,' instructed Barnaby. 'You greedy little scumbag.'

Craig squinted in that cross, imperious way that cats have when everything they desire is not immediately rushed to their side. Incredulity possessed his squashy, pugilistic features. Briefly he stood his ground then, no sustenance being forthcoming, mewed. Defeated by dryness and imminent starvation, it was no more than a pitiful squeak.

Resentfully, knowing he was being made a fool of, Barnaby had just started to cut off a sliver of meat when he was distracted by the arrival of his bag carrier who sat down opposite him with a loaded tray.

'Never much going on menu-wise Monday, is there, boss?' As Troy spoke he pricked a stout glistening sausage with his fork and watched the juice run out. 'I suppose they haven't really got into their stride.'

Apart from the sausages, his plate held a tottering pile of chips, two fried eggs, a bright orange puddle of baked beans, mushrooms and several chunks of black pudding.

'Do you mind sitting somewhere else with that lot?'

'Sorry?' Troy was always alert to the chance of a real or imagined slight. Now that he had actually received one, he looked as if he could hardly believe his ears. In fact, when it came to his expression and that of the cat, there was hardly a whisker to choose between them. Genuinely hurt, he picked up his tray, uncertainly looking about him.

'There'll do.' Barnaby pointed directly to the chair behind.

'Fine by me, sir.'

It was plain by his tone of voice that Troy had not only

distanced himself physically. Barnaby came as close to a smile as any man could faced with a pile of shredded root vegetables and a cat with attitude. Behind him the clash of metal on metal rose to a wild crescendo. It was like wandering into the last act of *Hamlet*. There was a satisfied pause, a final clatter when the irons were laid to rest then a soft squeak as the plate was mopped clean with a crust of bread.

'Right.' Barnaby heaved himself upright. 'Let's go.'

'I haven't had my pudding.'

'Pudding is for wimps, Sergeant.'

The National Westminster was in the High Street just a few minutes' walk from the station. Recoiling from this last, the unkindest cut of all, Troy followed his superior officer across the simmering car park and through the main gates. Immediately they were engulfed in a reek of exhaust fumes overlain with fried onions and recycled fat from a nearby hot-dog stand.

Troy strode in a crisp martial manner, emphasising his extreme machismo. *Wimp*. What a cheek! Fair did your head in, a remark like that. In fact, if it wasn't such an insult it would be laughable. Himself – a man with a personality so masculine and seductive it had been known to mesmerise any bit of yum-yum going at twenty paces. Muscular, good-looking, over the side so often he was known round the lockers as Maxie. Still on both feet after ten lager and blacks and father of one. Female, true, but plenty of time to rectify that. He was jealous, old porky. What else could it be?

They waited at a pedestrian crossing. The flagstones burned through the synthetic soles of Troy's highly polished tasselled black loafers. An elderly man came towards them draped in sandwich boards heavy with biblical instruction. Troy noted his approach sourly. The man, no doubt overcome by that irritating compulsion to share his convictions, which afflicts the overly religious, gave Troy a sugary smile. He said, 'Jesus loves you.'

'Jesus loves everybody, mate,' snapped Sergeant Troy, well equipped to recognise the emotionally promiscuous. 'So don't think you're anything special.'

The bank was air conditioned, which was heaven. Barnaby, newly bathed in moisture at every step, could feel the sweat drying on his shirt, the fabric easing away from his skin.

Freddie Blakeley did not keep them waiting. Once inside the office he indicated two extremely uncomfortable-looking seats, all leather straps and writhing chrome. They looked like a harness for some exceptionally gruelling medical examination. Or the practice of bizarre sexual shenanigans. Barnaby passed over his magistrate's order.

Blakeley did not wave it aside or give it a casual once-over, as was usually the case. He sat behind his huge teak desk with an air of great solemnity, plainly prepared to give the piece of paper as much time as it took to extract each scrap of meaning or sniff out any fraudulence.

Barnaby watched this performance with interest while at the same time absorbing every detail of the man's manner and appearance. After thirty years of practice, he did this almost unconsciously and without the slightest effort. Today he was especially well rewarded. The contrast between the bank manager's orderly desk and namby-pamby ways and his appearance was most striking. Not to mince words, Freddie Blakeley looked like a gangster.

He was short and square with meaty, muscular shoulders and meaty lips. Though thick, these were very sensuous and beautifully shaped. His skin was tough-looking but very pasty as if permanently deprived of daylight. A steel-blue shadow showed through his lightly powdered jowls. He wore a charcoal suit with broad, chalky stripes, a satin tie embroidered with golden peacocks and, tumbling in vast folds out of his breast pocket, an emerald Paisley silk handkerchief.

Hoping to share his pleasure in this unlikely phenomenon, Barnaby sought eye contact with Sergeant Troy who immediately averted his gaze and stared stonily out of the window.

Blakeley folded the order neatly twice, smoothed it flat on his unmarked blotter and seemed about to speak. Barnaby braced himself for a gravelly, Neapolitan rumble making him an offer he dare not refuse. Inevitably he was disappointed.

'A terrible business.' Blazered Home Counties, sieved through a tennis racquet. The smile had all the empty courtesy of a diplomat's. 'Terrible,' repeated Mr Blakeley. He looked at the policemen with distaste as if, by invading the portals of his hallowed establishment, they had brought in with them a most unpleasant smell. And in a way of course they had. For what could be less fragrant than the stench of murder? 'So how can I help you?' He touched his wide, hairy nostrils with the outrageous *mouchoir*.

Barnaby felt it sensible to approach the terrible core of his business obliquely and so began by asking about the general health of Alan Hollingsworth's company.

And Mr Blakeley replied in general terms. In front of him were several pages of A4 covered with neat columns of figures to which he hardly referred. Although without large reserves, Penstemon, it appeared, was presently stable and ticking over nicely. Unlike the majority of the bank's business customers, they did not have an overdraft. Alan Hollingsworth's personal account, though also permanently in the black, was somewhat more volatile. After volunteering this vague snippet of information, Mr Blakeley zippered up. Plainly the run of unsolicited information was over.

Barnaby's first direct question, relating to the upset between Hollingsworth and Gray Patterson, got pretty short shrift.

'You really can't expect me to comment on an affair of which I know next to nothing.'

'I believe the cause of the trouble was Hollingsworth's need to raise a lot of money rather quickly. Did he ask the bank for a loan?'

'Yes.'

'And you refused?'

'I did. The business is a small one. I could not regard it as reasonable collateral against such a sum.'

'Do you know if he tried to borrow the money elsewhere?'

'I've really no idea.' Elsewhere in any case, implied Mr Blakeley's disdainfully curling lip, must of necessity have been a deeply inferior source.

'Could you give me the exact date when the sum was eventually paid in?'

Two stapled sheets were passed over. Barnaby saw immediately the payment from Patellus. Two hundred thousand pounds on 18 March.

'I'm surprised a sum this size wasn't paid into a deposit account. I assume Hollingsworth had one?'

'Indeed.' Mr Blakeley passed over a third sheet of paper. 'And normally one would expect this. But, as you will see, the money did not stay around for long.'

'Ah, yes.' Four days to be precise. The minimum clearance time. 'He obviously needed it in a hurry. Do you happen to know who the relevant cheque was made out to?'

'I thought you might need that information.' Mr Blakeley admired his own foresight with a little *moue* of self-esteem. He looked down at his notepad. 'F. L. Kominsky.'

'I suppose it's too much to hope . . .' Barnaby was sure the name of the payee's bank was somewhere on the pad also but he never minded colluding with another man's quirks and vanities in a good cause. In this he was quite unlike Troy who, though prepared endlessly to indulge his own dreams and self-deceptions, gave short shrift to those of others.

'It was paid into Coutts. Their Kensington branch.'

'Thank you, Mr Blakeley.' The Chief Inspector was now running his eye down the balance column of Hollingsworth's high interest account. For a man who owned a reasonably successful business, it was pretty modest. He pointed this out.

'That's true,' agreed Blakeley. 'He was a heavy spender.'

Barnaby, recalling the house and Mrs Hollingsworth's wardrobe, could not but agree. He said, 'Now, to bring us up to the distressing present . . .' The bank manager immediately assumed a becoming gravitas, stuffing the larger portion of his rowdy kerchief out of sight. 'We know that, shortly before his death, Hollingsworth was again attempting to raise a sum of money.'

'Really?'

'In fact, I believe that on Sunday, June the ninth, round about mid-morning, he discussed this matter with you on the telephone.'

'Goodness.' Mr Blakeley appeared discomposed. Plainly

he preferred it when all the knowledge lay on his side of the fence. 'You must have magical powers. Or were you tapping his phone for some reason?'

'He was simply overheard.'

'I see. Well, it was a most awkward conversation.' A compulsive straightener, Mr Blakeley aligned his pens on his blotter before pausing rather awkwardly himself.

'I understand Mr Hollingsworth was extremely distressed.'

'Very much so. He'd rung up a few days before—'

'Could you give me the exact date, Mr Blakeley?'

'Yes, I can.' The bank manager pulled a large desk diary towards him, opened it and smoothed out the perfectly flat surface. 'I remember because a customer, who had an appointment about a bridging loan, complained at being kept waiting.'

Sergeant Troy admired the constrained order of Mr Blakeley's desk as he turned over a page in his own notebook.

'Here we are, Nine thirty on Friday, June seventh. He said he needed fifty thousand pounds straightaway and that it was desperately urgent. Although that amount, unlike the earlier request, was not completely out of the question, I still needed a certain amount of time to review Penstemon's affairs. I told him it might take a couple of days and he should really come in for an interview.'

'What did he say to that?'

'He became quite distraught. Almost . . . abusive.' Mr Blakeley's pale, suety cheeks warmed to the recollection. 'He asked how long it would take and expressed great distress when I said these things couldn't be hurried. I'm afraid this reaction made me extremely wary. You may think that sounds rather heartless, Chief Inspector.'

Barnaby made a vague gesture negating any such judgemental conclusion.

'It is not hearts, however, that should be relied upon when dealing with other people's money but a calm and rational mind. The calmer I remained, the wilder Mr Hollingsworth became. He rang several more times during the course of the day, always striking roughly the same note. Finally I had to instruct my secretary to say I was out of the office. I did what I could on the matter then, as I was going away for the weekend, left early. My wife and I went to a wedding in Surrey and stayed overnight, returning around eleven Sunday morning to at least a dozen frantic messages on my Answerphone. I rang him straightaway.'

'That was the call we know about?'

'Yes. I assured him that I was doing everything I could to speed things up. He seemed furious that I hadn't stayed at my desk until I'd got the matter sorted.' Mr Blakeley gave a sniff of outrage so forceful it briefly closed his hirsute nostrils. 'He was so hysterical that I pulled out all the stops and got the loan arranged early the following morning. And then, would you believe, he refused to come and pick it up! Said he was too ill to drive and, I must say, he did rather sound it.'

'So what did you do, Mr Blakeley?'

'Put the money – he'd insisted on small denomination notes which I didn't like at all – into my briefcase, locked it and drove over to Fawcett Green. All highly unorthodox.'

'And how was Mr Hollingsworth when you got there?'

'Most unwell. I hardly recognised him.' Mr Blakeley noted a hairline fracture between the A4 pages and closed it. 'And inebriated, though I'd guessed that from the phone calls.'

'Did he at any point say what the money was for?'

'No.'

'Didn't you ask?'

'It really wasn't relevant from our point of view. The business could more than cover the debt should we need to call it in.'

'But you must have been curious, Mr Blakeley. Didn't you have any ideas of your own?'

'Well, one doesn't wish to appear melodramatic,' said Mr Blakeley, melodrama incarnate in his Jimmy Cagney threads, 'but I did wonder if he was being blackmailed. Hard to imagine of course – a person of one's acquaintance.'

'What about the rest of the conversation during your visit?'

'There wasn't any. He virtually snatched the bag and showed me the door.'

'Did you hear from him again after this meeting?'

Mr Blakeley shook his head. 'The next thing I knew, Penstemon was ringing with the news of his death.'

'Do you have any idea what the future of the company will now be?'

'None whatsover. But I hope to be meeting with their Mr Burbage early next week.'

'What about Mrs Hollingsworth, sir? Did she have an account here? Perhaps jointly with her husband?'

'No, none at all. Even so, I have obviously written offering my sympathy on her sad loss. And any support or advice she may need.'

Big deal. Sergeant Troy was tapping and shaking his Biro fruitlessly before taking a spare from his breast pocket. What she needs, poor cow, is a fully armed section of the Flying Squad charging up the path to wherever it is and kicking in the cellar door.

'I'm afraid the lady is no longer at Nightingales,' Barnaby was saying. 'She disappeared a week ago.'

'More theatrics.' Mr Blakeley sighed, plainly washing his hands of the whole messy business. 'Are the two things connected, do you think?'

'We're at a very early stage in our inquiries. Impossible to say.'

'Heavens, I didn't want to *know*.' Huffily easing a cuff with an edge like a samurai sword away from his wrist, Mr Blakeley revealed a flashy timepiece. 'Well, I have an appointment in—'

'Just a couple of final questions, sir.' Barnaby was already anticipating his departure from this cool, constrained environment into the sweltering outdoors and feeling rather sorry for himself. 'Did Mr Hollingsworth have a deposit box here?'

'He did not.'

'And do you know of any other accounts he may have had? Perhaps offshore or overseas?'

'I am personally not aware of any such transactions. And, even if I was, the release of such information does not fall within the jurisdiction of the Bankers' Books Evidence Act. As I'm sure you are aware, Chief Inspector.'

The Chief Inspector got his own back for this little dig by informing Mr Blakeley that, as a visitor to Nightingales, his fingerprints would have to be taken for the purposes of elimination. He thought the bank manager was going to pass out.

'Queer bloke,' said Barnaby as they found themselves once more sticking to the boiling tarmac. Believing 'gay' to have, by now, firmly established itself as the accepted alternative for homosexual, he had used the term in the old-fashioned sense.

'Is he?' Though still sulking in his heart, Troy responded in a friendly manner for he could not bear to be lonely for long. 'I thought that snot rag was a bit over the top.'

They walked along for a few moments in silence, Troy pondering the recent interview, Barnaby dreaming of a nice cool drink.

'Think Patterson's in on this, guv?'

'I wouldn't be surprised.'

'Going to give him a tug?'

'Oh, yes.'

Once more the boarded salvationist approached.

'They never give up, do they?' said Troy.

'Don't knock it,' said Barnaby. 'This could be your chance to take the veil.'

'Nah, I'm doomed. Frying tonight, that'll be my lot!'

When Barnaby got back to the station, the driver on the Fawcett Green to Causton bus route was being interviewed by the officer-in-charge. The Chief Inspector sat in but made no attempt to take over, merely indicating to the officer that he should continue.

'Yes, I do remember her.' He was looking at Simone's picture.

'Are you sure, Mr Cato? It's over a week ago. And you must get an awful lot of customers, one way or another.'

'Yeah, but the market-day runs round the villages are special. You see the same faces, week in week out. Pensioners, youngsters with toddlers. I remember this one 'cause she'd never been on my route before. Plus she was a real looker.'

'What was she wearing?'

'Dress with flowers all over and a little coat thing to match.'

'Did you get the impression she was by herself?'

'Hard to judge. She was just in the queue.'

'Did you see who she sat with?'

'Can't say I did, mate.'

'And where was she going?'

'Causton. Asked for a single which was very unusual. Everyone always gets a return. It's only ten pence more, y'see.'

'And she got off?'

'Outside Gateways. There's only the two stops. The other's by the post office in the main square.'

'Notice her direction when she walked away?'

'Sorry. I was helping somebody with a pushchair.'

After Barnaby had once more declined to put any questions of his own, the driver signed his statement and left. In spite of the paucity of information obtained, the Chief Inspector felt quite cheerful. He had expected, given the jam-packed vehicle, absolutely nothing. Now he knew that Mrs Hollingsworth had not planned to return to Fawcett Green – at least by public transport – and where she had got off. It was a start. And there might well be a scrap or two extra once all the other passengers had been interviewed.

Dribs and drabs of information began to filter in. It appeared that Mrs Hollingsworth had no bank account at Lloyds, as her husband had suggested to PC Perrot at their first meeting. This was no surprise. Nor was the fact that British Telecom confirmed that there had been no fault reported on Alan Hollingsworth's line. And his bills were itemised.

Sergeant Troy's response to this snippet of information was predictably cynical. 'Now we know why she was using the public. To ring up her bit on the side.'

Having offered his deduction of the day, Troy vanished in search of a nicotine fix and Barnaby was left pondering this pretty obvious, but not necessarily correct, conclusion. Taking Hollingsworth's unstable and jealous temperament into account, his wife could quite possibly have simply been talking to a female friend. Always assuming she had any. Perhaps the newly started investigations would turn up an ex-colleague or two. Simone Hollingsworth must have met a fair amount of people during the time she had been doing all the jobs described by Avis Jennings.

A severely cropped wedding photograph showing a close-up of the bride had been sent out by the press office. Coupled with news of the kidnapping (and assuming that nothing even more appalling happened within the next few hours), it should make the front page of the next edition of the *Evening Standard*. Tomorrow the tabloids and perhaps even one or two of the broadsheets would carry the story, hopefully also on the front page.

Actually, asking members of the public for their assistance, though routine by now in the matter of serious crime, was undoubtedly a mixed blessing. Occasionally it could be a godsend. Much more frequently the procedure would prove to be a waste of precious time and resources. All manner of people fancied being attached to the fringe of an official inquiry. Most were ordinary, honest citizens who genuinely thought they had seen or heard something that would help the police. But the rest – they were something else.

You got to recognise them after a while. The same old sad sacks plainly believing they were important characters in a larger than life drama. This quaint conceit would lead to endless posturing, embroidery and exaggeration. Struggling to say what they thought the police wanted to hear, some of them ended up spinning a tale worthy of Hollywood at its most inventive. Anything to be in the movie. Then there were the anonymous tipsters who were often utter liars acting either from motiveless malice or to wrongly accuse some real or imagined enemy. None of these people could be safely ignored.

Barnaby turned his mind to the next item on his mental list, Messrs J. Coutts. These bankers to the great and the good had, naturally, been chary about revealing details regarding the person in receipt of Hollingsworth's weighty cheque. They would not even tell him if the name described an individual or an institution. However, they did agree to inform the owner of the account in question of the present situation and pass on to him DCI Barnaby's telephone number.

And so it was, at around four o'clock, shortly after Barnaby had despatched a car to collect Gray Patterson, a call came through on his direct line from a Mr Kurt Milritch. A courteous, softly spoken man with an accent that Barnaby thought was possibly Polish, he described himself as the director of the jewellers F. L. Kominsky of Bond Street and asked how he was able to assist. Barnaby explained the situation.

Mr Milritch remembered the cheque, indeed the whole transaction, very well. The piece in question, an emerald and diamond necklace, was extremely beautiful with a most unusual clasp, a pair of chased silver swans which linked magnetically. The purchaser asked for the piece specifically, not wishing to look at anything else. After the necessary checks to confirm that the funds to cover the purchase were available, the necklace was locked into its case and handed over.

'I asked if the customer needed to insure the jewels on his

home journey – a covering note – but he declined,'
continued Mr Milritch. 'We offered him tea – I presumed he
would be waiting for a car – but he merely slipped the
necklace into his briefcase and left. I watched him on the
pavement hailing a taxi and I must say my heart was in my
mouth until he got safely into it. Two hundred thousand
pounds is a lot to be swinging casually from one's wrist in
a busy London thoroughfare.'

'Indeed it is,' said Barnaby. 'You'd remember Mr
Hollingsworth by sight, would you, sir?'

'I believe I would, yes.'

'We'll send a photograph. Perhaps you'd be kind enough
to give us a ring just to confirm that it is the man in
question.' Barnaby took down the fax number, still talking.
'Had he been in the shop before?'

There was a slight hiss from the other end of the line
which proved to be the entente cordial icing over. Barnaby,
at a loss to understand the reason, was quickly enlightened.

'Certainly I don't recall seeing him at any other time in
our showrooms.' Shop? *Shop!* 'However, when the photograph arrives, I will be glad to show it to my colleagues, if
you think that will help.'

Barnaby assured him that it would. 'The reason I ask is
that it is surely unusual for anyone to buy something so
valuable within moments of first seeing it.'

'Oh, we get a lot of impulse buys,' said Mr Milritch
breezily. He might have been speaking of a box of matches.
'Anyway, that doesn't mean the party for whom it was
purchased hadn't seen it. She might have been here on
several occasions, looking round. Whittling items of her
choice down. They have the time to spare you see, the
ladies.'

Barnaby decided also to fax a picture of Simone but

without much hope of success. Although she'd certainly had plenty of time to look around and whittle, he couldn't imagine her being let off the leash for long enough to do so. He was about to thank Mr Milritch for his help and ring off when the salesman spoke again.

'Of course she could always have seen a picture of the necklace. In *Harpers*.'

'Where?'

'The magazine, *Harpers and Queen*. A full page. February issue. It looked breathtaking. We had heaps of inquiries. Nothing,' concluded Mr Milritch firmly, 'stimulates feminine interest like a well-faceted diamond.'

'Still a girl's best friend then?' Barnaby got another earful of chill in return for such levity. He thanked Mr Milritch and rang off.

The Chief Inspector was still reflecting on this conversation when Sergeant Troy came back from the jakes, the only place where smoking was now allowed. The scent of high tar tobacco drifted in with him. Virginia's finest.

'That's better,' he said, falling into a tweedy arm chair. 'Keep me going for a bit.'

'Just the opposite, I'd have thought.'

'You can live like a monk for years then get run over by a bus.'

'In a monastery?'

'So.' Troy, bored with any conversation that did not immediately present him in a good light, changed the subject. 'Anything fresh come in?'

'I've found out who F. L. Kominsky is.'

Barnaby went over his conversation with the salesman, or gem consultant as he was no doubt termed around the shebeens of Mayfair. Troy listened closely, both impressed and bewildered. Impressed by the amount of money involved; bewildered by the use to which it had been put.

'Unbelievable,' he said when Barnaby had finished. 'You could get a brand new Ferrari for that.'

Barnaby had made a note of the date. Almost three months ago. It seemed significant to him for a reason other than the purchase of the necklace. He frowned, teasing his memory.

'Give a lot to know where it is now, eh, chief?'

'Indeed. One thing's certain, either she took it with her, along with the engagement ring, or it had already gone by the time she disappeared.'

'Is that a fact?'

'Hollingsworth would hardly have fought his way through all that misery with Blakeley if he could just have gone to Kominsky's and flogged the necklace back.'

'Whoever tries to unload it will have their work cut out. Your average High Street jeweller, he'd be very wary. The top end of the trade would certainly ask questions. And a receiver will only divvy up a fraction of what it's worth. And that's assuming the man who did the snatch is savvy enough to find one.'

'We'll get some feelers out. See if anyone's heard anything.'

'I wouldn't be surprised if we're talking collusion here, chief.'

'What?'

'I reckon this chap she was meeting in Causton, or wherever, asked her to bring the necklace along.'

'She'd have to be pretty dim not to be suspicious.'

'But she thinks they're running away together, see? Starting a new life and that.'

'Mmm.'

Sergeant Troy sprang out of his chair then and walked

towards the window for he hated being still, or even in one place, for long. Forgetful of the heat, he laid his hand on the glass, then snatched it away. He said, 'Reminded me of something said at Nightingales, you mentioning that magazine.'

'What? Scenes of Crime?'

'Them or Parrot. Hang on a sec.' Troy frowned. Now he, too, surfed the memory bank, though making much more of a show of it.

Barnaby watched his sergeant. Troy would be longing to produce an intelligent and really helpful comment. And if the one he was genuinely seeking didn't come to mind, he would make one up. Anything rather than be found wanting.

Troy sighed and his frown deepened. Tell the truth, as the magazine's connection to the present situation continued to elude him, he was starting to regret having mentioned it at all. He should have remembered what it was before he had spoken out. Then he could have simply dropped the perceptive insight into the conversation, all casual like. If commended, he would conceal his delight and shrug it off.

All this Barnaby understood and, up to a point, sympathised with. Perhaps the most touching aspect of it all was that Troy had no idea he was so transparent and would have been mortified had it been pointed out to him.

'I know.' Relief and satisfaction slackened the tight, frowning mouth. The tips of his ears rosied up. 'It was old Polly. On the landing. Said there was a stack of magazines in the spare room, one with a page torn out. What d'you bet that was the advert for the necklace?'

'Easy enough to check. See to it, would you?' Then, because in a couple of hours he would be going back to

Joyce and Arbury Crescent where there would be asparagus and salmon and salade Niçoise, and because he was in the giving vein that day, Barnaby added, 'That was very sharp, Gavin.'

Troy's sallow cheeks glowed. Immediately he began to recount the scene to his even greater advantage. The old man – great in his time, of course, but his memory isn't what it was – said he didn't know what he'd do without me. Yeah, his very words. Relying on me more and more.

Problem was, who to recount it to. Certainly nobody round the station. Troy might not win prizes for self-awareness but he wasn't that stupid. Maureen would only fall off the settee laughing. His mum had always dinned it into him that self-praise was no recommendation, so she was out. That left Talisa-Leanne. Only three, admitted, but very intelligent. Also she listened when he spoke to her. Which was more than you could say for the rest of the world.

Fawcett Green could talk of nothing but the unexplained death of Alan Hollingsworth and the possible fate of his wife. The news of Simone's kidnapping, released by the door-to-door team in pursuance of their investigations, spread through the village like wildfire. People rang other people the minute they had had what Mrs Bream referred to as their turn. Becky called it 'being done' as if it was a vaccination.

What sort of thing did they ask you? I hear they're calling in the Yard. They didn't ask *me* that. I never believed that story about her mother. You know they found her cat? I thought it was his mother. Poor thing, thrown into a ditch and left to die. People who flash their money about are asking for trouble. I heard it had turned up in Gerrard's

Cross. Well, they won't have to look far for the prime suspect. With some kittens. Getting his own back, isn't he, Patterson? His cash, more like.

It was cleaning day at Arcadia. By now Heather had become, at least in her own evaluation, a key witness. After going over the fateful bus journey at least twice for the police, she was now going over it all again for the benefit of the assembled company.

'I'd commented on her bag – ever such a nice raised beaded design. Then I said it must be a bugger to clean, pardon my French, Mrs M. She just smiled then looked out the window for the rest of the journey though I chatted away to her. I said to the Bill, if I'd known it was going to be fatal I'd have been a bit more probing like.'

Mrs Molfrey, who had long since switched off her hearing aid, nodded. Cubby, in the kitchen shelling broad beans, had simply tuned out.

'The stress is really getting to Colin Perrot. I met his wife when I was collecting our Duane from playgroup. They've been horrible to him, that flash lot from Causton.'

There was a knock at the door heard only by Heather who opened it, admitting Avis Jennings. Avis was carrying a cream patisserie tart smothered in cherries, freshly picked from her orchard. And a tiny parcel of newly candied angelica of which Mrs Molfrey was very fond.

'We must have a morsel, toot sweet,' cried Mrs Molfrey as she unwrapped it.

Cubby, hearing only the last two words and assuming they were addressed to himself, put his head round the door.

'Yes, my love. What is it?'

'A confection without parallel, Cubs. Pop the kettle on and we'll all have a nibble.'

Heather, already hardly able to shoehorn her rear end into size twenty tracksuit bottoms, decided to pass on this one. Her mum sometimes picked up one of Mrs Jennings' confections at the WI so Heather knew them of old. She made her excuses, said, 'Ta-ra then,' and lumbered off.

Answering Avis's opening question, Mrs Molfrey admitted she had not yet experienced her door-to-door visit. 'I expect,' she continued, 'that nice Mr Barnaby will be calling personally.'

Avis, inexperienced though she was in the ways of the upper reaches of the CID, thought this a touch unlikely and murmured something to this effect.

'Not at all.' Mrs Molfrey firmly justified her flight of fancy. 'He gave me his direct telephone number. In case I remember what it is I've forgotten.'

'What was that then, Elfie?' Avis spoke absently as she went into the kitchen for plates and some cake forks.

'All I can tell you is that it's something to do with a sound,' shouted Mrs Molfrey. Like a lot of deaf people, she found it difficult to pitch her voice accurately when people moved even a small distance away. 'Unexpected, wrong or not there at all.'

'I see.' Avis knew better than to attempt a shared glance of amusement at these quaint juxtapositions with Cubby. Years ago she had learned that the slightest trace of jocular condescension would evoke a very cool response. She guessed that what others saw as elderly foolishness became transmuted, in his affectionate regard, to charming eccentricity. She watched him pour the fragrant tea then float some marigold petals in Elfrida's beautifully painted, shallow, gold-rimmed bowl.

'It happened on the day Simone went off,' added Mrs Molfrey.

Plainly she had not yet picked up the news of the kidnap. And Avis had no intention of distressing her by passing it on. When they were all sitting round eating, Avis, thinking back to Elfrida's previous remark, said, 'Would it be something to do with our bell-ringing practice, Elfie?'

'In what wise?'

'If you remember, we'd been asked to do Oranges and Lemons for Mr Rouse's funeral. That might be called a wrong sound. A bit jolly for such a solemn occasion.'

'I don't *think* it was that. Although the word "chimes" reverberates somewhat.' Mrs Molfrey frowned. She speared a cherry with a shining green sliver of angelica and sucked on it. 'I expect it will come to me suddenly at dead of night. Or when I'm in the bath, like Archimedes.'

'You must write it down,' said Avis. 'Before it goes again.'

'I shall shout Eureka!' cried Mrs Molfrey. 'And then I shall write it down.'

'Some more tea, my love?' asked Cubby.

'It occurred to me yesterday,' said Mrs Molfrey, handing over her dish, 'that Simone may not even know that Alan has died. It is all so mysterious and distressing. Especially when one remembers how happy they were.'

Avis, who knew all about Simone's bruises and her need for the occasional tranquillising dart, remained silent. Naturally any such conversations with her husband never became public property. Aware now that her friend was becoming genuinely upset, Avis, rather clumsily, tried to change the subject.

'I was wondering if the Brockley girl had gone on holiday.'

'Brenda? I've no idea.' Mrs Molfrey dabbed at her cyclamen lips with a whisp of embroidered lace. 'Why do you ask?'

'I haven't seen her walking Shona for a day or two.'

'I had noticed,' said Cubby hesitantly, not wishing to be thought a gossip, 'that her car is missing.'

'Iris hasn't been out either. I usually spot her in the post office in the early part of the week.'

'I've seen her staring out of the bedroom window,' said Mrs Molfrey. 'Several times, actually.'

Aware of the Brockleys' collective yearning for anonymity and passion for not drawing attention to themselves, all three fell unaccountably silent.

Then Cubby said, 'I did too, about half past five yesterday morning.'

'I hope there's nothing wrong,' said Avis. She spoke with absolute sincerity, for enough sorrow washed through Dr Jennings' surgery to more than satisfy the normal human impulse to take pleasure in the misfortune of others.

'I think perhaps we should call.'

'They won't like that, Elfie,' said Avis.

'But if we contrive an "accidentally on purpose" meeting?' suggested Mrs Molfrey. 'What about when he next goes into the garden? One doesn't wish to pry but sometimes the very people who need help and support the most are the least able to ask for it.'

Cubby, feeling rather awkward and embarrassed, made a non-committal 'mm' sound. He recalled the solitary figure at the window and it now seemed to him that there had been both desolation and yearning in Iris's face. For no reason, he felt she had been standing there for a very long time. A little later, walking along the herringbone path with the milk, Cubby had glanced up again. This time Reg was standing next to his wife with something – a cup or mug – in his hand. She seemed to be ignoring him.

'I will if you really wish it, Elfrida.'

As if this small decision had already been acted on, and that successfully, Mrs Molfrey beamed at everyone. By the time Avis left (carrying a second cardboard box), she was asking for another helping of patisserie and some more angelica.

The second cherry tart was for Sarah Lawson. Avis did not make a habit of such bountiful behaviour. In fact it was the first time she had gone to Bay Tree Cottage bearing a gift of any sort. The truth was she felt awkward calling without a reason. It struck her suddenly that this was the only house in the village where such strictures might apply.

What was it about Sarah? Avis put her carton down on the parched grass and heaved the gate back into position. Her off-putting neutrality, perhaps. Neither friendly nor unfriendly, kind or unkind, Sarah was the sort of person with whom, as the saying went, you never knew where you were. Like most people, Avis was uncomfortable with that.

Not that Sarah gave herself airs and graces. She might be indifferent to everyone else but there was never any hint that she thought herself their superior. But perhaps that was how the truly superior behaved. And there was something about her, a deep involvement in her own thoughts and a general unwillingness to comment on anything that went on outside her own front door, that made one feel quite gross producing even the mildest snippet of gossip.

Of course Avis's real reason for calling was to try and discover Sarah's thoughts on Simone's abduction. This, together with Alan's death, was far too exciting merely to chat about in a general way. Avis wanted to discuss it with the one person whose responses she could not have predicted in her sleep.

She picked up her box again, hesitated then told herself she was being foolish. After all, the woman couldn't bite her. And if, after one or two subtle opening gambits, it was plain Sarah was either bored or irritated, well, thought Avis, I can always change the subject. Or leave.

She knocked on the door. As she did so a cry came from inside the house. Later she was to realise that the two sounds were so close it was impossible that one could have been evoked in response to the other. At the time she thought Sarah had simply called 'Come in'. And so, awkwardly clutching her present, in she went.

Sarah stood by the dusty window. A dead fly hung in the remains of a web in the corner. She was tugging fiercely on a silk scarf, brilliantly striped in olive and aquamarine, knotted round her waist; looping and twisting it through her narrow fingers, almost tearing the thin silk. Gray Patterson was standing in the centre of the room. You could have cut the atmosphere, so Avis told her husband later, with a knife.

Convinced she had interrupted a lovers' quarrel, Avis stumbled into speech. 'I'm so sorry, I'll just leave this . . . I didn't mean, um, that is . . .'

But it was not a quarrel. At least, not as most people would understand the word.

Gray had turned up, as he did almost every day now at some time or other, given a slight tap on the knocker and walked in. Lately she had invariably invited him to do this so he thought it would be all right.

Sarah had been leaning against the old stone fireplace, her arms gripping the far edges of the mantel, her head pressed against the edge. Still as a statue.

Gray, thinking she may not have heard him come in, gave a quiet cough. Sarah whirled round, gasping as from a sudden blow. Although Gray had made no attempt to approach her, she raised her arm as if to fend him off.

'What on earth is it?'

'Go away.'

'Sarah, what's the matter?'

'How dare you just walk in here without knocking!'

'I didn't. That is, I did. Knock. I don't think you heard me.' He took in her white, strained face and staring bloodshot eyes. She was biting her mouth, making a great effort at self-control. A great welt, so red it looked almost raw, lay across her forehead.

'Have you been crying?'

'No.'

'But your eyes—'

'It's the pollen. *All right?*'

'Don't be angry.' She must have been rubbing, almost banging her head against the stone to make a mark like that. 'What on earth's wrong?'

'Go away.'

'How can I just—'

'It's simple. There's the door.'

'With you looking like—'

'*Go away!*'

'I'm worried about you.'

'Mind your own bloody business.'

Back to square one then and with a vengeance, thought Gray. It was as if their amiable conversations in her ramshackle house and lovely wild garden had never happened. He had not deluded himself that these had ever been of a romantic nature but he did think that he and Sarah were slowly becoming friends. Foolishly he had imagined a bond between them.

Well, friends or no friends, he had no intention of

leaving her in this state. He walked into the kitchen and started to fill the kettle.

She shouted angrily, 'What are you doing?'

'Making some tea. After you've drunk it, if you still want me to, I'll go.' He sensed that she had followed him; then saw her shadow fall across the old wooden table. 'Unless you feel the need to tell me about it.'

'I just want to be by myself.' Drained of all vitality, she was leaning her full weight against the door frame. Her gold and silver hair was a damp, lustreless tangle. 'Please don't mess around with that.'

'Sorry.' Gray hesitated then switched the kettle off. He noticed that the front of her sky-blue shirt was covered in damp patches. She must have been crying for hours. Tentatively he reached out and touched her hand which was cold and heavy as a stone.

'Look, Sarah, plainly something dreadful's happened. Won't you let me try and help?'

Ignoring him, she moved back into the sitting room with a slow, dragging walk painfully unlike her usual confident stride. Touched now as much by pity as by concern, Gray followed. As he passed the marble slab, he noticed the warrior's head had disappeared. In its place was a heap of dirty clay, deeply indented as if from many severe blows.

'*Please* tell me what's troubling you.'

Tears of rage and despair sprang into her eyes. She shuddered then gave vent to a harsh explosive sound. 'You make me laugh. You're no different from everyone else in this nosy cesspit of a village. Always on the look-out for a juicy bit of tittle-tattle.'

Her misery made the injustice of this remark irrelevant. In any case he was sure that, even as she mouthed the words, Sarah knew they were not true. She made a few more vaguely unkind, rather rambling comments then faltered into silence.

He watched her gradually become calm but in a terrible apathetic way which was worse than her original anger. Her mouth was haggard with grief.

Yes, thought Gray, that was the word exactly. Grief. She was mourning someone. A dear friend? A lover? Not a parent, for he knew both of them had been dead for some years.

And then, for absolutely no logical reason except perhaps propinquity, Alan Hollingsworth's name came into his mind. And though it seemed a baseless, even cranky notion, it would not go away. He told himself this was nonsense. Sarah had never mentioned the man, appeared barely to know him. But he could not let the idea rest.

'You've been . . . bereaved, Sarah, is that it?'

'Yes, oh yes,' cried Sarah. As if alarmed at this spontaneous outburst, she pressed her hands over her mouth.

Gray knew that the balance of the scene was his. Bereft and fragile, she would have neither the energy nor the concentration to deceive. The phrase 'strike while the iron's hot' seemed brutally appropriate.

Shamedly telling himself that he was acting purely in Sarah's interests, Gray said, 'Was it Alan?'

She was standing over by the window with her back towards him. For a few moments he thought she was going to pretend she had not heard the question. In which case he was quite prepared to put it again. But then she turned to face him. Though pale, she was struggling to compose herself. Only the fingers were busy, tugging at her clothes. Her voice was low and still husky from crying.

'Why did he do it, Gray? I mean, take his own life over a woman like that, trivial . . . greedy . . .'

There was a pause during which Gray realised his teeth were so tightly clenched together his jaw ached. Eventually he said, 'I'm sorry but I don't understand why you are so upset.' Deliberately he emphasised the 'you'.

'It's a question of responsibility.' This was said after some hesitation. It seemed to Gray that she had been searching for an explanation that would be credible yet removed from all intimacy. 'He must have been hiding behind those curtains in absolute despair. Drinking, maybe weeping. If someone had gone in, talked to him . . .'

'It was tried. He wouldn't open the door.'

'I didn't try.'

'Why should you?'

'Aahh . . .' The cry of anguish flared around the room. Neither of them heard the knock at the door. And then suddenly, to Gray's surprise and intense disappointment, there was a third person present.

He watched Sarah struggle to regain her equilibrium. She seemed almost to welcome the interruption and asked Mrs Jennings, who was plainly embarrassed and poised for flight, to stay.

Understanding that this invitation had been made solely for the purpose of getting rid of him, Gray saw no point in hanging around. The moment of revelation had passed and, in retaliation for his momentary cruelty, he had received naught for his comfort.

Serve me right, he thought as he hurried home. He wondered what he should do now. Offer his shoulder as a staunch friend? He couldn't, in all honesty, be sympathetic. Was it possible that an intelligent, lovely woman like Sarah could really have cared for *Hollingsworth* of all people?

That boring, screwed-up, money-grubbing slime ball.

Making his way past the blue piceas that screened his house, Gray discovered a police car parked on the drive. He did not object to the officer's request that he come down to the station to help them further with their inquiries. In fact, he rather welcomed the distraction.

It was all rather different this time round. Perhaps it was the alien setting: a cheerless room with cold blue walls, a floor of some dimpled black synthetic stuff and hard, wooden-backed chairs. The only bright spot was an extremely detailed poster of a Colorado beetle in full technicolour with instructions as to what to do should you be lucky enough to obtain a sighting.

He had been given a cup of tea by the detectives who had previously called at his house. They, too, looked different. Sterner and less approachable, inevitably at an advantage on their own pitch. The older one switched on a recorder, dated the tape, described who was present. The younger, the man who had been so nice to Bess, paced about, unsmiling.

'Thank you for coming in, Mr Patterson.'

'I got the impression I didn't have a lot of choice, Inspector . . . Sorry, I've forgotten your name.'

'DCI Barnaby.'

'Been a long while since I've been chauffeured any-where.' Patterson laughed awkwardly. Whilst not exactly ill at ease, he appeared puzzled at his sudden transportation into the heart of Causton CID.

Barnaby smiled in return. No reason not to at this stage.

'Do we have to have that thing on?'

'I'm afraid so, sir. And as much for your sake as ours.' No one ever believed that, but it was true.

'What do you want to see me about?'

'Just one or two more questions.'

'But I've told you everything I know.'

'The day Mrs Hollingsworth disappeared, Thursday, June the sixth. Do you remember where you were then? What you were doing?'

'Why?'

'Just answer the question, please, Mr Patterson,' said Sergeant Troy.

'I sign on on Thursday. A touch humiliating but I'm getting used to it. Beggars can't—'

'Where would this be?'

'Causton DSS. I went in just before half twelve. Did the deed, felt depressed as one always does afterwards. Went into the Job Centre to no effect then decided to go to a movie.'

'Which one?' asked Troy.

'*Goldeneye*. The new James Bond. I thought I could do with a spot of escapism. And the seats are cheap in the afternoon.'

'What time would that be?'

'Around two thirty, I guess. They'd have the exact time, I assume, at the cinema.'

'And when did you come out?'

'Five-ish.'

'Where did you go then?'

'I drove straight home.'

'Did you go out again that night?'

'No.'

'Did you see anyone you knew, if only by sight, all the time you were out?'

'Not that I noticed. But that doesn't mean no one saw me. Look, what on earth's the point of all this?'

'We feel it may be relevant to our inquiries, Mr Patterson.'

'How, relevant?'

Barnaby saw no reason not to explain. He took the latest edition of the *Evening Standard* from his desk drawer and laid it, front page uppermost, in front of Patterson.

He picked up the paper and gazed at it blankly. He shook his head once or twice then stared, first at one policeman and then the other, in stupefied amazement.

Barnaby stared calmly back. Stupefied amazement neither fazed nor impressed him. Neither did deep incredulity or gobsmacked disbelief. The last time he had seen such a convincing representation was on the face of a multiple rapist for whose capture he had been directly responsible. Proven guilty beyond all shadow of a doubt, the man had left the dock throwing his arms in the air in utter bewilderment that so many learned people could come to such an unbelievably erroneous conclusion.

'Kidnapped? Simone?'

'That's right,' said Sergeant Troy. 'Know anything about it, do you, sir?'

'What?'

'They've asked a ransom of fifty thousand,' Barnaby explained. 'A nice, round figure, wouldn't you say?'

Patterson hardly looked capable of saying anything. Eventually he made a noise that sounded like 'crark?'

'Add on the sparklers,' said Troy, 'and there's you with your money back. Plus fifty for your trouble.'

'Or perhaps you regard it as a redundancy payment, Mr Patterson.'

'Sorry . . . um . . .' He peered at them both, straining as if through a fog. 'Sparklers?'

'A diamond necklace worth over two hundred thousand

pounds has vanished from Nightingales. And also, we believe, an extremely valuable ring.'

'Well, I didn't take it.'

'You don't deny you've been there?'

'I only went into his office. I told you.'

'Is that a fact?' The house having been cleaned many times since Patterson's visit, there would be no trace of his prints. A comforting bit of information that Barnaby saw no reason to pass on.

'Two hundred . . . ?'

Barnaby watched the numerical coincidence take hold. Patterson's eyes became even rounder than the O of his mouth.

'Do you know when he bought it?' Patterson asked.

'Three months ago.'

'Just after . . .'

'Immediately after,' affirmed Sergeant Troy, regrettably with some pleasure.

'Are you trying to say that my life has been ruined,' Patterson lurched to his feet, *'for a piece of bloody jewellery?'*

Troy took a seat then, next to his boss. Both detectives sat quietly, waiting and watching. The tape hissed.

'I find that . . . Oh, shit, what a bastard . . . bastard . . . bloody hell . . .'

Patterson rambled on in this manner as the anger slowly leaked out of him. He slumped back into his seat. 'I suppose it was for her.' He sounded flat and tired. 'His wife.'

'Unless he's been sleeping around. Do you think that's very likely?'

'No. As I've said before, Alan just gets obsessed with one person. Runs them into the ground. Then starts all over again on someone else.'

The Chief Inspector, having heard Hollingsworth's anguish after the disappearance of his wife so graphically described by both Perrot and the Reverend Bream, had not seriously expected any other reply. A further thought occurred.

'Do you remember if he lashed out like this during his first marriage?'

'Lashed out?'

'Financially.'

'Oh.' He thought for a moment then said, 'I think he might have. I know he bought Miriam a fur coat once after they'd had a row and he was feeling very remorseful.' Patterson laughed briefly. 'It wouldn't have cut much ice with her.'

'How well did you know the second Mrs Hollingsworth?'

'You asked me that the other day.'

'Well, we're asking you again,' snapped Sergeant Troy.

'Nothing's changed,' said Patterson shortly. 'I hardly knew her then and I hardly know her now.'

'Did she ever visit your house?'

'No.'

'Or ring you up?'

'No.'

'Did you meet on any occasion outside the village?'

'*No!*'

'Did you know Mrs Hollingsworth at all before she met and married her husband?'

'Of course not.' There was no trace of anxiety in Patterson's voice, only irritation, increasing by the minute.

'When did you last see her?'

'Umm . . . I suppose that time in the phone box. I told you, the other day.'

'Ah yes.'

'I don't understand why—'

'Were you aware that Hollingsworth left a suicide note?'

'How could I be?'

'On a computer. Trouble is, there were no prints on the keyboard.'

'Really?' Gray Patterson frowned. He looked interested but in a detached way, like a man faced with an interesting problem. 'Why would he do that? Wipe them all off?'

'Why indeed.'

'Did he print the message out?'

'No.'

'Very strange.'

'We are considering the possibility that Mr Hollingsworth did not, in fact, key the note himself.'

Barnaby watched that go home. Observed Patterson's sudden unnatural stillness. The way his palms pressed on the metal table. And how the skin tightened along his jaw. Even his curls seemed flattened as if the force of what he had just heard was blowing against him like a gale. He sought consolation and shelter.

'You mean it was an accident?'

'People who die by accident don't spring up again for a few last words,' said Sergeant Troy.

'Of course not.' His face was wiped clear of all impression. 'So that leaves . . .'

'I can see you're way ahead of us, Mr Patterson.'

'And naturally you thought of me.'

'That's right.' Barnaby noted his suspect's continuing immobility. And wondered whether it was due to extreme caution or extreme shock. 'So you will understand that I must question you again about your movements on the night of Alan Hollingsworth's death. And ask you to think very carefully indeed before you reply.'

'I've no need. As I said the other day, I was at home all Monday evening. Out in the garden until around nine and then in the house.'

'Did you, late that evening or early the next morning, visit the property known as Nightingales?'

'No, I did not.'

'When did you last see Alan Hollingsworth?'

'I can't answer that. I don't remember precisely.'

Barnaby waited for a few moments then closed the interview, timed the tape and switched the machine off.

'We have a warrant to search your house, Mr Patterson. Also our Forensic department will wish to examine your car. You'll be asked to hand the keys over.'

'I understand. Can I . . .' He half rose then sat down again. 'Is it all right if . . .'

'You can go home, sir. But please keep us informed of your whereabouts.'

'Don't go taking any holidays in the Caribbean,' said Sergeant Troy.

This spark of levity did not even register.

'Also,' continued Barnaby, 'we'd like a recent photograph. Just a snap will do. Give it to the officer who runs you home, if you would.'

When his escort arrived, Patterson trudged leadenly off without having made eye contact with either of the two detectives again.

'What do you reckon?' asked Troy when they were once more back in Barnaby's office. 'In the frame, is he?'

'I don't know,' replied the Chief Inspector. 'Have to think about that.'

Troy nodded and sat back to wait. He would relax. He

would not bite his nails or run out for a fag. The minutes dragged by. Sergeant Troy's mind rolled back to when he had first been assigned to his present position, now nearly nine years ago.

Then he had found his new boss's refusal to produce an instant opinion on anything and everything somewhat alarming. Barnaby's dislike of drawing rapid conclusions also caused a certain amount of discomposure. But the sergeant had experienced his keenest unease when faced by the chief's willingness to acknowledge embarrassment or failure; the two great taboos of police culture. Barnaby had been known on occasion to admit publicly to both, which made some officers, especially the older ones, awkward in his presence. Resentful of his honesty and courage, in their own self-defence they transformed these qualities, in their canteen conversation, to foolishness and a need to curry favour with the younger element. No one ever suggested this to his face. And through it all the gaffer – Sergeant Troy glanced across the room at the bulky figure lost in thought and fanning itself with a manila folder – didn't give a bloody toss. You had to admire him.

It was nearly seven o'clock. Suddenly Barnaby got up and started stuffing things into a briefcase. 'Time we weren't here, Sergeant.'

'Right, chief.' Another ten minutes and they'd have been on overtime. Ah well, some of us could do with it and some of us are nice and comfortable already, thanks very much.

A brief 'goodnight' and the door slammed.

Troy put on his silky tweed jacket, adjusted his tie with immaculately clean hands and briefly admired himself in the mirror. Smoothing his hair and smiling, he checked his teeth for any foody bits. Finesse he might lack but you couldn't fault him when it came to a tidy mouth.

He unwrapped a stick of Orbit menthol, popped it on to his tongue and set off for the station bar and a glass of weasel piss. Plus a spot of amorous backchat which could well lead, should his cards fall sunny side upwards, to a nice little roll in the hay.

Chapter Seven

Think of a figure. Double it. Add on your weight in kilos, your National Insurance number and the National Debt. Take away the figure you first thought of and you'd still be hard pushed to come up with the degrees centigrade registered in the CID's outer office. The coolest place in the building was the inoperative boiler room.

The heatwave had been going on now for over a week. Chief Inspector Barnaby, gradually dissolving in his fourth floor office, thought the term singularly inept. Waves, whatever their temperature, moved. He was sitting in stationary air the consistency of thick soup. A large fan on his desk heaved hot gollops of it back and forth.

After sleeping badly, Barnaby was feeling bad-tempered and depressed. He had dozed off around half past four after spending hours turning the Hollingsworth mystery over and over in his mind.

There had been an extremely vivid and unpleasant dream just seconds before he woke. He was standing in the greenhouse watching a small, insignificant insect crawling up a pane of glass. He reached out and squashed it with his nail. A tiny spot of reddish brown liquid spurted out. This was followed by another, larger display which ran down the glass in a thin but steady stream. Then a quick gush of much brighter fluid followed by an absolute avalanche of thick, scarlet foam. Barnaby, his hands and jacket sleeves suddenly drenched, had recoiled in horror.

He pushed the image to the back of his mind by tackling the daily papers. Simone's picture was on the front page of all the tabloids, accompanied by some barmily imaginative headlines. Alan had been post-humously promoted to Gordon Gecko status: Dead Tycoon's Blonde Lovely Vanishes! Madonna Lookalike Kidnapped! Have You Seen Sexy Simone – Tragic Widow of Top Financier?

At least, thought the Chief Inspector, shoving aside the *Sun*, they'd been spared Phew! What A Corker!

He flipped through the small handful of house-to-house reports that it was thought were worth putting on his desk but discovered that all of them merely confirmed material that was already on record. He noticed, too, that so far Sarah Lawson had been unavailable on each occasion the police had called and decided he would attempt to visit her himself. As it was Saturday there was a fair chance he would find her in.

The SOCO report on Nightingales' garden and garage, also on his desk, revealed little of real interest. Fingertip searches had found nothing out of the ordinary. The baked earth yielded no footprints, nor were there any disturbed or broken plants. At the far end of the back garden was a tough and densely growing hedge of spiny berberis. Impossible to either climb or push through without leaving plenty of evidence that one had done so.

All the prints in the garage belonged to Alan Hollingsworth. Nothing untoward had been found there. Gardening tools and a mower. Boxes with half-empty paint tins and some wallpaper but no brushes, turps, rags or rollers. Presumably the Hollingsworths employed a decorator when they needed the place tarting up. It was the car Barnaby was interested in. He picked up his phone, buzzed Forensic and asked how long the report on this would be.

'Any minute now.'

'You mean next week?'

'You know your trouble, Chief Inspector?' said Aubrey. 'You've no faith in the system.'

'I can't think why.'

As Barnaby replaced the receiver, Sergeant Troy came in and placed a single cup of coffee on his desk. Barnaby immediately wondered what on earth had driven him to ask for it in this weather. Habit, probably. Yet the first sip was very enjoyable.

'Sergeant Brierley's in the incident room, chief.' Taut as a wound-up spring, he was, a quivery snap to the voice. 'You asked me to let you know when she came in.'

'Thank you.' Not all the door-to-door team had returned when Barnaby had left the previous night. He was particularly interested in discovering how things were at the Brockleys'.

'You sound rather sour, Gavin. Been putting you through it, has she, our Audrey?'

'Well, I wasn't going to say anything but since you mention it,' Troy's Adam's apple rose and fell rapidly, 'how come it's suddenly not OK for me to call her Miss Canteloupe of the year but perfectly OK for her to call me a talking dick?'

'It's called redressing the balance,' said Barnaby. Then, before the conversation could predictably touch on swings and roundabouts, he added, 'Anything worthwhile in over the last half-hour?'

'I notice she don't have to go on no Behavioural Correction Course.'

'I asked you a question.'

Troy pursed his lips. You were supposed to talk about what was worrying you these days in the new, caring sharing cop shop. Lob in for a spot of counselling if you were the wet, spineless sort.

'Well, there's been a call from that poncy jeweller in Bond Street. Recognises Hollingsworth's photo. He is definitely the bloke who bought the necklace. Didn't clock Simone though. Putting it all in writing for us.'

'Excellent.'

'Got the photo fax from *Harpers* on the actual article. Bloody spectacular, it is. Bet she had to spend some hours on her back to pay for that.'

'For Christ's sake, man.'

'What?'

'The woman's been put through hell. By now she's probably dead.'

Won't give a toss what I say then, will she? Troy watched the Brazilian disappearing down Barnaby's gullet and thought he was a funny bloke, the gaffer. If he hadn't seen him with his back against the wall fighting his corner, or making an arrest when the bloke was not only armed but high as a kite on amphetamines, or hanging halfway down a cliff trying to talk up some woman who'd drowned her baby – if Troy had not seen all these things and plenty more besides, he might well have got the impression that the DCI was a touch soft-headed.

They took the lift down to the incident room. Neither man spoke but the younger sneaked a couple of glances sideways. Barnaby looked stern. Imperturbable, you might say, should you be fortunate enough to have access to

Talisa-Leanne Troy's dictionary. The sergeant decided that the chief was cast down at the total lack of possible faces to put in the frame. He could not have been more wrong.

Unlike his bag carrier, who liked things cut and dried as soon as was humanly possible, Barnaby was quite happy to drift, for a short while at least, in what some early mystic once called the cloud of unknowing. He was also reflecting, with a considerable degree of satisfaction, on the recent departure of his *bête noir*, Inspector Ian Meredith, a smug Oxbridge know-all from Bramshill, the police training college for the elite. Deciding, like Alexander the Great, to declare himself a god at the age of thirty-two, Meredith had promptly been elevated to the Flying Squad. The whole station had been relieved to see him go. No one wanted the nephew of the Chief Constable sniffing round the place.

The incident room was not what you'd call lively. Phones were ringing, sure. Staff were studying the notice-boards. Material was being logged and there was a regular low buzz of conversation as information was exchanged, checked, or cross-referenced. But the near frenzy of barely contained activity that could be generated at the start of an urgent or especially dramatic investigation was markedly absent.

Sergeant Brierley not being immediately visible, Barnaby went to the reader's desk to catch up on what was currently coming in. As he had expected, there was more hearsay and suggestion than hard facts. Dozens of people thought they had seen Simone. On a ferry to France. Sleeping in a doorway in Glasgow. At a bistro in Old Compton Street, plainly under the influence of drugs. And dancing on a table in the Old Dun Cow, Milton Keynes.

But there was something really solid from the market-day bus passengers. Two women plus a toddler in a pushchair had followed Simone into Bobby's, Causton's only department store. She had gone into the Ladies, as they had themselves. Both had used the toilet but Simone had still not come out by the time they left. Now, wise after the event, both were convinced that 'poor Mrs Hollingsworth' had been hiding 'from those dreadful people who were after her'.

Alan's first wife had been traced and interviewed in Birkenhead where, after remarrying, she was still working as a general practioner. Barnaby picked up the facsimiled sheets and settled at a desk to read them.

Miriam Anderson, as she now was, had last heard from her previous husband just before his second marriage. He had sent her and her husband an invitation accompanied by what Dr Anderson described as a pathetic and childish letter. This described his present happiness in glowing terms. It also dwelt at some length on the youth, beauty and sweetness of his bride. And on how much she adored him.

'I suppose the idea,' read Barnaby, 'was to make me realise, now it was too late, what I'd thrown away. To be honest, it just made me laugh. I was never more glad to escape from anyone than I was from Alan Hollingsworth. And it was not easy by a long chalk. For weeks after I came back up here he was either on the telephone begging me to come back or driving up to the Wirral and making a nuisance of himself. It was only when I threatened to go to the police that he kept away. Even then, for several months, I was bombarded with letters. In the end I used to chuck them in the bin, unopened.'

Asked in more detail about her first marriage, Dr Anderson more or less repeated what Barnaby had already heard from Gray Patterson. On hearing of Hollingsworth's death, she had assumed it was suicide. Although he had never threatened her, he had threatened to harm himself on more than one occasion when she talked about leaving him.

Dr Anderson could contribute nothing useful as to the matter or manner of Simone's abduction. On both dates relevant to the inquiry she had been provably elsewhere.

Not much meat there – Barnaby pushed the sheets of paper aside – but it was useful to have at least part of Patterson's statement confirmed.

'Good morning, sir.'

'Audrey.' He smiled at the sight of her. At her shining cap of blonde hair and peachy skin and tranquil, shining eyes. You couldn't help it. She gave him a slight but grave smile in return.

'I was going to wait for briefing but Gavin said you were looking for some feedback on the house-to-house straightaway.'

Gavin – not Skipper, not Sergeant. Since Audrey had been made up, such respectful distinctions had melted away. And oh, how Troy resented it. The years of pulling rank – and no one pulls rank like the chronically insecure – had come to an end overnight. Barnaby watched with some amusement as Audrey more than came into her own.

'That's right. How did you get on at the Brockleys'?'

'They're absolutely distraught about their daughter. She still hasn't come back.'

'And there's been no more messages?'

'Nothing. They seem to think we're actively looking for her. It was a bit awkward, sir.'

'I'm sure.'

'I couldn't tell them there's no way we can spend time or resources on a missing person's file unless special circumstances make it necessary.'

'Well, let's hope they don't.'

'As you suggested, I asked if they had noticed anything

at all in the way of comings and goings next door. And I got a really good result.'

'Excellent. Let's have it then.'

'Neither of them have been sleeping much. I gathered that most of their time's been spent staring out of the window, more or less willing Brenda home. Unlike Mr Dawlish, they not only heard Hollingsworth drive away the night he died, but they also heard him come back just before eleven. What's more, they saw him.'

'Ahh,' said the Chief Inspector aware, even as he spoke, of the muscles in his throat slowly tightening. 'Clearly?'

'Very. There's a powerful halogen lamp by Nightingales' garage. Any approach switches it on. He didn't get out of the car – the garage is remote-controlled – but Iris is absolutely sure it was him. They both paid very close attention. Being excited, you see, when a car turned into the close.'

'They would be, poor devils. Was he by himself?'

'Yes. Reg said you could see right into the Volvo. There was no one else in the car.'

'And afterwards?' His stomach became still and cold, then squeezed itself up into an apprehensive ball, as if in expectation of a blow.

'I'm sorry, sir. Nothing.'

'Don't do this to me, Audrey.'

'No one came to the house, Chief Inspector. Iris watched until nearly one. Then she had a rest and Reg took over till daylight.'

'Which window was this?'

'Brenda's bedroom. It overlooks the drive next door.'

'One or the other must've dozed off.'

'They say not.'

'Made some tea, then. Went to the loo. Christ, they're only human.'

'Yes, sir.'

'It would only take a minute. Seconds, even. All we need is Brockley momentarily distracted and whoever murdered Hollingsworth would be across the forecourt and knocking on Nightingales' door.'

'You think they were waiting, then? Concealed somewhere?'

'Yes, I do.' Because the alternative, that there was no one waiting and that Hollingsworth, alone in the house, had taken his own life, was insupportable. Barnaby had abandoned that possibility for good and all within minutes of finding the body and he had no intention of reclaiming it.

'They saw no one leave?'

'No, Chief Inspector.'

'Anything else?'

'Not really. They kept watching but after this only caught what everyone else did. SOCO about the place, officers guarding the house. That sort of thing.'

'Sod them, then.'

'Yes, sir.'

It was just about that time, almost to the second, in fact, that Mrs Molfrey cried out, 'Eureka!'

Not in her bath, as things turned out, but while rootling around with a little hoe among the foxgloves and delphiniums. It was always the case, she thought, flinging down the implement and tottering up the garden path as fast as her twiggy old legs could carry her. Dwell and dwell upon something, seek it out, give it your undivided time and attention and where were you? Up the proverbial gum tree. But put it from your mind, thumb your nose at it even, and here it was, high-kicking its way into your consciousness for all it was worth.

Mrs Molfrey had placed Barnaby's card directly underneath the heavy Bakelite telephone so had no need to hunt for it. She picked it up with trembling hands. Her fingers trembled as she dialled the number and her lips trembled as she prepared to speak. Her mind shook and trembled under the load of this surely revelatory snippet of information.

She was reminded of *The Case of the Chocolate Scorpion*. In this rather racy thirties crime novel an elderly lady, not all that unlike herself (except rather eccentric) had overheard a fragment of conversation through her ear trumpet whilst playing baccarat. Meaningless in itself, she had had the wit to relate these few sentences to the larger pattern of a crime with which the police of five continents had been unsuccessfully wrestling. At the end of the story she was awarded the OBE. Mrs Molfrey exhaled wistfully. No one seemed to write books like that any more.

She got through to an answerphone. Much alarmed, for she had a horror of modern gadgetry, Mrs Molfrey immediately replaced the receiver. She had expected Barnaby to be in his office, awaiting her call. An unreasonable assumption, she now realised. Of course he would be out and about measuring footprints, analysing cigar ash or scraping telltale mud from a sinister pair of galoshes.

Pausing only to wonder if the single of galoshes was galosh, Mrs Molfrey made her way outside again. It was impossible to keep such a dazzling discovery to herself for more than a minute. Cubby had taken some calabrese to Ostlers but would surely be on his way back by now. Reaching the gate, Mrs Molfrey leaned on it to get her breath back. And then, oh joy! who should appear but Constable Perrot.

Hardly of a comparable rank to her would-be confidant, he was nonetheless of the same persuasion and, as such, a more than satisfactory courier. Mrs Molfrey cried, 'Cooee!' and fluttered her tiger-striped organza pelerine.

PC Perrot was just wheeling his Honda out of Nightingales' forecourt. He had made a point of arriving almost half an hour before the postman, to be on the safe side. He had even remembered to bring some gardening gloves, the only sort he owned, should there be any letters to handle. There were three. He stowed them carefully away in his pannier.

'Good morning, Mrs Molfrey.'

'I'm all of a tremble,' said Mrs Molfrey using, for the first time ever, a phrase much favoured by Heather's grandma.

'Is there something I can do?'

'Yes, indeed. There's good news to be taken from Aix to Ghent. Are you my man, Constable Perrot?'

'Pardon?'

'Can I rely on you?'

'Yes.' Perrot's reply was immediate and unthinking. He may not know precisely where Aix and Ghent hung out but reliable he knew, no question.

'Your chief is expecting to hear from me. Indeed he gave me his personal number to that effect but seems to be out of his office at the moment. Hot on the job, no doubt.'

'More than likely, Mrs Molfrey,' said PC Perrot, mentally filing the conversation to entertain Trixie at suppertime.

'Will you be seeing him at all?'

'Going over to the station right now, as a matter of fact.'

'Then you'll pass the information on.' She explained her message clearly.

It made no sense to Constable Perrot. Indeed, he wondered briefly if it was in some sort of code. There was that word Youree? Uri . . .? Yewree something.

'Eureka?' Questioned, Mrs Molfrey told him not to worry. 'You can leave that out. It's not really germane.'

Perrot, already wondering how much of the rest he could safely leave out, mounted his Honda and revved up.

'Remember, not a chink or chime!'

'With you, Mrs Molfrey.'

'And why not, Constable? Why not? That is the question to which we must now address ourselves.'

Perrot lifted a hand in salute, realised he was still wearing his emerald and bright yellow cotton gloves and took them off. Halfway up the lane he passed Cubby Dawlish and saluted again, this time with feelings of the deepest sympathy.

Barnaby was still in the incident room when Constable Perrot arrived at the station proudly bearing his envelopes. He placed them on the desk in front of the Chief Inspector, took a modest step back and waited.

'Left your prints all over these, have you, Constable?'

'Damn!' Perrot leapt into explanation. 'I was – that is, I only. Gloves off a moment. Gardening – I remembered specially. Waylaid the postma—'

'Spare me the sordid details.' Barnaby regarded the envelopes sourly. An AA magazine, an electricity bill and a *Racing Green* catalogue.

'Anything else to report?'

'Well, I hardly like . . . I'm sure it's nothing really . . .'

At this point Sergeant Troy strolled up. He placed himself directly behind the Chief Inspector's desk, parted his thin, dry lips and bared his teeth.

'Wotcha, Poll.'

'Good morning, Sergeant.'

'Quark, quark.'

As Perrot stood there in the painful spotlight of Troy's sneering regard, he imagined himself stumbling through Mrs Molfrey's message. If it had sounded more than a little wonky in the quiet country lane at Fawcett Green, how much wonkier would it sound here?

Perrot looked around at the busy room; all professional ordered activity. *Intelligent* ordered activity. Don't show yourself up, Colin.

'Get on with it then.'

'Pardon?'

'Whatever it is that's "nothing really".'

'I'm afraid it's slipped my mind, sir.'

Troy laughed out loud at this. A harsh, raucous bark.

'I should clear off back to the village then, Constable,' said Barnaby. 'And when you get there I'd like you to do something for me.'

'Yes, Chief Inspector.'

'It's a bit complicated but I'm sure, with a modicum of serious application, you can handle it.'

'Sir.' Perrot straightened his back in readiness.

'Pick up the keys to Nightingales from the solicitors Fanshawe and Clay and check whether or not the switch for the halogen light, which you'll find in the garage, is in the On position.'

'Yes, sir.'

'And – Oi! Poll?'

PC Perrot, now halfway to the exit, halted, sighed and turned round. His cheeks still glowed as a result of the Chief Inspector's irony.

'Sergeant?'

'Canteen's in the basement if you want a bite of lunch.'

'Oh, thank you.'

'It's seed cake on Wednesdays. And cuttlefish omelette.'

'Don't you ever get tired of playing Long John Silver?' asked Barnaby when the door had closed on the hapless policeman.

'Who?'

'A pirate.'

'Well endowed, was he?' asked Sergeant Troy.

At that moment a messenger from Forensic came in bearing a stout envelope containing SOCO's report on Hollingsworth's Audi.

There were few surprises. The boot had been empty but for the spare wheel and a jack. Apart from a single set of unidentified prints on the handles of the rear door, all the fingerprints in the car were those of Alan Hollingsworth, as were some hairs found on the driver's head rest. There were none on the passenger's side or in the rest of the vehicle. Indeed, someone had put a note in the margin to say it looked as if the Audi had been recently valeted.

Valeted. Barnaby, who loathed all such posey phrasing, sucked his teeth with irritation. Anyone would think the bloody thing was being steam-pressed, wire-brushed and a stitch taken up in its upholstery. No doubt during these ministrations it would be asked if it had been on its holidays yet.

Valeted! For God's sake.

The village shimmered in the blazing heat. The white-washed edges of the kerb dazzled the eye and the hedges were thick with dust. At the side of the road the straw coloured grass verges dried and crackled.

In the garden of Arcadia, Cubby Dawlish took an old zinc bowl with a wooden handle, lowered it almost to the very bottom of an ancient barrel and poured the silky rainwater round the base of his Glen Moy raspberries.

As he did this he wondered about Elfrida's new piece of information. He was glad she had passed it on to their local bobby instead of the Chief Inspector who had called at their house. Not that Barnaby hadn't been a very pleasant man but, placed very much at the top of the tree, as it were, he was bound to be extremely busy. Cubby could not bear the thought of Elfrida being brusquely dealt with. Or, much worse, being passed over to a younger person who might not appreciate just how much respect she was naturally entitled to. Who might even, God forbid, have a bit of a laugh at her expense.

As for the recollection itself, Cubby could not pretend he understood its significance. Secretly he suspected it would prove not to have any, though he would not have admitted this to Elfie for the world. She was already awaiting the CID's response with such eager anticipation. Over the hedge Cubby could see Colin Perrot and wondered whether to call across and check out the situation. But before he could come to any decision on the matter, the policeman disappeared inside the garage.

Constable Perrot had made a detour on the way to Fawcett Green to pick up his camera. He was determined not only to obtain the exact information that the DCI had requested but to have photographic proof of same. Carefully he photographed first the sensor switch and, secondly, its immediate surroundings.

After this he wrote a short summary (a novella, merely) of the situation. He read it through, keenly aware, after his boob with Hollingsworth's post, of the need to carry out this next allotted task with speed, efficiency and correctness. Barnaby's threat of an alien posting was never far from his mind.

Once certain the report could not be improved, he locked up and roared away, relieved at having avoided both the inhabitants of Arcadia. Sooner or later he knew one of them was going to ask how Mrs Molfrey's red-hot, number-one star clue – which was how she described it – had been received. And then he was going to be in a right old pickle.

Fortunately Mrs Molfrey was hardly likely to run into Barnaby and ask. Ignorant of the top echelons as he was, even Perrot knew that the officer running a murder investigation spends nearly all his time in the incident room.

Minutes after Perrot's departure, Barnaby's Rover turned into St Chad's Lane and pulled up outside Sarah Lawson's cottage. A shabby red and white Citroën Quatre Chevaux was now parked on the spare patch of oily grass. Sergeant Troy stared at it, a sneer twisting his thin lips.

'Toys R Us, that's where you pick them up. With one hand tied behind your back, most likely.'

Sweltering, mopping his brow with a large cotton handkerchief, Barnaby hove alongside.

'Kiddy cars,' continued Sergeant Troy. 'And foreign at that. If more people bought British, we might not be in the mess we are today.'

'Got rid of the Nissan, have you then, Gavin?'

As well you know, you sarky old bugger. Troy made a mental note to watch his step. When over-heated, the boss was inclined to lash out, willy-nilly. A bit like Long John himself, no doubt.

Clouds of tiny butterflies, like scraps of fawn silk, fluttered over wallflowers and night-scented stock. Barnaby stood in the shade of the bay tree which presumably gave the cottage its name and admired them. Troy knocked on the front door with little result.

'She must be in if the Meccano set's outside.'

'Not necessarily.' Barnaby moved to the nearest window. The type with lots of small panes framed in white painted metal. He glanced inside.

A woman was lying on a sofa covered by what looked like a brightly patterned rug. She had long hair which fanned out across the cushions that supported her. One of her arms hung limply over the side of the sofa, the other lay across her breast. Barnaby was reminded of a Burne-Jones illustration. Or the Millais painting of Ophelia in her watery grave.

He began to feel alarmed. There was no way, unless she was in a drugged stupor, that she would not have heard Troy's knocking. The Chief Inspector tapped gently himself, this time on the glass, without result. Then, just as he was seriously considering breaking in, she sat up. And, very slowly, made her way across the room.

The first thing that struck him was that she looked very ill. The second that, even looking very ill, she was strikingly attractive. She opened the window slightly. He heard the music then. 'Softly Awakes My Heart' from *Samson and Delilah*. It was sung in French, he guessed by Jessye Norman. Or maybe Marilyn Horne.

She said, 'What do you want?' Her breath was sour and cold. In the searing heat of the day, Barnaby shivered.

'Miss Lawson?'

'Yes.'

'We're police officers. We'd like to talk to you for a moment about Mr and Mrs Hollingsworth from Nightingales.'

'Why me? I hardly knew them.'

'We're not choosing you specially, miss,' said Sergeant Troy who was now also at the window. 'This is part of a house-to-house.'

'A what?'

'We're visiting everyone in the village. Just gathering general background information.'

'Oh. I see.'

'I believe someone has called once or twice before,' said Barnaby.

'Have they? I may have been in bed. I'm not well . . .' Here she broke off, making a vague gesture with her left hand in the direction of the front entrance. The two detectives, rightly assuming they were now to be admitted, retraced their steps.

Once inside, having produced his warrant card and introduced himself and Sergeant Troy, Barnaby looked about him.

They had stepped straight into a room crowded with sunlight; the golden beams sought out powdery gatherings of dust and illuminated webby corners. It was a place full of colour and a certain ragamuffin charm. Apart from the sofa, there were a couple of saggy armchairs concealed under vividly striped and patterned dhurrie. Several original paintings hung on the walls, mainly abstract but including one watercolour – pale sand, a limpid almost colourless sea, and sky like a taut sheet of amber silk. Books were everywhere. Stacked on the floor, jumbled about on shelves, piled on the furniture. None looked new. There were art and travel books, some essays. The Chief Inspector recognised the black spines of several well-worn Penguin classics. And marigolds: a blaze of orange in a black and white stone Dundee marmalade jar.

'May we?'

'I'm sorry, yes. Please. I'm sorry.' She switched off the music.

Troy sat down on a ladder-back chair painted with birds and flowers. Barnaby shifted a weighty Thames and Hudson volume on Goya then balanced his bulk on the edge of the sofa.

Sarah Lawson, having the air of someone poised for flight, remained standing. It was the intruders who appeared most at home.

'I understand,' began the Chief Inspector, 'that you had arranged to visit Mrs Hollingsworth on the day she disappeared.'

'That's right.'

'Could you tell me why?' asked Barnaby when the ensuing silence had lasted a full minute.

'She had some stuff for my white elephant stall at the church fête. I went to pick it up. Knocked on the front door, got no reply. Tried round the back and found she'd left the box on the patio.'

'You were invited for tea as well, I believe.'

'Yes.'

'Was that a regular occurrence?'

'Not at all. No.'

Troy made a brief note and looked surreptitiously about him. As always when surrounded by evidence of any sort of creative or intellectual existence, he saw it as a criticism of his own life. Typically, he began to redress the balance.

All these books, snob music. His eye fell on a stained glass panel and a heap of clay. Fancy messing around with that stuff at her age. Like a kid with Plasticine. Pity she didn't take a few minutes off to sweep up some of the grot. Or iron her clothes. He noticed with some satisfaction that the floorboards beneath the soft, washed out but still beautiful rugs were dirty. As a woman, he decided, she was a complete anachronism and it took a man of his cognisance to recognise it.

Delighted at this felicitous conclusion, he tuned back into the conversation. The governor was asking Sarah Lawson when she last saw Mrs Hollingsworth.

'I really don't remember.'

Barnaby was both patient and encouraging. 'When she invited you for tea perhaps.'

'Ahh . . .' Plainly she was grateful for the suggestion. 'That was it. I don't recall the exact date, I'm afraid.'

'The news of the kidnap must have come as a great shock.'

'It did to all of us. I still can't quite . . . I mean, it's not something that happens to people you know.'

The times the Chief Inspector had heard either that remark or a close variation on the theme. Every day thousands of people were burgled, mugged, beaten up, raped, murdered, arsonised – if there was such a word – yet the confidence of the human race that they, their loved ones and acquaintances had personally been granted divine immunity was uncrackable.

'You work in adult education, I understand, Miss Lawson.'

'That's right. At Blackthorn College, High Wycombe.'

'And Mrs Hollingsworth came to your course for a while.'

'Yes, she did.'

'How did that come about exactly?'

'I'd been designing four glass panels for a conservatory. Just finished autumn – fruit, hips and haws, woodsmoke. It was resting up against the car waiting to be wrapped while

I sorted out some sacking. Simone came by and pronounced it "totally wonderful" and said she'd "positively adore" to do something like that.

'Thinking she was only making conversation, I suggested she came along to a class sometime which she said she'd even more positively adore if only she had the transport. So then of course I felt constrained to offer her a lift which was a bit of a nuisance as I didn't always want to come straight home.'

'Is that another of the pieces?' Barnaby had noticed it when he came in, leaning against the stone fireplace. Engraved with glittering snowflakes, stained dark green and crimson. Winter, no doubt.

Sarah nodded. Slowly she reached out a hand and brushed a speck of dust from a holly berry, glowing like a ruby. Then she rubbed a thorny stem gently with her sleeve. This involved turning her back on her visitors and Barnaby sensed a great relief as she did so.

'It's very beautiful.'

'Thank you.'

'You must have more work than you know what to do with.'

'Not really. There are a lot of arty-crafty people in this part of the world. And some of them are very good.'

'Do you ever do puppies or kittens, Miss Lawson?' asked Sergeant Troy. It was Maureen's birthday soon and she loved a nice ornament. Be cheaper, he reckoned, to buy direct, especially from an amateur. Cut out the middle man.

'I'm afraid not.' There was a shred of colour in her voice for the first time – a faint shadow perhaps of indignation.

'Mrs Hollingsworth's was an afternoon class, I take it?' asked Barnaby.

'Oh yes. I don't think she was allowed out in the evening.'

'Her husband kept her on a pretty short leash, it seems.'

'A choke chain, I'd call it.' For the first time her voice and expression became animated. As she turned away, her high cheekbones flushed, a soft dusky rose. She shook her head, it seemed to Barnaby, with irritation. The loose knot of hair loosened further, tumbling over her thin shoulders and concealing her long silver and carnelian earrings. Her pale gold hair, coarse and very thick, had several silver threads which glittered in the sunlight.

The Chief Inspector wondered how old she was. Somewhere, he surmised, between thirty and forty, probably nearer the latter. He got up and walked about with the air of a man needing to stretch his legs, thus bringing himself into a position where he could once more see her profile which was gravely intense. Noticing him, she gave a disturbed, nervous cough and again turned away.

'Could you give me the dates that Mrs Hollingsworth attended your course, Miss Lawson?'

'Roughly, the last half of February. Part of March. The college will have an accurate register.'

'And do you know why she dropped out?'

'Apparently she hadn't informed Alan what she was up to. I discovered later that it was his habit to ring up during the day to see if she was "all right", though what on earth could happen to her in a fast-asleep place like this . . . Anyway, after the first class she told him she had been at Elfrida's when he'd rung. The next week that she'd been having tea with Avis Jennings. The third that she'd just popped up to the shop. The following Wednesday he decided to be persistent. Rang several times during the four hours we were out and demanded to know just exactly where she had been when he came home.

'She told him. God, you'd think it was innocent enough.

He said of course he couldn't stop her but if she persisted he wouldn't have a minute's peace. He asked if she really wanted to load all this extra worry on to his shoulders. What about the fumes? he said. Weren't there chemicals involved in that sort of thing? Simone rang up that same evening and said she wouldn't be coming again. I think she'd been crying. She certainly sounded very subdued. I got the impression Alan was standing over her.'

'You didn't attempt to persuade her differently?'

'Good heavens, no. What would have been the point?'

She was quite right, of course. No doubt any such approach would merely have made matters worse. 'It's some distance to High Wycombe, Miss Lawson.'

'About forty minutes.'

'So, adding up the sessions, that's several hours you must have spent in Mrs Hollingsworth's company.'

'I suppose. Though, if you're driving, most of your attention's on the road.'

'Did she tell you anything about her past life at all?' asked Barnaby. 'Or discuss her marriage?'

'No to your first question. And all I know about the marriage is that she was bored. But then, I think Simone would be bored anywhere. Except perhaps in Harrods.'

'What did she talk about?'

'Oh, rubbishy articles she'd read in magazines. Her stars. What was happening in *Brookside* or *EastEnders*. All Greek to me as I don't have a set.'

'No TV?' Troy gaped in astonishment. He had noticed the absence but assumed it was in her bedroom. He had never in his life met anyone who did not own a television.

'That's right.' She turned to face them then, almost smiling. 'I'm part of the one per cent.'

'So, what with one thing and another, you must have

been quite relieved when she gave up?' Barnaby said.

'Well, I certainly had no objection. And there's always a waiting list.'

He saw her loosen up. Her shoulders slackened, the planes of her face became less tautly defined. Barnaby got the impression that some precarious corner in the conversation had been safely turned. Or a minefield successfully negotiated. Was he being overly dramatic? It could be that she was simply getting accustomed to their presence.

'Was there anyone in the class that Mrs Hollingsworth was especially friendly with?'

'They were mainly pensioners,' said Sarah. She added drily, 'Not at all Simone's cup of tea. She was pleasant enough to them, I suppose. But no, no real friends.' She sat down on one of the armchairs, her narrow, brown hands banded with many brilliant turquoise rings, loosely clasped.

Barnaby didn't like this new composure at all though he found it hard to understand his resentment. After all, if there was no reason for her to feel guilty, why should she not appear calm? Perhaps it was simply that such a state of mind was not conducive to further revelations. He ought to ruffle things up again. Cast around for a remark or question that would really strike home. Difficult when you know next to nothing about your target. So, a shot in the dark it would have to be.

'Did you know he was violent, Hollingsworth?'

'What? To . . . ?'

'To her, yes.'

'No, I didn't.' Her fingers flew, touching her breast, as if to soothe a thudding heart. Her mouth shook. 'I hate that sort of thing. Why women put up with . . . God, how can . . .'

Sergeant Troy, never averse to seeing others all of a twitch, especially when they so plainly regarded themselves as his superior, bit his lip to keep back a grin. Personally he had never hit a woman though it couldn't be denied that they spent half their lives begging for it. Especially Maureen. He regarded this restraint as worthy of a medal.

Barnaby, pushing now, asked Sarah when she had last seen Alan Hollingsworth.

'One never "sees" Alan. Just the car zooming in and out.'

'What about last Monday?'

'No. That was the night he . . . ?'

'Died, yes. Were you at home?'

Sarah shook her head. 'Not in the evening. I went to a film. Farinelli *Il Castrato*.'

'Good, was it?' asked Sergeant Troy, thinking, bloody hell, we've got a right one here.

'The music was wonderful. Which was the reason I went.'

'Alone?'

'That's right.'

'Where was it showing, Miss Lawson?' A page in the notebook rustled loose and was flipped over.

'The Curzon at Slough.' She looked at Sergeant Troy and then across to the Chief Inspector. 'All these questions – you make it sound very serious.'

'An unexplained or suspicious death is always serious,' said Barnaby.

And there and then it happened. There had, after all, been a single undefused mine. Now, as they watched, she stepped on it. And fell apart. She uttered a sort of moan and clutched at her face savagely with her hands. Then keeled over, dropping first to her knees and then, face forward, on to the wooden boards.

'Get some water!'

As Troy ran to the kitchen, Barnaby knelt by the unconscious figure on the rug. But even as he attempted to take her pulse, Sarah Lawson started to come round.

'Sorry . . .' Already she was struggling to get up. There were deep half-moon nail marks on her cheekbones.

'That's all right, Miss Lawson. Take your time.' He gripped her left hand then, putting his other arm round her waist, helped her back into the chair. She felt very thin and light.

'Drink some of this.' Barnaby took the none too clean glass from Troy but she pushed it away, slopping the water over her faded blue skirt. Little crystal droplets settled on the velvet surface and rolled about.

'I don't know what happened. I don't usually . . .'

'When did you last have something to eat?'

'I don't remember. Thursday perhaps.'

Three days ago. 'No wonder you're fainting on us.'

Troy watched the old man bring, in every sense of the word, the woman round. Barnaby had many personas that he drew upon when conducting an interview and this one, everybody's pet uncle, was the sergeant's favourite. Listening to the soft, concerned comments, the suggestion that a friend or doctor should be contacted, Troy was lost in admiration. He acknowledged that it was not a technique he would ever be able to employ. He could not bear to be thought gullible. Or less intelligent than the person he was in conversation with, no matter how much of a simpleton that man or woman might be. It was a matter of pride. The chief, on the other hand, couldn't care less. Whatever means were needed to winkle people out of

252

their protective shells, those means would be brought into play.

Now he had stopped speaking and an atmosphere of persuasive calm took over the room. Into this pool of silence, as Barnaby had known she would, Sarah Lawson eventually voiced the real reason for her nervous collapse.

'I was surprised to hear you say that, about Alan. People in the village . . . we all thought he had committed suicide. I mean, wasn't there a note?'

'Not really,' said the Chief Inspector.

'I see.' She took a deep breath. You could see her, gathering both energy and wits together, as if for an affray. 'Was it an accident then?'

'We're in the middle of our investigations, Miss Lawson. I'm afraid I'm not able to discuss the matter in any sort of detail.' He wondered if she would be able to bring herself to take the next step and speak the unspeakable. The M word. So much more appalling, to the Chief Inspector's way of thinking, than what is coyly called the F word, and yet bandied hither and yon in polite society, heard daily on Radio Four without a single squeak of complaint from Outraged, Tunbridge Wells, and printed on the spines of books in respectable libraries everywhere. Miss Lawson chickened out.

'Of course. I understand.'

He decided to leave it there. For now. A day or two to recover, to settle into the reassuring belief that she had seen the last of them, and he would have her brought into the station and find out precisely why she had fainted from emotion on discovering that Alan Hollingsworth had not died a natural death.

'That woman's a dyke,' said Sergeant Troy as they made their way towards the car.

'Oh, yes?' Barnaby laughed. 'How do you make that out?'

'Going out of her way to watch a movie where men's todgers are chopped off.'

'Balls, not todgers.'

'Oh well,' said Sergeant Troy, attempting a little low-key irony of his own for once, 'that's all right then.'

Several hours later Barnaby, his face by now grey with fatigue though lightening by the minute, was in the kitchen at Arbury Crescent shaving thin curls of Parmesan from a large knobbly lump, holding the cheese steady with the palm of his hand and using a potato peeler.

He had a little grater described by his daughter as a 'piss elegant Italian job'; a souvenir from Padua. However, though extremely smart in matt black and chrome, the top kept falling off and Barnaby had soon reverted to his old familiar ways.

In a square wooden bowl he had placed some young globe artichoke hearts, black olives, strips of red pepper and chunks of his neighbour's home-grown Ailsa Craig tomatoes. Now he tore up the heart of a cos lettuce, cut some anchovies in half and added garlicky croissants, kept hot in an iron pan. Unwinding slowly, feeling his joints loosen, the tightness across his shoulders ease, little by little, he put Fawcett Green, the Hollingsworths, Penstemon *et al* from his mind. Gradually, over the years, he had become quite good at this. One had to survive.

Joyce had already prepared a vinaigrette with herbs from the garden, lemon juice and olive oil. She made salad dressing, toast and cups of tea and that, unless she was on her own and had only herself to please, was that.

Barnaby's wife was a dreadful cook. Not dull or

unadventurous; on the contrary, she had quite a bold, if rather haphazard, way with a chopping knife and an egg whisk. No, she simply had no gift for it. This in itself, of course, might not have mattered. Plenty of people with no talent for cooking manage to turn out perfectly edible meals. Some of them even earn a living at it. But Joyce was further handicapped in that her taste-buds seemed to have had some sort of bypass surgery early in their career. Her palate was, as you might say, tone deaf. She had once been memorably described, though not by him, as the Florence Foster Jenkins of the chafing dish.

He took a couple of glasses from the fridge, filled them with Montana McDonald Chardonnay and wandered into the conservatory. There, surrounded by ferns, grasses, orange and lemon trees and fluorescent blossoms the size of frisbees, Joyce reclined, like Titania, on a flowery bed.

'Oohh, lovely.' The *Independent* slid to the floor.

'Budge up then.' Barnaby gave his wife her drink and sat beside her on the bamboo sofa. He took a long, deep swallow of the wine which was truly marvellous: silky soft and smelling of melons and peaches.

'This is a bit of all right,' said Joyce.

Barnaby put down his glass, took hold of one of Joyce's slender brown feet and started to stroke it gently. She watched him for a moment then sighed.

'They're always the last to go, feet.'

'Don't talk such rubbish. Nothing's "gone", as you put it.'

This was only partly true. Her ankles were still slender, the skin on her burnished calves and plump upper arms remained unwrinkled, her curly mop of hair was still more brown than not. But the blurred line of her bottom jaw would soon become a double chin. Nose to mouth lines, barely sketched in a few years ago, were now engraved. Her eyelids drooped. She would be fifty in two weeks' time. Where had the years gone?

'Will you still love me when I'm old and grey?'

'Good lord, no. I'm already planning a new life with Audrey.'

'Is that why you bought those polka-dot boxers?'

'We're thinking of New South Wales.'

'Supposed to be very nice there.'

'Great grazing land. And a mighty fine place to raise youngsters.'

'Oh, Tom.' She caught his hand, pressed it to her cheek, against her lips. 'Do I still look forty?'

'You've never looked forty, sweetheart.'

Barnaby sympathised with his wife's gloomy apprehensions. Time was when birthdays had a proper sense of the order of things, strolling along at more or less regular yearly intervals. Now they turned up every other Thursday. Importuning, leering, tapping you on the shoulder. Best not look round.

'Come on, I'm starving. Let's eat.'

He was starting to wonder whether new perfume was a good idea after all. Barnaby was keenly aware that, even after buying gifts for nearly thirty years for someone he knew better than anyone else in the world, he didn't always get it right. Lack of time and, though he didn't like to admit it, defective artistic vision were largely responsible.

Cully was something else. Even as a young child with very little money, his daughter had had the knack. She would scour charity and junk shops and, later, auction rooms, dress agencies and the posh sales, always coming up with the one thing that the grateful recipient vowed they could never live without.

One Christmas, aged eight, Cully had been with her father rootling through what he described as 'a box of old rubbish' when she had found a soft leather bag, dark blue in the shape of a lotus. It had a broken zip and a long, frayed strap. Unable to dissuade her from spending twenty-five pence, he had then seen the rest of her money go on three brilliantly coloured feathered birds and some vivid crimson tissue which she had then made into paper roses. Nestling the birds inside the flowers, she had tucked the whole lot inside the lotus.

Joyce's cries of delight had to be heard to be believed. The birds were still perched on a house plant in the spare bedroom. The lotus eventually disintegrated after years of constant use as a peg bag. Her husband's gift of an expensive cardigan with a snowflake design had hardly seen the light of day.

As they wandered into the dining room she said, 'Will you be here on Tuesday evening, Tom? Cully's coming over to pick up the movie we taped.'

'I thought she'd changed her mind about watching it.'

'She's still not sure.'

Their daughter was about to start rehearsals for a revival of Pam Gem's play *The Blue Angel* at the Haymarket. The 1930s film had recently been on television and, the Bradleys' video being on the blink, Joyce had done the honours.

'So, will you?'

'I shouldn't bank on it.'

'But you'll try?'

They sat down, talking about their only child. About her career; flourishing. And her marriage; still in existence but, according to her father, hanging by a thread.

Joyce was more optimistic, believing that outsiders – and

especially parents – never really know exactly what's going on. It was true there had been plenty of friction. The last splendid display ended with a Coupe Jacques whizzing across a table at La Caprice and a month's trial parting.

The reconciliation, just as melodramatically staged and verbally inventive, took place on the roof garden of their Ladbroke Grove flat. It brought out half of Oxford Gardens who, when the champagne was finally broached, spontaneously broke into loud applause.

'Actors,' murmured Joyce, and turned her attention to the meal.

Cold lemon and tarragon chicken with Jersey mids. Followed by the salad, a fruity piece of Mimolette and a dish of golden Mirabelles. Barnaby was reaching out for some more potatoes.

'You can't have those and French bread. And cheese.'

'I'm having second thoughts about all this dieting.'

'Put them aside, Tom. The doctor said—'

'I'm beginning to wonder if excess weight is really harmful at all. I think it's a canard put about by the manufacturers of slimming products and all those loathsome magazines.'

'You know very well—'

'The words "low fat" should be stricken from the English language.' He tucked in. 'I shall become more relaxed about this whole food thing. Let it all hang out.'

'Sergeant Brierley won't like that.'

'Seems to work for Gerard Depardieu.'

'Gerard Depardieu's French.'

Having run amiably through this not entirely unfamiliar routine, the Barnabys finished eating in a comfortable silence. They had coffee in the garden, sitting on a bench in the rose arbour. The twilight air was heavy with perfume. A

Himalayan musk rose clambered above their heads.

In the dusk the trees and shrubs were that strange steely colour, not quite blue, green or grey, which, if seen in the sky, would indicate a coming storm. Already their outlines were indistinct as they merged into dark clumps. The sky was thick with pale stars.

The birds were quiet but, three or four houses away, someone was playing a piano. Satie, the third *Gymnopédie*. Stumbling through it, repeating a phrase over and over again. Rather than breaking, it emphasised the silence.

Barnaby put his coffee cup on the grass and his arm round his wife. He kissed her cheek, her lips. Joyce relaxed against him, slipping her hand in his.

In the house the telephone rang. Barnaby cursed.

'Don't answer it.'

'Joycey . . .'

'Sorry, sorry.'

'It might not be the station.'

'With that timing?'

'At least we've eaten.' The words were called over Barnaby's shoulder as he strode across the lawn.

Joyce gathered up the cups and followed more slowly. When she came into the sitting room he was already putting on his jacket. Half a lifetime of moments like this did not make them any easier.

'I suppose we should be grateful it isn't Saturday week. We might have all been rollicking around singing "Happy—"'

He turned aside but not before she had seen the expression on his face. Immediately Joyce's whole demeanour changed.

'It's something terrible, isn't it, Tom?'

'I'm afraid so.'

'What's happened?'

'They've found a woman's body.'

'Oh God. Do you think it's—'

'How the hell should I know who it is?' It was quicker that way. But lying made him even more irritable. He moved into the hall, scrabbling in his pocket for the car keys and shouted, 'Don't wait up.'

Chapter Eight

It was a member of the NCP staff who first spotted the woman. She was lying, almost completely concealed, behind a large Buick. He could see that she was unconscious and badly injured and immediately notified Heathrow police station to which each of the car parks had a direct line.

The duty officer arrived, closely followed by a doctor from the Medical Centre of the terminal, who pronounced life extinct. They were followed by a police unit from the station proper and an ambulance. It having quickly been decided that the death could be suspicious, the body was covered, the coroner's office contacted and the whole floor sealed off. At this point no one had any idea of the corpse's identity.

The numbers of every car on that level were checked on the Police National Computer and attempts were begun to trace the owners. Quite a few of them turned up unsolicited within the first couple of hours of the investigation and were not best pleased at finding themselves unable simply to climb into their vehicles and drive away.

The Forensic Laboratory Liaison Sergeant came out and examined the body in queasily precise detail after which, some five hours after it had first been discovered, it was transported to the mortuary at Hillingdon Hospital. There its fingerprints were taken and all of its clothing bagged and sent to the nearest forensic department should analysis eventually prove necessary. Scenes of Crime then began an analytical assessment of the area.

By nine o'clock the following evening the police at Heathrow believed they had possibly discovered the identity of the dead woman. The owner of every vehicle but one on the level where she was killed had been traced and interviewed either in person or by telephone. The exception was the possessor of a dark brown Mini. This was registered under the name of Brenda Brockley at an address within the jurisdiction of Causton police who were duly contacted. It was this notification which led to the call that had so rudely interrupted Tom Barnaby's sweet dalliance with his wife.

Heathrow police station is situated in a web of arterial roads about a mile from the airport proper and surrounded by an unlovely mass of hotels, petrol stations and factory buildings. In the office of Inspector Fennimore, DCI Barnaby and DS Troy were given the background to the discovery of the body. They in their turn gave what information they had on Brenda's disappearance.

The postmortem was due to be carried out at eleven the following morning by a Home Office pathologist. Until then the precise cause of death would not officially be known but the doctor who had first examined the body was of the opinion that a savage blow to the head was to blame.

'There were other injuries,' explained Inspector Fennimore, 'consistent with the girl being struck by a car. I think it's likely this flung her to the wall against which she was found rather than her being put there after death.'

'You mean we're talking about a hit and run?'

'It's the most likely conclusion. Scenes of Crime photographs may help us there. Certainly there were tyre marks on her skirt. Why, have you any reason to suspect a deliberate killing?'

'Perhaps.' Briefly Barnaby explained the situation at Fawcett Green. 'Is it possible you could run a check for us on cars parked there on Monday the tenth of this month? From around eight p.m.?'

'We can do that for you, yes. Are you looking for anything special?'

Troy passed over the registration numbers belonging to Alan Hollingsworth and Gray Patterson. Inspector Fennimore made a careful note and returned the card.

'Were you given any idea of the time of death when she was first examined?' asked Barnaby.

'Dr Hatton thought it had probably occurred around three days ago. Which would put it at some time Monday evening.'

'It's incredible she wasn't found earlier,' said Barnaby. 'Aren't these places patrolled at all?'

'Good heavens, yes. Every hour, according to the NCP staff. But they don't have time to go all round and in between every single vehicle. Mainly they're on the look-out for any cars that have been damaged or dodgy people. Anyone dealing, passing stuff – that sort of thing.'

'Even so, sir,' interrupted Sergeant Troy. 'A body—'

'You'll see when you get there how it could have happened. She was lying in the corner at the junction of two walls hidden by this big American car. Our Forensic guy thought she had probably been thrown clean over it.'

'Christ,' said Barnaby.

'And though the place is designated short-term, people

leave their vehicles for varying periods. The Buick has been there for nine days. The driver went on a weekend trip to Basle and ran it on a bit.'

As Inspector Fennimore now seemed to have come to the end of his information, Barnaby nodded to Troy who produced an envelope and handed it across the desk. The inspector drew out three photographs.

'I'd like all of those circulated around the Terminal One complex,' explained Barnaby. 'Shops, cafés, check-in desks, bureaux de change. And include the National Car Park staff, if you would.'

'No problem.' He studied the pictures. 'That certainly looks like the dead girl. Is this the man you believe to have been murdered?'

'That's right. The other woman is his wife, a probable kidnap victim.'

'Surely she won't have been seen here then,' said the inspector.

'I'd still like it included.'

'Fine by me. There'll have been some plane spotters on the top level during daylight hours. Several of them are regulars. We'll show them the pictures as well.'

'Thank you. I really appreciate this.' The Chief Inspector spoke with sincerity. Generous and wholehearted cooperation between varying police authorities could never be taken for granted.

'I'll arrange for a copy of Scenes of Crime findings and the postmortem report to be sent to you direct.'

'And the dead girl's prints to be sent to our Forensics, if you would.'

As Barnaby rose to leave, Fennimore rang the airport and arranged for him to be met and escorted to the place where the body had been found.

* * *

The tape barriers had been dismantled. The Buick coupé, its examination complete, rested in all its glittering two-tone emerald and apple-green glory. Chrome fins, fenders and twin exhaust, their shining surfaces somewhat subdued beneath the residue of SOCO's powdering, writhed and twisted around and about.

Sergeant Troy, vastly impressed, immediately saw himself in the car – hood back, naturally – coasting along, à la *American Graffiti*. Lightly caressing the ivory-padded steering wheel with his right hand, his left arm negligently draped along the back of the passenger seat. By his side an exquisite girl with a tumble of blonde hair, glossy scarlet lips and wearing shorts a man could tuck into his glove compartment and still have room for the halter top. Music blasting out of the car radio. 'Earth angel, Earth angel . . . Puleeze be mine . . .'

'You in a bloody trance again?'

'No, sir. Of course not.' Troy was furious at being shown up in front of the policeman who had accompanied them. He stepped closer to the car, studied it intently and nodded several times. He pictured cool things, hoping this would bring his colour down.

'Where exactly was she found?'

'Just here, Chief Inspector.' The constable moved down the side of the car and Barnaby followed.

He could see now what Fennimore meant. The Buick was last in line almost parallel to the exit and flush against the wall. A body lying behind it could easily have remained unnoticed for several days.

There were smears of blood on the concrete about two feet above ground level, presumably from the injuries to her head. Whether she had received these after being run over or not until hitting the wall, later analysis would no doubt determine.

Crucial also was where the vehicle that struck her had been parked. It must have been going at a fair old lick. Travelling from the far side of the bay it would have been possible for someone in a hurry to pick up the necessary speed. The nearer one came to the point at which the body was found, the harder this would become. Really close and you were talking about a deliberate revving up and stamping on the accelerator.

Barnaby sighed. He went and stood in the centre of the white exit line and stared up the empty ramp and tried to picture Brenda Brockley in the last moments of her life. Had she been running after someone? Or running away? Plainly she had been knocked down by a moving vehicle but was it this impact that had thrown her over the gaudy Buick? Perhaps she had been crammed into that ugly grey stone corner by the driver, anxious to gain time to put some distance between himself and the result of, at the best, dangerous driving.

Two cars were now approaching at a sedate 5 m.p.h. Barnaby stepped to one side and watched them pass, thinking what an old cynic it would be who made any connection between their tortoise-like progression and the presence of a uniformed copper.

The next step was Hillingdon Hospital to which Sergeant Troy drove with no great eagerness. After a cup of tea and a longish wait in the security office, both officers were directed to the mortuary.

Though the experience was nothing new to either of them, they reacted in very different ways. Barnaby, though never completely detached, had over the years come to accept what now lay all about them with a certain amount of saddened resignation.

Troy who, until he was around twenty-five, had been convinced he was immortal, was still not a hundred per cent sure that he would be going the way of all flesh. He knew it was true but he couldn't believe it. A bit like hearing Terminal Cheesecake had made the Top Ten. In any case, the way things were shaping up right now, what with science and all, some magical potion or process of suspended animation was bound to be discovered long before his turn came round. Perhaps he could be frozen. Rich people in the States were. One man had just had his head done – lowered into a cylinder accompanied by clouds of dry ice. Troy had seen it on the telly. He pondered now on what bit he might have preserved should the chance arise, on what portion of his anatomy had given the most happiness to himself and the world about him.

'Up this end, Sergeant.'

'Right, guv.'

The attendant had already folded back the unstained, white sheet. Barnaby stood looking down at a youngish woman of scarcely describable ugliness. Her head was lying at an unnatural angle along the twisted line of her shoulder. A great beak of a nose, no chin to speak of, a tiny puckered drawstring mouth. Although her eyes were closed they still bulged, fish-like, beneath swollen blue lids. Her brown hair, stiff with dust and grit, was short and plainly cut.

Barnaby had a sudden vivid recollection of his own daughter who was so insistently lovely there was no getting away from her. No one pretended life was fair but unfairness on this scale must indicate a quite savage whimsy on the part of the Fates. To what despair must such a profile have reduced this poor girl?

Having called Sergeant Troy over and now sensing his approach, Barnaby felt a need to shield Brenda Brockley from any comments. He flung the sheet over her face as he had once, long ago, pulled down the skirt on a corpse lying in a muddy ditch.

'Sorry, Audrey. I thought, as you'd already met and talked to them . . .'

'That's all right, sir.'

It was not the first time Sergeant Brierley had travelled alongside a male colleague on his way to break the news dreaded above all other. Not the first and, she had no doubt, not the last.

She sometimes thought her approach up the path or arrival on the doorstep might alone be enough to telegraph the reason for their visit. So many people realised now, from watching various police programmes, that a female officer invariably accompanied the bearer of ill tidings. A pastoral presence; that was the idea. Someone to make the tea. To listen while the bereaved wept and shouted, rambled with repetitive and confused anguish or brought out photographs of the newly dead. Sometimes they would just sit silently, grief breaking them apart, like a hammer shattering a stone.

Chief Inspector Barnaby rang The Larches' bell. Two thirty in the morning but there was still a light on downstairs. Like Audrey, this was the part of the job he hated most. And it was not only psychologically uncomfortable, it could be dangerous. As in ancient Greece, the messenger's report could sometimes bring about quick and savage retribution. Barnaby knew of an officer detailed to inform someone that his pregnant wife had been killed by a drunken driver. In a fit of agonised rage, the man had snatched up the first weapon that came to hand – a set of fire irons – and struck out with them. The sergeant had almost lost an eye.

As soon as Barnaby rang the bell, the dog had its paws up on the windowsill. She wasn't barking this time. Just staring silently out. There was a full moon, a great circle of glowing alabaster. The close was flooded with cold, silver light.

Reg opened the door. He looked at them both. Stared into their faces, one at a time, with great intensity. His pallor, already very pronounced, deepened to a ghastly whitish-grey. He stood aside so they could enter.

Iris, wearing a quilted nylon housecoat over her nightdress, was seated bolt upright on the settee facing a blank television screen. She got up quickly when Barnaby entered. Unable to read his expression as her husband had done, her drawn face plumped up with anticipation.

'Is there any news?'

'I'm afraid it's bad news, Mrs Brockley. The body of a woman was found earlier this evening at Heathrow Airport—'

'No!'

'I'm very sorry but we believe it to be that of your daughter.'

A long pause. Then, with one swift movement, Iris doubled over and started to howl. Bloodcurding sounds interspersed with little snorts and grunts of agony. Audrey crossed over and tried to comfort her but was pushed away.

Reg remained standing, staring desperately around. He seemed to be seeking a third person. Someone perhaps with new information rendering that which had suddenly brought death into his house null and void.

Barnaby repeated himself. 'I'm so sorry.'

'What . . . how did . . . ?'

'She was hit by a car.'

'Are you sure?' The words were blurred, spoken through flabby lips. 'I mean that it's Brenda?'

'Obviously the body has not been officially identified—'

'Well then!' shouted Reg, a parody of a sergeant major on parade with his ramrod stance and bristly moustache and unfocused, staring eyes. 'You can't know for sure. They don't know, Iris. Not for sure.'

'Don't know?'

This was terrible. Barnaby saw the beginnings of hope in Iris's tortured face. He spoke quickly before it could gain any sort of focus.

'It is the person in the photograph you left at the station, Mr Brockley. There's no doubt about that.'

At this, Iris began to scream silently, opening and closing her mouth with great energy and drawing her lips back in a savage snarl.

Barnaby said, 'I think you should ring your GP, Mr Brockley. Is it Jennings?'

'You can't do that. He might tell someone.'

'Your wife needs a sedative.' The Chief Inspector could hardly believe he had heard aright. 'I imagine you could do with some help as well.'

When Reg did not reply, Barnaby picked up a tapestry address book by the phone and opened it under J. Then under D with more success. While he dialled, Sergeant Brierley asked if she could make the Brockleys some tea. Iris, even *in extremis*, was then compelled to do the correct social thing. Somehow she got herself into the kitchen but then just stood gazing blindly around, unable to remember where the teapot was, let alone the tea.

Shona, having long since appreciated the abandonment of all previous rules and regulations, was lolling in an armchair on a mass of scatter cushions. She jumped down when the two women left and followed with a melancholy swagger. As Barnaby replaced the receiver, Reg began to argue.

'Photographs aren't real life. You should get someone who knew her to do a proper identification. Try Mr Marchbanks, from the office. Or Miss Travers from Personnel. They thought the world of Brenda.'

To his shame, Barnaby became aware of a flicker of irritation, as if this man's refusal to accept the loss of his only child was somewhat irrational. After all, it was not as if such a reaction was out of the ordinary. Shock took different people different ways and one of the most common was an inability to believe that what had truly happened, had happened. And who would not use every ounce of energy to hold the smashing of their entire world at bay? How would I cope if it was Cully? wondered the Chief Inspector. And knew that it would finish him.

'Why don't you sit down, Mr Brockley?'

'Yes.' Reg walked hesitantly to the nearest chair, running the tips of his fingers over the arm before lowering his body, like a blind person. He said, almost to himself, 'Why on earth would Brenda have been at Heathrow?'

Unable to answer, Barnaby asked if there was anyone Reg would like the police to contact.

'What?'

'A neighbour? A relative perhaps?'

'What for?'

'You and your wife will need some support, sir.' Silence. 'And help, if only of a practical nature.'

'We're a very private family.'

It seemed unnecessarily cruel to point out that they would not be very private for much longer. The fact that their daughter had lived next door to a couple who were themselves currently making lurid headlines would not be missed by the tabloids. In next to no time journalists and photographers could be swarming all over their neat little pea shingle drive. Barnaby wondered if he could perhaps prepare the Brockleys for this invasion without being too blunt about it. He suggested they might like to go and stay with friends for a few days. Dully, Reg explained that they had no friends.

Audrey, having brought Iris back into the sitting room, was handing round cups of tea when the doorbell rang.

Barnaby had been brief on the telephone, simply telling the Brockleys' GP that they had received very bad news and that his presence was urgently required. Audrey let Dr Jennings in and spoke to him in the hall, explaining the situation in more detail. He entered the room looking deeply shocked, went over to Iris and began to talk quietly. Eventually he persuaded her to get up and he and Audrey half led, half carried her upstairs.

As soon as they had gone, Barnaby began to speak. He did this from regretful necessity knowing, from long experience, that there was no way to make the sudden transition from the personal to the practical sound anything but crude, even heartless.

'I was wondering, Mr Brockley . . .'

Reg did not respond. He was sitting quietly, resting his elbow on one knee and his forehead in the heel of his hand, as if shading his eyes from an unspeakable catastrophe.

'. . . if you feel up to answering one or two questions.'

'About what?'

'Well, Brenda. Time is very important in a situation like this. Your daughter has already been dead for perhaps five days. The sooner we can start to gather information, the better our chances are of catching whoever brought this tragedy about.'

In normal circumstances this sort of fudge-up would have rung an extremely loud warning bell, for there was no logical reason why knowing the background to a random hit and run victim's life would help trace the driver responsible. Barnaby was banking on Reg's devastation not to spot this. And on his remarkable subjection to authority.

'So if you could tell me a little—'

'She was very highly respected.'

'I'm sure—'

'You won't find anyone to say a word against her.'

'Forgive me if I recap on ground you may have covered at the station,' he would look over the couple's earlier interview when he got back, 'but it's obviously very important that we get every detail absolutely right. She dashed out of the house – I think that was how you put it – at around about seven thirty.'

'*Watchdog* was on.'

'Did Brenda say anything at all as she went out?'

'She just ran off.'

'Nothing about meeting anyone?'

'No.'

'Did she take a coat?'

'No.' He was becoming querulous. 'I *told* them all this.'

'Yes, I'm sorry, Mr Brockley. You said Brenda had no special friends. Was there anyone at work perhaps she was close to?'

'No person more than another. She got on with everyone.'

Barnaby took this with a grain of salt. No one got on with everyone, but the pitifully unattractive needs must develop their own defences and stratagems against rejection. Perhaps Brenda's had been a continuously compliant and ingratiating manner. Well, he would soon find out.

'They bought her a lovely brooch,' said Reg. 'With her name on.'

'What about telephone calls at home? Or letters?'

'From men, you mean?'

'Not necessarily, sir.'

'Brenda was very choosy.'

Barnaby narrowed the circle, asking about possible acquaintances in Fawcett Green. He got nowhere. Brenda Brockley had got up, gone to work, come home, had her tea, walked her dog and gone to bed. That was it. The life plan.

'Although . . .'

'Yes?'

'It's nothing, really. Just that, over the last few days, she has been, well, different.'

'In what way?'

'Abrupt. She's always had a lovely way with her. Mummy and I insisted. Courtesy costs nothing. But then she started getting all reserved. Not joining in the conversation. Refusing to answer questions about her day. That sort of thing.'

Barnaby, who lived half his life in just such a manner, much to his wife's annoyance, hardly knew what to say. But it was interesting that this change in Brenda's behaviour seemed to have taken place around the time of Simone Hollingsworth's disappearance.

'I suppose we'll never know what the problem was now.' Reg's voice had become strained and forlorn.

There seemed little point, at this stage, in being any more precise or stringent. It could even be counterproductive. Iris, when she was in any sort of state to answer questions, might well be more helpful.

Barnaby explained that it could be necessary to make

Brenda's room available for examination some time during the next few days. Bearing this in mind, would Mr Brockley have any objection if he, Barnaby, had a look around right now?

'Normally I'd have to say no,' replied Reg. He got up quickly, as if glad to have a definitive objective. Almost bustling across the carpet. 'Her door was always locked, you see.'

'Oh?' Barnaby was immediately intrigued as to why a blameless spinster, long past the adolescent 'Keep Out – This Means You!' phase, would do such a thing.

'But she dashed off in such a rush she didn't take her bag.' As they climbed the stairs he added, unhappily, 'We've spent a lot of time up here, over the past few days.'

He hovered wretchedly just inside the door while Barnaby, who would much rather have had the place to himself, looked around the silent, abandoned room.

A pink candlewick dressing gown was draped over the back of a chair. The curtains and bedspread were of a matching trellised print of insipid leaves and flowers. There was a clock radio and a couple of framed country scenes so completely characterless they could have been set almost anywhere. Above the bed was a large framed print of two small street urchins, a boy and a girl, holding hands and crying. Tears, in the form of several tiny, clear glass beads, were glued to their cheeks.

Barnaby, who had seen the likeness more than once before, remained bewildered. What sort of person would want, permanently displayed in their home, images of distressed children?

He opened the wardrobe and looked briefly inside. Dun-coloured suits, a single patterned dress (brown and olive green), several pairs of highly polished black and navy court shoes, all on trees. A drab overcoat. Dressing-table drawers revealed some plain cotton underwear and several pairs of heavy denier, flesh-coloured tights. They held no perfume or make-up. Perhaps she had long ago recognised the futility of any attempt at cosmetic improvement, let alone transformation.

Close to the narrow, single bed was a glass shelf supported by curly metal brackets, painted white. This held soft toys and a small stack of romantic novels.

Barnaby turned his attention to the pretty antique desk placed by the window. He lifted the lid. The desk was empty but for a flat, dark green, beautifully marked book which he took out and opened. An action that finally provoked Reg into speech.

'Inspector, if you wouldn't mind. I think that could be rather personal.'

'It's the personal that might help us the most, Mr Brockley.' Barnaby switched on the little goose-necked lamp, adjusted the pink shade, opened the pages at random and began to read.

April 3rd: Today a new departure. A has discovered where I work! Emerging from the office I literally 'cannoned' into him. And there was something about his expression – slightly guilty but at the same time eager and excited – that told me this was no coincidence.

After this accidental (quote unquote) collision there was nothing for it but that he absolutely must take me to lunch. We went to the Lotus Garden where much hilarity ensued due to my complete incompetence vis à vis chopsticks. He insisted on advising me which, needless to say, involved a lot of 'hands on' tuition. His fingers are slender but so strong. Did they press a little too firmly and with unnecessary warmth? He has such laughing eyes. When they met mine I think we both realised that something hugely significant had just occurred.

The Chief Inspector, his expression one of amazed disbelief, flicked through several more pages of vivid green script that should surely have been purple, and picked up the thread.

May 7th: Strictly against instructions A has started to ring me at the Coalport. Need I say 'raised eyebrows all round'? Trish Travers commenting on his sexy voice, everyone asking questions. I maintained a discreet silence, simply saying 'no comment at this stage'.

I'm determined not to succumb but he is so good-looking. Persuaded into another lunch – this time at the Star of India. He confessed then what I have long suspected. That his marriage is an empty sham and his life desperately unhappy. Little does he know that I also have experienced loneliness, that special He having proved elusive. Until now. Much against my better judgement and purely out of sympathy, I allowed my hand to rest briefly on his. Those laughing eyes became deadly serious and seemed to look directly into my soul. I think I knew then that there was no turning back.

Barnaby dipped into the saga three or four more times. The gist, style and content did not change. On the point of closing the diary, he noticed a photograph pasted inside the front cover. He passed the book over, saying, 'Have you seen this, sir?'

Reg's stretched out hand was tentative. Longing to be privy to his child's innermost thoughts when she was alive, he now experienced feelings of severe unease at such an intrusion.

'It doesn't seem right.'

'Just look at the photograph, if you will.'

Reg stared at the picture, his eyes and mouth circles of stupefaction. He handed the diary back. 'It's Alan.' Then, as if trying to clarify an impenetrably murky situation, 'From the property adjacent.' He walked, stiff-legged, to Brenda's pretty little mother-of-pearl seat and leaned on it. 'What does this mean? What is she writing? I don't understand.'

'There are several meetings of a romantic nature described here, Mr Brockley. A courtship, as it were.'

'With *Hollingsworth?*'

'No name is mentioned in full.' Though a closer reading, he hoped, would prove otherwise. 'But the initial A does recur from time to time. And this, coupled with the photograph—'

'But we hardly knew them. I told you that the other day.'

'You and your wife may hardly have known them but—'

'Oh God! You don't think it was Alan who . . .' Reg's face was contorted, crazed with pain. 'Could that be why he took his own life?'

At this point Audrey appeared in the doorway to say that Iris was now asleep and that Dr Jennings had left but would call again first thing in the morning.

Reg cried out, 'My little girl. Brenda, oh Brenda.'

Audrey helped him up and persuaded him to go downstairs. As the two of them left the room, Barnaby thought about Reg's agonised suggestion. Until the motorist responsible was apprehended, no one would know precisely when Brenda Brockley died; even after a postmortem, there was always a certain amount of uncertainty. But if she had been killed last Monday night before, say, ten thirty Hollingsworth could have been responsible. He was out and about and on wheels. And it was certainly possible, given reasonable traffic conditions, to drive to Heathrow and back in under three hours.

So, means and opportunity may turn out to be not so problematical. But motive? That was a facer. Barnaby found it difficult to believe that Alan Hollingsworth was sexually involved with the Brockleys' daughter. His guess was that her secret writings were as much a work of fiction as the Mills and Boon novels on the little glass shelf. Not that extremely ugly women were inevitably unable to hold a man in thrall: history had plenty of examples to prove otherwise. The Duchess of Constantinople, whose lovers were legion, was said to have warts on her nose, one shoulder higher than the other and breath to set the Bosphorus on fire.

But in this particular instance Barnaby felt convinced he was right. Perhaps because Hollingsworth's obsession with his wife was so consuming as to make an interest in any other woman appear unlikely. But how had Brenda viewed next door's marriage? Did she, keeping herself to herself in this sad little cell, really know anything about it at all?

Working on the open mind principle, Barnaby considered, for one wild moment, the idea of the Brockleys' daughter as Simone's kidnapper. She may well have been jealous of Simone, and even wished to do her harm. And deliberately driving Alan half mad with anxiety was also not entirely out of the question. Unrequited love could spawn behaviour both cruel and perverse. But when would she have had the time? Unless subsequent interviews at the Coalport and National proved absenteeism, every moment of her blameless, tightly organised life seemed to have been accounted for. Which meant an accomplice.

Rapidly painting himself into a more and more impossible corner, the Chief Inspector shook the whole muddle from his mind and turned once more to the diary.

The viridian script, tightly crammed, jigged about on the page. He flicked back and forth and then, suddenly, there was a breathing space. A cool expanse of blank lemon paper. It was broken by two lines, calmly written in pencil. He addressed himself to the brief paragraph and the words flew like arrows, straight to his heart.

People say what you've never had you never miss. That isn't true. You dream of what you're missing all night long. And then you ache, all through the day.

By 8 a.m. on Monday morning the incident room was as busy as a hive of bees. There was still a certain amount of fresh information coming through regarding the Hollingsworth case, including several sightings. Desk staff, civilian and uniformed alike, listened and transcribed.

In Brick Lane, Simone had worn a gold and scarlet sari and bells on her toes. In Telford she posed as a nun, in Devizes as a traffic warden. Near Stratford-on-Avon she sported on the deck of a canal barge in Gipsy earrings and little else.

More sensibly and closer to home on the day of her disappearance, Mrs Hollingsworth had appeared at Uxbridge Tube station loaded with Marks and Spencer's shopping and constantly looking at her watch 'as if she was waiting for a friend'.

On a Country Route bus to Aylesbury a passenger had

sat next to someone wearing a shocking pink linen jacket over a flowered dress with a pattern similar to Simone's. Though this person had auburn hair and was wearing dark glasses, she still bore a close resemblance to the kidnapped woman. As the informant left the bus at Flackwell Heath she had no idea of the woman's final destination.

Thirdly, and most promising of all, Simone had been spotted getting into a shabby white van parked only a few yards from the department store where she had last been genuinely sighted. The person who reported this had not noticed the number but did recall that the vehicle was unmarked. In other words, not trade.

Barnaby, refreshed after a Sunday spent pottering in his garden and lying in the deck-chair, caught up with all the other salient stuff, then asked that an 'anxious to trace' notice be put out on the van driver. Also that every store in Causton, including charity shops, be questioned over the sale of an auburn wig and a pink jacket. For Mrs Hollingsworth had certainly not been carrying either item when she boarded the market bus at Fawcett Green.

Finally he asked for some posters of Simone showing the relevant time and date of her supposed sighting to be plastered all over Uxbridge Tube station, entrance hall and platforms. You never knew your luck.

After this he retired to the quietest corner he could find. A briefing had been called for eight thirty which was in about twenty minutes' time. The Chief Inspector took with him some strong coffee and Brenda Brockley's diary which he had been perusing, on and off, since breakfast.

A closer reading had not revealed the significance of the gold and silver asterisks and little scarlet hearts and Barnaby doubted now that he would ever understand their significance. But if they remained mysterious, Brenda's adventures were proving to be sadly conventional. There was no breaking of banks in Monte Carlo or skiing in Gstaad. No yachting on wine-dark seas beneath a brazen Aegean sky. She did not even go to Ascot or Cowes.

She had wanted so little, poor girl. Dinner at a pub on the river bank at Marlow, 'with white swans so very graceful bobbing at their reflections in the water. Daintily they ate some petty fours straight from my hand.' A concert at High Wycombe with a slow drive home in the moonlight 'which Alan begged and pleaded might never end'. Yet another Chinese, this time at the Kyung Ying.

The room was filling up. Some people had gathered in front of the notice-board on which were pinned blow-ups of Brenda's studio photograph along with the SOCO pictures of Alan on the hearth rug, the happy nuptial portrait and the Polaroids of Simone. Others were making themselves familiar with the latest developments to date. Barnaby closed the diary and returned to his official place.

'All right, everyone.' The jabber lessened only slightly. He gave the surface of the desk a smart blow with his fist. And tossed a cold 'Thank you' into the ensuing silence.

'Now, this is what we've got and so far it isn't much. Brenda Brockley was last seen by her parents at seven thirty last Monday evening. She left the house in the clothes she was wearing when she died. She said nothing as to where she was going. Just jumped into the car and drove off "like a mad thing", to quote her father. She didn't even take a handbag and scraped the gatepost as she went by.

'At nine o'clock she called to say she had met a friend and was going for a meal and they weren't to wait up. Her father, who took the message, got the impression, from the background noise, that she was ringing from a railway station. We now know that it was almost certainly

Heathrow. All of this information is already on a Four Two Eight which is being photocopied and should be up here shortly, so make yourselves familiar.

'The body was found on the top level of the Short Stay Car Park that serves Terminal One, as was her car. The injuries are commensurate with being struck by a vehicle moving at some considerable speed. The PM's being done this morning so we should know more by tomorrow at the latest. Her photograph, together with that of Hollingsworth and his wife, are being circulated at the airport. She could have had the meal she was referring to on the concourse itself, in which case she may well have been noticed. She was an . . . unusual-looking girl.'

Someone said something at the back of the room and someone else laughed.

'What was that?' Barnaby's voice cracked like a whip.

'Sorry, chief.' A throat was cleared. 'Got a bit of a cough.'

'We can't all look like Ava Gardner, Constable.'

'No, sir.'

'The Heathrow police are being very cooperative and, as more stuff comes in, we shall know better how to proceed. Now, as to the Hollingsworth inquiry, any more catching up for me to do? Yes, Beryl?'

Detective Sergeant Beryl, whose surname was the bane of his life, said, 'I talked to someone in St Chad's Lane yesterday, sir. A Mr Harris. He was working in his front garden and actually saw Alan Hollingsworth drive away at the time Dawlish said he heard him.'

'Excellent. Get in touch with him again, would you? Find out if he saw the Brockley girl leaving as well. It sounds to me as if they set off within minutes of each other. And bear in mind, everyone, that this was the evening of the day that Hollingsworth received the money. I don't think it's stretching matters to assume that he was on his way to hand it over. And if she was following him . . .'

There was an interested and lively murmur of speculation then a plainclothes inspector, leaning against the water cooler, said, 'Has there been any feedback from her parents at all? I mean, any suggestion as to why she might have been pursuing Hollingsworth?'

'She fancied herself in love with him.' Barnaby glared around the room as if daring it to respond risibly. Everyone was quiet. 'As far as we know, she never even went inside the house, though once we've got her prints, we may find otherwise.'

'I'm holding back on any large-scale inquiry at this stage mainly because it's possible we might simply be looking at an accident. But I would like her photograph, together with Hollingsworth's, shown at all the cafés and restaurants in Causton. See if anyone remembers seeing them together.' Though Barnaby firmly believed the diary to be a complete work of fiction, he couldn't risk not checking the matter out.

'I shall be visiting her place of work in half an hour and hope to fill in the background somewhat. The next briefing's at six o'clock. So, go to it. Gavin?'

Sergeant Troy picked up his jacket and followed his boss from the room. As the door closed behind him, the man who had laughed said, 'Who the hell's Ava Gardner?'

Approaching the Rover where his chief was already installed, Sergeant Troy, carrying two cans of iced pop from the iced pop machine, was laughing silently to himself. His expression was bemused and his head moved back and forth in disbelief as he climbed into the driving seat.

'Thanks,' said Barnaby, holding out his hand. 'I could do with one of those.'

'Oh. Right.' Troy, who had bought both cans for himself, handed over the least pleasant. 'This one's supposed to be pretty good.'

'I wouldn't deprive you, Gavin,' said Barnaby, seizing the alternative. 'What were you chortling at?'

Troy explained. 'There was this old tramp downstairs trying to make a complaint. Apparently he'd been sitting on the pavement, everything he owned in the world packed into a fraying carrier, when some smart Charlie walks up. "I represent Sainsbury's," he says. "Penny for your bag?" Chucks the coin down and walks off with all the old geezer's stuff. They were still wetting themselves in reception.'

'Made your day, did it?'

'Pretty near,' said Sergeant Troy, opening his Cherryade and taking a long swig.

'Well, you're not here to enjoy yourself so knock that back double quick and get a move on.'

'Right, guv.' He drained the can, wedged it behind the gear box and turned on the ignition.

They had been asked to go to the back entrance of the Coalport and National but, on arriving, found it locked. Barnaby peered over half-mast lace curtains into what proved to be a kitchen/rest area. A girl who was washing up dried her hands on a tea towel and let them in.

'Sorry. I was supposed to watch out for you.' Easing past them, she opened the inner door revealing a large, high-ceilinged room with several desks and a counter at the far end at which one person was standing. 'I'll just let the manager know you're here.'

After the customer had left, Mr Marchbanks, a Lowry

stick-figure with a mass of pale lemon curls, eyes like boiled gooseberries and a handshake like a damp flounder, admitted the two policemen to the main office.

'I was sure you would wish to discuss matters undisturbed,' he said, indicating the notice on the glass door. The side facing them said Open. 'But I do hope . . .'

'I'll try not to take up too much of your time,' replied Barnaby. 'May I?'

As he sat down at an empty desk, a great sepulchre of a woman, very tall and wide with more bristles on her top lip than an Oral B, came out of an office marked Personnel. The Chief Inspector presumed this to be Trish Travers.

Everyone looked subdued but not overly distressed. Not even Mr Marchbanks, who had thought the world of Brenda.

'This is devastating news,' he said, with the air of a man about to pare his nails. 'The whole office is in a terrible state of shock.'

'I understand,' said Barnaby. 'And I do appreciate your cooperation.'

Troy selected a high stool at the counter, laid his notebook down next to the Day At A Time calendar and took stock of the talent. Four in number (you couldn't count Adolf) and of variable delectability.

There was the very short one who had let them in: a proper little butter ball, completely round with long eyelashes and a ginger fringe. Fringes, Sergeant Troy thought, always made a girl look saucy. An only half-decent looker with floppy wings of silky fawn hair, a complexion like the wrong half of the Flash floor ad and a long pointed nose. Fine if you liked Afghans. An irritable, harassed-looking one with worn hands, too much jewellery and a habit of screwing up her face and blinking. And Troy's fancy; tall, red-headed like himself, wearing enormous tortoiseshell glasses perched on the tip of her pretty nose. Long fragile legs folded away beneath her chair. A juicily deluscious eye-boggler. Viewing alone fair brought a lump to your trousers.

He waited till the smoky lenses glinted in his direction and gave her a brilliant, uncomplicated smile.

She parted her own lips, wet and glistening like newly washed cherries, in acknowledgement.

'It would be helpful,' the Chief Inspector was explaining, 'if we could discover a little about Miss Brockley's background and private life. I know that girls often—'

'Women, I believe you mean,' put in the tired hands.

'Indeed,' said Barnaby. 'I beg your pardon. Women will sometimes tell their colleagues in the workplace things they might not discuss with immediate members of their family. I wonder if Brenda perhaps . . .'

There was an uncomfortable silence. Barnaby took the room's temperature and was not encouraged. He had already suspected that the sterile pattern of Brenda's life as described by her parents indicated the type of withdrawn personality that did not communicate easily with others.

'Was she . . . well-liked here?'

'I wouldn't say well-liked,' said Mr Marchbanks.

'But not disliked,' the roly-poly girl, Hazel Grantley from Accounts, interrupted quickly.

There was an immediate chorus of over-emphatic agreement which died down into another awkward pause.

Barnaby recognised their collective dilemma, for it was not uncommon. Many people who thought nothing of speaking ill about the still woundable living could not bring themselves to breathe a syllable against the indifferent dead.

'So no one here was what you would call close to Brenda?'

There was a negative mumble. Not a single person looked directly at him.

'What about outside the office? Did she ever mention anyone she regularly went about with?'

'Not to us.'

'A boy friend, perhaps?'

Everyone looked surprised and then ashamed of looking surprised and then cross at looking ashamed.

'I don't think she had a boy friend,' said Mr Marchbanks.

'Brenda didn't go in for that sort of thing.'

'She was a born singleton,' said the girl with the Bambi legs.

Barnaby winced as much at the casual unkindness as at the excruciating terminology. 'What about personal telephone calls? Did she receive or make many?'

'They're not allowed.'

'Officially,' said the girl with the long nose and everybody started to giggle until they remembered how solemn the occasion was.

'She got one,' corrected the woman clanking with jewellery. 'The first morning she didn't come in. A man rang and asked to speak to her. About nine thirty, it was.'

That would have been her father. Barnaby asked then how long Miss Brockley had been working at the Coalport and National.

'Since she left school,' said Mr Marchbanks. 'That would be thirteen years.'

Unlucky for some, thought Sergeant Troy. Appreciating the fan standing next to the calendar, he eased it more directly towards him, loosened the collar of his check sports shirt and flicked over the first page of his notes.

'What about when she was up at the counter?' persisted

the Chief Inspector. 'Did she have any long conversations with anyone in particular? Perhaps the same person on more than one occasion?'

'Well,' Mr Marchbanks cleared his throat, 'she didn't do a lot of, erm . . .'

'One-to-one customer relations.' The Afghan helped him out.

'That's right. She seemed to prefer to work more quietly.'

'By herself, like,' said the woman from Personnel.

Barnaby had a quick apprehension of the abyss of loneliness on the edge of which Brenda must have existed at the Coalport and National. Arriving in the morning to conversations about boy friends, problems at school, family rows, how would she have responded? By nodding and smiling while listening to described situations completely outside her own experience? Perhaps, appreciating that any attempt properly to participate must necessarily be known to be false, or even condescending, she had pretended not to hear – and may well have been thought stand-offish for her pains. Perhaps she simply sat quietly at her desk, hoping not to be noticed – no doubt the empty one in the far corner of the office on which now lay a solitary bunch of roses, swathed in shiny, white-spotted paper. He wondered if they had ever bought flowers for her when she had been alive.

Barnaby asked about the midday break. Had anyone ever called to take Brenda out to lunch? No. Never. Did she perhaps spend time during this period with any of her workmates?

'Not really. We all had things to do, you see.'

'She'd stay here, make herself a coffee and eat her sandwiches.'

'Sometimes she went to the library.'

'We'd come back absolutely fagged. Racing round the

shops buying food and stuff. She'd be sitting there, feet up, reading one of her romances.'

'I think her mother did everything.'

'Yeah, she had it dead cushy.'

'Wouldn't do for me. Nearly thirty and still living at home.' The needling words were delicately shaded with spite. Troy directed a glance of warm admiration at this lovely girl, so after his own heart. She recrossed her slender, breakable legs and smiled to herself. He noticed that her identity brooch read 'Jacqui Willing' and hoped it wasn't having him on.

Mr Marchbanks began tousling his limp curls with a worried hand at this point, Trish Travers looked at her watch and the heavily ringed fingers on the tired hands crept towards the nearest keyboard. Someone knocked on the glass front door.

Realising there was probably little else to be gained at the Coalport and National, Barnaby thanked the manager, handed over a card should any of the staff remember anything that they might consider helpful, and prepared to leave.

Bambi was detailed to show them out. As she opened the back door, with Troy's zealous and quite unnecessary assistance, she said, 'Poor Brenda, she was really over-sensitive about her looks. Many's the time I've tried to cheer her up. "Bren," I used to say, "beauty's only skin deep." But you just can't help some people, can you?'

Barnaby could have hit her.

By the time the Chief Inspector had concluded his building society interview, the *Evening Standard* had already published its midday edition under the headline 'Mysterious Death Of Kidnap Woman's Neighbour'.

This time the village, genuinely and deeply shocked, kept its distance when invaded. Journalists, asking in the Goat and Whistle for the Brockleys' precise whereabouts, got nowhere. The fact that the couple were not well liked did not enter into the matter. As is the way of the fourth estate, they quickly sussed the address anyway and were soon giving The Larches' push button bell some really serious stick.

Shona jumped up at the window, barked and had her picture taken. Next day it appeared under the caption 'Dead Girl's Pet Pines Away'. Several people rang the *Mirror* wanting to adopt the dog.

Few people could cope easily with such an onslaught. Brenda's grief-stricken parents were prodigiously ill-equipped. They cowered behind their starched net frills. Iris wept, Reg wrung his hands and rained blows on the walls and furniture. The poodle, desperate to go out, scratched and whined for half an hour then did a puddle in the hall. When a bearded face pressed up against the kitchen window, Iris started to scream.

It was at that moment that Constable Perrot, accompanied by the vicar, arrived. Perrot, alternately cajoling and threatening arrest for trespass, eased the press out of the Brockleys' garden and back into the lane. Then supposing, rightly, that the door chimes must have by now worn out their welcome, he ignored the bell and reprised his earlier star turn at Nightingales. Bending down he spoke, very clearly, through the letter box.

'Mr Brockley? This is Constable Perrot. I'm your local community police officer.' He felt this explanation necessary as he had never actually spoken to Brenda's parents before. 'The vicar is with me. We're anxious to help in any way we can. Please open the door.'

Reg and Iris looked fearfully at each other. Having heard the noise from the army of pressmen diminish slightly, Reg had peeped through a narrow gap in the curtains and seen Perrot firmly shepherding them away. Gratitude alone thus inclined him to admit the visitors. Common sense reinforced the idea. After all, sooner or later he and Iris would be forced to let someone in. Or, horror of horrors, go out themselves. And at least these people's interest would, hopefully, be impersonal.

It was nothing new for the vicar to enter a house of mourning. Years of experience had equipped him with suitable responses and to spare. To give him his due, he tried to empathise afresh in every case and not sound platitudinous or mechanical. But as soon as he stepped into the Brockleys' private hell, he knew that the situation was beyond him. Childless himself, he understood that anything he might have to say could only be cruelly impertinent. He hovered in the hall, one foot spongily sinking into the dog's puddle. Shona herself crouched on the stairs, isolated and lonely, her nose between her paws.

Perrot, quietly and with concerned sympathy, took charge. In the lounge Iris lay full length on the sofa, her stout legs stretched out, her arms by her side. She looked as if she was on a bier. Reg stood in the centre of the room. He seemed lost, as if waiting for someone to tell him what to do.

Perrot made some tea and cut some bread and butter. As he did this, he asked one or two questions in a soft, uninsistent way. Had the doctor been? Was there a prescription to be filled? Could he make any telephone calls on the Brockleys' behalf?

Reg said, 'We've stopped answering the phone.'

Watching Perrot's skilful ministrations, the vicar began

to feel not only *de trop* but utterly useless. He moved awkwardly across to where Iris was lying, sat down on the fringed pouffe and took her hand. In spite of the hot, stuffy room, it was icy cold. She did not open her eyes or appear even to notice his presence.

He was reminded of that other occasion, ten days ago, when he had found himself in a similar position at the house next door. He had been of no help there either. And the result of his daily prayers for the restoration of order and the wellbeing of each and every parishioner in Fawcett Green had been yet another violent death. If the Reverend Bream had ever doubted that God worked in mysterious ways, he doubted no longer.

'My wife,' he said, clearing his throat with nervousness. 'Food. Anything at all, happy to bring. If you would like to come and stay, just for a few days. I mean, that is, as long as you like . . .'

Everyone ignored him.

Perrot, having placed a cup of tea in Reg's hands and made sure he was grasping it firmly, sat close by, talking quietly. He also offered plenty of encouraging silence, which Reg occasionally broke. Perrot explained that the police might very well need to talk to both him and Iris again, but there would be no pressure. He, Perrot, would ask to be present if they felt it would help. Should they go to stay with relatives or friends, please make sure to let him know.

The vicar whose eye, having once been snagged by the leaping butterfly clock, found it could now settle on little else, was glad when the dog started whining and scratching again and he had a practical task to perform.

On Perrot's advice he took her into the back garden. Shona, already shamedly conscious of her disgrace in the hall and desperately afraid she was about to disgrace herself even more profoundly, streaked off down the path with a yelp of gratitude. She relieved herself on Reg's flawless green lawn, dragged her bottom around on the grass then stood up. She looked expectantly at the vicar who stared uncertainly back. Neither he nor Mrs Bream cared for animals although they did look after the Sunday School hamster when the necessity arose.

There was a sudden flash. Rightly suspecting a concealed photographer and mentally composing the subsequent headlines, 'Vicar Abducts Bereaved Parents' Sole Comfort', the Reverend Bream hurried back into the house.

Barnaby was in the canteen squaring up to two tomatoes, some wholewheat bread, a small wedge of Double Gloucester and a Comice pear when the news came through from Heathrow that a witness had come forward. Someone who had seen not only Brenda Brockley on the night she died but also Alan Hollingsworth. A double whammy. The girl, a counter assistant in an ice-cream parlour on the Terminal One concourse, finished her shift at three thirty.

The first part of their second drive to the airport in as many days took place in virtual silence. Barnaby was lost in recollections of the case so far, mixed with hopeful anticipation of what might shortly be thrown in his lap. Sergeant Troy was seeking a grievance to while away the fleeting hour.

After picking a few over, he settled for an old favourite, the iniquities of the car mileage system. Or: Why Did They Always Have To Use The Rover? Forty-two point one pence a mile allowance straight into the gaffer's pocket. A nice lump sum every twenty-eight days, even after you'd taken the petrol off. And it wasn't as if he needed it. Fat salary, pension assured, no kids, mortgage paid off, but would he be driven around in Troy's Cosworth? Would he buggery. OK, OK, he's a big bloke and the Cossie might be a bit of a squeeze but the response had been the same whatever car Troy had had.

Course he was music mad, old Tom. And there was no doubt the equipment in the Rover was stellar. Waste of space, though, with the tapes he'd got. So-called singers warbling and gargling like canaries on speed. Musicians – *musicians* – scraping and sawing and twanging away.

As if reading his sergeant's mind, Barnaby reached out, slipped a tape in the deck and turned up the volume. Rich and full, the singer's voice filled the confined area of the car and poured out of the window on to the still summer air. She kept it up until they were entering the slipstream of traffic aiming for the Short Stay Car Park. Troy had to admit it was one of the less offensive numeros. At least she stayed in tune, which was more than you could say for some. Big Lucy and his football aria excepted.

'She can give it some welly, chief,' said Sergeant Troy as he searched for a parking space. 'That that Cecily Bertorelli, is it?' He tried to remember the odd name. Show an interest.

'No,' said Chief Inspector Barnaby. 'That's my wife.'

Barnaby had decided to talk to the girl in her place of work, where she would be more relaxed, rather than in the police offices. Also he would need, at some stage in the interview, to look at the scene from her point of view.

They were offered delicious iced coffee in the Häagen-Dazs spotlessly clean kitchen. Eden Lo, a pretty Chinese girl, was taking off her maroon overall and yellow-banded forage cap. The three photographs which the Causton CID had circulated lay on a freckled Formica table with those of

Alan Hollingsworth and Brenda set a little apart.

'These are the people that I saw.' She pointed at the two pictures.

'They were here, in the café?'

'Not together. He was in the café. She was, well, sort of hiding. At least I got that impression.'

'How was it you saw her then, Miss Lo?'

'I came out to clear just after I had served this gentleman with his coffee. She was standing behind the notice-board outside the fish restaurant next door. I noticed because she was so,' she hesitated, being a kind girl, unlike Bambi, 'different-looking.'

'Quite.'

'Also she was peering over this way. As if she was keeping an eye on someone.'

'And the man you served. Tell me about him.'

'That was rather strange as well. He took his coffee to the middle table. The circular one that runs—'

'Show me, would you, please?'

They left the kitchen to stand behind the chill cabinet and Eden Lo pointed out the round rim table overlooked by the blow-up of the radiantly lascivious half-dressed guzzlers. Sergeant Troy had a knee-jerk reaction (well, to be honest, it wasn't his knee) and transferred his jacket to his other arm where it could be more tactfully disposed.

'And then,' continued the Chinese girl, 'he didn't drink it.'

'You mean he just sat there, waiting?'

'No. He sort of leaned against the stool for barely a second. Put the cup down and walked away.'

'Which direction?'

'Towards those stairs. When the girl who was watching realised he'd gone, she rushed after him. I saw her on the steps staring down all over the floor. She was really upset. I heard her cry out, "Oh, what'll I do? What shall I do?"'

'Was that the last you saw of her?'

'Of both of them, yes.'

'And what happened to the coffee?' asked Barnaby, leading the way back to the kitchenette.

Sergeant Troy raised his eyebrows at the frivolity of such a question. If he'd asked it there'd have been a bloody lecture afterwards on how not to waste a witness's valuable time.

'That's the odd thing,' said Miss Lo. 'When I looked again there was this old woman drinking it. I thought, what a cheek!'

'What was she like?' Barnaby leaned forward, intent and purposeful.

'Really dirty. Some old bag lady.'

'Had you seen her before?'

'No. The airport police are quite strict about people like that. They usually move them on.'

'I meant before, that same evening. In the restaurant.'

'Not really. She just seemed to appear out of nowhere. To tell you the truth, I wondered if she'd been hanging around in Garfunkels. Or maybe the Tap and Spile next door, keeping an eye out for a half-empty glass, that sort of thing. It's all open here, as you can see. She could have spotted a coffee going begging and just nipped across.'

'Did you talk to her?'

'Well, I started to go over but when she saw me coming she picked up this grotty string bag and hurried away.'

'Now, this could be very important, Miss Lo. Did you notice if the man who bought the coffee had a bag or case of any sort with him?'

'He certainly didn't have one with him at the counter. He used both hands to carry the tray.'

'But he could have put it down by the table he intended to occupy?'

'He could have but I didn't see that. I'm sorry.'

'So the first time you caught sight of the string bag was when this old woman ran off with it?'

'That's right.'

'Did you get any idea of the contents?' Barnaby didn't have much hope. The whole incident seemed to have happened within seconds.

'Um, just newspaper, really. Parcels wrapped in newspaper.'

'Little parcels?'

'I'm sorry.' She opened her arms, turned up the palms of her hands and shrugged.

'Did you clear the coffee cup away then?'

'Yes, I did.'

'And you're sure of the date on this?'

'Quite sure. My friend on the Air Indonesia desk has been trying for ages to get me a cheap flight to Hong Kong and it was Monday it came through.'

'Could you give me a time at all?' asked the Chief Inspector.

'Not really. I came on at eight and I'd been here maybe an hour. Maybe longer.'

Brenda had rung her parents at nine o'clock. Barnaby tried to fit this into the fragment of knowledge, far too slight to be called a pattern, that had just now come his way.

It wasn't easy. If she was trailing Hollingsworth, she would hardly have risked losing him by taking time off to make a phone call. So it must have been made later after Brenda, by then 'really upset', had completed her survey from the top of the staircase. Had she spotted Hollingsworth in that great swarming mass of people? Caught up with him? Arranged to go for a meal? It seemed unlikely but if she hadn't, who was the friend she had talked about?

'Was there anyone else on duty with you, Miss Lo?'

'Yes, but not out front at the time it happened. They were working in here.'

'Right. I'm going to ask you to come along to Heathrow police station and sign a statement. And you may also be asked if you could assist in compiling an Identikit picture of this elderly lady.'

'But I only saw her for a second.'

'That doesn't matter. Just do the best you can.'

She collected a white lacy cardigan and they left together by way of the steps that first Alan and then the frantic Brenda had descended.

But Barnaby was never to know about the dark-skinned boy in the sweaty T-shirt. The boy who had agitated the war machines and asked for change and laughed at Brenda's distress and who could have helped them most of all. For he had long since taken a flight into Egypt.

Chapter Nine

By the following morning there had been a considerable falling off in sightings of Simone Hollingsworth. Plainly she was becoming yesterday's news. And Brenda's death, in spite of all the tabloids' nudging, exclamatory prose hinting at a possible connection, had not obtained the same imaginative grip. This made for a rather less frenetic atmosphere in the incident room which did not please everyone. Sergeant Troy, for example, blossomed when the adrenaline flew.

Information both positive and negative was still coming in but was proving helpful rather than exciting. Clearing useless stuff out of the way rather than shedding light into dark corners.

The man with the white van phoned to say he was innocent of all knowledge of what he called 'the missing Mrs Haitch'. She was definitely not the blonde who had been seen climbing into his vehicle outside Bobby's department store on the afternoon of her disappearance.

He rang anonymously on 999, unaware that the number from which all such calls are made is automatically displayed to BT as they come in. He was furious when someone from the station later called at his house. But not as furious as his wife who had thought he was working on the Friday in question over at Naphill.

The check on the possible purchase that same day in Causton of a pink jacket and auburn wig had also proved negative. The nearest the inquirers could manage was the sale of a size 20 cerise blazer with diamanté buttons and sequined lapels from the British Heart Foundation shop. A coronary-causing little number if there ever was one.

Mid-morning Barnaby received a call from the coroner's office to say that a death certificate had now been issued for Alan Hollingsworth and the remains released for burial. In the absence of the deceased's wife, notification had been made to his brother.

There was some news on Simone Hollingsworth's first husband although he had not yet been physically traced. While not actually the 'bad lot' as described by Hollingsworth to Gray Patterson, Jimmy Atherton, born and dragged up in Cubitt Town, certainly seemed to be swilling around somewhere near the bottom of society's barrel. Runner of iffy errands and deliverer of highly flexible packages; selling from a suitcase in the West End; bookie's messenger; bag carrier and front man for a casino near Golden Square; street trading from a suspiciously mobile lorry and kiting dud cheques.

The word on the street was that Jimmy's wife had been mad about him and he was mad about her and both were mad about money but he was worse. And so, when a new project with the possibility of immediate potential and long-term growth came up, you didn't see him for the proverbial. She cried fit to float a P&O liner but he still cleared off.

Incredibly, given such a profile, this jammy dodger had somehow managed to convince Australia House that he would be an asset to the country's community. Consequently, a mere six months ago, Atherton had set off, via Qantas, along the well-worn convict trail to the

Antipodes. Had this not been the case, the Chief Inspector would have got a search going, for Jimmy sounded just the sort to be mixed up in a plot to raise a stack of the readies on the ex-missus.

Thinking along these lines, Barnaby experienced a sudden powerful sense of coincidence which directed him back to Dr Jennings' surgery. Once more he attended to the descriptions of Simone Hollingsworth's bruised arms and her distressed condition. He found his notes and checked out the date of her first visit. March the ninth. He pulled a keyboard towards him, scrolled through Sarah Lawson's statement and hit on the lines: 'Simone rang up and said she wouldn't be coming again. I think she'd been crying. She certainly sounded very subdued. I got the impression Alan was standing over her.' That had been early March too, both incidents taking place just over a week before Simone had been given the necklace.

The pattern was not unfamiliar. A bullying partner brings pressure to bear to get his or her own way. Once achieved, at whatever the cost to the recipient, the victor is all smiles and affectionate generosity. Loving assurances are made that such a thing will never happen again. Gifts are quite frequently offered – in this case, one would have thought, of quite disproportionate value to the petty victory gained.

This train of thought led Barnaby to dwell on the disappearance and possible theft of the jewels. Their illustration in *Harpers* was being well circulated by the police both in legitimate and highly suspect circles but so far to no effect. And surely if they had been stolen, Hollingsworth would have reported it, if only for the insurance.

The Chief Inspector's opinion was that Simone had taken the necklace with her. No doubt she felt she'd earned it and it would certainly have fitted into her handbag, or even her pocket. This notion went well with the theory that she believed she was off to start a new life with a new partner, albeit without much in the way of luggage. Then one was left with the problem of why, with two hundred thousand smackers worth of razzle dazzle in his hot little hand (and perhaps the ring as well) the man had persisted with a possibly risky kidnap and ransom demand. Unless, as was so often the case, the original request was scheduled to be the first of many.

At this point in his reflections an update from Heathrow was put on Barnaby's desk. Of the two registration numbers he had left with Inspector Fennimore, one had come up trumps. Alan Hollingsworth's Audi convertible had definitely checked into the Short Term Car Park. A ticket found in Brenda Brockley's Mini indicated that she had been barely minutes behind him. There was no record of the second number, which belonged to Gray Patterson.

A fax of the Identikit portrait of the bag lady drawn with Eden Lo's assistance also arrived. This had only been in circulation around the airport for an hour or two so it was unrealistic to expect much feedback as yet. Barnaby drew it towards him and switched on his Anglepoise for a closer look.

It was not a pretty sight. The Chief Inspector was reminded of the drawing in the final box of the Have You Got Your Pension Sorted adverts. A jolly smile in the first, a couple of faintly sketched frown lines in the second, a much more definite network of anxiety as our improvident hero flirts with middle age, and finally something resembling a man with a densely woven spider's web stuck to his face.

This was a female, of course. Seamed and wrinkled as a

walnut, wearing a patterned headscarf loosely tied under her chin. Clothing listed alongside: stained dark skirt, shabby cardigan with some sort of design which might, Miss Lo suggested, have been Fair Isle. An ancient jumper, colour not remembered. Dirty tennis shoes.

Not bad for a glance lasting a couple of seconds. Barnaby, duly grateful, prayed that someone somewhere would recognise the woman and that the police would then be able to lay hands on her. He leaned back and closed his eyes, picturing the scene in the Häagen-Dazs café.

Hollingsworth coming in, buying a coffee, taking it to a table and walking away. Almost immediately the woman crosses over and starts to drink it. At Miss Lo's approach she hurries off carrying a string bag holding parcels wrapped in newspaper. It was not known whether she brought this in with her.

It seemed to Barnaby there were three ways of explaining this little vignette. She was a genuine transient simply keeping a sharp eye out for a free nibble or bevy; she was a transient who had been paid to go into the café, pick up the bag and deliver it elsewhere; or she was directly involved in the kidnap and ransom of Simone Hollingsworth.

Barnaby thought this last extremely unlikely and favoured the second notion. Which led to the interesting question as to why such a messenger would be necessary. The most obvious reason – because she was substituting for someone who would otherwise have been recognised – was not the only one. Presumably this person also needed to establish an alibi well away from where the drop was made.

The more Barnaby thought along these lines, the more it seemed to him that this old crone might have the key to the whole business. If they found her, they might well get a description of the man they were looking for.

Fingers crossed.

He pulled forward the next envelope and took out Perrot's report on the position of the Halogen switch in the garage and accompanying pair of photographs. Barnaby hardly knew whether to laugh or fling the whole caboodle up in the air and the over-scrupulous constable with it. All he had wanted was a simple message: 'on' or 'off'.

The pictures showed the main switch and the surrounding area from two points of view. Aesthetically there was not a lot to choose between them. One lawnmower and collection of garden equipment looked, as far as Barnaby was concerned, much like the next. But the interesting point, the ah! factor, if you like, was that the Halogen light which, according to Reg Brockley, came on when Hollingsworth drove home was now switched off.

Barnaby sat quietly, warmed by this tiny bit of information even more powerfully than by the summer sun, now streaming through the ivory plastic slats of the incident room's Venetian blinds. For if Hollingsworth had not pulled that switch, someone else had. Someone who needed to leave Nightingales without being observed. Which meant there *had* been another person in the house in spite of the Brockleys' insistence that no one had entered or left.

Barnaby looked around for Troy and singled him out, half hidden by a busy, moving crowd of people at the far end of the room. The DCI stood up, preparing to attract his assistant's attention.

Troy, unaware of the chief's regard, was about to embark on the most delightful method of time-filling imaginable. Chatting up every man in the station's favourite ingredient, Sergeant Audrey Brierley.

'Blimey,' he began, perching on the edge of her desk. 'It's a fair cop.'

Audrey wrinkled her lovely brow with irritation and moved an I Heart New York mug out of his way.

'Sometimes,' continued Sergeant Troy, gazing hungrily at the matchless profile, 'I wonder if you quite appreciate what a lonely person I am.'

'Whose fault's that?'

'Pardon?'

'If you weren't so . . .'

'So what?' Troy was genuinely curious. He could see no logical reason for this continual rejection for, while acknowledging that he had faults, being imperfect was surely not one of them.

Audrey, cross at having allowed herself to be provoked into a personal exchange, decided she might as well continue. 'I just think you'd be happier if you weren't so spiteful.'

Troy blinked with surprise. This was not a connection he would have made himself. If anything, the reverse was true. Life, if you didn't put the boot thoroughly into it from time to time, would pretty damn soon walk all over you. A cruel aside could put people in their place before they had a chance to screw you into yours.

Memory sparked. A small boy with his dad, sober for once, climbing on a swing in the park. A slightly larger boy coming along and tugging on the chain. Not violently, probably only wanting to play. Told to stand up for himself and push the intruder away, the younger child had started to cry. The man had seized his son's fist and swung it hard against the other boy's jaw. The boy fell down, hurt. It struck Troy now that this was possibly the very first occasion that he had got his retaliation in first.

'Where was I, Aud?'

'Lonely, "Gav".'

'Ah, yes. Reason being,' sorrow weighed down his voice,

darkened the pupils of his eyes, 'my wife doesn't understand me.'

'Oh, I bet she does, sweetheart. I bet she understands you till it's coming out of her ears.'

'I sometimes feel I'm—'

'Whatever would men do for conversation if the letter "I" was abolished?'

'What?'

'You'd be absolutely dumbstruck.'

'God, skipper.' He slid off the desk. 'It's a business doing pleasure with you.'

'I should give up then.'

'There's thousands be glad of it.'

'There's thousands watch Jeremy Beadle.'

Troy hesitated, unsure how to respond. Was it a joke? Or an astonishingly generous compliment?

'Get a grown-up to help you with that one,' said Audrey kindly. She half turned in her swivel chair. 'What's that roaring sound?'

Troy, who had absorbed the bellowing through the back of his head without giving the source much thought, now sprang to attention. He hurried to the gaffer's desk.

'Yes, sir.'

'Is that all you can find to do?'

'Developing good relationships with colleagues, chief. I mean, that's what it's all about, isn't that right? On the streets, in the field—'

'Credit me with some intelligence, Sergeant.'

'Righto.'

'I need something very wet and very cold from the Automat.' Barnaby rootled a pound coin from the jangling collection in his trouser pocket and passed it over. 'There you go.'

'Tango?'

'No thanks. You're not my type.'

It was not often Troy found himself in the position of being able to deliberately withhold laughter at his superior's jokes – the DCI hardly ever made them and when he did they were usually quite good. Troy kept his lips firmly closed now with some satisfaction.

'Make that two,' called out Barnaby as his leg man sauntered off. 'I'm celebrating.'

'Celebrating what?' asked Sergeant Troy on his return.

Barnaby made rings on the desk with two Lemon and Lime Fantas. 'An extremely—'

'That's another twenty pee, by the way.'

'Oh.' Barnaby continued speaking as he rootled some more. 'After Hollingsworth returned home on the night he died someone switched off the Halogen lamp.'

'Fancy.' The sergeant waited for the bit worth celebrating. The chief looked so pleased with himself Troy thought the murderer must have turned up while his own attention was wandering. Just presented himself at the front desk with a fringe of parsley round his mouth and an apple up his bottom.

'Which means the man wasn't alone.'

'Not necessarily.'

'What?' Barnaby, popping his first can, looked displeased.

'It could have been Alan.'

'What reason would he—'

'Habit. Probably did it every night, like winding up the cat and putting the clock out.'

'But they're specifically for use in the dark.'

'He knew someone was after him, then. Wanted to hide.'

'In that case, wouldn't he want the light to be working?

So he could see if anyone approached the house?'

'Not nec—'

'For God's sake!' Barnaby slammed his drink down. An effervescent fountain of spume shot up in the air. 'Whose side are you on?'

Tight-lipped, Troy produced a spotless handkerchief and dabbed at his newly spotted cuff. Typical of the force, this sort of thing. They asked you to use your initiative. You used your initiative. They threw Lime and Lemon over you. It was the way of the world. No point complaining.

'Sorry, Gavin.'

'Sir.' Old people today, thought Sergeant Troy, refolding his snowy cotton square and tucking it back into his sleeve. They couldn't care less. 'Want anything to eat with those, chief? Sandwich? Some crisps?'

'No thanks. I'm taking an early – yes, what is it?'

'The information you asked for from the Curzon cinema, Chief Inspector?' said one of the civilian telephonists. 'Programme times?'

Barnaby loathed perfectly straightforward statements that transformed themselves into questions almost as much as he loathed jargon. He grunted and took the print out, churlishly withholding any thanks.

And then he was sorry, for the girl had handed him one of the most interesting items to date. A nice little length of rope, you might say, to hang someone with. Or at least give them an extremely sharp tug.

'Have a look at this.' He passed it over.

Troy read the page and emitted a long, slow hiss. 'New programme starts each Monday . . . tenth of June we've got *Olivier, Olivier*. Whoever he is. *Farinelli* whats it finished Saturday night. Well, waddyaknow.'

'She's not very good at it, is she, our Sarah?'

'Got her head in the clouds, no doubt, creating and that.'

'A lie's a lie. Go and pick her up.'

'OK,' said Sergeant Troy, making a mental note to cover all extremities and wishing, for the first and only time in his life, that he had access to a cast-iron chastity belt.

'Take her to the interview room in the basement.' Barnaby passed over the Identikit drawing. 'And before you go, pin this on the board.'

''Strewth!' Troy regarded the sketch with disgust and disbelief. 'The granny from the black lagoon.'

Barnaby drained the first drinks can and Troy took it off the desk and placed it carefully in the waste paper basket. He tried to ignore the damp rings and certainly was not going to use his handkerchief to wipe them off. He made a mental note to bring a paper towel roll in and put it in the cupboard. He was a bit of a messer, old Tom.

'What I can't understand about this whole Häagen-Dazs scene,' Troy fished some drawing pins out of a Sharpe's toffee tin, 'is the business with the coffee.'

'Oh, yes?'

'Well, Hollingsworth goes and buys it. The girl says he needed both hands for the tray which means leaving whatever he was carrying, i.e. the loot, somewhere in the café. Highly dodgy. You don't turn your back on your valuables for a second in an air terminal. Thieves are everywhere.'

'Presumably that was the drop.'

'But the old hag turned up after he took the coffee to the table. Not while he was at the counter.'

'That was the first time she was spotted. Not necessarily when she first turned up.'

'And why buy the stuff and not drink any?' That had really niggled Troy. He hated seeing money wasted. 'It wasn't as if it was the sort of place where people are breathing down your neck if you don't immediately order.'

'Now Hollingsworth's gone, we may never know.'

'I hate mysteries.' Sergeant Troy saw nothing incongruous in the fact that a detective should make such a statement. Yearning for a society that was passive, ordered and static, he regarded police work as nothing so much as an endless and ever more stringent tidying. Sweeping the country's rubbish off the streets and into first the courts and then Her Majesty's detention centres.

Not that it always worked like that. Half the time you were no sooner out of the witness box after giving evidence for the Crown than the rubbish was back on the pavement giving you the finger and either laughing or spitting in your face.

'What's that?'

Sergeant Troy hadn't realised he'd been mumbling aloud.

'Restoring order, chief. The right balance. That's our job, isn't it?'

'Symmetry's for the gods, Gavin. We mustn't presume.' Barnaby got up, taking his jacket from the back of his chair. 'They don't like it.'

Sergeant Troy parked his beloved Cosworth outside Bay Tree Cottage. He got out and stood, in a blaze of oppressive sunshine, in the space where a gate should be. Briefly he lifted his face to the sun and revelled in it.

The Citroën was not there. Troy crossed over to the window, leaned on a pale windowsill bleached even paler by the consuming heat, and looked inside. The sitting room appeared empty.

He walked to the rear garden and studied the tangle of herbaceous and climbing plants, receiving no pleasure from what he immediately designated a right old mess. There was a wishing well with a small ornate arch made of cast iron wreathed in nasturtiums. Troy lifted the old wooden cover and peered down the shaft which was lined with damp moss and appeared very deep. It smelled sweet and clean. A pretty good sign that there was no one having a casual kip at the far end.

Disappointed that he was not going to be hurrying back to the station with news that he and he alone had found the body of Simone Hollingsworth, Troy replaced the lid. In the back yard – you couldn't really call it a patio – was a scarred and battered table covered with a right load of old junk – pebbles and driftwood and shells. There were lots of earthenware pots in all shapes and sizes containing assorted cuttings, trays crowded with leggy seedlings and some tomato plants. Although there was a length of hose close by already connected to a tap, everything looked as if it could do with a good soak.

Troy dragged the table out and had a gander into the kitchen. There was some dirty crockery in the sink. Normally he would regard that as a sign that whoever the stuff belonged to would be back soon but with a slut like Sarah Lawson you could never tell. He wouldn't put it past her to go off on a round-the-world trip without even putting the bin out.

At the front again, he lifted the letter box and peered through, hoping there might be some post on the hall carpet – that would at least give him some idea how long she'd been out – but no joy.

The sergeant drifted back on to the pavement, wondering what to do next. He had no intention of returning empty-handed to the station. He might not be able to produce Ms Lawson in person but at least he should be able to glean some information on her whereabouts. So where would be the best place to start?

He was facing Ostlers which was ideally situated for observing all the comings and goings at Bay Tree Cottage. In a matter of seconds, Sergeant Troy was in there. A red-faced woman with bobbing little sausage curls, wearing a floral pinafore dress and pearl stud earrings, sat behind the till. Troy did not recognise her. But Mrs Boast remembered him.

'So. It's you.'

'Pardon?'

'How you can show your face . . .'

'Me?'

'The Incident of the Curdleigh Posset?'

'Ohh . . . yes.' Troy smiled.

Mrs Boast pushed her red angry countenance close to his own until their noses were almost touching and snarled. It was very off-putting. She smelled of candles and lavender wax polish. 'That's the high spot in my talk. I can't culminate without my posset.'

Sergeant Troy essayed a spot of light relief. 'Whatever turns you on.'

'I reach my peak, I have the audience in the palm of my hand, I lift up my hedgehog and what do I see?'

Troy had had enough of this tomfoolery. He produced his warrant card and said, 'Causton CID need your assistance, Mrs Boast, in a matter of some discretion. I hope we can rely on you?'

'That depends,' said Mrs Boast, peering at his photograph with the deepest suspicion.

'On what?'

'Neither hubby nor myself would be prepared to do anything illegal.'

It was not often Sergeant Troy found himself lost for

words. Eventually he said, 'There'd be no question of that. It's a simple matter of surveillance.'

'I see.' Mrs Boast's eyes narrowed. Without moving a muscle she managed to strike an attitude. That of a woman of whom her country may demand great things at any moment and who would not be found wanting. She straightened her shoulders and said, 'Message received. Over.'

'We're hoping to interview Sarah Lawson—'

'What about?'

'That's the discreet bit.'

'I thought you meant—'

'She's not in at the moment. I wonder if you noticed what time she went out?'

'Her car hasn't been there for a day or two. In fact, she drove off not long after you and that other policeman, the one with the nice manners, called at the cottage the other day.'

'And she hasn't been back?'

'No.'

Ah shit. The boss was going to love this. 'Have you seen anyone calling at the house?'

'Not that I've noticed.'

'I see. Well, as you're so ideally placed, Mrs Boast, perhaps you or your husband would be good enough to give us a ring the minute she does return.' He placed one of Barnaby's direct line cards on the counter.

Mrs Boast studied it, plainly with some disappointment. 'Is that all?'

'It may not seem like much but it could be of great assistance.'

'Like in *Crimewatch*?'

'Exactly.'

'And should I listen out for any comments – on her possible whereabouts or suchlike? This place is a good clearing house for village gossip.'

Troy could well believe it. He hesitated. The DCI might not be prepared as yet for their interest in Sarah Lawson to get around. 'Listen by all means, Mrs Boast, but I can't stress how important it is that you keep this present conversation to yourself.'

'Have no fear.'

'And your husband too, of course.'

'There is no need for you to concern yourself over Nigel,' retorted Mrs Boast. 'He played Francis Walsingham in our last Tudor pageant so there's not much you can tell him about surveillance.'

Troy escaped but not without buying a pack of twenty Rothmans which cost seven pence more than those at his local newsagent.

While this conversation was going on Elfrida Molfrey reclined in her lovely garden on a slatted wooden steamer. The chair, like its occupant, was the genuine article, having been reserved for her personal use on the top deck of the *Cherbourg Orion* during its 1933 maiden voyage to New York. After the ship had docked, the Captain, at whose table every evening she had glittered and sparkled like the great star she was, had presented her with the lounger. It had been crated up and delivered to the Music Box where she was triumphantly to appear in a revival of *Oh Lady, Lady*.

For a while Elfrida's mind wandered, recalling the towering pagodas of flowers – red roses and lilies and Malmaison carnations that had filled her dressing room to the ceiling and lined the long stone corridors outside. She thought of dinner at Sardis and how everyone in the restaurant would get to their feet and raise their glasses when she came in. Of dancing in her white satin Worth gown at DeLanceys on Madison Avenue. And of the rope of rose gold Okinawa pearls that Jed Harris, the meanest man on Broadway, had looped round the neck of a pretty little marmoset and had delivered to her suite at the Astor Hotel.

Elfrida sighed but briefly for, unlike many people with a brilliantly successful past, she was extremely happy in what some might regard as a rather mundane present. Struggling to sit up, she looked around for Cubby. Not seeing him immediately, Elfrida closed her eyes and concentrated hard, for she believed her secret thoughts to have great carrying power.

And sure enough, a moment later, he came trotting round the corner of the house bearing a bunch of forget-me-nots and stephanotis.

'For your bedroom, dear,' he called across the herbaceous border. 'Which vase would you prefer?'

'I need my writing things, Cubby. If you would be so kind.'

'Of course.'

Cubby retrieved the cigar box, writing paper, envelopes and the gold and tortoiseshell lorgnettes from the trolley in the sitting room. One of the loveliest things about Elfrida, he thought as he made his way back into the garden, was her manners. And, though exquisite, they were in no way artificial. She just always considered other people's feelings.

'We simply must do something about those poor souls next door,' said Elfrida, proving his point. She opened her cigar box and took out a fountain pen. 'If it is only to express our sympathy and offer what help we can.'

'I doubt if it would be wanted.'

'This is no time to worry about being rebuffed, my love.'

'I didn't mean that. I just can't imagine what on earth we could do.'

'Sometimes just knowing that concern – and I'm not talking about prurient nosiness or the wish to meddle but genuine concern – exists can perhaps yield a grain of comfort.'

Cubby still looked doubtful. His whole nature shrank from entering the force field of another's agony. All he wanted was to be left alone to cultivate his garden.

Elfrida, understanding this, said, 'You don't have to be involved, sweeting.'

Then of course Cubby wanted to be involved, fearing that the Brockleys might think he didn't care.

'I shall write a little note which will naturally be from both of us and slip it through their letter box.' Elfrida selected a sheet of thick ivory paper with taffeta watermarks and a long narrow envelope. She uncapped her pen.

Coincidentally Reg Brockley, accompanied by Shona, was at the same time entering St Chad's Lane at the point where the very last house in the village abutted on to the barley fields.

Reg had neither seen nor spoken to anyone, except PC Perrot and the vicar, since the public announcement of his daughter's death. He dreaded the time when a confrontation would be forced upon him and had chosen to take his walk at twelve thirty for this very reason. For most of Fawcett Green's inhabitants would surely, at that hour, be either preparing or actually eating their lunch.

Shona had been allowed out again into the back garden and had, out of timid desperation, once more fouled that pristine velvet showpiece. She had crept back into the house with the deepest apprehension, peering round the kitchen door and cringing when Reg approached.

It was this as much as anything that had driven him to go out. He no longer gave a damn about the garden but this was his daughter's dog. Plainly anxious, bewildered and lonely, Shona had received no exercise since the evening Brenda disappeared, let alone any word of comfort or affection. Somehow Reg had made himself take the leash off the hook in the hall, as Brenda had done every night of her life. Then, after checking that Iris was still deeply asleep and the lane was deserted, he and Shona had set off.

They made a square round the nearest field, the poodle moping and sighing at Reg's heels. She never leapt and pranced now. He tried to make conversation but simply felt foolish and could think of nothing to say. Brenda would have chattered away to the dog about everything and nothing, using sweet pet names and baby talk. Unbelievably, he and Iris had sometimes been irritated by this.

On the way back and just a few yards from his house, a woman whose name Reg did not know but who lived in the village appeared. She was on a bicycle and travelling towards him. It seemed inevitable that they must pass each other.

Reg's stomach bucked and churned. In the throat-searing heat his upper lip and forehead became drenched in cool sweat. Convinced that she would know just who he was, he stared hard at the moving polished toecaps of his shoes.

But then, as they drew nearer to each other, an extraordinary thing happened. His gaze would not stay lowered. He felt his eyes being tugged upwards and sideways, again and again. A confused need for human contact overwhelmed him. And by the time she was barely a few feet away he was staring, hard and determined, directly into her face.

The woman started frowning; looking at her watch. She

shook her wrist, checked the watch again, tutted and sighed with an irritation that was plainly artificial. By the time all this had been accomplished she was well past him and pedalling quickly away.

Reg stood quite still, gazing after the departing cyclist, amazed at the distress he felt at the rebuff. It was as if he had suddenly become invisible. And, worse, untouchable.

Slowly he covered the remaining distance to The Larches. As he approached the gate, a figure draped in floating organza was just coming out. No problem with recognition on this occasion.

Forewarned by now, Reg braced himself. He stood aside for her to pass; Shona humbly came to heel.

'Mr Brockley.'

'Good . . . er . . .' Reg licked his dry lips and tried again. 'Good morning, Mrs Molfrey.'

'I just wanted to say how very sorry both Cubby and myself were to hear the terrible news about Brenda. We're close by, as you know, and if there is anything, anything at all we can do to help, please don't hesitate to ask.' Whilst speaking the last few words, she laid her hand gently on his arm.

It was this, or so Reg thought, long afterwards, that broke him. He had not shed a tear since his daughter's death. Now the frozen shell round his heart splintered, cracked, fell away. He stood there weeping in the street and pain ran through his veins like fire.

Sergeant Troy did not drive back to Causton straightaway. So far his purse was empty of all save bad news and he wanted to be able to offer at least a coin or two which had a positive ring.

Troy thought about Gray Patterson. He had had as

much to do with Sarah as anyone in the village. And even if his attempts to know her better had, as he had put it, 'got nowhere', he must have found out quite a bit about her background, family, friends and so forth during their conversations. He might also know where she'd hopped off to.

It took Troy all of three minutes to walk round the corner to Patterson's. That was about all you could say in favour of country life, in the sergeant's opinion. At least everything was near everything else. Pub, shop, post office. Trouble was they were all surrounded by miles and miles and miles of nothing.

The first thing he noticed was that the agent's For Let board had been taken down. It was lying on its side just behind the belt of blue piceas. Bess came rushing up, doing her stuff. Troy liked to think the welcome meant she remembered him.

'Good afternoon, Mr Patterson.'

'Hullo.' Patterson's greeting was much more cautious. He had plainly not forgotten their last meeting. As if sensing a certain reserve in the situation, Bess's tail began to wag less confidently. 'What is it this time?'

'Let the house, have you, sir?'

'That's right. Move out at the end of the month and, yes, I will inform you of my new address.'

'Planning to go far?'

'I'm going to look at a flat in Uxbridge this afternoon.' He had been cleaning up the drive when Troy arrived. Now he started again wielding the rake with smooth, sweeping movements, lightly dragging the pea shingle back and forth. Tugging up weeds.

'Thirsty work,' suggested Sergeant Troy through dry lips.

'What do you want?'

'A word about Miss Lawson, actually.'

'I'm not discussing Sarah behind her back.'

'Mr Patterson, refusing to help the police with their inquiries—'

'Don't give me that crap.'

Sergeant Troy reacted immediately to this insult. Colour flared beneath his near transparent skin. His cheeks became hollow with tension as he clamped his lips together. He concealed his annoyance by bending down to pat the collie, murmuring, 'Good dog.'

He used these few moments to ask himself some sensible questions. Such as, could he handle this supercilious bastard as the chief might in similar circumstances? Could he, just this once, not let himself be pushed all over the shop by his emotions? He decided to give it a whirl.

'Thing is,' Troy drew a deep breath and straightened up, 'we're rather concerned about her. Were you aware that she has been missing for the past two days?'

'I'm not sure I'd use such an emotive word as missing.'

'Could I ask when you last saw her, Mr Patterson?' God, this phoney civility stuck in his throat. Troy could not believe that the words This Man Is A Creeping Toad were not branded on his forehead in letters of fire.

'Well, it was four days ago actually.' Gray had no intention of saying how often he had called at the house. Or how, for no logical reason, anxiety as to Sarah's wellbeing had been gradually building up in him until, last night, he had been unable to sleep.

'And how did she seem to you then?'

Gray hesitated. He could just imagine what the police would make of the news that Sarah had been distressed beyond measure by Alan Hollingsworth's death. Yet he felt to prevaricate might look odd.

'A little bit down, I think.'

'Did she say why?'

'Look, a woman has disappeared here and two people have died in mysterious circumstances. Even if they weren't well known or liked, something like that seeps into the bricks and mortar of a small community. I think everyone has been affected to some degree or other.'

'And she'd be specially sensitive. Being artistic.'

'Up to a point, Lord Copper,' said Gray drily. Sarah had not been all that understanding when it came to his own feelings.

Troy did not reply and it was not until Gray glanced up again that he became aware that the other man appeared flushed and angry. It occurred to him that perhaps Troy had never heard the phrase before and thought he was being sarcastic. He said, 'It's a quote, Sergeant.'

'I'm aware of that, sir. Thanks very much.' Always more comfortable with a lie, Troy felt his flush subside. 'So, Miss Lawson didn't tell you she was going away?'

'There's no reason why she should.'

'Sounds a bit sudden.' Troy remembered the plates in the sink, the feeling he'd had that someone had simply walked straight out, leaving the house exactly as it was. Just like Mrs Hollingsworth.

'Isn't tomorrow her teaching day?'

'That's right.'

'Could you give me the name of the place where she works, please?' Troy produced his notebook and jotted it down, murmuring casually as he did so, 'We did actually talk to Miss Lawson on Saturday morning.'

'Really?' His voice was wary.

'Mmm. She hadn't quite realised that Mr Hollingsworth's death was being treated as suspicious. I must say when we explained this, her reaction was, well, rather extreme.'

'In what way?'

'She passed out.'

'Christ!'

'Which naturally gave one pause for thought, as you might say.'

'You surely don't think she had anything to do with it?'

'Who's to say?'

'I'm to say. I know Sarah. You're barking up totally the wrong tree.'

'Have you discussed the matter with her then, Mr Patterson?'

Gray paused then, realising that 'no' would not be believed. 'Briefly. And came to no conclusion, before you ask.'

'Did she ever mention any close friends or relatives to you? I'm thinking of where she might be staying.'

'Where you might be able to hunt her down, you mean.'

'I think hunt is rather an emotive word, don't you, sir?' Pleased with this natty bit of table turning, Troy put away his notebook. 'Thank you for your time, Mr Patterson. Oh, by the way . . .'

'Now what?' Gray had already returned to his raking.

'Your alibi for the sixth of June checks out. The cashier at the cinema remembers you buying a ticket.' All that meant, of course, was that Patterson had gone into the Odeon at the time he said he had. Nothing to say what time he had come out. Might have been sitting in there five minutes before climbing out of the toilet window. Still no point in saying so at this moment in time. Get them off their guard and keep them there.

Troy was quite chuffed with his performance. He went

into the phone box and gave the Coalport and National a bell. He asked for Miss Willing, left his name and explained that one or two things had come up regarding the Brockley case that he thought she might be able to help him with. He didn't like to disturb her at work but perhaps later?

Then he rang Sarah's college and was told that a supply teacher was taking the Stained Glass Design Course this week. Sarah Lawson had rung in saying she had had an accident which had left her incapacitated. She would not be returning until next term at the earliest.

Barnaby had withdrawn from the incident room to his office three floors away and was already thinking of going back. The atmosphere, merely soupy downstairs, was positively gluey up here.

The DCI's blue and white striped shirt had great dark patches of sweat under the arms. He had opened the front and loosened his tie the better to ease the collar away from the back of his burning neck. Even the desk fan, heaving its propellor blades slowly round, appeared to be on the point of grinding to a halt.

The idea was that, being quieter up here, it would be easier to think. He was struggling to put this notion into practice but his brains had become addled by the heat. He heaved himself to his feet and wandered over to the wall by the window on which was spread a map of the Thames Valley area.

He studied it with a certain amount of gloom. Somewhere in that great expanse of land and water existed – or, more likely, had by now ceased to exist – Mrs Alan Hollingsworth. And all the newspaper publicity and posters and flyers and handouts had failed to discover where.

Barnaby, though deeply disappointed, was not really

surprised. If it was easy enough to disappear under one's own volition – and Missing Persons files were heart-breakingly clear on this point – how much more easy to vanish from public view under duress.

And vanish was the word. Like the pretty assistant of a master magician, she had entered the magic box – in this case the ladies' loo in a department store – and apparently never come out again.

The key word, of course, being apparently. The store was very busy on market day, which was probably why none of the assistants or shoppers had noticed Simone leave. Certainly she must have walked through Bobby's to get to the street. The ladies' room was on the second floor so she could hardly have climbed through the window.

Barnaby closed his eyes and pictured the thronging streets, busy stalls with their bright striped awnings and bawling, shouting occupants, hot dog and fresh fish mobile vans, and the open-sided lorries selling clothes and china. Simone, or whoever was pulling her strings, had certainly chosen the right day for it.

A knock at the glass-panelled door and Sergeant Troy put his head round.

'About time.' Barnaby lifted his crumpled linen jacket from the old-fashioned hat stand. 'Are we fit then?'

'No, chief.' He came properly into the room. 'Sorry. She's scarpered.'

'What!'

'Left the house soon after our visit. Hasn't been seen since. Phoned the college to say she won't be in again this term.'

'Oh hell.' The Chief Inspector stumbled back to the old leather swivel chair behind his desk, slumped into it and groaned again. 'Bloody sodding buggering hell.'

CAROLINE GRAHAM

'Yeah, it's a pisser all right.' Troy closed the door and leaned against it. 'I tried Patterson on the off chance. Him doing a bit of courting, like. Or trying to. But he doesn't have a clue where she's gone either. Or so he says.'

'Of all the stupid, *stupid* . . .' Barnaby's voice shook with self-directed anger. It had been plain, talking to the woman, that she was emotionally entangled in some way with what had been going on. He had known of her friendship with Gray Patterson, the main man in the frame. He had seen her trembling with nervous distress throughout their whole interview and passing out with shock on discovering Hollingsworth had not taken his own life. On coming round she had wept.

And still he had not taken her in. Just how serious an error his decision was to leave matters for a day or two now became plain. A breathing space was how he remembered regarding it. Time to 'settle into the reassuring belief that she had seen the last of them'. What a grave miscalculation. What swaggering hubris.

And now she had turned the tables on her tormentors with a vengeance, presenting them with the alarming proposition that it was they who might well have seen the last of her.

Barnaby returned to his desk in the incident room to wade through the latest backlog of information and kill time till the five o'clock briefing. He found clarification from Scenes of Crime who, having received a facsimile of Brenda Brockley's fingerprints from Heathrow, were now able to inform him that they had not been present anywhere in Nightingales. No more than he had expected.

Also pretty predictable was the postmortem report. Brenda had died from a subdural haemorrhage following the fracturing of her skull. She also had a broken tibia in her left leg, a fractured pelvis and three broken ribs. The accompanying SOCO report described the marks on her legs and dress as being made by Pirelli tyres identical to the ones fitted to the Audi convertible. The Heathrow team had already liaised with Causton Forensic and would be coming over to examine Hollingsworth's car within the next two days.

No luck with the letting agencies as far as discovering the hiding place for the kidnapped woman was concerned though the checking procedure had borne some rather unpleasant fruit. A two-bedroomed flat in Princes Risborough had been found to be in use for highly immoral purposes. And, nearer home, a lockup with dripping walls and no proper ventilation proved to be doubling as a sweat shop in which over twenty Asian women and young girls spent their days inhaling kapok while making soft toys.

Barnaby drank some tea, a cold drink, more tea and tried not to dwell on the fact that it was now twelve days since Simone had taken the market bus to Causton and never returned. And almost eight since Alan Hollingsworth and Brenda Brockley had died. He reminded himself that all investigations moved at their own pace. That some, lacking witnesses perhaps or forensic detail, never got off the ground and others, like this one, could be submerged in such a wash of assorted information that any movement that was at all subtle could very easily be overlooked.

He recalled the moment in the lift, not all that long ago, when he felt himself content to be submerged for a while in a 'cloud of unknowing'. And tried to be unbothered by the fact that the cloud now seemed to have transformed itself into a sea of blind ignorance in which he was floating, rather more quickly than he would have liked, to a watery grave.

The room was filling up. At 5 p.m. precisely the Chief Inspector got up to speak.

'I'm afraid there's been a disappointing development,' he began and went on to describe Sarah Lawson's disappearance. 'I'm now quite convinced that Lawson is seriously involved in this matter. She lied about where she was on the evening of Hollingsworth's death. On the other hand, she appeared absolutely devastated when I told her that we were regarding it as suspicious.'

'P'raps they were lovers, sir,' suggested Sergeant Beryl. 'On the Q and T.'

'More likely she was devastated on Gray Patterson's behalf,' said Troy. 'I reckon she knows something about his movements that really puts him in the frame.'

'That level of concern implies some sort of genuine involvement. He led us to believe he was keen but getting nowhere.'

'Men have been known to lie,' said a young red-haired girl. And immediately ducked down behind her VDU.

Barnaby cut the jeering short. 'The crucial thing now is to find her. The college will be open tomorrow at eight thirty. Talk to the staff and administration and get a photograph if they have one. And it's the day her class meets so talk especially to her students. Find out everything you can about her background, especially any friendships or close relatives she may have spoken of. She might be staying with one of them. Ask the students their opinion of Simone Hollingsworth while you're at it. She wasn't on the course for long but it will be interesting to see what they thought.'

'Will we be searching Sarah Lawson's house, sir?' asked a fresh-faced young constable with an extraordinary moustache; very curly and totally out of control. 'There might be some clue there as to her present whereabouts.'

'Probably within the next day or so, Belling, yes.' Barnaby nodded, half smiled. They asked questions now, the youngsters. Were encouraged to do so which was quite right. Thirty years ago he would never have dared.

'Unfortunately we can't spare anyone to watch the cottage full time in case she returns but our man on the beat will keep an eye. Details of her car have already been circulated. It's a red and white Quatre Chevaux. Far from unique but out of the ordinary enough perhaps to catch someone's eye.'

'Be well tucked away by now, sir, though, won't it?' asked Sergeant Brierley. 'Garaged somewhere.'

'Not necessarily,' said Barnaby. 'She may not realise we're searching for her. It could be, of course, that her disappearance has nothing to do with my visit and we're in a muck sweat over nothing.' He paused, looking round. The famous eyebrows lifted slightly, evoking a response. It was plain from the expression on their faces that no one believed that. Barnaby didn't blame them. He didn't believe it himself.

'Well,' he got up and stretched his legs. 'Until eight o'clock tomorrow then. And that's eight sharp.'

'Yes, sir. I certainly will. I'll be over there, on the spot, within the next half hour.'

Trixie Perrot, keeping an eye on her youngest child who was just learning to feed himself, drying the hair of the oldest and trying to keep the dog from mangling her husband's slippers, shouted across the room, 'Tell him it's your rest day.'

'Sorry, Chief Inspector? No, no, that's the television set. It's a bit loud.'

The Perrots had had a lovely afternoon. Trixie's parents had brought around a bright blue plastic paddling pool. Colin had inflated it in the garden and filled it from the hose. Back from school the kids had laughed and screamed and splashed about while the grown ups sat in the shade and ate scones and freshly picked raspberries with Devon cream.

In half an hour, when the children were upstairs, there would be chicken salad, an ice cold lager and Keith Floyd who Colin and his wife loved to watch. More for the tears before bedtime factor than the recipes if truth were told, the sense that any minute the whole boiling might well go up in smoke.

'Daddy . . .'

'What was all that about?'

'Daddy!'

'Sarah Lawson's disappeared. They want me to keep an eye on the house.'

'But you're off duty.'

'It's my beat. There's no one else.'

That this was true in no way mitigated Trixie's distress. 'What are you supposed to do then? Sit on her doorstep in case she turns up?'

'I suppose. Well, on and off.'

'That's ridiculous. And surely you don't have to go this minute?'

'*Dadee, look.*'

'Good grief, Jamie.' Colin pulled out his handkerchief. His son's face was covered in ice cream, as was his hair. There was even a certain amount up his nose. 'Have you eaten any of that?'

'Eaten *all*,' cried Jamie proudly.

'At least stay until they're in bed.' Trixie tried to keep the irritation out of her voice but she hated seeing him like this, so anxious to please. Running round in circles the minute that sneering lot at Causton blew the whistle.

'Can I go and watch TV now?'

'No.' She ran her fingers through the hair of the child on her lap. 'You're still damp.' Then, to her husband. 'They won't think any more of you.'

'You know how things are, Trix. The mistakes I've made. I've already been threatened with a transfer.'

'Well, they shouldn't expect you to do CID work. That needs special training. You're a village bobby. And the best there is.'

'Don't get upset.'

'I'd like to see them come down here and do your job.'

Constable Perrot stayed to see his sons to bed then got his Honda out and rode over to Fawcett Green. He parked outside Bay Tree Cottage, walked up and down the lane a bit and visited the Goat and Whistle for a quick half. Then he sat in the warm evening sun in Sarah Lawson's back garden. The time passed very slowly. Next time, he decided, he would bring something to read.

While Perrot kept his lonely vigil, Barnaby was enjoying the pleasure of his wife's company and a chilled glass of Santara Chardonnay. He was suffering rather than enjoying a series of more or less painful pinpricks in his knees.

'Those trousers'll be ruined.'

'Leave him alone. He's all right.'

Eighteen months ago the Barnabys' daughter and her husband, having signed up for a three-month European tour, had left behind their newest acquisition, a Russian Blue kitten, Kilmowski.

Barnaby pointed out sourly that he thought the period

wherein your offspring begs for a pet, promises to wash, groom, feed and exercise it to the end of its days then promptly dumps the whole procedure on to you drew to a natural close around the fifteenth year.

Joyce, enchanted by the adorable little creature, told her husband he was an old grump. Barnaby, just as deeply disenchanted, soon had his worst fears realised. Food nicked off his plate while he wasn't looking, his newspaper torn up then wee'd on. He counted the days to his daughter's return.

But by the time Cully and Nico got back, the kitten had seduced him utterly and it was not only Joyce who was unhappy at the thought of giving it back.

However, as things turned out, Cully was barely unpacked before she had to leave for Manchester Royal Exchange and *Hedda Gabler*. Nicholas had a surprise chance to go to Stratford where an actor had broken his contract and taken a movie offer. They decided to let their flat for the next six months. By the time they had stopped vagabonding and had once more settled in London, Kilmowski, though still richly endowed with beauty, elegance and playfully winning ways, was plainly no longer a kitten. He had, as Cully put it with sorrowful wit, transmogrified. She and Nico both agreed that it would be not only selfish but cruel to whisk him away to a window-boxed flat when he had all of Arbury Crescent to roam around in. So Kiki, as he had been called almost from the day of his arrival, stayed put.

'What time are they coming?'

'Not they. It's Cully on her own.'

'Oh, we're not starting all that again, are we?'

'Of course not. Nico's got to be at Pinewood by half past seven in the morning so he's having an early night. I told you.'

'You always say that.'

'It's always true.'

'I meant to tell you,' Barnaby changed the subject, 'I played your Amadeus rehearsal tape yesterday—'

'Oh Tom, that's really nice.'

'Gavin thought you were Cecilia Bertoli.'

'Perhaps I've misjudged that boy.'

'No you haven't.'

'No, I haven't.' Joyce laughed.

The doorbell rang. She left to answer it. Barnaby put the cat down and went to the kitchen where he retrieved his gazpacho from the fridge and began to crack some ice.

Cully entered (no other word would do), crossed centre left and gave him a kiss. She wore a very short plain white linen dress and black espadrilles, the laces cross-gartered almost to her richly bronzed knees. No make-up, hair tumbling every which way. Beauty unadorned.

'Hullo, Pa.'

'Hullo, darling. You've decided to watch this film then?'

'Almost. I think. I wanted to see you and Mum, anyway.'

Barnaby, ridiculously pleased, said casually, 'Nice to see you, too.'

'Yum yum.' She dipped her finger into the gazpacho and sucked it. 'What else is there?'

'Crab and rice salad and gooseberry— Don't *do* that.'

'We're all family.'

'Licking your fingers then sticking them back in the food, that's not how we've brought you up.'

Cully giggled. 'Shall I go and stand in the corner?'

'You can help your mother with the plates. And help yourself to some wine.'

'You sure I'm old enough?'

Barnaby got out three white soup bowls with a blue fish

---

on the bottom. Souvenirs from Galicia. He set them in slightly larger bowls packed with crushed ice and poured in the soup. Put French bread on the tray and a dish of pale, unsalted butter from Brittany.

'Shall I open another bottle?' said Joyce through the serving hatch.

'I shouldn't.' He had noticed Cully's car keys, swinging from her little finger.

The food was set out on a low coffee table in front of the television. The tape of *The Blue Angel*, set to Rewind, whizzed, hissed and finally clicked off. Joyce picked up the remote control and looked at her daughter.

'Do I press Play?'

'Sure. Why not?' Cully pushed an imaginary trilby to the back of her head with the edge of her thumb. 'Let's hear it for Marlene and the professor.'

Barnaby, as far as he could remember, had never seen the film. This made the score two out of three. Joyce had caught it at the Hampstead Everyman 'years and years ago'.

Supposedly a new print, it was still pretty grainy. But nothing could mar that astonishingly flawless face. A face whose mysterious perfection no words could even begin to describe. Beautiful was hopelessly inadequate. And where could you go from there?

Cully sighed deeply. She said, 'I will never, ever again believe that cheekbones are merely deposits of calcium.'

Watching the character played by Emil Jannings, twisting and turning in the fatal net, Barnaby thought how useless a weapon intelligence was against the inscrutable devouring onslaught of sexual passion. Here was a man fighting for his honour, his marriage, his very life even with no weapons but his mind. When physical obsession took over, it seemed that common sense and even sometimes sanity itself fled.

Barnaby put the film on Pause and went to dish up the crab and rice salad. When he came back, his wife and daughter were discussing Dietrich, then and now.

Cully was saying, 'It's impossible for us to react to the film, and especially to her, as people did in the thirties.'

'I don't see why.'

'Because then she was simply a stunning-looking woman at the start of her career. Now she's an icon. And whatever else icons might be, they are not sexy. Isn't that right, Dad?'

'Hang on a sec.' He forked up some of the rice and tasted it. 'Not enough nutmeg.'

'Don't put your fork back into that when it's been in your mouth,' cried Joyce.

Cully started giggling again but stopped when her father refused to refill her glass. There was a fairly brisk argument which ended with the youngest Barnaby deciding she had had enough of the film, the dinner and her parents, thanks very much and vanishing abruptly into the night.

Chapter Ten

The next morning Barnaby awoke with a vaguely depressed feeling that he could not shake off. It stuck with him all through his fruit-filled, fibre-rich, niacin-laced breakfast, any benefits from which were surely cancelled out by the long, self-fumigating crawl along the A412. He decided it would probably be quicker to jump out and swim to work in the Grand Union which was running along beside him.

It was partially the previous evening's disagreement, of course. He did not regret refusing Cully another drink. Or sticking to his guns when she started playing up. But he hated it when they had even a minor tiff. However his daughter, though a champion flouncer, was, thank God, not a sulker. She had rung up before he'd gone to bed to say he was right, she was wrong, she loved him and not to forget her mother's birthday.

Thinking of his wife reminded Barnaby that he had reluctantly promised to listen to a tape she had pressed upon him the other day. *Four Last Songs* by Richard Strauss. He'd argued that he only liked the popular classics. Joyce had said this was a popular classic and it was high time he broadened his mind. Knowing the only occasion he would sit and listen to something all the way through was in his car, she had slipped the cassette in the appropriate slot and taped over the opening a blank postcard on which she had drawn a large ear.

Barnaby's love of what he thought of as 'musical music' went back a long way. As a little boy he would listen for hours with his father to heavy shellac records on a wind-up gramophone enclosed in a fumed oak cabinet. When the voices started to go all yawny and flat he would rush to turn the handle and speed them up so they would sing normally again. Sometimes, when the tips of the needles got all rough and scratchy, he was allowed to put a new one in.

A lot of the songs were performed by the Carl Rosa Opera Company. Gems from *The Merry Widow, Die Fledermaus, The Gipsy Baron*. All great stuff. Wonderful tunes the heart could waltz to. Barnaby sighed and dutifully pressed the Play button.

Joycey's pupils seemed to want to perform the most extraordinary things. Occasionally Barnaby was at home when his wife was giving a lesson and, during any brief moments he was compelled to leave his study, could hardly believe his ears. It seemed incredible to him that people would actually pay good money to be taught how to squawk off key. No wonder the cat disappeared under the sofa.

The glorious voice of Kiri te Kanawa poured out of the car. The man in the vehicle creeping along parallel to his own stared. Barnaby turned the sound down and closed his window. Ever since the advent of that opera-loving cop on the telly, he had had moments of feeling self-conscious, as if caught out in some affectation when idling musically in a queue or at the traffic lights.

He was aware that this was nonsense. After all, no one knew he also was a Detective Chief Inspector in the CID. And even if they did, *tant pis*. If life could not occasionally imitate art, what was the world coming to?

Arriving at the station, he pulled into his private parking space and switched off his tape. Nice enough, but not a patch on the Easter Hymn from *Rusticana*.

The incident room was ominously quiet. All right, you could say it was barely eight o'clock. That the people manning it were just coming to the end of a long shift and that the great British public was too busy scraping the sleep out of its eyes to be on the blower feeding helpful information to its local nick. Even so, there was no escaping the sense that things were grinding slowly to a halt.

The Chief Inspector poured himself some coffee from the hot plate. It had been stewing for some time and was quite bitter.

The day dragged on. Barnaby, with little that was new to work on, recapped on the story so far. Read through all the Fawcett Green interviews, those at Penstemon and the Coalport and National and the one with Freddie Blakeley.

His mind was beginning to feel like a bowl of alphabet soup. One stir and certain letters floated up, a few would join briefly and seem to make some sort of sense before sinking once more to the bottom of the dish. Another stir would produce only disconnected gibberish.

Troy, an old hand at assessing the chief's moods, was also an expert at being both present and absent at the same time. Positioned so that he was immediately available should old misery guts happen to look around for him or call out, he had also organised enough space between them to remove himself from the turbulent range of Barnaby's bad temper.

He understood the reason, of course. Felt the same himself. There were times when you wanted to get hold of a case and shake it till its innards rattled. Shake it until the entire shape of it changed or until someone caught in the frame started to sing a completely different tune.

Like Sarah Lawson, for instance. Troy would have handled that interview the other day quite differently. Seemed to him the time to put pressure on someone was when they were at their most vulnerable. Now, even if they picked the woman up within the next twenty-four hours, she'd had over three days to sort herself and her story out. Go over and over it. Make it question-proof.

Mind you, having said that, it paid to be a bit cautious when dealing with a member of the middle class. You couldn't really let yourself go as you might with a steaming pile of lowlife from the average tower block. They would sit there, the Lawsons of this world, looking as if they couldn't afford a pot to piss in and all the while they were shagging the local MP. A wise man watched his back in these matters.

Sergeant Troy was a bit off women anyway at the moment. They were, it seemed to him, deceivers ever. Take Jacqui definitely non-Willing. What a teaser she'd turned out to be. An extremely spicy wrapper, no question (four chillies, Troy would have said, asked to grade that luscious exterior) but more of your three hundred cals a portion when it came to tasting time. One quick lager and lime in the Turk's Head and she'd had to dash off to get her husband's dinner. Seemed that if he didn't have something hot on the table the minute he got in, there was no handling him. Troy said sourly he knew just how the man felt.

It was at this point in the sergeant's irritable musings that the fax machine leapt into life. He went across, read the results and tore the paper off with some satisfaction. This would cheer the boss up.

'Something from Heathrow, sir.' He placed the fax on

Barnaby's blotter. 'Bit of a breakthrough, wouldn't you say?'

The gist of the matter was this. Someone working in the Left Luggage department and seeing the photographs of Alan Hollingsworth and Brenda Brockley pinned up in the office recognised the girl.

Gordon Collins had seen Brenda, on the evening of her death, standing just underneath the stairs in the section where cases were deposited. She had at no time joined the queue. At one point she had been reading a paper. Like Eden Lo, the Left Luggage clerk got the impression that Brenda was hiding from someone.

Inspector Fennimore had left unasked no question that Barnaby himself would have put. The Chief Inspector read on with increasing satisfaction not unmixed with gratitude that he would be spared a sweltering drive to Heathrow to talk to the man himself.

In spite of being asked to look and think and look again, Mr Collins could not recall ever seeing Alan Hollingsworth either passing over his luggage or collecting it. He pointed out that three handlers were on duty at any given time and he may not have been the one to take the case in question or issue the ticket.

The other two men on the same shift were equally unable to help. Hundreds of passengers used the system every day. A customer would need to be really remarkable either in manner or appearance to stand out.

The excellent Inspector Fennimore had worked out the next step in the puzzle with admirable speed. Hollingsworth had gone to the Häagen-Dazs café, ordered a coffee he didn't want and immediately walked away. So why buy the drink? Because he had been instructed to leave the ticket under the saucer.

Fennimore had shown the baggage handlers the Identikit

portrait of the old lady and asked if any of them had seen her. Receiving a negative reply, he then wondered what the situation would be if she had presented herself at the counter and handed over Hollingsworth's ticket.

All three men agreed that it was unlikely the item would be released without question. Normally this would be done, for there was nothing in the rule book to say that the party who handed in the luggage had to be the party who picked it up. But some dirty old transient?

So, wrote Inspector Fennimore, this meant surely that the old woman had merely taken the ticket for someone else. And take it she certainly did for Miss Lo cleared the cup away immediately after chasing her off and it had not been there then.

The fax's concluding paragraph gave the date of the preliminary inquest on Brenda Brockley as Thursday week at Hounslow Civic Centre. It also offered continued assurances of assistance should Causton CID feel the need.

Barnaby pushed the letter aside. The upsurge of interest, the feeling that at last something was happening to move things further forward or show them at a new angle was fading fast. For what had they got now that they didn't have before? Only the knowledge that the ransom money was not in the old biddy's string bag, as previously supposed, but in some sort of container in the Left Luggage department.

'Get that acknowledged, would you? Include our thanks.'

'Right, sir.' Troy, dismayed at the quick return to surly withdrawal, added. 'After that I thought I'd take a break. Grab a bite in the canteen. You coming?' This last sentence was prompted by the sight of Barnaby unhooking his jacket from the hat stand.

'No. I'm off to the bar.'

Troy stared then glanced, as he thought surreptitiously, at the clock. It was barely twelve thirty.

'Got a problem with that, have you, Sergeant?'

'Of course not, sir.' Not what you'd actually call a problem. Admitted, he had never known it happen before, the gaffer taking a drink in the middle of a shift; still, he supposed there had to be a first time for everything.

But he felt uncomfortable as he picked up the letter from Heathrow and set about organising the reply.

As things turned out, Barnaby only had a half of mild and a cheese and tomato farmhouse bap. A farmhouse bap was indistinguishable from the common or garden bap but for a smattering of white flour on the top and an extra penny on the price.

It was while chewing away at this uninspiring slab of tasteless stodge that the perfect solution to the problem of what to do with this completely unproductive lunch hour presented itself. He would go and buy Joyce's perfume.

The slip of paper with the address of the nearest stockist was in his wallet, as were some credit cards. He also carried his cheque book. Barnaby drove to Uxbridge, filled up with petrol, took the A4007 and got into the city centre about thirty minutes later.

Policewoman Titheridge, who had chased up the details, had thoughtfully asked for the precise position of the shop and the Chief Inspector was glad of it for La Parfumerie was in a tiny cobbled street behind a Norman church. He could have been wandering around for hours searching.

It was a lovely little place, the interior a glittering octagon of mirrored walls which multiplied again and again the crystal bottles and cellophane-wrapped and beribboned boxes that lined the shelves.

A pretty woman with a cloud of dark hair wearing a pink cotton wraparound overall smiled at Barnaby and asked if she could help him. He said he was looking for some Joy.

'The perfume, sir? Or the eau de toilette?'

'Oh, perfume. It's for a special occasion.'

'We're out of the one ounce size.' She took down a glistening gold and white box striped with red. 'But we have this which is the two ounce. Or the fifteen millilitre.'

This second box was very much smaller. Almost minuscule, it seemed to Barnaby. Not much to offer the wife of your bosom on the occasion of her big five oh.

'I'll have the first one.'

'Thank you.' The girl smiled at him and started to wrap the larger box first in fuchsia tissue paper and then in a sheet of shining metallic gold. She tied it up with wide satin ribbon, making several lavish bows. Then she reached under the counter, produced a velvet rose slightly deeper than the colour of her overall and wound the stem round the ribbon.

'That looks lovely,' said Barnaby who had unfolded his cheque book and uncapped his fountain pen while all this was going on. 'Now, what's the damage?'

She described precisely the extent of the damage then said, 'Oh dear, you've dropped your pen.'

'Yes.' Barnaby bent down and retrieved it off the floor. The sudden movement made him dizzy. But not nearly as dizzy as he felt already. 'Four . . .' He realised he was croaking and cleared his throat. 'Four . . . ?'

'Four hundred and seventeen pounds and eleven pence, please, sir.' She watched as his pen jerked around, pecking at the paper eventually, almost, one would have said, against its will, inscribing the correct words and figures. 'Someone's a very lucky girl.'

It struck Barnaby then that she thought the gift was for his doxie. A furtive, guilt-absolving donation to some tucked-away mistress in a service flat.

'The perfume is for my wife. Her fiftieth birthday's coming up. I wanted to get her something really special.'

'Goodness.' She blinked, plainly at a loss. 'Have you been married long?'

'Thirty years.'

'Thirty . . . ?' Not even the excuse of a newly revived lust then. 'Well, all I can say is, she must have made you very happy.'

'Happiness,' said Barnaby, picking up his box and turning to leave, 'is not the word for it.'

'That looks a bit of all right,' suggested Sergeant Troy as his boss put the conspicuously decorated box in his desk side cupboard.

Barnaby gave a noncommittal grunt. Normally he would have simply left such a thing in the car. After all, the vehicle was locked and standing on a police station forecourt. But the value of the perfume had made him extra cautious. He gave a final squint at it as he closed the cupboard door. The gift wrapping already appeared to him both garish and tawdry.

'I've got two birthdays coming up next week,' volunteered Troy. 'Maureen and my mum.'

'What are you getting them?'

'Maure wants that beauty book by Joan Collins. I said to her, "Maureen, if everybody could get to look like Joan Collins simply by reading a book, Joan Collins wouldn't be worth shit."'

'That must have gone down well.'

'The old lady's a doddle.' This had always been the case.

Mrs Troy was invariably overwhelmed by the smallest kindness demonstrated by her children. Or anyone else, come to that. Self-esteem was not her strong suit.

This year Troy planned to give her the video of *Martin Chuzzlewit*. He had missed at least half the episodes and it would give him a chance to catch up. The sergeant liked a good costume drama. Lace-up boots, frilly bonnets, powdered wigs. And that was only the horses.

Troy waited for an appreciative laugh for this sally in vain. The boss appeared distracted and remained so for the rest of the afternoon.

In the incident room all the leg men were back from Blackthorn College in time for the five-thirty briefing. The good news was that each staff member, as well as the students, had to carry an identity card complete with photograph. Only one had been needed from Sarah Lawson's strip of four and the rest, still on file in the office, had been willingly handed over. The bad news was that there was no more good news.

Each member of her class had been interviewed but could tell the police nothing apart from the fact that their tutor kept herself to herself. During the class's tea break she usually stayed in the studio. It was felt that, though encouraging and plainly interested in their efforts, Sarah remained very detached.

About Simone the group's opinion was also united. A pleasure to look at, she had also been very popular. Friendly and always ready for a chat though not talking much about herself at all. Often she would laugh or whisper in class which could be a bit distracting. Sometimes Miss Lawson would give her a telling off. Everyone was sorry when she stopped coming.

The administration department and the rest of the staff

were likewise unhelpful. Taking only one mid-afternoon session a week, Sarah never made use of the senior common room. Asked to describe her last telephone call in more detail, the woman who took it said the accident which was keeping Sarah away for the rest of the term was a fall from a stepladder. She had a badly strained arm and displaced shoulder. No, she had not sounded unusually distressed. Just her usual rather dry, sardonic self.

'Wonderful,' said Barnaby when all this came to an end. 'Nothing minus nothing. Which leaves us with?'

The room, infected by his pessimism and recognising the question as purely rhetorical, remained silent. Eventually Sergeant Brierley offered a consoling observation.

'At least we have Lawson's picture now. Get that circulated, someone's bound to catch sight of her somewhere.'

'Like they did Mrs Hollingsworth?'

'All due respects, sir, Mrs Hollingsworth was being deliberately concealed.'

Barnaby's expression did not lighten. It was now past six and no overtime in the offing. Indeed the next shift, with little to check out, follow up or run a search on would definitely be overmanned.

Everybody started to collect their gear. Barnaby's telephone rang; his own line. He had been waiting for a call from Heathrow Forensic. They had been examining Hollingsworth's car hoping to find proof positive that it was the one responsible for Brenda Brockley's death. But it was not Heathrow Forensic.

Barnaby turned his back on the others, mumbled something, left the room. In the corridor he pressed the elevator button for the next floor up.

Troy, who had followed him out at a respectful distance, knew what that meant. So he didn't go home with the others but stayed behind, hovering near the lift doors, pretending to study the notice-board. Just in case the chief wanted to let off steam when he came down. Talk things over. Maybe go for a quick drink.

But his presence was not required. Half an hour later Barnaby stormed out of the lift, his face black as thunder, dived into the incident room, seized his briefcase and left via the stairs without even noticing the presence of his faithful sidekick.

Sergeant Troy had never come across the phrase 'darkest before the dawn' or surely would have added it to his well-worn list of aphorisms. Like most hoary old sayings, it only applied to some of the people some of the time but Barnaby would have gone to sleep a good deal happier that miserable Wednesday if he had known just how soon it was going to apply to him.

What happened was this. When Troy got home, his deeply loathed cousin Colin, girl friend Miranda and Maureen were sitting under the B&Q umbrella in the backyard drinking champagne. Talisa-Leanne was flinging around a Mickey Mouse drinking cup half full of Buck's Fizz.

Torn between the pleasurable novelty of a bibulous homecoming and resentment at Col's 'great surprise' (he and Miranda had just got engaged), Troy sat down with the intention of making serious inroads into the Asda non-vintage.

Conversation dawdled. The four really had nothing in common. Troy was tired, Maureen distracted by the toddler, Colin and Miranda were simply doing the rounds as people with wonderful tidings to impart have always delighted in doing.

'How's work then, Gav?' inquired Colin. 'Still making the streets safe for muggers and pushers?'

Maureen laughed.

Miranda said, '*Colin.*'

'Looking for someone who taught at your place actually,' said Troy to Miranda. 'Crafts department. Wednesday afternoon.'

'I wouldn't know them then. I'm full-time Business Studies.'

'Sarah Lawson?'

Miranda shook her head. 'Disappeared, has she?'

'That's right. Three – no, four days ago.'

'What do you do now?' asked Miranda. 'I mean, how do you set about finding someone?'

'Don't encourage him, sweetheart,' said Colin.

'It's interesting though.'

'Yeah. Like watching paint dry.'

'Don't do that, Talisa-Leanne!' yelled Maureen.

'Whaaahhh . . .'

'Pass me that cloth, Gav.'

'Well,' said Troy, passing the J cloth, 'we circulate a photograph, if we have one. Ask the press and public to help. Talk to people who knew her. Perhaps run a check on estate agents and letting agencies in case she's renting a hidy-hole somewhere. If it's a really big fish, some absconding financier or suchlike, we inform the sea and airports.' It sounded quite exciting, put like that. Very different from the dreary foot-slogging actuality.

Miranda said something inaudible under Talisa-Leanne's righteously indignant bawling.

'Give her back her mug,' instructed Sergeant Troy.

'And have it thrown over everybody?'

'She's only three.'

Tight-lipped, Maureen returned the mug and sponged the orange juice off her skirt. It was always the same. She's only one, she's only two, she's only three. Maureen could see handsome young men thronging the doorstep only to be told Talisa-Leanne couldn't come out to play because she was only twenty-one.

'Sorry, I missed that,' said Troy to Miranda.

'I said, have you tried the college accommodation bureau?'

'Didn't know they had one.'

'They find bedsits and digs for students. And sometimes flats if people want to share.'

'Is that a separate department?'

'No. They work from the main office.'

And so, the very next morning, Sergeant Troy left home an hour early – absolutely no hardship there – and burned up the M40 on his way to High Wycombe.

He had no expectations of success. In fact, as he waited at the counter in the main office having shown his card and stated his business, he began to think what a waste of time coming here had been. Because if Sarah Lawson had disappeared on impulse, and then only because of the visit from himself and the chief, she would hardly have a room all sorted out and waiting.

Automatically Troy gave the women in the office the once-over. All middle-aged with hips like, well like a hippo's. A motherly one smiled at him. Troy smiled back but ruefully, trying to get across that much as he appreciated the come-on, he wasn't in the toy boy market.

The woman, who had simply felt sorry for a man who was plainly desperate for a good square meal, said something to her colleague and they both burst out laughing.

Troy did not notice. His gaze was fixed on the girl who had been sorting out his inquiry. She was returning to the counter. *And she had a card in her hand.*

He told himself not to get excited. It might simply be an ordinary record card. The girl would say: Is this the Miss Lawson you mean? Bay Tree Cottage, Fawcett Green? I'm afraid we only have the one address for her. And that would be the end of that.

'We did have a request for accommodation from Miss Lawson. Just over a month ago. Her cousin was coming on a visit from America. She was looking for a studio flat.'

'Did you find something?' Troy was amazed at the way the words came out. Deep and crisp and even – just like the carol. His skin might be creeping and crawling with excessive and rapid temperature changes and the back of his neck prickling like a thousand copulating porcupines, but the voice – you couldn't fault it.

'Yes, we did. A small one-bedroomed place in Flavell Street, High Wycombe. There wasn't a phone but she didn't seem to mind.'

'Could I?'

'Be my guest.'

This girl, the most beautiful, Troy was beginning to realise, that he had ever seen in his entire life, handed over a Biro and a notepad. He wrote the address down. Then, unable to offer what she deserved, the moon and stars, the world, the universe and everything he simply thanked her and left.

Shortly after this a great shout was heard outside the administration department windows. Everyone rushed over. A few yards away in the car park they saw the thin, red-haired, good-looking man who had just been inquiring about accommodation.

As they watched, he shouted again, raised high two clenched fists and jumped into the air.

The flat at 13 Flavell Street was situated in a busy but decidedly scruffy area, directly over the Sunbeam Washeteria. The launderette was one of a small terrace containing four trading places. The others were a halal combined butcher and greengrocer, a branch of Joe Coral and a Homeless Settlement Charity shop.

It might be thought that someone wishing to hide another person or conceal their own whereabouts might do well to choose an isolated area many miles from what is called, for the sake of a better word, civilisation. Barnaby did not go along with this. Like the man who suggested that the best place to hide a book is in a library, he believed the best place to hide a human being was in a crowd.

There was nowhere to park and, rather than draw attention to their presence by stopping on a double yellow line, Troy drove around until he found a large empty space reserved for the clients of Fenn Barker, Sols, Commissioner for Oaths, and pulled in there.

Today the weather had broken. The two men made their way back to Flavell Street under a sky thundering with darkness; clouds clashed and rumbled over their heads. They were passing a hairdressing and massage parlour, the Cut and Come Again Salon, when the first drops of rain fell. These were so heavy that little puffs of dust bounced up where they hit the paving slabs.

The only access to the flat above the launderette was up a dirty iron staircase. Troy kicked aside some orange boxes, old cabbage stalks and rotting fruit and started to climb. He knocked sharply on the door of number thirteen then brought his face close to the single window and tried to peer through. But the yellowish-grey net curtains, rigid with age and grime, were impenetrable. While waiting for a response, he passed the time reflecting, with a pleasure so intense it was almost painful, on his recent triumph.

While driving to the station Troy had naturally anticipated over and over again the moment when he would hand over his slip of paper bearing the information, obtained entirely on his own initiative (he had already forgotten all about Miranda), that would reshape the whole landscape of the case.

First he pictured keeping quiet for a while then lobbing the information casually into the pool at the nine o'clock briefing. Then he thought he might write it up on the board and see how long before somebody noticed. Or should he casually put a note on the chief's desk? This might be of some use, sir.

In the end, of course, he did none of these things. Just walked extremely briskly from the parking lot to CID reception; gathered speed during lap two along the main corridor and erupted into the incident room shouting, 'Hey! Hey! Guess what?'

Joe Cool he would never be. But for a man whose soul yearned above all else for praise and admiration, the response to the news he carried left a glow that was with him still.

Now, as he rapped hard on the shabby door for a second time, Barnaby wandered along the balcony, peering in through the windows of the other three flatlets. Only the furthest from number thirteen seemed to be in use as a normal domestic habitat. The one over the bookie's was crammed with packs of stationery, catering-size drums of instant tea and coffee and towers of polystyrene cups wrapped in polythene. The third was completely empty.

Troy crouched down, lifted the scarred aluminium flap of the letter box and peered in. No sign of human life. 'No one here, chief.'

Troy was disappointed. He had plotted quite a different scenario. Sarah Lawson would appear, then, distraught with amazement and alarm at being discovered, try to make a run for it. Alternatively she'd attempt to shut the door in their faces. In either case Sergeant Troy would have no problem bringing her to heel.

'Not to worry.' Barnaby was resting his elbows on the waist-high brick wall and enjoying the sensation of rain upon his face. 'She'll be back.' He had not waited that morning to organise a search warrant. Apprehending the woman was what mattered. This place and Bay Tree Cottage could be gone over tomorrow, the next day, any time. 'There's a kebab house across the way. Let's get some coffee. We can keep an eye on the flat from there.'

But as things turned out, their drinks were left untasted for they had barely sat down when they saw their quarry making her way aimlessly along the pavement on the far side of the road.

Barnaby said, 'Get the car.'

The interview room in the basement of the CID building was windowless but brightly lit by two long fluorescent strips. The walls were white perforated plasterboard, the chairs had tweedy seats and padded arms and the table was pale grey. Functional but hardly sinister. Nothing there, you might say, apart from the location of course, to inspire discomfort let alone despair.

But Sarah Lawson, from the moment she had been brought in, exhibited symptoms of the deepest unease. Barnaby could see it was the room that was at fault rather than her situation for, until she entered it, her demeanour had been quite different.

When he had blocked her way outside Joe Coral's, repeating her name and saying he wanted to talk to her, she had stared hard at him as if he was some mysterious stranger. Eventually she said, flatly, 'Oh, it's you.'

Barnaby knew then that he had got it wrong. Realised that, whatever the reason she had left Bay Tree Cottage in such a hurry, her departure had not been prompted by a visit from the police. This threw him somewhat and he had still not quite recovered his balance.

Not that Sarah Lawson had been happy to accompany them to the station. She had asked if it would take long and why they could not just talk where they were now. As she climbed reluctantly into the car, she was still staring up and down the street and continued to gaze out of first one window then the other until they were well away from the centre of the town.

As she was plainly looking out for someone, Barnaby said they would be happy to wait if she wanted to leave a note at the flat. He did not add that they would insist on knowing the contents of any such communication. But the offer was declined.

Sarah had politely accepted the tea which had been brought to the interview room but left it untasted. The questioning had been going on for half an hour. She slumped, blank-faced, in her chair, showing a lack of interest in the whole proceedings so deep and total that Troy thought they might as well be tossing the questions down the well in Bay Tree's back garden.

Her appearance, mildly unkempt when they had last seen her, had deteriorated to a marked degree. She wore the same saxe blue dress which was now none too clean and still damp from when they had all stood together in the rain. She was thinner. Her dull hair had become matted and was lying over her shoulders in heavy hanks. The skin on her face seemed looser and more coarse and, although there was a small but efficient fan on the table, her forehead was beaded with sweat. She plucked at the neck of her dress with thin fingers, pulling it away from her throat as if it was constricting her breathing. She spoke then for only the third time since they had entered the room.

'Can we talk somewhere else, please? I can't . . . this place . . . it's choking me.'

'I'm afraid there's nowhere else available at the moment.'

This was not true. And Barnaby, having finally discovered a weak spot in a previously mute suspect, now prepared to exploit this for all it was worth.

'Once the formality of our interview is concluded, Miss Lawson, we can go and talk in my office.' He added, 'It's on the fourth floor.'

She said nothing but her eyes, her whole face lightened.

The Chief Inspector wondered if she was seriously claustrophobic. If so, he would have to play this very carefully. A clever brief could get great mileage out of an interview conducted under that sort of psychological stress.

'As I said earlier, Miss Lawson, you are allowed to have a solicitor present if—'

'I don't know any.'

'A duty solicitor is provided by the courts.'

'Why would I want such a thing?' Then, receiving no reply, 'Can't we just get on?'

'By all means. First I'd like to recap on our earlier interview. There seems to be some discrepancy in the matter of dates. You told us you went to see *Castrato* on the evening of Monday the tenth of June. In fact, the last showing of this film was on the previous Saturday.'

'Oh. In that case it must have been then. Or earlier in the week perhaps. What does it matter?' She sounded not only as if she genuinely did not know why it should matter but that she did not care.

'Do you remember what you actually were doing?'

'Loafing around in the garden, I suppose.'

Barnaby, taking a softly, softly line, did not press the matter. Did not point out that Gray Patterson had called 'around eightish' to find both Sarah and her car missing. The time for that sort of punch would come during round two. He moved on to the subject of Alan Hollingsworth's demise, inquiring first how well she knew the man.

'You asked me that before.'

'Refresh my memory, Miss Lawson.'

'I didn't know him at all.'

'Then I would have thought your reaction to his death rather inappropriate.'

'When you said it was suspicious I was shocked. Violence introduced suddenly into a conversation can have that effect. Perhaps I'm over-sensitive.'

That could be true. Barnaby recalled how distressed she had been at the news that Hollingsworth had physically ill-treated his wife.

'When Mrs Hollingsworth asked you round for tea on the Thursday she disappeared, did she give any reason for choosing that particular day?'

'Not really.'

'Perhaps it was the only occasion you were available?'

'No. I'm free every afternoon except Wednesday.'

'Why do you think she asked you at the same time that she'd made a hair appointment?'

'I should think she just forgot. Simone was a bit on the dizzy side.'

'And that same evening, Miss Lawson,' continued Barnaby. 'What did you do then?'

'What I always do. Read a bit, listen to music, potter in the garden.'

'So that wasn't the night you saw the movie?' suggested Sergeant Troy.

'Oh, well, I suppose it could have been. I really . . .'

'Don't remember?'

'Look, will this take much longer?' During the last few minutes her breathing had changed. It was now so rapid and shallow she seemed to be almost panting. Barnaby asked if she would like some water but she declined. 'I'll be all right once I'm outside.'

'I'd like to ask you next about the flat at High Wycombe,' said the Chief Inspector. 'I understand you told the college you wanted it for a cousin who was coming over from the States.'

'Yes, I did.'

'And is that the truth?'

Her eyes roved constantly around the concrete cube. Searched every corner, raked the floor and ceiling. She seemed to shrink into herself as if for protection. As if the room was not inanimate but a physical threat.

'Miss Lawson? Is that the truth?'

'Why would I make something like that up?'

'Could you give me the details then, please?'

'What do you mean, details?'

'We mean,' said Sergeant Troy, 'your cousin's name, address and telephone number.'

'He . . . travels. Moves around a lot. Usually I wait for him to contact me.'

Barnaby inserted a pause into the conversation; a long one during which he made plain his disbelief. Quite honestly he was surprised at such pitiful transparency. She must surely have had time to work out something more credible than a mythical relative from America.

Troy, taking his cue from the boss, merely leaned against the wall and sighed, shaking his head. Though enjoying himself he was, like Barnaby, somewhat disappointed at the lack of invention on offer. After all, what was the point of being creative if you couldn't make up a really good story?

'So you'll be keeping on the flat till you hear from your cousin?'

'Yes.' For some reason this question, answered only in a whisper, brought Sarah to the brink of tears.

Barnaby waited, not for her to recover but because he was unsure just how and where to press on this plainly weak point. The fact that it had been revealed only by a lie didn't help. In the end he said, 'You were looking for someone when we met earlier today.'

'No.'

'Waiting then?'

'You're mistaken.'

'Very well.' There was no point in wasting time trying to prove the unprovable. 'Let's talk about your accident now, shall we, Miss Lawson?'

'What acc—' She stopped herself just too late.

'Quite,' said Barnaby, and waited.

'I needed a break from teaching. To be honest I was simply tired but I didn't think the college would rate that very highly as an excuse.'

'Is your health poor then?' asked the Chief Inspector.

'No, why?'

'I wouldn't have said three hours teaching once a week was especially exhausting.'

'Perhaps you've been going in for extramural activities?' Troy's polite tone did not conceal the offence in the words. Nor was it meant to. 'Private lessons like.'

'Look.' She had turned her attention now to the table top, brushing a little ridge of dust backwards and forwards with the index finger of her left hand. 'You said . . . you . . .'

Barnaby leaned forward, experiencing some concern. She was opening and closing her mouth quickly, like a fish gasping for breath. He was about to offer her some water again when she began repeating herself.

'Said. You said. We could go upstairs. To the fourth floor.'

'After the interview.'

'I can't breathe in here.'

'Sergeant. Open the door.'

Reluctantly Troy did so. He didn't hold with pandering to the whims of the incarcerated. They had enough of their own way as it was what with the entire Social Services and half the legal profession on their side.

'You don't understand, it's not lack of air.' Troy closed the door. 'But there's no daylight.'

'Just one or two more questions.'

'I'm sorry. I have to get out!'

'We won't be long.'

'I need to go to the lavatory.'

'Right.' Though this had plainly been a spur-of-the-moment improvisation, Barnaby could not refuse. 'Find someone, would you, Gavin?' He timed the tape and switched off.

When the policewoman arrived, the Chief Inspector

beckoned her over and said, 'It might be an idea to take another officer with you.'

'You don't think Lawson's going to do a runner surely?' asked Sergeant Troy when the women had left.

'That's not what I'm worried about.'

Though the toilets were only a short distance away, it was ten minutes before voices were heard in the corridor, arguing and persuading. Eventually Sarah Lawson was half coaxed and half dragged back inside the interview room.

'Sorry we've been so long, sir. It was all a bit troublesome.'

'I'm trying to be patient, Miss Lawson,' said Barnaby when Sarah was once more sitting down. 'But you're making things very difficult.'

'I'm sor—'

'The more you cooperate with us, the sooner all this will be over and done with. Which is what we both want, right?'

Sarah nodded. The break, far from doing her good, seemed to have made matters worse. She was shaking in every limb and her lips trembled.

'I'll ask you now about your relationship with Gray Patterson. Are you friends or lovers?'

'Friends.'

'Close friends?'

'Not at all. The relationship is very casual.'

'Have you conspired with him in any way to bring about the kidnap and consequent ransom of Simone Hollingsworth?'

'No!'

'Has he ever discussed such a possibility with you?'

'Never.'

'Has he talked about revenge? Ways of getting his own back after Hollingsworth swindled him?'

'No.'

'When you met, what did you talk about?'

'Nothing. Day-to-day trivia.'

'How well did you know Alan Hollingsworth?'

'What?' She stared at him, mesmerised and bewildered.

'The question was,' snapped Troy, 'how—'

'You've asked me that! What are you trying to do?' She jumped up, her cheeks blazing. She shook her head in anguish and the damp pleats of hair fell against first one and then the other of her sunken cheeks. 'Why are you dragging it out like this?'

'All right, Miss Lawson, calm yourself. One final question and that's it.' For now. 'What were you doing on the night Hollingsworth died?'

'I've *told* you. I was at home.'

'Gray Patterson called at Bay Tree Cottage at eight p.m. Neither you nor your car were anywhere to be seen.'

That stopped her. Stone cold in her tracks. And her mental state was such that she could not gather her wits even to the degree necessary for the simplest response.

'I shall be obtaining a warrant shortly to search the flat at Flavell Street. And also your house at Fawcett Green. It would help us if you would hand over the keys, otherwise I'm afraid it's a forced entry which can mean quite a lot of mess.'

She did not reply but pushed her bag across the table. Made from Liberty's peacock fabric, it was floppy and unlined with a drawstring neck.

After Troy had made a statement to the effect that the suspect had now willingly surrendered her handbag and its contents, the tape was once more timed and switched off.

Then, to Sarah Lawson's loud and continuing distress, she was told she would be further detained at least until the results of the search were available.

This meant a cell. There was only one with bars and it was occupied. Barnaby had a word with the duty sergeant. He explained the extreme stress his suspect was suffering and that her psychological condition could only deteriorate should she be put in a room with no window. At this, the inhabitant of the first cell was transferred.

Once Sarah Lawson was installed, the duty sergeant wondered if it would be wise to remove her belt and shoe laces. Also, bearing in mind that a remand prisoner had managed to hang herself earlier this year with a bra . . .

The Chief Inspector weighed the possibility of attempted self-damage against the added distress caused by the forcible removal of his suspect's clothing and decided against such a step. However, he did ask that the usual four times an hour surveillance should be increased to a check every five minutes. Ignoring the disbelieving and resentful glances spreading around an understaffed and overworked front office, he also suggested that a doctor should have a look at the prisoner.

After obtaining a warrant and while waiting for his car to be brought round, Barnaby went back to the cell block. He let the door flap of number three down and looked in.

The cell window was way above the sightline even of someone as tall as Sarah Lawson. So she had climbed on to the rim of the toilet and seized the bars to pull herself level. The tips of her toes rested on the porcelain and her face was turned towards the sky. A golden rectangle of sunlight fell across her eyes like a blindfold.

No one took the slightest notice of Barnaby and Troy as they climbed the iron staircase once again. Or even when they put on some latex gloves, produced a set of keys and let themselves into the Flavell Street apartment taking a dustbin, which proved to be empty, from the balcony in with them.

The first thing that hit their nostrils was the smell of stale fat – in the air, in the curtains and carpets and, no doubt, the furniture as well. Decades of greasy fry-ups. Troy felt around for a light switch.

They were standing in a narrow hall with three doors off, the cheap, hollow type filled with wadding and varnished light brown. One opened on to a bathroom – cracked green and black tiles and an old, once white bath. The second revealed a scruffy kitchen – a couple of odd, free-standing cupboards, a stained Formica table, two plastic chairs, one with the seat slashed, and an extremely grotty fridge. Barnaby poked distastefully at some chipped pots and pans in the sink. He unlocked the back door. Another set of iron steps, this time leading down into a deserted little back alley bordered by a row of garages.

He was locking up again when Sergeant Troy called loudly, 'Guv! Quick, in here!'

Barnaby lumbered away into the sitting-cum-bedroom. Troy was standing in the centre of a hideous black and yellow carpet staring at the wall.

'Aahhh,' cried the Chief Inspector.

'Geronimo, yes?'

'Too right,' agreed Barnaby. Longing to demonstrate the passionate satisfaction consuming him but a bit heavy for anything more taxing than a saunter round the room, he slammed his right fist into the palm of his left hand and said, more loudly, 'Too bloody right.'

Though the paper on the wall was deeply unattractive and none too clean, both men devoured the pattern of narrow ribbon stripes and sentimental puppies as if it was the latest from the brush of Michelangelo.

'OK, that's enough gloating. Now, where's the camera?'

'Shouldn't be difficult.' Sergeant Troy, bringer of good fortune and turner of tides, swaggered. 'Place is no bigger than a flea's bumhole.'

They both started to look. It didn't take long. Troy pulled out the furniture – one armchair covered in rusty red nylon fabric and a well-snagged mustard tweed Put-U-Up. While he checked down behind the cushions and opened out the single bed, Barnaby went through the dressing table's drawers and the wardrobe which took no time at all as they were both empty but for two sheets, a pillow and a couple of blankets.

Physical elation gradually draining away, the Chief Inspector inspected the kitchen cupboards. They held a few storage jars and tins with nothing in them, some tea bags and a carton of milk. That was it.

'One toothbrush.' Troy came in from the bathroom. 'One towel, one bit of soap. The Ritz it ain't.'

'Well,' they wandered back next door, 'it was only needed as a place to hide Mrs Hollingsworth.'

'And use her as a punch bag.'

'As you say.' Barnaby stared morosely at the capering canines. He was remembering Aubrey Marine's comment on the wallpaper when they had first seen the ransom pictures: 'It was everywhere, that,' declared Aubrey, 'a few years ago.' A sharp defence could make persuasive headway on such popularity.

'Cheer up, guv. It'll be at her cottage – the camera.'

Barnaby did not reply. He stood quietly, regarding the plain bevelled mirror on the wall opposite the window, and wondered if Simone had been dragged in front of it to see the results of her captor's handiwork. He thought about constraints and how they had been managed. Had Simone been tied to one of the kitchen chairs? Or drugged? Or simply promised more violence if she made any move to draw attention to herself and her plight? He remembered how her hair had been wrenched out and her mouth bloodied. Threatened with another helping of the same, who wouldn't keep quiet?

He was surprised the room retained no sense of any of this. He remembered crossing the Bridge of Sighs once in Venice and the very fabric seemed to groan in sad recollection of the prisoners' tears.

'There's two of them in this, isn't there, guv?'

'Oh, yes.'

'Patterson?'

'I don't think so. I believe Sarah Lawson's working with someone entirely unknown to us. Which is why, if she decides to keep schtum, we're going to be in real trouble.'

'What about Simone? Do you think she's still around?'

'I doubt it. Hollingsworth's gone, which means no more money. Alive and able to identify them, she's a continuing threat. My guess is they've already got rid of her.'

'Christ.'

'Well.' Barnaby turned briskly towards the poky little hall. 'No point in hanging around. We'll get Aubrey's lot over and see what they can dig up.'

'With a bit of luck, Patterson's fingerprints.'

'Don't hold your breath.'

Before returning to the station they talked briefly to the owner of the Asian greengrocery who gave them the disappointing news that number ten, the only other flat in the terrace that was occupied, was owned by his uncle, Rajni Patel. And that Mr Patel had flown to Bangladesh a month previously to join the family celebrations on the birth of his first male grandchild.

Asked if he had seen anyone entering or leaving number thirteen, the available Mr Patel described only Sarah Lawson, whom he referred to as a thin, wild woman.

So it would be back to more foot-slogging and photo-flashing and persistent questioning up and down Flavell Street and nearabouts. Which meant there would be no reason at all for the Chief Super to cut Barnaby's team by half, as he had threatened to do the previous evening. So in that respect, at least, life was definitely looking up.

Fawcett Green had also caught the rain. A certain amount of dampness still marked the ground in St Chad's Lane and clung to the grass borders. The air was fragrant with the scent of newly washed leaves and flowers. Sergeant Troy pulled in off the road and parked on the spot previously occupied by Sarah Lawson's Dinky toy.

'I thought the home guard was supposed to be keeping an eye on this place,' said Troy.

Poor Perrot. He had been staunch and true but, like all human beings, occasionally needed a rest and something to eat. Give or take an hour here or there, he'd been hanging around Bay Tree Cottage for nearly two days. It was just his bad luck that, after a lengthy early-morning shift, he should have popped home for a quick shower and a bowl of Coco Pops.

Barnaby and Troy had donned their gloves and were standing on the front steps when the decelerating cough of the Honda's engine preceded his return. A picture of dismayed disbelieving guilt, the policeman hurriedly lifted his bike on its stand and ran towards the broken gate.

'Chief Inspector—'

'Ah, Constable. Nice of you to drop by.'

And that was that as far as Perrot was concerned. As he

told Trixie later, 'Something snapped and everything went red.' Driven by the injustice of the remark and convinced by now that he was done for anyway, Perrot threw himself into his swan song.

'Actually I haven't just dropped by, sir. I have just dropped back. I have stayed close to this house and its immediate environs for the last forty-eight hours as per your instructions. I have hardly slept and I have eaten on the hoof. I was not able to attend the Infant Cyclists' Time Trials yesterday as I have done every year since I moved to this posting. Likewise the Old Reliables Bowls Tournament. My wife and children have hardly seen me since this case began. I have tried to carry out my duties to the very best of my ability and all I've had is sneering remarks and cruel comments. It's . . . it's not right.'

Silence, open-mouthed and thick as treacle, followed this intemperate outburst. Then Troy walked slowly over to Constable Perrot, squared his shoulders, thrust out his chin and said, 'You give the DCI any more lip, Poll, and I'll squeeze your cods till your eyes bubble.'

'Don't call me Poll.' Perrot spoke up boldly though his lips were stiff with misery and fear. 'I don't like it.'

'Who the fuck do you—'

'All right, Gavin. That'll do.' Barnaby stood on the doorstep regarding Constable Perrot. Now that all restraint had been removed and his bolt was shot, the policeman stood silently quaking. His face was white going on grey; his eyes were ringed darkly with exhaustion. Asked for a comparison from the animal kingdom, Barnaby would have suggested a panda on the edge of a nervous breakdown. 'There's no need for any further surveillance here, Perrot. We'll be keeping Sarah Lawson at the station for the present. Better go home and get some sleep.'

'Yes, sir. Thank you.'

'And I should think twice before you give a senior officer the benefit of your private opinions in future.'

'I will, Chief Inspector. Thank you very much.'

'You let him off light, guv.'

'Poor sod,' Barnaby turned the key in the Yale. 'Out of his league, out of his depth, desperate to please. All he wants is a kind word.'

'He's in the wrong bloody job then,' said Sergeant Troy.

Remembering how withdrawn and subdued and lacking in energy Sarah Lawson had been during their previous interview at Bay Tree Cottage, Barnaby was surprised at how plainly the house reflected her absence. It seemed to have shrunk. It had a collected air of seclusion, a quietness that also seemed somewhat sterile. He was put in mind of a rarely visited museum.

Even Troy sensed it. He stood awkwardly on the glowing, shabby rugs and finally said, 'Where should we start, do you think?'

'I'll look in here. You take next door.'

Sergeant Troy, remembering the dirty plates, sighed. He braced himself to check the sink first and get it over with. One plate was already wearing a greenish grey fur collar.

He pulled out all the drawers including those in a battered Welsh dresser. Wooden spoons, old but hand-carved, all sorts of cooking pots and utensils in different styles and colours, bowls and dishes painted all over with flowers and fish and stars and suchlike. A proper junk shop. Troy recalled his mum's kitchen which was *Diary of an Edwardian Lady* throughout, including the tea towels. That'd open Sarah Lawson's eyes all right.

Barnaby, for reasons that he could not quite determine,

was reluctant to get going. This was unlike him. Rooting determinedly through other people's most private possessions was all in a day's work. He tried to disentangle his thoughts but to no avail and eventually wiped the wretched image of an incarcerated Sarah Lawson from his mind and simply began.

He started on a little writing table with a brass rail littered with used cheque books, bills and sheaves of loose paper, most of which were covered with sketches. He was hoping to find something personal; a note or letter, perhaps a photograph, but he was out of luck. Nothing was concealed in any of the books nor inside the covers of the vinyl records which Sarah still seemed to prefer to tapes or compact discs. Perhaps she couldn't afford a CD player. This theory led Barnaby into wondering about his suspect's financial affairs. Just how poor was Sarah Lawson?

The Chief Inspector was well aware that middle and working class ideas of what constituted poverty were very different. True, she had no television set but Barnaby suspected this was from ideological reasons rather than lack of money. She must have some sort of private income, though. At the most, three hours' teaching would bring in sixty or seventy pounds. Who could live on this, pay their council tax and bills (in her case electricity, phone, Calor gas), and run a car?

Plainly, from the state of the house, she had no spare money to chuck about. But Barnaby could not believe she would have got involved in something as alarming and dangerous as the abduction and wrongful ill-treatment of another human being for the sake of a few thousand quid to do up Bay Tree Cottage.

'Look at this, guv.' Troy, going through the last stack of

books by the window, held a study of Picasso open at a page showing a portrait of Dora Maar.

'Mmm.' Barnaby waited to hear that the drawings from Talisa-Leanne's playgroup made more sense and you didn't have to know anything about art to know what was crap.

'Look.' Troy came over and sat down on the old sofa. 'She's got a red eye looking one way, a green eye the other and a yellow face.'

'Nobody's perfect,' said Barnaby, stealing the great line without a qualm.

'What do you think he's getting at?'

'Search me.'

'I mean,' he gestured angrily at the shelves of books, the music and stained glass, the beaten-up pile of clay on the marble slab, 'what's it for, all this?'

'Supposed to make life more bearable.'

'Give me a good shag and a double Scotch any day.'

'Upstairs.' And, when they were on the tiny landing, 'You take the bath and loo.'

There was just one bedroom which ran the length of the house and had windows at both ends. These had unlined curtains made from faded velvet patches hanging from thin metal rods. Barnaby glanced out of the window facing the lane and noticed a group of three women on the other side of the road staring at the house. When they saw him they immediately turned their backs and started to chat among themselves but he had no doubt that the news of his own and Sergeant Troy's presence (and Sarah's continuing absence) would be zinging along the village hotline in no time.

He turned his attention to the room which was as austere as the one downstairs was rich and colourful. The divan had a cover made from crushed velvet the colour of moleskins. A raffia stool by the bed held a flat dish full of beautifully marked stones, a paperback novel by Barbara Trapido and a jar of honey.

The bare walls had been painted white then washed in a soft, powdery blue but so thinly that the original colour showed through giving them an almost luminous glow. A very delicate scent in the air could be traced to a bunch of white violets in an egg cup placed on an old linen chest. The room was crowded with sunshine.

Barnaby put the egg cup carefully on the bare wooden floor and lifted the lid. As he did so, Troy came in.

'Dead basic in there, guv. One of them old-fashioned baths – ball and claw foot.'

'Is that right?' Barnaby took out some unironed shirts and blouses and a long skirt patterned with wild irises.

'They're in again now. You can pay a fortune for something your granny used to scrub the old man down in.'

'Well, you know what they say . . .' An embroidered jerkin, a three-quarter length coat with a sheen like hammered bronze, some boots made of patterned skin and fastened with six tiny silver buckles, a frayed straw hat. 'What goes round . . .'

'You never know what to chuck away these—' Troy broke off. Though the DCI was facing the other way, there was that about the quality of Barnaby's attention – a sudden rigidity in the spine, an abnormally still line to the shoulders – that reminded Troy of a Jack Russell at a rabbit hole.

'You've found something.' It was not a question.

Barnaby sighed then and raised his head and looked around the room. A room which, when he first entered it, had seemed so full of quiet innocence.

'Yes, I have,' he said and held up his left hand. 'I've found the camera.'

* * *

The next interview with Sarah Lawson took place, as he had assured her it would, in Barnaby's own office.

He had charged Sarah in her cell on suspicion of kidnap and obtaining money by ransom and repeated the caution twice until he was sure she understood the importance of what he was saying. She seemed quite dazed and the duty sergeant explained that the doctor had left two tranquillisers at the desk which the prisoner had taken 'docile as a lamb'. Offered food, it had been refused.

Barnaby also urged, given the seriousness of the offence, the importance of having a legal representative present. Until this was sorted, he made notes and reviewed the case so far, attempting to pare away the dross of rumour, suspicion and supposition and leave bare only incontrovertible facts. He had just completed this when Troy came in with the suspect and John Starkey.

There is a general feeling abroad that altruism is a highly perishable commodity and that solicitors only offer legal aid if they can't get enough of the other stuff to keep the practice going. Though this was not always the case, it certainly was with Starkey. If he had been very sharp or the sort to sail close to the wind, Sarah might have been better off. But he was idle, nearly always ill-prepared in court and, as he usually had the sort of clients whose apathy and lack of expectation matched his own, complaints against him were rare.

Some investigating officers might have been glad to have a suspect under interrogation so poorly protected but DCI Barnaby was not of their number. Sergeant Troy, on the other hand, thought it evened things up somewhat. It seemed to him the chief had already given enough ground letting Lawson dictate where the present interview should be held.

Starkey, who wore a white shirt which was far from pristine and had a faint whiff of Newcastle Brown about his person, already seemed to have drifted into a light trance. Barnaby started the tape, gave precise details of the present set-up and began.

'Let me explain, Miss Lawson, what has led to the present charge being made against you.'

He described the search of the flat in Flavell Street and Bay Tree Cottage and what had been found there. He did not point out that, until forensic reports had been completed, the evidence was merely circumstantial. That was Starkey's responsibility. A fact which appeared to have completely passed him by.

Barnaby then turned over three enlargements of the ransom pictures and placed them one at a time and in order of harrowingness in front of Sarah, describing his actions for the tape.

If he had had the slightest doubt that she was involved in the kidnap of Simone Hollingsworth it would have been extinguished by her response. It was immediately plain that she had seen all of the photographs before. There was a bitter twist to her mouth as she placed them in a neat pile. Barnaby could not help noticing that the final picture was on top and that she was regarding it with apparent indifference. Such callousness provoked in him a harsh response.

'Were these taken at number thirteen Flavell Street?'

'You don't have to answer that, Mrs Lawton.'

'For heaven's sake, Starkey. Can't you even get your client's name right?'

'What?' The solicitor bent his head and rustled his papers. His bald spot shone greasily under the fluorescent strip. 'Oh, I do beg your pardon.'

'I'll repeat the question. Miss Lawson, were the photographs I have just shown you taken at number thirteen Flavell Street?'

'Yes, they were.'

'With the camera that I discovered in a wooden chest in the bedroom of Bay Tree Cottage?'

'Yes.'

Troy, who hadn't realised he had been holding his breath since the question had first been put, now let it go. A lengthy, jubilant exhalation. In one day – no, tell a lie, half a day – they had moved from floundering in a desert of ignorance getting practically nowhere to being home and dry.

He turned to glance at the chief – they were sitting side by side – expecting to see the same triumphant flush on those brawny, slab-like cheeks that he could feel warming his own. But Barnaby's profile was motionless. Cold and judgementally grave. A chill seemed to emanate from the large frame so close to his own and Troy then began to chill out in his turn. Though not an imaginative man, he began to comprehend in a more sharply focused, fresh and vivid manner how cruel were the actions to which Sarah Lawson had just confessed.

John Starkey also seemed to be waking up to the fact that his client was in the process of laying herself open to a very long jail sentence. He began to close the stable door.

'You know you're allowed to remain silent—'

'Miss Lawson is fully aware of that fact,' said Sergeant Troy. 'She has been properly cautioned. Twice.'

'Well, um, Sarah, I advise you not to say anything else for the—'

'What does it matter?' She drew one long, shuddering breath. 'What does anything matter? It's all over now.'

Barnaby stared at Sarah across the desk. She was sitting very still, her head bowed, her face expressionless. She looked even more haggard than when they had first talked. Her skin was as thin and fine as tissue paper and the bones at the base of her neck stuck out like sharp little wings.

'Where is Mrs Hollingsworth now, Sarah?'

'Don't know.' It was little more than a whisper.

'Is she still alive?'

'I . . . I doubt it.'

'When did you last see her?'

'On Thursday. I went over—'

'Hold on, which Thursday are we talking about?'

'The day she disappeared.' Her voice became crowded with agitation. 'If only she'd done exactly what we said, none of this would have happened!'

'Who's "we"?'

'I can't tell you that.'

'Can't?' asked Sergeant Troy. 'Or won't?'

She did not reply and Barnaby did not press the point. The vital thing was to keep the information coming, not dam up the stream for the sake of a single detail. They'd fish it out sooner or later.

'I think you'd better tell me about this from the beginning, Sarah.'

'I wouldn't know where to start.'

'Well, how the whole thing was set up, for instance. And why.'

'We were desperate for money. My . . . friend—'

'You mean your lover?' said Troy nastily. The middle classes could be so mealy-mouthed.

'He's being pursued in the courts by his ex-wife. Been forced to sell the house and, because she found a really sharp lawyer and there are two children, he got next to nothing. I would have been happy for us to just live at the cottage, we'd have managed, but he's used to . . . well, finer things.

'Then one day – this was before she had started my classes – Simone invited me round for coffee. She was always asking people to the house, looking for company. I must have been miles away and said yes without thinking. It was like spending time with a silly child in a toy shop. She ran around chattering away, showing off all her ghastly clothes and make-up. Then she produced this jewel box and flashed the contents about. There was a diamond engagement ring that apparently had set Alan back sixty thousand pounds. It was just so . . .'

'Gross?' Troy had a quick fantasy of pretty, golden-haired Simone prancing innocently about her bedroom showing off her trinkets.

'I told—' She stopped suddenly, glancing across at Barnaby. 'Sorry, it's not that I don't want to carry on. But it's difficult.'

'Look. You're going to be talking about this man for some considerable time and on more than one occasion. It'll be simpler all round if you make up some sort of name for him.'

'That seems . . . Oh, well,' she shrugged, 'why not? Tim then.'

'Right. You told Tim about Simone's collection of jewellery?'

'Not in the way you've made it sound.'

'Leading the witness.' John Starkey briefly broke the surface of his subterranean doze.

'It was in passing. During general conversation. We were simply catching up on what we'd been doing since the last time we met. When I described the scene at Nightingales

Tim said, "A fool and her knick-knacks are soon parted," and laughed. Nothing more was said about it at the time. Then, a few weeks later, Simone started coming to my classes.

'I didn't tell you the truth about our journeys to and from the college. They weren't straightforward. The very first time she attended, Tim met us as we left the building. Didn't tell me he was going to, just turned up. She was smitten by him straightaway. People were. It wasn't just that he was very attractive. He had a gift, an air about him that made you think he was on his way to a really wonderful party and that all you had to do was stretch out your hand and he'd take you along.'

'A useful accomplishment,' said Barnaby.

'You make it sound calculating. It wasn't like that.'

It sounded exactly like that to Sergeant Troy. He thought, of all the tricks a con artist could draw on, this sounded like one of the neatest. The guy sounded like the Pied Piper in Talisa-Leanne's picture book. Except that he was one of the rats.

'We went for some coffee and stayed so long I only just got Simone home in time. All she could talk about in the car was Tim. Just one meeting and he had her in the palm of his hand. I was very upset of course. I rang him that night.'

'Where does he live?'

'I'm not prepared to tell you that.'

'All right. What happened next?'

'He said he had a wonderful plan, the answer to all our troubles. We would be able to buy a house – he mentioned Ireland – and live together. No money worries. The thought of it – to be able to sculpt and paint all day. And, in the evening, to be with him. It seemed too good to be true.'

'And did he tell you what this plan was?'

'Not then. He just said that, at the beginning, it would involve Simone and, however things looked, I was to trust him.' Her eyes brimmed with tears, some of which splashed down on to her cheeks. She brushed the moisture away with the back of her hand and wiped it thoughtlessly on her skirt. 'The next week Simone asked if we could go in an hour earlier than usual as she was having lunch with Tim. I could see that she didn't expect me to be present. After class we all went for coffee again and she was all over him. This routine happened every Wednesday until, as you know, Alan stopped her coming. But by then she was hopelessly in love with Tim who had no trouble at all persuading—'

'Hang on, hang on,' said Barnaby. 'I don't want the fast track *Reader's Digest* version. I want it unexpurgated and a step at a time. First, at what point did Tim tell you what he was actually planning?'

'When he asked me to sort out a flat. It's cheaper, going through the college. Also, though this didn't strike me till later, he didn't want to do the rounds of estate agents and get his face known. The idea was that Simone would "disappear" and then ransom demands would be made. She was sure Alan would do anything to get her back and, as things turned out, she was right. I've never seen anyone so excited. She was like a captive bird watching someone coming to open the cage door. Of course she believed that she and Tim, after they'd got as much as they could from her husband, would be going away together.

'As fellow conspirator I was naturally privy to it all. She was for ever popping into the cottage going on about how exciting it was, plotting and planning. Discussing the latest twist or turn.'

'You say "plotting and planning",' said the Chief Inspector, 'but from what you say all the plotting seems to have been done by other people. What was left for Mrs Hollingsworth?'

'Oh, nonsensical dramatic flourishes. She decided when she was running away that it would be fun to be disguised. So she put a wig and some dark glasses in her handbag. That sort of thing. And wore an outfit with a little reversible coat which she could turn inside out.'

'I see.' No wonder Simone had been so long in the Ladies at Bobby's department store. Barnaby tried not dwell on the wasted man hours checking on the sale in Causton of pink jackets.

'Didn't you find that a problem, Miss Lawson?' asked Troy. 'Listening to her burbling on while all the time the shakedown was for you and your fancy man.'

'It's not as if her feelings were deeply involved. She was a silly, spoiled woman and very shallow. And I assumed once we'd got enough money, she would simply be returned to her husband who would be so overjoyed to have her back he'd spoil her twice as much.'

'But something went wrong?'

'Yes, from the very beginning. She was supposed to take the two thirty market bus to Causton and the four o'clock from there to High Wycombe. Tim, who had already moved into the flat, was meeting her at the bus station. But, I suppose unable to wait to begin her "great adventure" as she kept calling it, she caught the twelve thirty instead and took a taxi to the flat.

'It was so like her that we should have anticipated it. Anyway, knowing there might not be another chance of being alone together perhaps for some weeks, Tim and I had taken advantage of this last opportunity and gone to bed. The street door wasn't locked and she just walked in on us.'

'Holy Moses,' said Sergeant Troy.

'Simone was devastated. She stood staring for a minute then tried to run away. Tim grabbed her, told me to clear out and bundled her into the kitchen. I got dressed and left straightaway.'

'So what on earth was the point of then turning up at Nightingales in the afternoon?'

'For the same reason that Simone didn't cancel her hair appointment. We wanted to put the idea in people's heads that she had definitely expected to be back home at that time. In other words, that she was not absent of her own free will. I thought, as I had no idea what was happening back at High Wycombe, I'd better just carry on.'

'I'm sorry, Miss Lawson, I really don't see the rationale behind all that. What on earth did it matter what people in the village thought?'

'I suppose we saw it as a check against the idea of collusion, just in case the news of the kidnap somehow got out.'

'Which did actually happen.'

'Yes. Alan did everything we asked. Except burn the photographs.'

'What about the jewellery?' asked Barnaby. 'There's a necklace missing as well as the engagement ring. I'd have thought that would indicate collusion all right.'

'That was entirely Simone's doing. We had no idea she was bringing them.'

'A nice little bonus then,' said Sergeant Troy. 'Put them in his pocket when he scarpered, did he, our Tim?'

Sarah Lawson did not reply but became so pale Barnaby thought she was going to faint. He asked if she would like some water and when she said yes, decided this might be a good time to take a break.

'Get some tea sorted, would you, Sergeant? And sandwiches.'

Troy pushed his chair back and attempted to conceal his contempt that this latest diversionary ploy by the suspect had borne such a quick result.

'Try not to disturb our legal eagle as you go. I think he's hibernating.'

'Milk and two sugars,' said Starkey as Troy moved towards the door. 'And I prefer corned beef and pickle. I hope, Chief Inspector,' he turned the desk fan to an angle more advantageous to himself as the door closed, 'that the full extent of my client's cooperation will be drawn to the court's attention at the proper time.'

'Rest assured,' replied Barnaby, turning the fan back. 'Although, if you can't soon talk her into eating a few square meals, I fear there'll be nothing left of her at the proper time.'

Sergeant Troy brought, as well as the glass of water, tea, ham sandwiches and four Wagon Wheels. All the men tucked in although Sarah would not be persuaded. Starkey ate three of the biscuits.

After about fifteen minutes Barnaby restarted the tape and the interview continued. To Troy's disappointment the DCI did not pick up where he himself had left off, on the matter of Mrs Hollingsworth's jewellery.

'So, Miss Lawson. On Thursday the sixth of June things were left in a rather fraught state at Flavell Street. What did you do then?'

'I stayed at Bay Tree Cottage till I couldn't bear it any longer. Tim wasn't able to tell me what was happening, you see, as there isn't a phone at the flat. I drove back about eight o'clock that same evening. When I knocked, he opened the door. The place was very quiet. There was no sign of Simone. Tim took me into the kitchen. He said he had got the first letter and a photograph off to Alan. I wanted to—'

'Just a minute. If he was able to leave the flat to post a letter, why couldn't he ring you from a public box?'

'Can I just tell this in the order that things happened? Then you'll understand.'

'All right,' said Barnaby. 'So, you're both in the kitchen.'

'I asked if I could see Simone but Tim said she was asleep and not to go into the other room. I should have been more persistent. I knew, after what she'd discovered earlier, she wouldn't cooperate willingly. But then I told myself that somehow he had managed to talk her round.' She looked back and forth between the two men, urging them to see the inevitability of her actions.

'He told me to stop worrying, go home and make sure I was seen about the village over the next couple of days. And that he would ring me after the weekend. Tim did this on Monday afternoon and said that Hollingsworth was paying up. He didn't give me any details. Just that he was collecting the money that same night and I should come to the flat around one o'clock the next day and help him count it. I asked about Simone, if she was all right and how he was going to, well, hand her over but he cut me short and rang off. When I arrived on the Tuesday he'd gone. There was no sign of Simone and her handbag was missing. I waited there for an hour or two. But I knew, in my heart, he wasn't coming back.

'I thought at first that I'd simply been betrayed. That he and Simone had taken the money and gone off together. But then, in the sitting room next to my camera, I found the photographs. He'd obviously taken more than one at each stage and calmly chosen the most . . . the most . . .' Here

Sarah broke down in a torrent of despair which completely overwhelmed her. She folded her arms on the edge of the desk and hid her face. There was little any of them could do but wait until the storm passed.

When she finally became calmer, Barnaby asked if she felt ready to continue. And Sarah replied, with great weariness, 'Why not?'

'How long did you stay at the flat after this?'

'I suppose until the evening.'

'And you kept going back, even though you knew he had gone for good?'

'Hope springs eternal.' Everything about her belied the words.

'And then?'

'I heard that Alan had killed himself – at least that's what people were saying. I was devastated. I knew he'd paid the ransom so I thought it must mean he'd been told Simone was never coming back. Then, when you told me it was an unnatural death I – God, I couldn't believe it. There seemed no sense in it. And then I realised that was probably why Tim had had to run away.'

'You mean because he was responsible?'

'Well, there must be some sort of connection. The coincidence is too great.'

'I'd agree with you there,' said Barnaby. 'But what reason do you think he'd have for killing Hollingsworth?'

'All I could think of was that something had gone wrong when Alan handed over the money. That he'd tried to follow – Tim. Or recognised him.'

'*Recognised* him?' This time it was Sergeant Troy quick off the mark.

'I mean, would have recognised him if he'd seen him again. In a . . . what do you call them? A police line-up?'

'I don't think that's what you—'

'Look, Sergeant, my client is answering all your questions willingly and to the very best of her ability. And this in spite of being in an extremely distressed condition.' For the first time John Starkey spoke with some authority. In fact he sounded quite dynamic, as if he had been stoking up the few scraps of conviction he naturally possessed to let forth in one splendid salvo.

Sergeant Troy was indignant. 'We have a right—'

'You have no right to badger people. Especially those who . . .' The imperious dialogue tapered off. Barnaby guessed that the man had been about to say 'who have done nothing wrong' and then recalled the precise details of Sarah Lawson's situation. Everything about Starkey suddenly deflated. He began to wobble, looking rather like a shabby jellyfish in his tight brown Terylene suit.

Barnaby asked if they could please get on.

'Yes, Chief Inspector, of course. Absolutely.'

'Let's recap for a moment, Miss Lawson. I'd just like to confirm that you have not seen or heard from this man, who for the moment we have decided to call Tim, since he telephoned you on Monday the tenth of June?'

'That's right.'

'He did not come to your house late that night or during the early hours of Tuesday morning?'

'No. I've just told you.'

'You have no idea where he is at the moment?'

'None at all.'

'And you are not prepared to help us further in this matter?'

'I'm not sure what you mean.'

'By giving us his home address, for instance.'

'No.'

'I'm wondering if you fully realise the gravity of your position. Apart from the part you have played in the kidnap and ransom of Mrs Hollingsworth, you now appear to be shielding someone who may well be guilty of murder.'

'I do understand how serious it is, yes.'

'And do you understand that you could be looking at a very long custodial sentence? If you couldn't cope with a couple of hours in the station interview room, how will you cope with ten years in a prison cell?'

'I shall never have to.'

'If you think you're going to get off light,' Sergeant Troy was truculent, throwing in a sarcastic laugh for good measure, 'on the ploy that you didn't know exactly what he was up to, you can think again.'

'That isn't what I meant.'

After this Sarah Lawson would not speak and, fifteen minutes of fruitless questioning later, Barnaby drew the interview to a close.

Over the next two days both the flat in Flavell Street and Bay Tree Cottage were subjected to a scrupulous Scenes of Crime investigation. The results were disappointing.

Only Sarah Lawson's prints were found at the flat where Simone Hollingsworth had been held. And only she appeared to have handled the camera. This seemed to indicate, as Barnaby pointed out to his team at their next full briefing, a pretty cold-blooded and thorough clean-up by her lover before he moved out.

The much more neglected interior of Bay Tree Cottage yielded a richer and more complex haul although, alas, no hint of the identity or natural habitat of the man still only known to the police as Tim. But there were many and various prints, all of which took some time to identify and

CAROLINE GRAHAM

disentangle. Sarah's own, those of Avis Jennings and Gray Patterson, and several that had still to be identified. Some from a very small hand matched precisely those taken from toiletries in the bathroom at Nightingales and were thus presumed to be those of Simone Hollingsworth. Several strands of very fair hair were taken from an armchair cushion, carefully analysed (they proved to be dyed) and optimistically filed. The white-gold filaments would be useful should the body, for that is how everyone's thoughts by now inclined, be discovered.

But everyone was to be proved wrong, for on Saturday, 22 June, two weeks and two days after she had disappeared from her home in Fawcett Green, Simone Hollingsworth was found.

Indeed it would have been hard to miss her for she was thrown out of a van, alive if not actually all that well, barely ten yards from the main entrance of Causton police station.

Chapter Eleven

It was not long before the identity of the woman was revealed, even though she was unable to give her name or even talk at all with any degree of sensibility. Famous only for fifteen minutes and that a whole fortnight ago, several people at Hillingdon Hospital immediately recognised Simone.

And so it was that Barnaby and Troy found themselves hanging around reception. It was as depressing as such places always are. People sat about either with sluggish apathy or nervily on the edge of their seats, as if wired to receive dreadful news. Children ran about shouting with laughter. Others whined, begging money for the snacks machine. Old people, with little to gain and nothing to lose, glared about them, tutting severely at anything that moved.

The staff, having barely a second to draw breath, remained efficient and cheerful. Mrs Hollingsworth was in G ward, third floor. The two policemen were told to go first to the staff nurse's office.

'Turn right,' recalled Troy in a subdued voice as they got out of the lift. He hated hospitals.

Shown into a corner cubbyhole, it was some time before Staff Nurse Carter arrived, though the wait was far from dull. Nurses were in and out, the phone rang nonstop and the lift doors hissed. Through the top half of the glass door the two policemen could see people passing endlessly back and forth along the corridor as if on a concealed conveyor belt.

'Sorry to keep you.' Jenny Carter hovered just inside the doorway, plainly on the wing.

'Mrs Hollingsworth?' inquired Barnaby. 'In for observation.'

'Ah, yes, our celebrity. Well, physically she's not bad. Scratched and bruised – I understand this is due to being thrown out of a car on to the pavement.'

'Partly. Fortunately it wasn't moving but, according to witnesses, there was still a certain amount of force employed.'

'But mentally,' Staff Nurse Carter shook her head. 'That's something else. She hardly seems to know who she is or what's going on. The doctor seems to think the amnesia's temporary. It happens sometimes after a severe blow to the head.'

'Has she had any visitors?'

'No. Not even a telephone inquiry.'

'What about the press? Has anyone here talked to them?'

'Certainly not. We've better things to do with our time.'

'Quite. Well, being aware of Mrs Hollingsworth's story, Nurse Carter, I'm sure you appreciate that we'd like to interview her as soon as possible.'

'I wish you luck. Perhaps,' she plucked a pen from the top pocket of her uniform and moved over to the desk, 'you have the name of someone we could contact. She's not ill enough to be kept here, you see, but we can't discharge her in her present confused state except in someone's care. And we desperately need the space.'

'I'm sure you do.' Like everyone else, Barnaby was familiar with stories of lengthy waiting lists, patients on trolleys in corridors waiting for beds and dramatic dashes from one hospital to another trying to find a unit available for someone in need of intensive care. He wondered how long it would be before hospital administrators, tapping their feet, sucking their teeth with impatience and checking their watches, would be positioned at the bedside of the dying, silently urging them to get a move on.

'She is married, I believe. Perhaps her husband—'

'Mrs Hollingsworth is a widow.'

'Of course, I forgot. What about the name of her doctor?'

'Now there I can help you.'

'Excellent,' said Staff, writing it down then reaching for the telephone.

'Oh, one more thing. We shall need to examine everything she had on when she was brought in. Someone from Forensic will call and collect the stuff.'

'What on earth is she going to wear when she leaves?'

'Whoever collects her will no doubt bring something.'

As Barnaby and Troy left the office, Staff Nurse Carter was already punching buttons.

'Mrs Hollingsworth's right at the end,' explained a probation nurse brightly over her shoulder. Her soft shoes squeaked slightly on the shiny composition floor. The ward, which was flooded with sunlight, fell silent as the two men marched along behind her. Everyone capable of sitting upright stared with avid interest changing rapidly to disappointment as the nurse drew the brightly flowered curtains round the patient.

There was a single chair which Barnaby drew up to the bedside. Troy moved closer, looked down on the still, small figure in the bed. And fell instantly and wordlessly in love.

What is there to say? It happens. It's a fact of life. One could say it was *the* fact of life. But it had never happened to Sergeant Troy before.

He had fallen into lust, oh yes. As easily and naturally (and almost as often) as he scored at snooker or washed the Cosworth. And, in his simplicity, he had thought that was it. The many-splendoured thing of which the poets sang. The stuff that was always just around the corner when I'm around you. How could he have been so blind?

'Mrs Hollingsworth?' Barnaby spoke very softly.

'She's asleep, sir.' Immediately defensive on behalf of the unconscious girl, Troy was not aware that his tone verged on the indignant. He gazed down in a passion of protective concern. How small she was. Her hands rested on the counterpane with the fingers, badly scratched, curling loosely inwards like a child's. There was a dressing taped to her temple and the left cheek was badly bruised. Her white-gold hair, chopped and torn about, was dirty.

Rage directed against the bastard who had ill-treated her swept over Sergeant Troy like a tidal wave. The volume and intensity of the experience alarmed him, for he could not bear to be out of control. It was as if someone had attacked Talisa-Leanne. He stepped back a little and took several deep breaths, averting his eyes from the girl in the hospital bed who was now opening her eyes.

'Mrs Hollingsworth?' said Barnaby again. And then, when she did not respond, 'Simone?'

'What is it?' Her voice was so faint Barnaby had to bend over the bed to make the words out.

'I'm a policeman. From Causton CID.' He paused. When

she did not respond he went on, 'I realise that you've just been through a dreadful ordeal but the sooner you can bring yourself to talk about it, the sooner we'll be able to get after the people responsible.' He paused again and with much the same result. 'Do you understand what I've been saying, Mrs Hollingsworth?'

'Yes but . . . I . . . I can't remember anything.'

'Nothing at all? Even the smallest thing might help. Do you recall any names?'

'No.'

'Sarah for example?'

'Sarah.' Though Simone repeated the word tiredly and without any recognition, the colour ran suddenly under her pale skin and her lips trembled.

'Or the name of Sarah's friend.' Sensing concealment, Barnaby began to push. 'She calls him Tim. Did she call him something else when you were all together? Did she perhaps use his real name?'

'I . . . I don't know . . .'

'You were planning to leave your husband and run away with this man.' He was leaning over her now. 'Surely you remember something about him.'

It was terrible. Like watching somebody bullying a child. Troy stepped forward, positioning himself directly behind his boss's shoulder where he could see Simone and she him. He said, 'Not to worry, Mrs Hollingsworth. It'll all come back to you, in time.' He smiled, received the faintest sketch of a smile in return and a sour look for the interruption from his chief.

Then someone came up with a note from the staff nurse. She had explained the situation to Mrs Hollingsworth's doctor and his wife would be coming over to the hospital later that afternoon to collect Simone. They would be happy to look after her for the next few days or for longer should this turn out to be necessary.

Barnaby had got to his feet when the message arrived. Troy promptly whipped the chair some distance away, hoping this might dissuade his boss from sitting down again. But the Chief Inspector had already decided that pressing ahead under the present circumstances would probably be counterproductive. Now that Simone's immediate whereabouts when she left the hospital had been securely established he was happy to postpone any further interrogation until later.

Once more outside in the busy corridor, Barnaby disappeared into the visitors' toilet. Troy seized the opportunity to dash back to Simone's bedside. He stood feeling awkward, uncertain what to say but determined to dispel any anxiety that the enforced interview had aroused.

In the end they spoke together. Simone saying, 'Thank you for—' Sergeant Troy, 'You mustn't worry—'

'His bark's worse than his bite.' Her eyes were lovely. Huge, grey-green, terribly sad. But seen now, without make-up, he would never have recognised her from the glamorous wedding portrait. Her pinched little face looked almost plain. Mysteriously, his feelings remained unaltered. 'We understand what you've been through, Mrs Hollingsworth. Obviously we'll need to talk to you again but you mustn't worry. Until you feel able to cope there won't be any pressure.'

Tears started to trickle down Simone's wan cheeks.

With the greatest difficulty Troy resisted taking the small hand in his. He said, 'It's not the victims we're after.'

Troy caught up with Barnaby at the front entrance.

'You never give up, do you, Gavin?'

'What do you mean?'

'That woman's in no state for what you've got in mind.'

'Actually, sir, I don't have anything "in mind" as you call it.' They strode off towards the car park. 'And I can see for myself what sort of state she's in, thanks very much. Anyone would suppose,' continued Sergeant Troy, angrily yanking open the door of the Rover and climbing in, 'I was the sort of man who never thought of anything else.'

That afternoon, in response to a request from DCI Barnaby, the person who had reported seeing Simone Hollingsworth wearing a wig, shades and a pink jacket on the Aylesbury bus called in at the station.

She was a sensible body, not at all the sort to put herself forward for the sake of it and was pleased that her contribution had been of some help. They settled her down with a cup of tea and a biscuit and left her with a graphic artist describing, in as much detail as she could remember, the style of the wig and design of the sunglasses.

Within a couple of hours a detailed sketch of Simone wearing both had been circulated by the press office to the newspapers and to the television programme *Crimewatch*. In both instances the public was asked to communicate with the police if they had seen the woman in question at any time within the last two weeks.

Barnaby put a call in to Avis Jennings and asked that she keep in constant touch with the station once Simone was living at her house. He would be coming over himself to talk to Simone again within the next day or so. If her memory appeared to return or if she showed any signs of wishing to leave, even if it was only to return to Nightingales, he should be informed at once.

He read through the statements of people who had been present at the incident with the van. One woman said

Simone had 'sort of rolled out'. Another that she had been pushed by the man behind the wheel. A third witness thought that she had been thrown with some force. All agreed that there had been no struggle. The person who sat with her until the ambulance arrived had the impression that she was unconscious even before she hit the pavement.

So concentrated was the attention on Simone that hardly any attention had been paid to the driver. But a youth with quick wits and sharp eyesight, who described the van as dirty yellow and very rusty, had made a note of the number plates. On checking, these proved to have been stolen.

So far the investigative interviews in and around Flavell Street, now in their second day, had come up with only one really interesting result. But this certainly seemed, at least in part, to bear out Sarah Lawson's story.

A couple, backing their Ford Fiesta out of one of the lockup garages behind the flat, had seen a man running up the iron staircase. He had entered number thirteen by way of the kitchen door, going straight in without even knocking. They said the man, wearing jeans and a black T-shirt, had dark, curly hair and was not very tall. As he had his back to them they were unable to describe his features. From the way he moved they believed he was youngish. Pressed, they suggested no more than the early thirties. This had occurred at around two thirty on Tuesday, 11 June.

Shown photographs of Sarah Lawson and Simone Hollingsworth, the couple recognised only Sarah. There were half a dozen other such confirmations, mainly from people in the launderette or Mr Patel's greengrocery. More than one person described her as wandering about like a lost soul.

The following morning Sarah Lawson was due to be

arraigned before the magistrate. Bail, due to the seriousness of the offence, would probably be refused. Certainly it would be opposed by the police.

Once officially on remand, she would be transferred to a woman's prison, probably Holloway. Barnaby took this last opportunity of interviewing her on his own patch. Though he had been told she was still not eating, he was shocked at the rapid change in her.

She was crouched, shivering in the corner of her cell on a foam mattress, knees drawn up under her chin, long skirt covering her legs. The bones of her cheeks and forehead were jutting forward as if they would break through the skin. She stared around wildly as the door was opened, shame and despair ravaging her face.

'Miss Lawson,' said Barnaby. He couldn't bring himself to ask how she was. He sat down on the edge of the toilet. 'What are you hoping to gain by all this?'

'I just want to get it over with.'

'What?'

'Everything. This long disease, my life.'

'You won't be allowed to starve yourself to death, you know. You'll be taken to hospital and fed, one way or the other.'

'So it'll be later rather than sooner. What does it matter?'

'I wonder if you understand the process—'

'Far better than you, I suspect.'

'What I mean is that fasting can inflict serious and permanent internal damage. What if you decide, after all, that you want to survive?'

'I shan't change my mind.' Though distracted and full of suffering, her profile was set as if in stone.

He couldn't leave it there. In some muddled way he felt he had to try and talk her round. Yet all he seemed to be capable of was reducing the situation to banality. Trite phrases fell from his lips. Her betrayer was not worth it. The world was full of people. She would meet someone else. (Sergeant Troy would have been proud of him.) At least he avoided time heals all wounds.

'You're wrong,' said Sarah, 'about meeting someone else. I believe Plato got it right and that we partly exist until we find the single missing person who will make us whole. Only then shall we know true happiness.'

'Goodness. I wouldn't like to calculate the odds on that. They must be worse than the Lottery.'

'And yet, by some wayward calculation of the stars, I found mine. So you see, Inspector, there's no point in searching again. And, once you have known that completeness, being torn apart is simply unbearable.'

The calm finality behind the words made further discussion of the matter pointless. Barnaby got up and walked towards the door, turning back as he reached it. 'You know Simone has been found?'

She cowered at the words. Flinched as if a bucket of icy water had been thrown in her face. 'Yes. They told me. Is she . . . all right?'

'Physically, yes. But she's still confused. He threw her out of a van, did they tell you that? Your charming better half?'

'Out of . . . ?' She stared at him as if he had suddenly broken into a foreign language.

'We've got a description of him. He was seen going into Flavell Street via the back entrance. Not too tall, thirtyish, dark hair. That accurate, would you say?'

'What . . . what are you . . .'

And then, as Barnaby received the stare and returned it with an equal force and intensity, Sarah Lawson began to batten down the hatches.

The Chief Inspector was reminded of a film he once saw, a costume drama where a distraught, unhappy heiress, discovering the man she loves is only after her money, runs around the great dark Victorian house in which she lives barring it against his next visit. He could still hear the shutters. Slam, slam, slam, slam. Slam.

And so it was now.

'Yes.' When Sarah eventually spoke she sounded very tired. 'Yes, I think that's a fairly accurate description.'

'Is there nothing you won't say, Sarah? Nothing you won't agree to to help out?' Pitiful though she was, Barnaby still experienced anger. 'No lies you won't tell?'

'No. None.'

Barnaby let down the flap then and shouted for the duty officer to unlock the door.

Next day, following the publication of the drawing of Simone in her dark glasses, some reports of sightings started trickling in. These were nowhere near as numerous or as full of exotic detail as happened at the beginning of the case. Either the public was by now fed up with the Hollingsworth extravaganza or Simone had been very securely hidden away after she was removed from Flavell Street. Of the few that were reported, nearly all in or around London, none proved to be worth the time and effort spent following them up. *Crimewatch*, which should flush out many more, was not due to go out for another three days.

Just after lunch Barnaby received notification from Rainbird and Gillis, Causton's most well-established undertakers, that the funeral of Alan Hollingsworth had now been arranged and would take place in two days' time. The service would be held at St Chad's parish church, Fawcett Green, and the internment directly afterwards in the burial ground adjacent. No flowers by request.

Barnaby, wondering by whose request, scribbled a note on his pad. The last thirty-six hours had been so crammed with new incident and revelation that trying to absorb and assess it all had pushed the deaths of Hollingsworth and poor Brenda Brockley to the fringes of his mind. Now he turned his attention to both.

Brenda was the one that depressed him most, perhaps because he felt that it was the one he could do least about. They knew she had been killed by Hollingsworth's car. Presumably, if not inevitably, he had been driving it. What chance now, though, to find out exactly what had happened?

At least, in the matter of Hollingsworth's own death, they had a suspect. The faceless, false-hearted and falsely named Tim. Sarah, at her second interview, had seemed to imply it was he who was responsible.

Of course there was also Gray Patterson who fitted the bill to perfection. A powerful motive, no alibi and a friend of Sarah Lawson. However, set against this must be the fact that there was absolutely no forensic evidence to put him inside Nightingales the night of Hollingsworth's death. Also, on the afternoon Simone absconded, he was sitting in the Causton Odeon watching *Goldeneye*. Thirdly, and surely most telling by far, Patterson could by no stretch of the imagination be described as a short man with dark curly hair.

And it was this man that they now had to lay their hands on.

The storm of two days ago had really broken the weather. The day of the funeral, though warm, was patchy. The sun was inconstant, clouds scudded about and the branches of the elms and yew trees in the churchyard bent and rustled in the slight breeze.

The Reverend Bream, a snowy surplice covering his shabby cassock, read the elegy. His voice was grave and rich and full of quite genuine-sounding sorrow. It was at such moments that he came into his own.

Barnaby and Troy did not go to the service. Neither did they join the tiny group at the graveside but stood some small distance away on a grassy knoll – outsiders with no part to play but that of spectres at the feast.

'For man born of woman has but a short time to live . . .'

And who could argue with that? We give birth astride a grave, as the poet said. At least Barnaby thought it was a poet. Or maybe he remembered it from one of the plays that Joyce's group put on. Whatever, the writer was spot on. Looked at in cosmic terms, it was as fast as that. Now you see the sun shine, now you don't.

Although quite a large collection of people hovered at the lych gate, there were only eight mourners at the graveside. Avis Jennings was there next to Simone, her arm round the girl's slender shoulders. Constable Perrot, his helmet in the crook of his elbow, stood more or less to attention. The accountant Ted Burbage, representing Penstemon, was next to Elfrida Molfrey. She and Cubby Dawlish held hands and gravely bowed their heads.

The other two mourners were strangers to Barnaby. He guessed at the dead man's brother and his wife. She must be a wife for surely such an upright, stern-faced, joyless countenance could not belong to a man frivolous enough to bring along a mistress. He wore a black suit of dull, heavy cloth. She a limp dress the colour of dirty water with an uneven hemline and a black velvet band stitched round one sleeve. Her expression was even more sour than her husband's. Barnaby was reminded of his mother's phrase, 'Fit to turn the milk.'

'Ashes to ashes, dust to dust . . .'

'If the booze don't get you the tax man must.' Troy spoke almost absently, his gaze fixed on the window's pale, distressed face. He trembled unaccountably and felt rather queasy.

'What on earth's wrong with you?'

'Ay?'

'Shaking about.'

'It's the heat, guv.'

The baked meats were laid out at the doctor's house. Mrs Jennings had been quite restrained. Flamboyantly showy cakes and delectable confections of cream and sugar were absent. The most elaborate item on the table was a many-layered *millefeuille* made with fresh raspberries. There was half a York ham on an old-fashioned white china stand and a herby salad freshly picked from the garden. Dr Jennings began to carve but was interrupted by an urgent call, whereupon he disappeared and the vicar took over.

Conversation was subdued and remained so, perhaps because the only liquid offered was Indian or China tea. Simone, naturally the focus of everyone's concern, appeared overwhelmed. She sat between her husband's relatives on a velvet chaise longue looking, to Sergeant Troy's way of thinking, like a soft and lovely rose between two cacti. The hospital dressing on her temple had been removed and, though she was carefully made-up, the bruise showed through.

Mrs Jennings had made it plain to both himself and Barnaby that they would be welcome to partake of the refreshments but Troy still felt extremely uncomfortable.

Being neither friends nor family their presence could only underline the dark provenance of the situation. How could he simply go up and offer his condolences to Simone, no strings attached? For the first time since he joined the force, Sergeant Troy wished he wasn't a policeman.

Barnaby did not mingle. He was in the kitchen tucking into some home-baked Ciabatta with a piece of runny Brie and a bowl of salad. He was also talking to Avis Jennings who had discovered she was a cake fork short and was rummaging in the cutlery drawer.

'I understand from your husband that Simone is getting better.'

'She's quite a bit better, yes. Her memory's returning in fits and starts. Jim says it's often like that. She knows us and Elfie and remembers all sorts of things about the village but not much about her . . . ordeal. It's not surprising, is it? I mean, that she wants to block things out for as long as possible. Ah, there you are!' Avis scolded the missing fork and started to polish it on her skirt. 'I know I would.'

'Perfectly understandable.'

'I took her round to the house just to get some fresh clothes and stuff. But she didn't want to stay.'

'How did you get in, Mrs Jennings?'

'Jill Gamble let us have the key.' She looked at Barnaby somewhat anxiously. 'I hope that's all right. We were only there a few minutes.'

'And were you with Mrs Hollingsworth all the time?'

'I was, actually.' Avis was deeply puzzled. 'She just put a couple of dresses and some underwear in a bag. They are her own things, Inspector.'

Barnaby, his mouth full of delicious cheese, merely nodded.

'Well, I must to my muttons,' said Avis. 'I wish the

Scottish contingent would tuck in. It's not as if they're overwhelmed by grief. Simone said Alan hadn't spoken to either of them for years.'

'Some people would think such behaviour perfectly proper for a funeral.'

'Hm.' Avis sniffed. 'In my opinion a pinch of rectitude goes a very long way.'

Troy, in the odd moments that his eyes strayed from Simone, had noticed a general eddying towards a door at the far end of the room which led directly to the kitchen. Although there was definitely not what you could call a queue, Sergeant Perrot was hovering near the opening and slipped in as Mrs Jennings emerged. Mrs Molfrey was also gently whirling in that direction followed by Cubby Dawlish, whirling counterclockwise while hanging on to a plate of ham and salad and a nice strong cup of Ridgeway's Breakfast Blend.

As things turned out, all three arrived together. Perrot remained standing but the other two sat down. Cubby drank his tea. Elfrida, delighted to be tête à tête once more with the top brass, turned her glowing face towards Barnaby.

'I'm not reproaching you of course, Chief Inspector. I know how incredibly busy you must be. But I was disappointed not to hear from you, after the news of my revelation.'

'I'm afraid I'm not with you, Mrs Molfrey.'

'No chink, no chime. Didn't—' Elfrida glanced over the Chief Inspector's shoulder and, in the nick of time, saw Colin Perrot's expression of horrified apprehension, '—you get my message? I spoke into your answering machine.'

'Sorry,' smiled Barnaby. 'They're not always reliable, I'm afraid. What was it about, Mrs Molfrey?'

'As I think I previously told you on the day Simone disappeared, I walked up the lane with Sarah Lawson and she was carrying this large box. She said it was some Kilner jars that Simone had promised for her white elephant collection at the fête. But then, when we got to her gate, she sort of hefted it up in her arms, like this, oof oof—'

'Careful, dearest,' murmured Cubby.

'—and there was not a single sound. This from a box supposedly full of glass. Then I thought to myself, what on earth would Simone be doing with such things anyway? She could hardly cook, let alone bake bread or make jam. Certainly I can't imagine her ever bottling fruit or vegetables. Also,' Elfrida gave Barnaby a look he immediately recognised. It was identical to the one worn by Kilmowski when he brought a particularly large and succulent corpse into the house and laid it proudly on the doormat. 'You could tell by the way she was hanging on how heavy the box was. There was more in there, believe you me, Inspector, than a few empty jars.'

'That's very interesting, Mrs Molfrey.' And it was too. There had certainly been no such box either in Bay Tree Cottage itself or the garden shed when they were searched. 'When is this fête?'

'Not until August Bank Holiday Monday.'

'And who would Sarah pass them on to?'

'No one if she was running her own stall. You could ask Mrs Perrot – she is on the committee again this year, I believe, Colin?'

'That's right, Mrs Molfrey.' Perrot, still metaphorically wiping the sweat of relief from his brow, smiled warmly at his rescuer. 'I'll certainly ask, sir, if the stuff has been passed to someone else.'

'If you would, Constable.'

'I should tell you both perhaps, although you'll no doubt hear it on the news tomorrow, that Miss Lawson has been charged with taking part in the kidnap and ransom of Mrs Hollingsworth.'

'Oh! But that's . . .' Mrs Molfrey could not continue. With trembling fingers she adjusted the anthracite chiffon veiling draped over her ringlets. It was trimmed with marcasite which sparkled as it caught the sunlight pouring through the kitchen window. 'I can't believe. No. No.'

'That's right. No,' echoed Cubby firmly. His bright blue eyes shone with conviction. 'She's too . . . what is the word I want, Elfie?'

'Proud.'

'That's right. Proud.'

'You've got it wrong, Inspector,' said Elfrida. 'I'm sorry, I know how presumptuous that must sound—'

'We don't charge people without strong evidence, Mrs Molfrey. Also, Sarah Lawson has confessed.'

'But she doesn't *care* about money. You've seen how she lives.'

'She may not care about money. But the person she was working with cares very much indeed.'

This shocked them both. He watched new and terrible complexities crowding their minds. Neither spoke again. They sat on, bewildered, for a few moments then got up and went away, Cubby patting Elfrida's hand in tender consolation.

'Perrot?'

'Sir.' Constable Perrot moved smartly up to the pine table and rested his helmet.

'I'm putting a twenty-four-hour watch on this place. To be transferred to Nightingales should Mrs Hollingsworth decide to move back.'

'Do you think she's still in some sort of danger then?'

'Perhaps. In any case we need a sharp eye kept. She's a very important witness. I'll leave it with you.' Barnaby pushed his chair back. 'You'll be relieved once the shifts get sorted.'

'No problem, sir.'

'Are you all right for tea?' Avis popped her head round the door.

'I could do with another cup,' said Barnaby. 'But I'll take it out there.'

The scene in the Jennings' drawing room had changed slightly. Elfrida and Cubby were no longer present. Edward Hollingsworth had moved to the window seat where he was deep in conversation with Penstemon's accountant. His wife was stacking used plates at the table and putting them on a large wooden tray. Troy was sitting next to Simone on the green velvet chaise longue.

Barnaby, unnoticed by either, watched them both. Simone was speaking, pausing to bite her lip and frown, hesitating, speaking again. Her hands fluttered constantly, at her white bruised forehead, over her heart, smoothing her shaggy silver gilt hair. She was wearing a simple cotton dress, pink and white stripes with a sprig of mignonette pinned to the collar. Beneath it the slender outline of her body was tense.

Troy, his whole attitude one of absorbed tenderness, listened. Every now and again he nodded his head. Occasionally he said something. Barnaby thought he lip-read the words, 'I'm so sorry.'

He stepped sideways to the woman at the table and introduced himself.

'Oh, I know who you are.' Each word came out well-rounded, hard and individual, like polished pebbles. She had a strong Scottish accent. 'It's taking you long enough to find out who's responsible for my brother-in-law's death.'

'When did you arrive, Mrs Hollingsworth?'

'Yesterday. We had a communication from Alan's solicitor and have a meeting tomorrow morning. We shall be getting straight back then. My husband has to prepare his weekly sermon.' Then, just in case Barnaby had not fully understood the importance of her spouse's position, 'Edward is a minister of the church.'

Yes, thought the Chief Inspector, glancing at the bloodless profile and sanctimonious curling lower lip. I guessed he might be. 'I understand your husband and his brother had been estranged for some years.'

'Not at all. They may not have communicated all that frequently but there was no estrangement. In fact over the past few months they have spoken on more than one occasion.'

'But I am right in thinking you didn't approve of his second marriage?'

'As we do not acknowledge divorce there can be no such thing as a second marriage.' She picked up her tray and bared her yellow tombstone teeth at him. 'Fornicating liaison, I think the Lord would call it.'

Blimey. Barnaby watched her ramrod back, long and thin and stiff as a poker, marching off to the kitchen. I wouldn't fancy trying to warm my feet on that on a winter's night.

He made his way over to the couple in the corner relishing, even before he reached it, the pleasant change in the scenery.

'And how are you feeling today, Mrs Hollingsworth?'

'Ohh, Inspector.' They were like white doves, those hands. Her prettiness, her loveliness was returning. Cosmetics had been lightly applied but with such art as to appear artless. How long and silky her lashes were.

'Much better, I can see.'

'Yes. Thank you.'

'Sergeant, there's going to be a police presence here until further notice. This needs to be explained to Mrs Jennings. So if you'd do the honours?'

'What, now?'

'Yes. Now.'

There was no mistaking the emphasis on the second word. Troy reluctantly rose to his feet. He gave Simone a smile, a mixture of comfort and encouragement, and retreated. Unluckily for him, Mrs Jennings chose that moment to disappear through the French windows into the garden. Still looking anxiously over his shoulder, Troy followed.

'Avis has been so kind,' explained Simone. 'And her husband too.'

'Even so, I expect you're looking forward to going home.'

'Home?'

'Nightingales.'

'I'm never going back there.' The palms of her hands pressed violently against her knees. 'I hate it!'

'You remember being unhappy, then?'

'Yes.' She looked at him uncertainly. 'Some things more than others.'

'I understand. I want to ask you a question, Simone. And,' her eyes had already widened in alarm, 'it's nothing to do with . . . Well, perhaps very indirectly. Please don't be alarmed.'

'You must think I'm very foolish.'

'Not at all.' Barnaby smiled. 'Do you recall, just before you . . . went away, leaving a box with some glass jars on your patio for Sarah Lawson to collect.'

'Jars? What sort of jars?'

'Apparently they were Kilner jars. For bottling fruit.'

'I can't . . . Wait a moment. Yes. They were for the fête.'

'That's right.' He barely stopped himself saying 'good girl' for, having produced the right answer, she appeared as delighted as a child.

'Now, can you tell me where you got them?'

'Um, let's think.' She frowned and sighed and frowned again. 'The church jumble. Everyone is always expected to buy at these dos. And then, as nearly everything's usually pretty horrible, when the next fête or bring and buy comes round, it goes back in. There's been a dreadful table lamp apparently doing the rounds for years.'

'Excellent,' said the Chief Inspector. 'That's tidied up, then.'

'Is that all?'

'At the moment.'

She relaxed; lifted her hands from her knees. But so fierce had been the pressure that their imprint remained in the fabric of her dress. 'What did you mean when you said to Gavin there'd be a police presence here?'

'It's for your own protection, Mrs Hollingsworth.' Gavin, is it? We'll see about that.

'But isn't it all over?' Under the cosmetics her face paled. 'I mean—'

'Passed the message on, sir.' Sergeant Troy was once more urgently present. Standing four square on the carpet and daring anyone to shift him.

'Right.' Barnaby got up. 'Let's away.'

When they reached the car, which they had left parked outside Bay Tree Cottage, Gray Patterson was leaning up against the bonnet. He moved towards them anxiously.

'I recognised the Rover, Inspector,' he said. 'Didn't like to intrude at the Jennings' or come to the church. Especially with Alan's brother there. I thought it might look rather two-faced.'

'I've no doubt it would,' replied Barnaby. 'Given your past history.'

'I'm trying to find out what's going on regarding Sarah. I heard she'd been arrested so I went down to the station. But they wouldn't let me see her.'

'I shouldn't fret about it, Mr Patterson.'

'But she'll need me. To help get this stupid mistake sorted out.'

'There's no mistake, I'm afraid.' Barnaby repeated the information he had so recently given to Cubby and Mrs Molfrey and with much the same result. Patterson was absolutely devastated.

'That can't be right. *Sarah?*'

'Working with her lover,' said Sergeant Troy. Still peeved at seeing Simone bullied yet again, he was determined to take it out on someone. 'I expect that's why she suddenly got all chummy with you. To deflect attention, like.'

'Rubbish.'

'Not caught up with him yet, but we will.' Smiling, Troy delivered the *coup de grâce*. 'A very passionate affair, by all accounts.'

Patterson turned from them then. Turned away and walked straight into the road, which was fortunately empty. After this, stumbling and wavering, he wandered off along the grass verges in the direction of his home.

We are all in the lap of the gods. When Barnaby listened to criminals whining during interrogations or later from the dock that they had never had any luck, he was not overly sympathetic.

Though he himself had had the luck – affectionate parents, a stable and happy marriage, an intelligent and healthy child – he was not a man to pour libations or even offer up a grateful prayer. Like most people in such a fortunate position, he took it all for granted.

But now, entering the final stage in what was to be called, in the first of many books dealing with the subject, *Twist and Counter Twist: The Mysterious Lives of Alan and Simone Hollingsworth*, the Chief Inspector became keenly aware of the part that the Fates had played in his investigation.

They always did, of course. And you soon knew if they were for you or against you. For instance if someone – and Barnaby didn't believe for a minute that that someone was Sergeant Troy – had not had the idea of questioning the college accommodation bureau, the chances were the flat at Flavell Street would never have been discovered.

And if Eden Lo had been looking elsewhere during the few seconds that it took Alan Hollingsworth to put down his coffee cup and walk away, the Heathrow connection might never have been made.

And now the most vital link of all was winging its way along the ether. At first, it looked like nothing much. Just another sighting, in fact. A woman on the blower, a genuine Bow Bells Cockney, rang in the morning after the funeral. Barnaby picked up the extension and listened in.

At the time he could not have said why it was this call out of all others that spoke to his condition. It was only a couple of hours later, on the spot as it were, that he recognised the connection.

Her name was Queenie Lambert and she lived on the Isle of Dogs. The woman sketched in her copy of the *Sun* had been staying in a flat across the walkway. Although she hadn't been out and about as such, Mrs Lambert had glimpsed her a couple of times, once opening the door to the postman and later watering the window boxes on the balcony.

Mrs Lambert sounded elderly and Barnaby imagined her life to be somewhat constrained. She probably spent much of it taking keen note of what the neighbours were up to. Probably regarded as a nosy nuisance around the buildings, such people could be an absolute godsend to the police.

Although, like everyone else, both detectives were aware that massive development had been taking place around the quays and docks of Canary Wharf, the scale and magnificence of the enterprise was pretty breathtaking. Great towers of glass and steel surrounded by piles of rubble glittered in the sunlight. Diggers roared and trundled about, raising huge clouds of dust. New apartments, soon to be sold for hundreds of thousands of pounds, rose up just a few yards from old thirties-style low-rise council estates, broken down and boarded up poverty fisted by brazen, upmarket cash.

Driving out of the Blackwall Tunnel, Troy gave an impressed whistle of appreciation and even Barnaby was much taken by the hugely confident operatic splendour that lay spread out before them.

As it was nearly twelve thirty they stopped at the George, Westferry Road, for a pint of Webster's Yorkshire bitter and some excellent sandwiches. Sergeant Troy threw a few darts. Barnaby sat quietly thinking. The atmosphere between them seethed and simmered. Troy was still angry that his passionate concern for Simone's wellbeing had been crudely interpreted as creating an opportunity to get his leg over. He was also smarting over a follow-up lecture against the advisability of getting involved, on any level, with someone so severely entangled in a case that was presently under investigation.

He knew what that meant, all right. It meant the chief did not trust him to keep his mouth shut. Thought that he, Troy, was so careless and dim that any bit of fluff could wind him round their little finger, ask any questions they fancied and get the right answers. Talk about a fucking insult.

'You fit then, Sergeant?'

'Yes, sir.' Troy hit a bull's eye, drained his glass and put his black leather jacket back on.

Mrs Lambert's flat was on a small development of Peabody buildings, just behind Thermopylae Gardens, two storeys high with balconies running all round, some strung across with washing. Most of the windows on the ground floor were either barred or covered with wrought-iron grilles. One or two people had bought their homes and personalised them by painting the bricks blue and orange or replacing the original doors and windows. But mostly they remained uniformly drab, grubby-looking and in need of repair.

'Don't drive right in.' Barnaby recalled an occasion when his car had been parked outside a tower block for barely ten minutes while he had struggled to arrest someone on the eighth floor. When he came out every removable part of the vehicle had vanished, including the seats. 'Over there'll do.'

Troy parked neatly facing a little row of single-fronted shops and climbed out. The Chief Inspector picked up his mobile phone and followed. They walked across the open well of the courtyard and past smelly communal rubbish bins that were taller than they were. As they climbed the metal staircase, Barnaby wondered again at the strange compulsion that had brought him way out of his own manor to investigate something a local man could have checked out in no time.

He could see Mrs Lambert agitating her curtain, watching them approach. The old lady snatched open her door before Troy could even ring the bell. Showed into a sparklingly clean sitting room so overstuffed with furniture they practically had to walk sideways, and having declined the offer of a cup of tea, Barnaby asked where Mrs Lambert had seen the woman in dark glasses.

'I'll show you.' She hobbled painfully towards the window. 'Directly over the way, see? Where them boxes wiv the red geraniums are.'

'And could you tell me – I'm sorry,' the Chief Inspector interrupted himself, 'perhaps you'd like to sit down.'

'I'm better upright, if it's all the same to you.' She wore large men's checked slippers bulging round the toes. 'Uvverwise the blood rushes to me bunions.'

'When did you last see this woman?'

'Oohh, must be four or five days now.'

'Could you possibly be more precise, Mrs Lambert?' Barnaby's heart plummeted in his breast. Five days ago Simone Hollingsworth was lying in Hillingdon Hospital.

'Well, let's see. It was the day before our Elaine came round to take me to the chiropodists. They won't send transport if you can dig up somebody wiv a car. Mean buggers.'

'And that was?'

'Well, it's Thursday afternoon, Health Centre, so it would have been the day before I spotted her.'

'Wednesday?' Eight days ago. Barnaby held his breath.

'That's right.'

'And can you remember when you saw her first?'

Troy took no part in this. He told himself there was no

point. That it was a complete waste of time. But in truth a nervous apprehension, the like of which he had never known, was gradually seeping into his bones.

'I can't, in all honesty,' replied Queenie Lambert. 'But I do know it was after June the twelfth because that's when I come back from me holiday in Cromer.'

'Thank you,' said Barnaby feeling the phrase would prove to be shamefully inadequate but not knowing quite what to put in its place.

He and Troy had to go down to the courtyard again to get to the other side. Halfway across they passed some little girls skipping. One of them wore a T-shirt that caught the Chief Inspector's eye. The bold letters read: Cuba Street Carnival.

He stopped walking then and stood, stock still, engrossed in thought. Troy carried on for a few steps, realised he was alone and also came to a halt. Deciding he had deliberately been made to look foolish, the sergeant refused to backtrack. Instead he wandered over to the little girls, smiled and said, 'Hullo.'

They all ran away.

'Gavin?'

'Sir.'

'You got the London A to Z?'

'In my pocket.'

'Look up Cuba Street, would you?' As he waited, Barnaby couldn't help wondering what he was waiting for, why the word Cuba rang in his ear like a cracked bell, and what earthly connection this seedy environment could prove to have with the beautifully maintained hamlet of Fawcett Green. Yet the longer he stood there, the surer he became that he was in the right place at the right time. And for the right reasons.

'There you go.' Coolly Troy handed over the book, open at page eighty. 'Cuba Street. Square two C.'

Barnaby stared at the page. The River Thames, like a great white snake, twined through it, cutting off the Isle of Dogs from Rotherhithe and Deptford and Greenwich. He located Cuba Street at the West Indian Dock Pier. It meant nothing at all.

Sergeant Troy noted this and not without a certain amount of satisfaction. He hadn't a clue as to what the chief was after but recognised a letdown when he saw it.

Barnaby continued studying the map. And then he did find something. Troy knew this because an expression of recognition followed quickly by one of astonishment possessed Barnaby's solid features. Troy thought the boss looked like that daft bird in a story he sometimes read to his daughter. Left the safety of the farmyard to go walkabout and the sky fell on it. Say what you like about chickens, they may be stupid but they know where the action is.

'It's not Cuba, Sergeant. It's Cubitt.'

'Right, guv.'

'Cubitt Town.'

'Got that.'

'Mean anything?'

'Not offhand.' Here we go.

'Think about it.'

Yeah, think about it, Gavin. Give your mind a hernia, why don't you?

They negotiated the second staircase and walked along the balcony. The flat with the window boxes was the last in the row. As they approached, Barnaby's footsteps slowed. He was conscious of feeling extremely nauseous and slightly dazed. There was a lump the size of a ping pong ball stuck in his throat and his whole body felt as heavy as lead. Now, so close, his previous certainty wavered. Wasn't it rather foolish to build up such hopes merely on a single geographical coincidence?

Then he noticed, stretched along the balcony wall, yawning and sunning itself, a beautifully marked tabby cat. He bent down, stretched out his hand and called, 'Nelson?'

The cat jumped down and came straight to him.

'*Nelson?*' Sergeant Troy stared at the animal now weaving itself around and about Barnaby's trouser legs and purring. 'You mean that's . . .?'

'Simone's cat, yes.' Barnaby rapped hard on the door.

'What the hell is it doing out here?'

'I suppose they've been looking after it for her.'

'But how did it . . . I mean, who's they?'

Someone was moving inside. They could see through the small frosted panes of glass a dark formless shape approaching. A mortise was unlocked, a key turned, a chain rattled then fell, clattering against the frame. Slowly the door opened.

A middle-aged woman stood there. Thin, consumptive-looking, heavily made-up. Sucking in smoke through a slim cigarette. Frizzy henna'd hair. She smelled of vinegar and chips and wore a denim mini skirt and a semi-transparent nylon blouse with rhinestone buttons.

'Whatever you're selling I don't wannit. And that includes religion. So piss off.'

'Mrs Atherton?'

'Who wants to know?' This came from a man at the back of the hall. A man perhaps in his early thirties, not too tall with dark curly hair.

'DCI Barnaby, Causton CID,' replied the Chief Inspector. And got his foot in the door just in time.

* * *

One of the most infuriating things about the guv'nor was his refusal to talk until he was good and ready. Another, equally infuriating, was this habit of pointing out to his irritated bag carrier that the said carrier had all the information that he, the guv'nor, possessed and so should be quite capable of drawing his own conclusions.

That Sergeant Troy knew his chief well enough to appreciate that this attitude was neither spiteful nor motivated by any desire to show off only made matters worse. He was well aware that Barnaby was simply offering encouragement. Trying to persuade him to recall, reflect, deduce, connect.

But these were not Troy's natural strengths. He was sharp-eyed, fast and agressive. He was a good man to have on your side in a fight. But he was not patient. When they eventually got back to the ranch, there was no way he would be going over every statement and interview relative to the Hollingsworth case to find out where the words Cubitt Town had cropped up.

The two inhabitants of the council flat behind Thermopylae Gardens were being held at Rotherhithe police station pending a transfer to Causton CID for questioning. Queenie Lambert, already vaguely aware of playing some small part in what she suspected might prove to be a very large drama, had further consolidated her position by offering to look after the cat.

On leaving the East London nick, Barnaby had asked to be driven straight to Fawcett Green and now Sergeant Troy, his heart beating twenty to the dozen and his thoughts jumping like deranged fleas, was walking very quickly down St Chad's Lane to Nightingales, aware, as he almost ran along, of an urgency he could not put a name to, a compulsion that, at all costs, he must get there first.

Calling earlier at Dr Jennings' they had been told that Simone, accompanied by the attendant officer who had taken over from PC Perrot, had gone home to sort out a change of clothes and pick up any post that may have arrived. The place was otherwise unoccupied. Hollingsworth's brother and his wife, having resolutely refused to spend a single night under the roof of 'the devil's house of sin', were staying at the Vicarage.

As Barnaby walked up the weed-choked path to the front door for the last time, he thought how much longer it seemed than two weeks since he had walked up it for the first time.

The nicotiana in the Italian terracotta jars were dead and dried up and one of the pots had cracked open, spilling fine earth all over the doorstep. Thistles and nettles had got a stranglehold on the front garden and the window-panes were thick with dust. All the downstairs curtains were drawn. The whole place had a somnolent air and although the interior had been cleaned, a faint smell of stale food still mingled with that of lemon-scented furniture polish.

'Afternoon, Chief Inspector,' said the constable positioned by the front door which was standing open.

'Mrs Hollingsworth inside?'

'That's right, sir.'

Barnaby entered first but he was hardly in the hall before his sergeant pushed past. Troy blundered into the living room and from there to the dining room and kitchen. He returned and stood in front of Barnaby, breathing deeply. He appeared to be in a state of extreme physical discomfort and his face was transfigured by a passionate determination. There was a footfall overhead.

Troy moved quickly forward but found his way blocked.

'Gavin. Listen to me.'

'Someone's upstairs.'

'There's only one way out of this.'

'I don't believe you.'

'I'm truly sorry.'

'There's always more than one way. You told me that a long while ago.'

'Not this time.'

'Oh Christ.'

'Do you want to stay down here?' The words, spoken as Barnaby moved towards the staircase, were barely audible. Troy shook his head. 'Then keep quiet, OK?'

They ascended the stairs, Troy struggling to make his face blank and keep some sort of grip on his emotions. He felt as if he was being put through a wringer; the ventricles of his heart squeezed by a giant first. He thought, if this is love, give me a vicious kicking any day of the week.

The door of the master bedroom was wide open and they could see clear across it when they reached the landing. Barnaby rested a warning hand on his sergeant's arm – unnecessarily, for Troy could not have spoken for the world.

A woman, unrecognisable to both men though they each knew who she was, stood gazing into a full-length mirror. Lost in the happy contemplation of her reflection, she remained unaware of their proximity.

She wore a beautifully cut dress of rich black velvet, backless and a stitch away from frontless. On her feet were elegant sandals with dangerously high heels. She balanced easily on them, swaying slightly but in a poised and naturally graceful manner. She wore an ash-blonde shoulder-length wig, teazed and tousled into a cloud of soft, loose curls. At her throat, wrists, hands and ears a conflagration of light blazed.

419

Her face was both very beautiful and completely soulless. A dazzling example of cosmetic alchemy. Peach and ivory skin blushing coral over cleverly modelled cheekbones, huge, brilliant but very hard eyes enlarged and enhanced by layer upon delicate layer of shadows. False lashes dark, glossy and thickly curled.

But it was about the mouth where the most startling transformation had taken place. Her own rather thin lipline having been skilfully erased, a new crimson mouth, greedy and voluptuous, bloomed in its place.

She turned sideways, pausing briefly to admire the compelling perfection of her image, adjusted the diamond necklace then picked up a magnificent full-length blue fox coat from the back of a chair and draped it round her shoulders.

And it was then that she saw them.

Simone did not turn round but she did become very still, regarding the intruders silently in the mirror. Barnaby observed the calculation process at its most naked. Explanations, excuses, evasions, exits. She ran them all by with alarmed rapidity. It was like watching a fruit machine lining up the total. Ching, ching, ching. And every one a lemon.

'Good afternoon, Mrs Hollingsworth.'

'Oh. Hullo.'

There was nothing she could do now, thought Barnaby with some small satisfaction and a great deal of anger. No way she could revert to the shy, sad, winsome little scrap that the world had treated so cruelly.

'I just came over for some clothes.'

'So I see.' He glanced at the bed which was strewn with money. There were dresses lying there too. And underwear and shoes. Several real leather suitcases stood nearby with their lids open. 'I hope you're not thinking of leaving us.'

Simone ignored this remark. Her pretty pink tongue flicked out, wetting her already glistening lips. She glanced at Sergeant Troy and attempted a seductive smile, lifting her scarlet top lip to reveal sharp white incisors. But extreme tension froze the movement, distorting it into a half sneer.

'Hi, Gavin.'

Troy turned and walked back to the landing. He leaned over the stair rail feeling sick with betrayal and unhappiness. He felt his longing, poisoned beyond redemption, curdle in his heart.

From the bedroom he could hear Barnaby start to speak but the words seemed to come from a great distance and echo strangely. Troy wondered if, for the first time in his life, he was about to faint.

'Simone Hollingsworth,' began the Chief Inspector, 'you are under arrest on suspicion of the murder of your husband, Alan. You do not have to say anything . . .'

He was taken at his word. Simone had now been in custody for just under two hours and had remained silent apart from making a single telephone call to Penstemon's solicitor who was unable to get to the station until seven o'clock that evening.

Awaiting Jill Gamble's arrival, Barnaby organised a debriefing at thirty minutes' notice, inevitably garnering, in the incident room, only the immediate shift of men and women who had worked on the Hollingsworth case.

Audrey Brierley was present; Gavin Troy was not. He had cried off and Barnaby thought for once the term not inappropriate. Naturally, though perilously close to breaking down, Troy would have died rather than be seen weeping. He had turned the keen edge of his distress against himself and fallen on it like a defeated warrior upon his sword, mutilating his emotions, furiously attempting to kill what had been so newly born. Wounded and a fool for love, he was fit for nothing and Barnaby had sent him home.

People were scattered around the room, popping cans or queuing for the kettle to make coffee filters. Some peeled confectionery wrappers, others tore open crisps. The lines were diverted to the separate office and a couple of civilian telephonists detailed to take the calls. There was a slight air about the place of getting dug in.

The Chief Inspector had so far just given them the bare bones of the matter. They all knew that Simone Hollingsworth had been arrested and why. It was the sordid details, what someone had once called the 'shitty gritty', that now closely engaged their attention.

Naturally, as the subject of Barnaby's disquisition had yet to speak, his narrative would be in the nature of an imaginative re-creation rather than a straightforward listing of acknowledged facts. But he still looked forward to unravelling the tangled web in which they had all been ensnared. Like his daughter, he had been born to the sound of a drum roll. And now, ladies and gentlemen, before your eyes, before your very eyes . . .

But – Barnaby shuffled his notes – where to begin? No crime takes place in a vacuum and he had the feeling that this one had been in the making for a long while. Certainly since the beginning of the marriage and maybe even earlier. Perhaps since the very first moment the black widow spider spotted such a big juicy fly.

'So what made you first think to put her in the frame, Chief Inspector?' Sergeant Beryl kicked off.

'There was never one specific thing. Rather an accumulation of signs, scraps of information, conversations that meant nothing at the time but, viewed in retrospect, became significant.'

Perhaps that would be a good starting point. The village itself, Fawcett Green. And its opinion of Alan Hollingsworth's second wife.

'The first unusual thing I noticed about Simone was that everyone I spoke to described her in exactly the same way. Now, this is very odd. Usually, if you ask half a dozen people's opinion of someone, you'll get six varying replies. But the same adjectives turned up again and again in this case. Mrs Hollingsworth was wistful, lonely, childlike and not too bright. Easily bored, she remained a docile and loving wife even in the face of her husband's apparent cruelty.'

'Don't know about apparent, sir.' Audrey sounded a bit bullish. 'We've got the interview with her doctor to bear it out.'

'I'll come to that. The point I'm making now is that unlike the rest of us, who adjust our behaviour according to the situation and who we're with, Simone gave a rubber-stamp performance. So, what does this tell us?'

'That she was playing a part?' suggested PC Belling hesitantly, tugging at his curly moustache.

'Just so. The boredom I've no doubt was genuine. But apart from that, she was playing a part. And biding her time. She married for the cash and, as a quick look around her bedroom will show, very quickly got through a great deal of it. But, though this case appears to be all about greed, it is also all about love.'

'*Love?*' Sergeant Beryl rolled his eyes in disbelief. 'Seems to me she took him for all she could get then did him in.'

'Oh, she didn't love Alan! No, we're talking here about husband number one.' He flicked through his notes and

423

found the lines relating to the man dragged up in Cubitt Town. '"She was mad about him and he was mad about her and both were mad about money." But Atherton, or so the story goes, found a likely mark and disappeared.'

'So, you reckon she followed his example and found a mark of her own,' suggested Alan Lewis, a plainclothes inspector.

'And plotted her own kidnapping?' PC Belling sounded incredulous.

'With his help, yes. I don't believe they ever really lost touch.'

'Hang on, sir,' said Audrey. 'I'm not with you at all on this one.' There was a general murmur of agreement around the room. 'Surely Sarah Lawson and this bloke we're calling Tim were responsible.'

'That's right.'

'Lawson confessed.'

'And there's proof – she rented the flat where Simone was held.'

'We found the camera at her cottage.'

'You said she recognised the photographs.'

'Besides, Simone was infatuated with her boy friend. That's how it all began.'

'Everything you say – the last remark aside – is true,' granted the Chief Inspector.

'Then I don't see what you're driving at, guv,' Audrey finished where she had begun. 'Either Lawson and her boy friend set it up or Simone and her ex-husband set it up. All four of them couldn't have been involved.'

'But they were,' said Barnaby. 'Except it was all three.' He waited for a second baffled murmur to subside. 'However, only two knew what was really going on. I spoke of love a moment ago. The love of Jimmy Atherton and his wife. But I suspect this will prove to be a poor thing in comparison to that of Sarah Lawson. Unfortunately I didn't bring her in for questioning when I should have done and she was left with plenty of time to dream up an alternative scenario. A cover to protect the woman who so cruelly betrayed her. And I have not the slightest doubt she will stick to her story to the very end. For she has nothing to lose and, it seems now, nothing to live for.'

'Are you saying,' asked Inspector Lewis, 'that this man "Tim" doesn't really exist?'

'That's right.'

'When did you discover this?'

'The last time I spoke to Lawson. I told her he'd been seen going up the back steps at Flavell Street and into the flat. She was completely mystified. Just didn't have a clue as to what I was talking about.' In his mind Barnaby ran the scene again. Saw Sarah finally understand the true extent of her betrayal and watched her efforts, even as the knife plunged home, to protect the woman she loved.

'So why was it necessary to make him up?'

'It wasn't at first. Getting Hollingsworth to believe that someone had kidnapped his wife was a doddle. Locking her away, taking the photographs and posting them – no problem. But once the pictures had been dug up, things rapidly got much more complicated. And when the flat in Flavell Street was discovered, Sarah Lawson was really up against it.

'Not that she was worried on her own behalf. As we know, Sarah was at Fawcett Green the Friday evening following the kidnap and nearly all the following weekend so she couldn't have been the person responsible.'

'So . . . this was Atherson?' said Constable Belling.

'No, no.' Barnaby was starting to sound irritable. 'Don't

you see? There *was* no one else. The pictures were faked.'

'Faked!'

'They were a bloody professional-looking job then, sir.'

'You've picked exactly the right word, Belling. When I interviewed Avis Jennings she talked about Simone's early life. The various jobs she'd had.' He referred once more to his notes. '"Spent some time in a florist's, did a cosmetics course, demonstrated food mixers, was in television for a bit and a cashier in some sort of nightclub." I didn't have the nous to spot a possible connection between make-up training and television. I presumed she'd worked in one of the offices.'

'None of us spotted it, sir,' said Audrey. She could be quite protective at times. 'And we all read the interview.'

'Did that idea check out then, guv?'

'We're still waiting for feedback from the TV companies.'

'I reckon you could be right, chief. I watched *Casualty* last week. God, some of those injuries. Bleeding off your screen.'

'I suppose that's why she had to disappear for so long.'

'Precisely. She could hardly just wash it off and turn up. All the supposed cuts and bruises had to have time to heal.'

'Why risk coming back at all though, guv?' asked Constable Belling. 'She'd got the necklace, the ring, the ransom money.'

'But as Hollingsworth's widow she would expect to inherit all his worldy goods. Nightingales, Penstemon – that alone must be worth a fair shake.'

'So, is that why she killed him?'

'That's my belief, though I've no doubt there'll be a different version at the interview.'

'If she decides to cough it.'

'Yes.' Barnaby didn't really want to consider the alternative. In the brief period that he had spent in the company of the real Mrs Hollingsworth he had sensed a backbone of steel, a heart of stone and an iron will that might prove to be more than a match for his own.

'How she got him to drink the stuff we can only guess at at this stage but we do know how she obtained it. She visited her doctor twice, treating him to a pretty display of nervous distress plus a few bruises thrown in for good measure. Though it's interesting to note that when Jennings tried to examine them more closely, Mrs Hollingsworth, in his own words, "shrank away". There were two prescriptions given for haloperidol but Jennings became suspicious when she tried for three. He thought she might wish to harm herself.'

'That's a good one,' mumbled a machine operator at the back of the room, through a mouthful of Twix.

'To anyone who hasn't met her, all this easy manipulation of other people must sound a bit unbelievable,' said Barnaby. 'All I can say is, in all the years I've been at it, she's the best I've come across. I was deceived along with everyone else.'

Here Barnaby paused and glanced at the familiar face of his watch. Just on six thirty. Time to draw the briefing to a close. Time to have a wash, a cup of tea and a quiet reflective fifteen minutes in his office. Because for the next encounter he knew he would need to be very much on his toes. And that was putting it mildly.

Accompanied by Sergeant Beryl, DCI Barnaby entered the same interview room that was used when he had talked to Sarah Lawson. He had no particular course of action in mind. Nothing up his sleeve, no rehearsed rhetoric or cunning verbal games. Just prepared to play it as it lays.

Simone and Jill Gamble broke off talking as the detectives went in and Barnaby got the feeling that they had been in discussion for some time.

Simone was looking very composed. Obviously deciding to split the difference between the flamboyant splendour of her last public appearance and the milkmaid demureness of all previous ones, she wore a grey silk shirt dress, polished silver triangles in her ears and a carved coral bracelet. Discreet make-up lay on her skin like a natural bloom and her perfume was light and flowery. Barnaby was relieved to discover it was not Joy.

He shook hands with Jill Gamble whom he knew quite well. Sergeant Beryl set up the tape and the interrogation began. The solicitor spoke first.

'I should say straightaway Chief Inspector, that my client denies the charge that has been brought against her. She does not, however, deny that she was at Nightingales on the evening of her husband's death and is willing to answer frankly any questions that you might wish to put to her regarding this whole case.'

'That's very encouraging,' said the Chief Inspector. 'So, Mrs Hollingsworth—'

'Oh, Inspector Barnaby!' cried Simone. She leaned forward, clasping her hands. 'I can't tell you how glad I am that it's all over. At last.'

'I'm sure we're all—'

'You've no idea how unhappy I've been. I'd got to the stage where I was saving up the tablets I'd got from the doctor . . .' She looked anxiously at her brief who nodded encouragingly. 'I felt I'd rather be dead than go on living the way I was. I'd asked Alan for a separation, so I could go back to London and make a new life. But he said he'd never let me go. And if I ran away he'd find me wherever I was and . . . kill me . . .'

'So, you decided to get your retaliation in first?' The phrase reminded him sharply of Troy and his voice was harsher than it might otherwise have been.

'It wasn't like that. If you're going to make everything sound so calculated—'

'If pulling open thirty capsules, disposing of the casings, mixing the powder that was left with whisky and persuading someone to drink it isn't calculating I don't know what is.'

'You don't understand.'

'So tell me.'

'It's difficult.' Simone pulled a little silk square from her bag, dabbed at her eyes, slid the hanky through her bracelet and sighed. Then she said something so outrageous that Barnaby thought at first his ears were deceiving him. 'The thing is, I don't want to get Sarah into trouble.'

'Miss Lawson has already been arrested and charged, as you are well aware,' said the Chief Inspector when he'd got his breath back. 'She has also made a full confession as to her part in the conspiracy. Now, tell me about your relationship.'

'Well . . .' Simone settled herself comfortably, folding her hands in her lap. 'It all started shortly after I moved to Fawcett Green. She started asking me round for coffee. And I did go sometimes, out of sheer loneliness. But it was ever so embarrassing. All talk about art and music and stuff, showing me books with paintings in and trying to get me interested. Then she started putting her arm round my shoulder, moving in close, that sort of thing. She wanted to sketch me and I gave it a go but it was so boring. Just sitting there, not able to move, staring into space.'

'What sort of drawings were these?' asked Sergeant Beryl.

'I didn't take nothing – anything off, if that's what you're getting at.'

'If you felt like this about Miss Lawson,' said Barnaby, 'how on earth did you come to be doing her course?'

'She kept on and on about how art could change my life. Naturally I never believed that. But in the end I thought, why not give it a whirl? I'd get out of that poky hole and meet a few new faces. But the car journeys were that tense I couldn't stick it. She never actually *did* anything but I got all this hassle about women's friendships and how we were really sisters in heart, mind and soul. I thought, do me a favour. Then, after the third or fourth class, things really came to a head.'

Simone broke off here, took a sip of water and sat quietly for a moment before continuing. Barnaby understood the pause which he was sure would be the first of many, for although there had been plenty of time to work out both the plot and emotional subtext, the telling of the story was bound to be extremely complex.

'On the way home Sarah turned off into a little lane near Hellions Wychwood. I got quite twitchy – I was sure she was going to make a grab at me – but she was really calm. She just said she loved me more than anything in the world and wanted me to leave Alan and come and live with her. I was knocked sideways. She promised she would never make any demands on me. Well,' Simone gave a coarse chuckle, 'we've all heard that one.

'She said she'd sell the cottage and buy a house wherever I liked. I said I liked the Smoke and she'd be lucky to get a one-bedroom flat in Walthamstow in exchange for that old Bay Tree dump. She told me she had a bit of money put by and some things of her parents she could sell. It was all a bit pathetic, to tell you the truth.'

That'll be the day, thought Barnaby.

'So was that the last time you went to the class?' asked Sergeant Beryl.

Simone hesitated, frowning.

Barnaby said, 'It must be difficult, Mrs Hollingsworth.'

'What?'

'Trying to remember what comes next.'

'I don't know why you're being so sarcastic.' Her soft rosy bottom lip started to tremble.

'Perhaps I can jog your memory.'

'Please don't put words in my client's mouth.' Jill Gamble spoke with some annoyance. 'Perhaps you have forgotten that she is doing her very best to cooperate with you in every way.'

Sergeant Beryl bridged the following chilly pause by repeating his question.

Eventually Simone said, 'That's right. Alan discovered I'd been going. He was very jealous and could be violent. So I had to give up.'

'And he was so grateful,' said Barnaby, 'that he bought you a diamond necklace worth nearly a quarter of a million.'

'Alan loved giving presents. It was almost the first thing that attracted me to him.' She looked puzzled when both detectives laughed and murmured something to her solicitor.

Jill Gamble shook her head. 'It's all right. You're doing fine.'

'You know what he did to raise the money?' Barnaby said.

'Vaguely. But, me and business . . .' Simone lifted her

slender shoulders and sighed. Her pretty brow wrinkled with incomprehension. Plainly she was as a child in these matters.

'Why do you think he took such desperate measures?'

'Heavens, *I* don't know.'

'I suggest that, far from your husband being the forceful and domineering partner, all the power in that marriage lay in your hands, Mrs Hollingsworth. And that you told Alan, not for the first time, that if he didn't buy you exactly what you wanted you would leave.'

Simone shrank slightly at this and looked more waifish than ever. She remained silent but her response was written clearly in those ravishing eyes. Prove it.

And, of course, he couldn't.

'It was after this painful episode that the plan for your escape was conceived?'

'That's right. Sarah didn't give up. She came round to Nightingales several times and got that worked up at Alan's brutality she threatened to have a go at him.'

'Awkward,' commented Sergeant Beryl.

'Anyway, one day she turned up with the kidnap plan. She knew I'd worked in television; I'd told her all about making up actors as road accident victims and corpses and that. Her idea sounded really simple. I'd disappear, we'd mock up some piccies, collect the money and Bob's your uncle.'

'And afterwards?' asked Barnaby.

'Pardon me?'

'Did you lead her to understand that you would then be on the brink of a glorious new future together?'

'I suggested we just took it a step at a time.'

'How wise.'

'And I told her I couldn't possibly leave without my

darling Nelson. So we arranged that I put him in a box on the patio and she would pick him up. I put one of the tranquillisers Dr Jennings gave me into his breakfast so he'd stay nice and quiet. Poor sweetie.'

'You told me on Tuesday the box held Kilner jars.'

'But Inspector, on Tuesday I was still very confused.'

'So. On disappearance day you took the bus and Sarah took the cat.'

'She drove over with him at tea time to that absolutely foul flea pit she'd rented. She brought the stuff for my face – I'd given her a list earlier – food for me and Nelson, some magazines and a litter tray. Then she went back to Fawcett Green to make sure she was seen around the place. Sort of an alibi during the time I was banged up. She just came back here to collect the letters and take them to the post.'

'Your timing's a bit cockeyed on that one, isn't it, Mrs Hollingsworth?' suggested Barnaby. Aware of having caught her out, he felt the first glimmer of satisfaction since the interview began. 'We know from talking to Penstemon that you rang your husband at five fifteen the day you disappeared. How could you do that if you were already incarcerated at Flavell Street?'

She didn't even hesitate. 'Sarah bought me a sweet little mobile. We needed a phone, you see, to give instructions about the ransom though that first call to Alan was entirely my own idea. I thought it would get us off to a good start.'

Barnaby remembered the drunken anguish of Simone's husband as described by Constable Perrot. 'It certainly did that.'

'In fact the whole thing went like a house on fire. Sarah made all the other calls, disguising her voice, naturally, while I cried and kept shouting "Don't hurt me" in the background.' She made it sound like a jolly jape. When no one responded in kind, let alone gave any sign of admiration for such resourcefulness, Simone frowned again, this time somewhat peevishly.

It occurred to Barnaby then that a way through that impregnable composure might be found by the application of flattery.

'I must say the whole plan seems to have been very cunningly worked out.'

'I thought so.' The shadow of guileless petulance lifted.

'Especially the set-up at Heathrow.'

'Oh, that was fabulous.' For a moment he thought she was going to clap her hands. 'Sarah came over around four o'clock on Monday, bringing some shabby clothes she'd picked up in a jumble sale. I made her up to look like an old woman – quite brilliantly if I might say so – and around half past six, off she went.'

'We know all about what happened when she got there.'

'Do you really?' Simone looked both genuinely impressed and slightly alarmed.

'I presume she changed back into her own clothes before collecting your husband's briefcase?'

'That's right. She took them with her in a string bag plus a pot of removal cream.'

It was so obvious once you knew the trick. Barnaby felt he was being led around backstage by a magician. Shown the false fronts and distorting mirrors and concealed trap doors. And still to come was the grand finale.

'And what were you doing while all this was going on?'

'This is going to sound really awful,' began Simone.

'Come to a bad bit, have we, Mrs Hollingsworth?' asked Sergeant Beryl.

Barnaby couldn't help laughing again and Jill Gamble gave an irritated little cough.

'Sarah's a very dominant personality,' continued Simone. 'This was her plan, she was running everything and I was just a pawn in the game. I thought what if, once she'd got the money, she never came back? There wouldn't be nothing I could do about it.'

'Surely her feelings for you would have brought her back,' suggested Barnaby. He was finding it more and more difficult to keep his temper at this heartless reversal of the truth.

'Oh, feelings! All they mean is somebody's all over you till they get what they want then you don't see 'em for dust.'

'So you decided to keep an eye on her?'

'Yes. There was a scarf of hers in the flat. I wrapped it round my face as well as I could—'

'What on earth for?' asked Sergeant Beryl.

'Because I was all bashed up, why do you think?'

'Why didn't you clean it off?'

'There wasn't time.'

'I would have thought,' suggested Barnaby, 'that as the last photograph must have been despatched on Saturday and this was now Monday evening, you would have had ample time.'

Simone stared at him, her lovely face so blank she could have been dreaming. Her shimmering hazel eyes opened very wide, reflecting what they saw like pools of liquid light. Behind them he knew her mind was racing.

'A really complicated make-up such as I was wearing can take a long time to construct. Two or three hours at least. We had one last photograph to take and I didn't want to start again from scratch.'

'You were going to ask for more money?'

'No, no.' Perish the thought. 'But Sarah believed, and I'm sure she was right, that Alan would never give up looking for me while he thought I was still alive. After his first wife left he made her life such a misery she had to take a court order out against him. He didn't give up till she remarried. So, I was to become a corpse. Throat cut, probably. I do a very realistic knife job.'

It had taken her all of five seconds to come up with a completely convincing answer soundly based on an accurate assessment of her husband's character. Barnaby, who had been sure he knew the real reason for the non-removal of the make-up, felt his confidence slipping slightly. Not his belief in her guilt, never that. But in his ability to lay this guilt out, pin it down supported by scrupulous evidence, before a judge and jury. And prove it.

'So I rang for a cab and told him the airport. I'd no idea where Sarah might've parked but I knew exactly where Alan would be because he'd been given strict instructions. So I decided to check him out arriving with the money, wait till he came back and drove off, then go and find Sarah and give her a lovely surprise.' She chirruped with pleasure, sounding like an excited little bird. 'But it all went horribly wrong.'

Barnaby interrupted her there. Partly because the interview had already lasted over an hour and he needed to change the tape. Partly because he sensed that control of it had somehow slipped from his hands and he was determined to get it back.

He ordered some drinks and sandwiches to be brought up from the canteen. Simone sipped half-heartedly at a cup of very weak lime tea and said she couldn't possibly swallow a thing. The men dove in and all the edibles quickly disappeared.

Then the two women went to the loo and Sergeant Beryl

stepped out of the building for a cigarette. Barnaby was left alone with his thoughts which were not comfortable. So far he hadn't managed to make even the slightest dent in Simone Hollingsworth's slippery but totally convincing performance as a victim of bullying and gross injustice.

Feeling suddenly stiff and awkward in his chair, he got up and walked around. He flexed his shoulders and turned his head from side to side to loosen up the neck muscles. He felt the need of a sharp gust of fresh air to stir his sluggish mind but knew the atmosphere outside to be warm and humid. The complete silence in the room pressed upon him. There was not even the hiss of the tape for company. He should have gone outside with Beryl.

On her return, Simone picked up precisely where she had broken off. The taxi having put her down near the Short Stay Car Park, she made her way to the top level in the lift and walked to the far end. Barely minutes later the Audi convertible turned up. Simone ducked down behind a Landrover. Alan parked any old how, got out slamming the door and raced off without even bothering to lock it.

'And thank God he didn't because who should drive in then but that weird girl from The Larches. She got out of her Mini, crouched down behind the other cars and started creeping along by the wall! I scrambled into the back of the Audi just in time. I pulled a travelling rug over me in case she looked through the window. I waited – oh, I don't know, ten or fifteen minutes – and I was just wondering if it was safe to climb out when Alan came back!'

'Oh dear,' said Sergeant Beryl.

'There was shouting, quite near. Then, when Alan started the car up, the passenger door opened and someone tried to get in. I couldn't see any of this you understand, but I could hear the voices. She kept saying, "You're ill" and

"Let me help you". He told her to get out and I think he pushed her. Then he drove off but I could still hear her calling to him to stop. I think perhaps she was hanging on to the door handle or maybe her dress was caught up. Then there was this terrific bump and she screamed and he stopped the car. I heard him swearing. He got out and then there was another sound. More of a bang followed by a thud. Then he got back into the car and drove away.'

Here Simone paused, turned a fresh, untroubled profile to Jill Gamble and asked if she could possibly have a fresh glass of water as this one had got rather tepid in the heat. She listened gratefully to her solicitor's murmured encouragement. Then she tugged her grey silk handkerchief free of the confining bracelet and dabbed at her dry eyes.

Barnaby watched her, his hands resting lightly on the edge of the metal table. He was pleased to see that, whatever else she could do, Simone Hollingsworth could not cry to order. As he waited he was aware of a certain melancholy satisfaction that he would now be able to inform the Brockleys that the loss of their daughter was due to a tragic accident. After all, there was little point in raising a charge of manslaughter against a man already dead.

He recognised the drink of water ploy for what it was, a device to provide a necessary break in the questioning and, sure enough, once the glass arrived, Simone ignored it.

Barnaby became aware of a deepening tension in the room and then became aware that the tension was not within the room but in himself. There was a tightness in his breast and his breathing was shallow. His concentration, which had not faltered since the interview began, now narrowed to a degree where he felt it must be almost visible, like a pinpoint of brilliant light at the end of a dark tunnel.

'So, Mrs Hollingsworth. You now find yourself on your way home to Nightingales.'

'To my amazement and distress, Chief Inspector.'

'What happened when you arrived?'

'Alan drove straight into the garage. I stayed very still, holding my breath. I thought, once he'd gone into the house, I could maybe get out of the car and somehow work my way round into the back garden. Hide there till it was really dark. But then he leaned over the back seat to check the door, saw there was something underneath the blanket and that was that. He was overjoyed to see me, almost hysterical with relief but at the same time there was something black and despairing about him. He wrapped the rug round me and—'

'What happened to this rug?'

'Sorry?'

'It was not in the sitting room when the police broke in.'

'Oh, he took it upstairs, I think. Later.'

'Right. Carry on, Mrs Hollingsworth.'

'We got in the house and he started rambling wildly on about how the whole business had nearly killed him. And that it would happen again or that I would leave or meet someone else and his life would be over. I tried to calm him down and it seemed to work because he suddenly went very quiet. Said he was sorry he'd frightened me and that I wasn't to worry any more because from now on everything would be all right. I suppose I should have been suspicious at such a quick change but I was just so relieved he'd stopped raving. By this time—'

Barnaby interrupted her. He had a terrible premonition as to where all this was leading and a cold foreboding gripped his heart. He longed to stop the immaculate and callous recitation, if only for a minute.

'As you yourself have introduced the word suspicious I suggest it might be more likely to apply to your husband. Surely, once he had seen you really close to, he would know he'd been duped.'

'I only switched one lamp on.'

'Even so—'

'And he'd have had to touch my face which I'd already told him was extremely painful. That was when he went upstairs – to get me some Panadol, he said, though he came down without it. Told me we'd run out.'

'Then what happened?' asked Sergeant Beryl.

Barnaby drew in his breath sharply with irritation. He had wanted to explore that scene a little further. But before he could put a question of his own, she was off again, speaking now in an intense, gasping little voice as if short of breath.

'He talked and talked about how he'd missed me and asked a lot of questions but I said the whole experience was so awful I couldn't bear to talk about it and he seemed to accept that. After he'd run down he went very quiet for some time. Then he got up and made us both a drink. Whisky. It's not something I like but Alan said it would help me sleep. Then he went to get some water from the kitchen though there was already a siphon on the tray. He sat on the settee and started to knock it back. I just sipped mine but he kept urging me to drink up so I swallowed a bit more. He was terribly pale and sweating. I got quite alarmed. Then, when he leaned back and closed his eyes, I tipped the rest of the stuff away.'

'Where?'

'Into the ice bucket. The drinks table was next to my chair. When he looked at me again he smiled and seemed really content. He said, "Good girl." Then "Forgive me, my darling. We'll always be together now." I didn't understand what he meant.'

The hell you didn't, you lying bitch. Barnaby saw the brilliance of her solution now. Understood the final twist, in all its cruel clarity. He saw poor Hollingsworth beside himself with happiness from the moment his wife decided to reveal herself. Touched perhaps almost to tears when, despite her injuries and all that she had gone through, it was he to whom she showed concern. Mixing him a drink with her own fair hands; settling him on the settee. Making sure he drank it all.

Prove it.

'And when did you discover, Mrs Hollingsworth, that your husband had not simply fallen sleep?'

'But I didn't! After I'd washed up my glass—'

'Why did you do that?'

'I'm a tidy person.'

'The mess that kitchen was in,' said Sergeant Beryl, 'I wouldn't have thought one glass would make a lot of difference.'

'Also the smell of whisky in the room was most unpleasant.'

'Mrs Hollingsworth,' said Chief Inspector Barnaby, 'there was no trace of spirits in the ice bucket.'

'I rinsed that out as well before I went.'

'Did you not simply, once your husband had finished his lethal potion, throw your own undoctored drink down the kitchen sink?'

'Undoctored?'

'And if you were about to leave anyway,' said Sergeant Beryl, 'why worry about the smell?'

'Look, do you want to hear this story or don't you? Because I am just about getting—'

'You are harassing my client, Chief Inspector.' Jill

Gamble had placed a restraining hand on Simone's arm. 'And if you persist I shall be forced to advise her against assisting you so comprehensively.'

There was a brief silence during which Sergeant Beryl chewed his bottom lip, Simone once more ran round the eye area, this time with a pink tissue, and Barnaby tried to stifle the feeling that he was driving along the edge of a cliff in a car he couldn't control.

'Shall I continue?'

'Please do, Mrs Hollingsworth.'

'Not that there's much more to say. I left the house—'

'Haven't you forgotten something?'

'I don't think so.'

'Before you left you went upstairs—'

'I never went upstairs!'

'And typed a message on your husband's computer. What did you use to cover the keyboard? One of your many scarves perhaps? I noticed a couple of near transparent ones in your bedroom.'

Simone was utterly mystified. 'What did the message say?'

'It was a farewell note.'

'There you are then!' She turned to her solicitor and seized her arm. Exultant, vindicated. 'Ohh, isn't that . . . *He left a note!*'

This was unbearable. For a moment the Chief Inspector felt so enraged he could have thrown up. It was three or four minutes before he felt able to speak and move the interview on. Then he said, 'Tell me what time you left the house, Mrs Hollingsworth.'

'Around eleven, I suppose.' She still hadn't simmered down. Everything about her sparkled.

'And which way did you go?'

'Through the front. There were a couple of false starts till I thought of switching the halogen off. Mr and Mrs B next door kept peering out of the bedroom window. And then, of course, I had to get back to High Wycombe.'

'But why?' asked Barnaby, in mock puzzlement. 'With Bay Tree Cottage just two minutes away.'

'There was no one there. I knocked and knocked.'

'Wasn't it more the case that you could not afford to let Sarah or anyone else know you were in Fawcett Green the night your husband died?'

'But I didn't know he'd died *then*,' sighed Simone with an ever patient, sweetly resigned expression.

If Barnaby was disappointed that the trap he had cunningly placed in his suspect's path had been so neatly circumvented, he showed no sign of it.

'And anyway, I couldn't risk running into anyone while I was still supposed to be kidnapped.'

'So how did you get back to High Wycombe, Mrs Hollingsworth?'

'I decided to walk to Ferne Bassett and ring from there for a taxi. It's only about a mile.'

'A bit risky,' suggested Sergeant Beryl, 'walking along a country road at that time of night.'

'You're not the only one to think so,' replied Simone. She started to laugh in a merry, uncomplicated way. 'This old guy in a Morris Minor picked me up. He was actually going through High Wycombe and I thought, great! But when he saw my face he wouldn't drive me home, insisted on taking me to a hospital. So we ended up in casualty.' She could hardly speak now for laughter.

The two policemen watched, their faces expressionless.

Jill Gamble said, 'Calm down, Mrs Hollingsworth,' and offered the glass of water.

'Oh, dear, oh dear,' said Simone and her shoulders shook. 'It's all right, I'm OK. So I had to hop out the back way and grab a cab from the rank. And far as I know,' more peals of merriment, 'he's still there.'

'You're lucky you were picked up by someone so considerate,' said Sergeant Beryl.

'I'm a lucky person.'

By the end of the third session, weaponless in the face of such calm, bland resolution, Barnaby knew himself defeated.

There had been more tea and this time Simone, no doubt more relaxed now that the trickiest corner of all had been successfully turned, really tucked in. She ate a cheese and tomato sandwich and two Jacobs Club biscuits (fruit and nut). Her pearly little teeth were speckled with chocolate. She licked her handkerchief and daintily wiped her lips.

'Right. Tell me about the Athertons, Mrs Hollingsworth. Where do they fit into this elaborate fairy story?'

'I shouldn't use the word fairy in front of Ronnie—'

'Will you answer the bloody question!'

'I'm sorry.' Simone shrank away, blinking in distress. 'It was just a joke.'

Barnaby, furious that he had allowed her to provoke him, struggled to swallow his anger.

'I think my client has had more than enough bullying in her life already, don't you, Chief Inspector?'

'We are trying to find the truth here, Mrs Gamble, about the death of your client's husband. She seems to regard this extremely serious matter as a bit of a giggle.'

'I don't, I don't!' cried Simone. 'But different people react to nervous strain in different ways. And I get a bit hysterical. I always have.'

'If you say so. Are you ready now to answer the question?'

'Of course I am. I always was.' She patted her hair and briefly rested her fingers on her brow, smoothing it gently.

'Renee Atherton is my mother-in-law – ex, that is. We've always got on really well. Even after Jim and I split I kept in touch – went to see her and everything. Before I remarried, naturally. I used to ring her up from the box sometimes when stuffy old Fawcett Green got unbearable. Jimmy's brother – well, he's always fancied me but I only like him as a friend.'

'Someone you can turn to in time of trouble?'

'That's right.' She beamed happily, delighted at how quickly he had got the hang of the situation. 'So as soon as I got back to Flavell Street, I gave them a bell.'

'At that hour?'

'They're late birds. I knew they wouldn't mind. Explained I had to have somewhere to stay for a week or two, dead urgent.'

'So why the sudden need to move?'

'I dunno, premonition maybe. I just felt a bit panicky. Ronnie wanted to drive straight over.' She smiled, shaking her head in tender recollection. 'Talk about keen.'

'But that wouldn't have done at all, would it, Mrs Hollingsworth?'

'Pardon me?'

'Not much point in leaving empty handed.'

'If he's going to be spiteful,' said Simone to her brief, 'he can whistle for the rest.'

Jill Gamble murmured something conciliatory; Sergeant Beryl favoured the polystyrene ceiling tiles with a hard stare; Barnaby ground his teeth.

Eventually Simone, with a much put-upon air, condescended to continue. 'I told him best thing was to time it for around two o'clock the next day. Park in the multi-

445

storey and I'd give him a buzz on the mobile when the coast was clear.'

'I see. And where does your first husband come into all this?'

'*Jimmy*. He don't come into nothing. He's in Australia.'

'We're aware of that. But, even so—'

'He's hardly kept in touch with his family so he's not likely to have kept in touch with me.'

'Right.' One more cherished theory gone to pot. 'So Ronnie picked you up. And, presumably, put you down.'

'Don't.' Simone gently touched the bruise on her forehead. 'We wanted to make it look convincing but he pushed me a bit too hard.

'Sarah turned up about one. And, honestly, Inspector, if I'd ever had any doubts about running away . . .' Here Simone stopped speaking and trembled slightly. Her eyelids fluttered and one hand rested on her breast as if to ease her breathing. 'That woman seemed to think because she'd brought the money she'd bought me. She tipped it out on the bed and started throwing it into the air and laughing. I thought she'd gone a bit mad, to tell you the truth.'

'I can imagine,' said Barnaby, able to picture Sarah, now that the whole traumatic law-breaking procedure was safely accomplished, dancing around the room in joy and relief.

'She said, "Here, here – have some," and started stuffing it down my dress, trying to undo the buttons. Well, I weren't having none of that. I reminded her she'd promised we'd just be friends. I'd hardly got the words out when she started kissing me and pushing her hand up my skirt. It was bloody disgusting.'

Barnaby tried to imagine that also and failed. But he could see how powerfully such a scene would come across in a court of law. Especially when embellished by a few even more salaciously inventive details.

'She went out to get some things for lunch. Oh, what we weren't going to have. Salmon, foie gras, lovely cakes, champagne. She said when I'd had a few glasses I'd change my mind about going to bed. The minute she'd gone I rang Ronnie.'

'And left.'

'Wouldn't you?'

'Taking the money.'

'I took my *share*.'

'Which was?'

'Straight down the middle. I know it was all Sarah's plan but without the photographs it wouldn't have even got off the ground. So I reckon I'm entitled.'

'Our information is you took the lot.'

'Only Sarah knows what I took and she wouldn't make up a lie like that.' She smiled at both policemen, her confidence impregnable. 'Even if she is an old dyke.'

Barnaby thought of Sarah Lawson slowly fading from the light in her prison cell and Alan Hollingsworth in the cold ground. But he would not allow his anger to get the better of him a second time. Not when he was handling something as slippery as a basket full of cobras. Unkindness, well, that was something else.

'Quite a contrast between the pair of you, isn't there, Mrs Hollingsworth?' Simone stared at him. 'Here's you calling Sarah all the names under the sun. Yet she'd die rather than speak a word against you.'

'I should hope so too!' She blushed all the same. Just a shade.

'But you've known that all along, haven't you? Known that she loved you so much you would always be safe?'

Simone turned to her solicitor and said, 'All this is a mystery to me.'

She decided then, in the face of the ungrateful way all her efforts to help were being received, that she had nothing further to add. Shortly after this, the interview was terminated. Simone was taken downstairs. Barnaby sat on in the room with the pale blue walls and metal chairs and poster of the Colorado beetle. He sat with his head in his hands and his eyes closed. He was seeing, as vividly as if she was standing a few feet in front of him, Simone Hollingsworth in the dock.

Wearing flat shoes she would appear very small indeed inside the witness box. Slender though she was, he would not put it past her to lose weight before the trial began.

Her hair would have been allowed to revert to its true colour and she would be wearing the sort of make-up which, though remaining indiscernible, emphasised her fragility. Her clothes would be plain and inexpensive. Perhaps even a trifle shabby. There would be no jewellery apart from a wedding ring.

She would have an outstanding defence lawyer but would give her evidence throughout so shyly that the judge would frequently have to ask her to speak up.

The tale unrolled would be a tragic one. Abandoned after a brief marriage to a man she truly loved, she then fell under the spell of a cruel exploitative neurotic who watched her like a hawk. Though generous if she behaved exactly as he wished, this man responded with violence if she made even the slightest attempt to have any sort of interest outside the home. Mrs Hollingsworth's doctor would testify to this.

An offer of friendship from a local artist was seized on

with gratitude by this lonely and, yes, we admit it, ladies and gentlemen of the jury, perhaps rather simple and naive woman. A friendship which was to prove fatal to Simone's future wellbeing. For Sarah Lawson, an articulate, highly educated and extremely forceful personality, was also a lesbian. A woman who, having persuaded the now unprotected and deeply vulnerable Mrs Hollingsworth to leave her home, attempted to rape her.

Fleeing from this new oppression Mrs Hollingsworth found herself accidentally entrapped once more with her brute of a husband and this time was lucky to escape with her life.

And so on and convincingly on . . .

You could forget all about a murder charge. What evidence would the Crown Prosecution Service have been able to offer? That the prisoner had washed up a glass and an ice bucket? They'd be laughed out of the Old Bailey, all the way down to Blackfriars and over the river to Southwark.

If the more-sinned-against-than-sinning defence came off she might get away with three to four years. And as anything under four was automatically halved all the red-blooded males in the country could have a shot at the pleasure of her company in a mere eighteen months' time. The lucky bastards.

'Sir?' It was the desk sergeant.

'Oh, sorry.' Barnaby looked up. 'You waiting for the room?'

'We are Chief Inspector, actually.'

'I was miles away.'

'Going over the Hollingsworth case?'

'Well, at that precise moment, sergeant, I was thinking of Marlene Dietrich.'

'Really sir?'

'Saw one of her old movies last week on television.'

'Good was it?'

'Excellent,' replied DCI Barnaby. 'Very true to life.'

But there was some justice to be had, after all. Just a little. A short while later the Chief Inspector was pleased to discover, via the good offices of Fanshawe and Clay, that Alan Hollingsworth's will, carefully and very tightly drawn, left every single one of his assets and whatever monies accrued from these to his brother, Edward.

The bequest had one condition. Alan's widow was to be housed, fed and cared for in every way necessary to her basic wellbeing by Edward and Agnes Hollingsworth unless or until she remarried, upon which all financial provision would cease.

Barnaby would have given much to be present when Simone discovered that the day she walked out of Nightingales in her plain grey dress and simple earrings, leaving behind her entire wardrobe, her necklace and diamond solitaire and the ingeniously raised ransom money, the whole kit and caboodle already belonged to someone else.

Barnaby could not help but wonder, when he heard about all this, if Alan had not always had some inkling of the darker side of his wife's personality.

A happier side effect of this surprising legal document was when Edward Hollingsworth, informed of Gray Patterson's plight and discovering it to be the result of his own brother's immoral behaviour, decided to reimburse him fully.

Sarah Lawson was brought from Holloway Prison to Wood Green Crown Court where she was charged under

Section One of the Criminal Law Act, 1977, with conspiracy to obtain money by falsely claiming to have kidnapped Simone Hollingsworth. When requested to stand and face the court it became plain that Miss Lawson was unable to do so without assistance. She received the charge calmly and, when asked if she had anything to say, chose to remain silent.

Later that same week Renee and Ronald Atherton were charged on suspicion of obstructing a police inquiry. Neither had form, much to Barnaby's surprise, and would probably end up with little more than a caution or a suspended sentence.

Sergeant Troy came back to work, not quite his old self. In his first lunch hour he went out to W. H. Smith and bought the Joan Collins book for Maureen's birthday. He added a large box of Belgian chocolates from Marks and Spencer and a vast bouquet of flowers, which was really two put together. He chose a card with some care.

PC Perrot remained on the Chief Inspector's mind. Barnaby remembered the inexperienced constable's early lapse in reporting the interview with Alan Hollingsworth and compared it to his own crass error of judgement, after thirty years in the business, in relation to Sarah Lawson.

It seemed to Barnaby, after these reflections, that he had treated Perrot unreasonably. He then made the decision that it would be not only unkind but foolish to remove the policeman from a job that he was doing superbly well. He dictated a memo to this effect and received reams of thankful gratitude in response. Interleaved with the ten-page letter were details of all the coming events in every village on Perrot's beat and a request, if it was not too much trouble, that they be put on the station's notice-board.

* * *

Gradually, in the offices of Causton CID, the machinery of the case was wound down and the inquiry team absorbed into other ongoing investigations.

Detective Chief Inspector Barnaby licked his wounds in private. This was not his first failure and doubtless would not be his last but it was one that he found especially irksome. He imagined the station discussing the affair, not entirely sympathetically. Recalling the day a pretty blonde, with the face of an angel and the temperament of an assassin, ran rings round old Tom.

But one had to keep such things in proportion and, in the end, they did not really matter. What mattered was that in two days' time it would be Joyce's birthday.

Barnaby planned a tomato mousse to be served with slices of avocado and lettuce hearts. After this there would be grilled wild salmon with Hollandaise sauce and new broad beans from his garden. Cully and Nicholas were bringing an apricot tart from Patisserie Valerie and some Perrier–Jouet Belle Époque.

They would eat out in the garden and afterwards sit on together in the dusk under the diffused radiance of the stars. Barnaby and his daughter and her husband would sing 'Happy birthday to you' and then Joyce would sing to them, as she always did. 'Greensleeves' perhaps. Or 'There's No Place Like Home'.

A Place of Safety

Caroline Graham

'A pleasure to read: well-written, intelligent and enlivened with flashes of dry humour' *Evening Standard*

When ex-vicar Lionel Lawrence opens his rambling rectory to a stream of young offenders he has no idea the consequences will include blackmail and murder. But Chief Inspector Barnaby's sure he knows who's behind the worrying disappearance of Lionel's latest protegé – a defiantly elusive suspect whom he's convinced is the incarnation of evil.

'At last, the long-awaited new novel featuring Chief Inspector Barnaby, the favourite of 14 million TV viewers when ex-Bergerac actor John Nettles played him in *Midsomer Murders* . . . The mystery is intriguing, the wit shafts through it like sunlight . . . do not miss this book' *Family Circle*

'A treat . . . haunting stuff' *Woman's Realm*

'Read her and you'll be astonished . . . very sexy, very hip and very funny' *Scotsman*

'Satisfyingly enjoyable' *Woman and Home*

'Proves there's feisty life in the traditional English crime novel' Val McDermid, *Manchester Evening News*

'A delight' *Sunday Times*

0 7472 4971 7

headline

Now you can buy any of these other bestselling
books by **Caroline Graham** from your
bookshop or *direct from the publisher*.

FREE P&P AND UK DELIVERY
(Overseas and Ireland £3.50 per book)

The Killings at Badger's Drift	£7.99
Death of a Hollow Man	£7.99
Death in Disguise	£7.99
Written in Blood	£7.99
Faithful unto Death	£7.99
A Place of Safety	£7.99
A Ghost in the Machine	£7.99

TO ORDER SIMPLY CALL THIS NUMBER

01235 400 414

or visit our website: www.headline.co.uk

Prices and availability subject to change without notice.